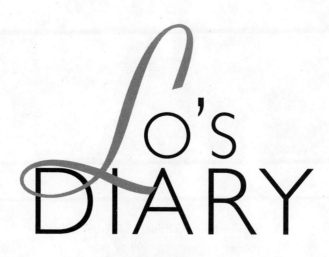

Pia Pera

translated from the Italian by Ann Goldstein

foxrock

© 1995 by Marsilio Editori S.P.A. in Venezia
Translation copyright © 1999 by Foxrock, Inc.
LO'S DIARY is based on LOLITA by Vladimir Nabokov.
Copyright © 1955 by Vladimir Nabokov.
All rights reserved, including the right of reproduction in whole
or in part in any form.

Preface by Dmitri Nabokov
Copyright © 1999 by Dmitri Nabokov.
All rights reserved, including the right of reproduction
in whole or in part in any form.

This edition of LO'S DIARY is published by arrangement with
the Estate of Vladimir Nabokov.

ISBN 0-9643740-1-3

Library of Congress Cataloging-in-Publication data is available.

Book design by Neuwirth & Associates, Inc.
Jacket design by Steve Brower

Foxrock Inc.
61 Fourth Avenue
New York, N.Y. 10003

Manufactured in the United States of America

Contents

On a Book Entitled Lo's Diary

*V*LADIMIR NABOKOV (henceforth "VN") has received
many splendid tributes in his centennial year—loving
ceremonies throughout the world by which he, a non–ceremonious
person, would nevertheless have been deeply touched.

VN has appeared on all the famous lists, and interesting works
by and about him continue to proliferate–the first Pléiade volume is
on its way; *Nabokov's Butterflies* is soon to be issued by Penguin in
England and Beacon Press in America. It will contain his invented but
plausible dedication butterflies, his scientific articles, and the butterflies in his fiction, including a substantial, never–published, projected
off–shoot of *The Gift*.

Some events leading up to the centennial year have been less
jolly, although I guess nearly everything has its jolly side. Outright
piracy persists in Russia, and in the Western world, as some readers
may know, one Pia Pera (henceforth "PP"), an Italian journalist,
author of some stories that I have not read and of a translation of
Eugene Onegin into Italian which I have, decided to seek inspiration,
fortune and fame from a book called *Lolita*.

Lolita, VN's third novel in English, has been translated into
some 20 languages, and sold over 50 million copies. During my
father's lifetime and thereafter, my family has been approached by a
perpetual stream of artists from around the world–filmmakers, play-
wrights, composers, choreographers, a graphic artist or two–who had
been inspired, moved, touched by *Lolita*. These suitors wanted to pay
homage: to take the novel, filter it through a personal vision, and

transform it into what the law of copyright defines as a "derivative work"—one that "recasts, transforms or adapts" something that has come before. Recognizing the derivative nature of their enterprise, would-be transformers—regardless of their celebrity or stature—gave a figurative knock on my family's door in Ithaca or Montreux seeking permission to offer their new works based on *Lolita* to an ever-curious public.

Like their works, *Lo's Diary* is based on my father's novel—as will be instantly apparent to anyone who knows *Lolita*. By explicit design, the characters, incidents, *sequences* of events, settings, articles of clothing, hair styles, personal effects, pets, gifts, even the bacon purloined from a breakfast tray—all of these ingredients and more will immediately seem familiar. Nevertheless, although PP has recast, transformed and adapted *Lolita*, she and her Italian publisher declined to seek permission, declined to acknowledge that *Lo's Diary* is a derivative work.

Depending upon whose flag was flapping, the resulting work was dubbed a legally permissible girl's eye view written in response to a challenge from VN, a sort of latter–day *Rashomon*, and/or an honorable addition to the catalogue of such "transformative" works as *My Fair Lady, West Side Story*, Stoppard's *Rosencrantz and Guildenstern*, Updike's *S*, Jean Rhys's *Wide Sargasso Sea*. When the New York *Times* presented the same seduction scene drawn from VN and from PP in parallel columns, stylistic considerations apart, feminists had mixed feelings about the calculating harpy that emerged. What PP called VN's "challenge to a literary tennis match," was, she quite forgot, a raving wish of Humbert's, not Nabokov's, to examine Lolita as a female doctor might. The comparison to *Rashomon* might have been persuasive if Kurosawa himself had not written all four versions of the rape/murder scene that figures in his own masterpiece: and as for the comparisons to earlier transformations—*Pygmalion, Romeo and Juliet, Hamlet, The Scarlet Letter, Jane Eyre*—all had been safely tucked into the public domain when the "transformations" were penned.

Lolita isn't in the public domain, and won't be until well into the next millennium when its copyright expires— notwithstanding which the Washington *Post* advanced the view that I should lighten up: *Lolita,* their editors urged, should be fair game in the fields of copyright because it has "come inescapably into common consciousness."

I thought then, and think now, that this is silly. Is *Lolita* to pay this price because it is too good, too famous? Are writers to strive for mediocrity lest their works similarly enter the "common consciousness?" Are icons of popular culture–*Star Wars* perhaps–to be made subject to plundering by free riders because they have entered the common consciousness? The *Post* urged me to "rethink" my stance, asking whether books like Madam Pera's "can truly do the original anything but homage?" By ignoring the fact that homage to *Lolita* can be and has been paid with bona fide licenses, the question seems naïve.

It is only fair to mention that before she published, PP did send her text to me in Sardinia. While there was no mention of permission or copyright, hope seemed to glimmer for evaluation and support from me. I try to be a nice guy. I did not know how to reply and therefore, if I recollect correctly, said nothing. My attorney, however, did advise PP's publisher that although *Lo's Diary* constituted copyright infringement, if they stuck to Italian, I would be disinclined to sue.

When *Lo's Diary* journeyed beyond its original Italian bailiwick, into Finnish, Dutch, then–courtesy of Macmillan of London and Farrar, Straus & Giroux of New York–into English translation, time came to put a stop to it. Menaced by serious court proceedings, the British and US publishers withdrew, for they understood that what was on the endangered list was not freedom of inspiration and expression, but the very principle of copyright that protects their own authors as well. As other pretenders to publication began to loom like ominous kinglets from *Macbeth,* it became evident that a new policy was needed. So a compromise was reached at the suggestion of Barney Rosset and Foxrock whereby, regardless of its literary merit, the *Diary* would not be denied publication, and I would not appear as a possessive, censoring ogre. A brief preface of mine would make it clear that my permission to publish was required by law, in the hope of setting a precedent without spending years and millions on trials and appeals, and of going on to more productive matters. To reinforce the notion of copyright protection, a portion of the proceeds would go to me. In order to banish any misunderstanding, that portion would be transmitted in its entirety to the International Pen Club for literary–philanthropic use. PP would be entitled to an afterword, a privilege that, after some vacillation, she decided to forego.

I see in today's All the News That's Fit to Print, however, that PP has had it both ways. Not only has her final attempt at an afterword been published, but so have her (odd) comments on this piece. I shall leave the matter in its mole–hole, other than to point out that it is not my intent to be ungracious, or to emulate my late father. It is simply to apprise the reader and the would–be plagiarist of the dry, legal aspects of the copyright issue. The rest may come soon, in a different forum. I also note that no mention has been made of the totally philanthropic destination of the meager proceeds one foresees. Perhaps that did not fit.

The path has been a rather tortured one; but the copyright to *Lolita* has been honored. *Lo's Diary* is in your hands.

DMITRI NABOKOV
Montreux, Switzerland
August 23, 1999

What if Dante's Beatrice were a poet
and Laura could sing of love's flame?
I encouraged women to speak . . .
My God, if only I could stop them now!

— ANNA AKHMATOVA

If I were a little girl
wrapped in soft curls
I wouldn't want to be Lolita
I'd rather be Natasha Rostov,
even though Lolita's image
is of astonishing beauty: so much
as an artist I understand, yet
for my own sake I
would rather be Natasha Rostov.

— DMITRI PRIGOV

Just to give you an idea, the following can be considered famous dropouts:
Holden Caulfield, Paperoga, Bill Clinton's brother, Robinson Crusoe,
James Dean, Arturo Bandini, Pinocchio, Nicu Ceausescu, Lolita, Tom
Sawyer and his whole crowd, Mowgli, Rusty the wild, Charles Bukowski,
Pippi Longstocking and Stephanie of Monaco.

—SANDRO VERONESI

Foreword

A NUMBER OF YEARS ago, a young American woman came to see me at the Olympia Press in Paris. She was slender and had a nice figure, and with her was a man who kept looking at her fondly, and a boy of about five, with thoughtful gray eyes and long chestnut curls.

"I am Dolores Schlegel, formerly Maze. This is my husband, Richard." Mr. Schlegel, a young man with raven-black hair, shook my hand a little too vigorously and said hello in the unnatural voice of a deaf person or a talking machine. They sat down on the other side of my desk, and Mr. Schlegel held the child on his lap while his wife dug through a large straw purse. She took out a package and handed it to me, and, holding it in my left hand, I unwrapped it with the right, which was still sore. It was a diary bound in a rough plaid material and fastened with a dented brass clasp. I ran my fingers over it.

"Goodness, I never imagined . . . " I said, realizing who it was I had before me.

"Yes," Mrs. Schlegel said, smiling. She crossed her legs, which glistened with a golden down. "But don't worry, what you published was a completely made-up story—not to take anything away from the author. Or maybe that was the way he saw it." She was chewing a piece of mint gum. Then, her eyes radiant with mockery, she added: "Apart from my death and some other nonsense . . . Maybe you'd take a look at my own impressions of that time. They're definitely less literary."

"But Mrs. Schlegel," I said, leafing through the diary of Dolores Maze (wondering, meanwhile, why Humbert Guibert had changed Maze to Haze), "what makes you think that the scribbles of a twelve-year-old are publishable?"

"Not all of it is relevant, of course, Dr. Ray. I'll leave it with you just like this, and you can decide what's worthwhile."

"I must compliment you on your French. Your accent is impeccable."

"You should compliment Professor Guibert. He was an extremely meticulous teacher. Only it's too bad that at a certain point your friend got a little out of control."

"I understand your feelings, but in a novel, after all . . . "

"Look, for a little while he told the story the way it happened, but when he began to run out of things to say, that is, when I ran out, he started making things up. So he could end with a bang."

"Do you mean that the actual novel begins when you're no longer there?"

"More or less. And also it's only then that we discover something about our dear Professor Guibert, who like all literary men . . . " Mrs. Schlegel concluded with a look of scorn.

"Which is?"

"To begin with, when he came to see me later I didn't say anything about the so-called Clare Quilty. Starting at that point, with my refusal to tell him how I managed on my own, he abandoned himself to his fantasies. You know how much fun he had sticking me in all those awful situations."

"Why, what really happened?"

"Worse, infinitely worse!" Mrs. Schlegel answered in a derisive singsong. "My God, I can just see him: gazing dreamily into the distance, he wipes away the tears with one of his perfumed batiste handkerchiefs, then looks at himself in the mirror with those big lost eyes of his to see the effect of the stains on his skin . . . He invented the most exquisite sentiments, my dear old dad . . . "

"Yes, of course, the hunt for Quilty and the murder—even a child could understand that that was a work of fantasy," I said, piqued that she should take me for a fool. "But I can't believe that after so many years together you haven't told him anything."

"You know, living with a deaf person, a real deaf person, after a while you get used to keeping what you have to say inside," Mrs. Schlegel explained, smiling at her husband. As we talked, he was making funny faces at the child, whose little cries, like the pealing of a bell, he couldn't appreciate. I reflected that he must be used to not hearing what was said around him. He certainly didn't seem very interested, and his wife didn't seem terribly sorry about it.

"Don't you know the deaf alphabet?"

"You're right, sooner or later I'll have to study it, but you see Richard understands a little from reading lips, and then he has his own way of listening to me," Mrs. Schlegel said languidly. Every so often her husband glanced in my direction—not, however, at my lips, as it had seemed to me at first, but at a painting behind me. I, too, had been curious about it the first time I was in the office, but I had forgotten to ask the name of the painter.

I was about to offer them something to drink, when Mrs. Schlegel rested a hand—with long thin fingers, pink oval nails cut short—on her husband's shoulder and said to me: "No, thank you, we really have to go. We still have so many things to see in Paris. I'll leave you my old diary. You can call me at the Hotel des Beaux-Arts."

"Just a moment. Tell me something about it." I tried to detain her.

"It's my diary, the only one I ever kept. I started it after we moved to Goatscreek, the Ramsdale of the book, and then . . . then, after Los Angeles, I stopped."

"And the loose pages inside?"

"From when I was traveling with Humbert. Obviously I didn't want him to be my first reader, so whenever I could get a few minutes alone, which was practically never, I wrote on any old scrap of paper. I want you to know, the attacks of constipation I had to fake . . . "

"What? You mean he doesn't know anything about this diary?"

"No, he never saw it, not even during that endless trip, that utter torture. If I made that trip again now, with Richard, I would write about it completely differently. Those were beautiful places, but I'm afraid that you'll find nothing but outbursts on my scraps of paper: you see, they were all I had."

"By the way, do you know that M. Guibert is in Paris?"

"Yes."

"Would you like to see him?"

"I don't think so."

"That's too bad, Mrs. Schlegel. After all, he has written, at least about the two of you, with disarming honesty," I said in defense of my author and friend.

"Yes, he's a strange man—he wasn't even embarrassed to tell how he robbed me. But you have to allow that he must have been a little ashamed about that check he gave us when Richard and I were in trouble: did you know it was worthless?" I didn't. Should I believe her?

"So how did you survive?"

"We rolled up our sleeves and toughed it out for a while, then I came of age and could dispose of my inheritance." Stroking the child's hair, she added, "Anyway, aside from his being too cowardly to use his own name, it hardly seems honest to call two people dead who are alive and well."

"Oh, that's not M. Guibert's fault. It was my suggestion: readers like stories with a moral."

"You mean those in which the characters can't have other stories?" Mrs. Schlegel asked as she got up to shake my hand. And then, in that small face with its delicate features, I saw the lineaments of the nymphet emerging, with her sardonic humor, her famous way of rolling her eyes, of talking while chewing gum, that mock vulgarity. Everything that had seduced my poor friend. "I never imagined I'd have you to thank for the brilliant idea of having me die in childbirth.

As long as it doesn't go badly for me this time . . . " she added, pressing her fingertips down on the desktop.

I noticed the round outline of her belly just visible under her blouse of raspberry-colored jersey.

"Dr. Ray, you speak with such good taste in your preface, but I must say that the device struck me as really macabre." We said goodbye.

Only then did Mr. Schlegel seem to remember us. "My son is deaf, too," he said proudly, pronouncing each syllable distinctly.

I was to see M. Guibert that evening. We dined in a Vietnamese restaurant that had opened recently. I told him about my encounter that morning.

"When did she write it?" He asked me for a detailed description, and I told him about the cramped writing, without margins, slightly slanting along the pages, about the obscene little drawings of women with enormous protuberances front and back, about curses written in big block letters, about pages so creased they couldn't be smoothed out, about the scraps of paper stuck inside, containing hastily scribbled notes or long, anguished outbursts. He couldn't conceal his agitation. He desperately wanted to read the diary that had been written under his nose without his being aware of it. I knew his irascible nature, and I wasn't sure that I could trust him. I told him that if the next day he brought me his photographs of the young Dolores Maze and let me put them in the safe, in exchange I would let him look at the diary in my presence. He accepted my conditions without hesitating to declare them offensive.

The next day he arrived early for our appointment. I glanced at the precious photographs, gave them to Mme. Houdenot, our editor, to put away in the safe, and handed over the diary. He held it for a long time, eyes closed, as if he wanted to take it in in a single mouthful. Then he opened the clasp, and the pages fell out, scattering all over the floor.

"I told you to be careful," I said reproachfully as I picked up those many-colored scraps. They seemed like messages from a prisoner.

In dismay, I wondered how I would put them back in order, for young Dolores Maze had never thought to indicate a single date, and as for Mrs. Schlegel she hadn't bothered to number the pages. With M. Guibert already deep in his reading, I attempted to reconstruct the sequence of events, going by external signs only when I could figure out from a season or a particular climate or geographical feature more or less what part of the trip a given note referred to. Otherwise I followed what seemed a logical progression in the state of mind of little Dolores Maze. Yet there, too, I faced gaps, because the irresponsible girl went from the most passionate hatred to the most dreamy-eyed love for no plausible reason, so that most of the time her outbursts seemed groundless. I asked M. Guibert to help me with some passages, but I got little out of him: he claimed he had never had the slightest idea what was going on in his young friend's mind, and he showed no interest in my reconstruction. It took him hours to get to the end, partly because the handwriting left something to be desired—everything had been written in such a rush. When he finished reading he gave it back to me and I returned his photographs. He offered no comments, nor did I ask him for any.

For an editorial opinion I turned to Mme Houdenot, who two days later gave a negative judgment. Sadly I locked the diary's ink-stained cover. And yet I didn't dare fight back: "No, it's not that interesting, but I thought it might make a different impression on a female mind." As I spoke I felt a shame I had long since forgotten: when, fearful of contradicting the opinions of my friends, I would wait to learn from them what I ought to think. Mortified, I added that we could not allow ourselves to publish pages and pages of childish nonsense, childish expressions . . .

"Not childish," Mme Houdenot corrected me harshly. "If only they were childish, how enchanting that would be! The trouble is, like all the adolescents in the world, this one believes she is special." Embarrassed, I lowered my gaze.

"Mme Houdenot, could you tell me who painted the picture

hanging behind my desk?" I asked, to change the subject.

"It's a work of the Maestro Esiguo. A reproduction, of course."

I telephoned Mrs. Schlegel, and told her that we had met to discuss her book, but, although we admired it, we were afraid that it didn't really go with our editorial line.

"Aha!" Mrs. Schlegel said, with amusement. "In your preface you make all those speeches about a difficult childhood . . . " I wanted to see her again, and I told her that I would come myself to give her back the diary. But when I arrived at the hotel the next day, I was told that the Schlegels had left early. I felt a pang of conscience. Mrs. Schlegel's ironic words now seemed bitter. I felt somehow at fault. It's true, I cared nothing about a difficult childhood, or, for that matter, about childhood in general. But there remained in me something of the literary pose of John Ray, the writer of the preface to *Lolita*. However false the words might be, I had written them. In some way they still clung to me. My usual failing. I have never managed to tell a lie without feeling it my duty to make a truth out of it. If I avoid a lunch by inventing a stomachache, I can be sure of getting the wretched stomachache. Thus I began to make up lies with less unpleasant consequences.

Surely there was a sense of irony and condescension in the tone I had used as the author of the foreword to the misdeeds of M. Guibert, and yet that moral parody had the effect of making me uneasy about rejecting the memoirs of Dolores Schlegel née Maze (not Haze).

Sometime later I read in a newspaper about educational games for deaf children invented by Mrs. Schlegel. I sent her a note of congratulations. Still later, when I left my job at Olympia, I found the diary in my desk. At a second reading, it seemed to me more childish than Mme Houdenot had thought. I brought it home and transcribed it. Some cuts were inevitable, and besides, for the reader's comfort, it seemed to me necessary to furnish the text with an introduction, rational punctuation, and some division, however arbitrary, into chapters. I left the names just as I found them: after all, nearly half a century has passed . . . As for my old friend M. Guibert, after teaching for some years in a college in California he retired to a peaceful town on the Riviera, not far from the Hôtel Mirana, the hotel his father owned, long ago. He is looked after by Annabel, the mulatto daughter of his cook, whom he dutifully married. I must say that he's not doing badly for eighty-five: he plays tennis every morning, takes long walks by the sea, and wins at correspondence chess.

John Ray
Paris, France
October 10, 1995

1.

A MAN IN KANSAS CITY is afraid that since the earth is hollow, the Bikini atomic bomb will make a hole in it, the ocean will get sucked in, and the world will stop turning and get lost in space. Another man says it will use up our oxygen supply and we'll have to breathe carbon dioxide. Mary Jo's father thinks that with the atomic bomb the next war will last only a couple of hours, and there won't be any more of those disastrous slaughters they get into in Europe. But it would be better to wait until next year because, according to a spiritualist hairdresser in San Francisco, if they explode the bomb now the Pacific will turn yellow, thousands and thousands of dead fish will float to the top, and it will stink to high heaven. Next year they can go ahead without worrying, nothing bad will happen. I've never seen the Pacific, and I wouldn't like it to turn the color of pee. Pee is pee, might as well stay here in Goatscreek looking down the toilet.

Just as I thought: Mom keeps rummaging through my drawers. Today she told me I worry too much about the bomb's effect on fish. What bomb? I ask. She looks at me like she's going to hit me, then acts like it's nothing.

"I told you to read that article about the experiments in the Marshalls."

"What experiments?"

"You know, you really ought to read the newspaper. All you read are those dumb comic books. You're not a child anymore."

"But it's vacation."

"The world goes forward even when you're on vacation." Said in the icy voice she uses when she doesn't want me to know she's angry. But she is angry, and how. She doesn't like it when I lie, but she likes it even less when I catch her lying. If she bugs me for lying,

I can accuse her of sticking her nose in my diary, and then who'll look worse, her or me.

An example of what an idiot my mother is. Last year, when my dad died, she told me not to be upset: I can write to him anyway, and he'll read my letters and answer them. Then she gave me a black notebook for this correspondence. Revolting, I thought. Other girls have a live dad, but I'm supposed to be happy with eighty sheets of purple-edged paper. A paper dad. They have a dad-dad and a diary-diary, while I have to settle for a notebook that's neither, a single thing to serve as both, like a camping knife with a can opener and a corkscrew.

Anyway, I wrote something more or less like this: Dear Daddy, today I was at the cemetery and I read on your tombstone: Gerald E. Maze, Goatscreek, 6/24/1893-Whiskey, 6/24/1945. It was like a stranger's grave. So you must be Mr. Gerald E. Maze. I hadn't ever thought about it. But they shouldn't forget that you're also my dad. Mom says you moved to heaven. I asked her if we could visit you. She told me that heaven is too far, and scientists are still working out a system for how to get there. I suppose that if they don't hurry up I'll join you by the old system. The conventional one. But there's one thing I don't understand: if heaven is so far away, how come you can see my letters? I'm asking because it doesn't make sense for me to keep writing if you don't read them. Try to answer me on this same page.

The next night I found this stuff here, in a bad imitation of my dad's handwriting: "Dear Dolly, of course I can read you. The eyes of the spirit know no bounds. From where I am, and where one day we will all be together again, you and little Nelson and Mom and I, I can see everything you do very clearly, so I hope you will never cause trouble and always do what your mother tells you." What my mother tells me! I'm not that stupid! I remember what my dad was like, and he would never have written anything like that. He *never never ever* told me to do what someone else says, especially Mom. Disgusting.

Nauseating. So I answered him: "Dear Daddy, since I have to do what Mom says, there's really no point in writing to you. Here's a hug, have fun in the kingdom of heaven, and wait for us. Sooner or later, we'll get there, too." I stopped writing to him, and Mom couldn't say anything. She's an idiot: she shouldn't have tried to trick me.

Then we moved, and Mom burned all the old stuff, even my toys—even my teddy bear. So I opened the jar that has her appendix preserved in formaldehyde, which she's kept since she was little, and I threw it in the fire. Mom ran up behind me and shouted how dare I, and if I don't stop behaving like that (like what?) she'll send me to reform school, like the Lucknows' daughter. Pig. She should be glad that thanks to me she won't catch appendicitis in heaven.

So that's the story of the fake correspondence with my dad. Which is repeated in the diary I bought for myself, with my own money, and is supposed to be from the me of now to the me of later. There's a reason to have a clasp that locks. That way it's clear that it's private. But not to nosy Mom, who immediately has another try at it. What a rat: she wants to know what I'm doing without having to ask me directly. She doesn't want to lower herself, not her. But I fool her just the same. Bobby, Mary Jo's brother, built me a hiding place: he shortened the drawer in my desk, and in the empty space he made a cubbyhole where I can keep my private things. Bobby is a genius carpenter. Mom would never be able to invent something like that.

If a diary has a purpose, which is to record what happened, it's absurd to start, for no particular reason, from this summer, from the day when Robert L. Hilton—Bobby to his friends—made me a hiding place. It's not the day I was born. There are all the days before this one, all the years, the time when there was my dad and the time when there was my brother. Nothing is left of those days, and you, Dolores Maze of the future, maybe you've completely forgotten them, and not even I, Dolores Maze of today, August 8, 1946, can remember what happened every day of my life. I don't want it to seem like nothing ever happened. Before I go to Scout camp (which I hope isn't gross like that repulsive Stinkhorn's, where they had the nerve to send me when I was nine), I want to write down at least the important parts of my life. I wish I could remember the moment when I was born, but there's no way. I remember the death of my little brother Nelson very clearly, but I'll write about that some other time, because it's complicated. Until last year we lived in Whiskey, Mom's home town, in Ohio. There are plenty of photographs of that house, so I don't have to describe it. After my father died we came here to Goatscreek, to my grandmother's house. She wanted to live with a friend in Pomona Beach, Florida. Grandma's house is big. There was a horse, too, which she kept at the club, but now it's in Pomona. Mom doesn't do anything athletic. She plays cards, reads, and does good works with the other ladies at church, which doesn't seem much of a way to spend your time, if you ask me. She took tennis lessons with me at first, but then she gave up and now I go by myself, with Martha and Daisy, because they live nearby and it's convenient. Grandma said Mom wouldn't grow old gracefully because she doesn't get any exercise. Grandma is always in motion, but when you get close to her she smells like saccharin, which makes you think of anything but the outdoors. I haven't seen her in a long time. Anyway, she stayed with her friend for a while, but one day they realized she was staring blankly at the marmalade jar, and they had to take her to a home for senile old people.

More news on the experiments. The problem with the fish is that the atomic bomb might alter their DNA so much that their children won't know what they're supposed to look like. The bomb was dropped on a fleet of ninety-two ships and on everything, dead or alive, in the water, which out there in the Bikinis is full of mollusks and crustaceans. There were lots of animals on the ships, including a very intelligent sow. Afterward they washed the radioactivity off her. That sow is amazing: when the ship sank she immediately learned how to swim, and they finally pulled her out before she drowned. Talk about the survival instinct. I told Celeste about DNA and how the bomb can change it. This scared her. It's terrible, she said, giant sharks could be born, or leviathans like the ones in the Bible, or huge monsters, like the ones from the time when we were apes. I don't get it. With new DNA we might become more beautiful, with longer legs and skin that's tan even in winter; we might always be young, or maybe even no one would die. No one ever said that change is always for the worse. Still, Mom doesn't want me to eat radioactive tuna— she must be afraid I'll become a hundred thousand times prettier and taller than she is.

My dad died last year, right on his birthday. It was a Sunday morning and he was sitting in his armchair, and on the radio they were saying to be careful not to drink liquids that are too cold, because they can cause stomach cramps. They were saying that now that the war is almost over air conditioners won't cost very much, and everyone will be able to buy one. Dad was happy because he thought that with the air conditioner he had secretly invented we would become millionaires, but right at that moment—*boom!*—he went. *Boom!* and Mom decided to move. She decided to move and then all of a sudden she was staring at me, with her evening glass of Dewar's White Label in her hand, looking like she couldn't understand what I was doing there with her. Maybe she was wondering whether or not to include me with the luggage.

I'm leaving for Scout camp soon. Last year Mom forgot about it. After Daddy died she even stopped sunbathing in the back yard. She forgot everything. She got in bed in the afternoon and never got out. In desperation I began to collect spiders. Here's how you capture them: you put a glass over the spider, then stick a postcard under it. After a while the spider dies, and you keep it in a box. Matchboxes are best. Now I have fifty of them, hidden in a place where Mom will never find them. The only problem is that when they're dead the spiders get stiff. Daddy used to do something to make them stretch their legs and grow long again, but I can't remember what.

I was at Mary Jo's and we ate canned tuna fish with potatoes: when I told her that according to my mother radioactive tuna could change our DNA she got scared and went to the bathroom to throw up. She wanted me to stick a finger in my mouth, too, so nothing would be left inside me.

"If you don't, you'll have monster children."

"What kind of monsters?"

"Children . . ." but she didn't know how to continue. She's so scared her DNA is already changed that she doesn't even dare to think what her children might look like.

Mom's got it in her head that when I grow up I'm going to be a nuclear physicist and invent big bombs like the ones in Hiroshima. She gave me a book, *Atomic Energy in Human and Cosmic Life*, and I leafed through it. It tells about this energy that's been around for millenniums and how it's going to be liberated and never imprisoned again, and for this very reason ought to be used for some grand purpose, like exploring the universe, and not wasted on some boring thing. This energy is in a totally weird state called metastability, and to understand it you have to imagine water enclosed in a large crater at the top of a mountain. If you make a gash in the crater the water pours out and produces a ton of power, like the power for electric light. That's because it's high up. As long as the water's closed up in the crater it can't do anything, but as soon as the crater's breached this water pours out with all the hidden force of water confined above sea level, that is, far from where it usually is. Coming down, it releases all the energy that was blocked on top of the mountain: it's like the genie in *The Thousand and One Nights*—he's shut up in a bottle, but just open it a crack and no one can stop him. So you have to pay attention, because afterward it's too late to be sorry—you have to think carefully beforehand what you want to ask the genie when he comes out, because afterward no one can shut him back up in the bottle. It's the same with the energy in atoms: every time you split one it's an opportunity lost forever.

Mom likes the mushroom cloud so much that she put the picture up on the kitchen door. I don't want to do something that's already been done. I want to invent stuff that's completely new. I'd like to study smells. Last year I studied Mom's smell, which was the only thing to do besides collecting spiders, sunbathing, and reading a little. One time Mom managed to stay in bed for days without getting bored, just staring at the fan blades. So I got in the big bed and put my nose against the yellow calluses of her feet. She didn't notice. I breathed very softly. I liked that odorless odor, sort of like butter, but stronger, like butter with a rind, maybe even slightly rancid butter. Her feet are whitish because she never goes out in the sun and never does any sports. She also has flat, translucent but darker yellow calluses on her heels. A color like the color of rubber. Feet of butter and rubber. I couldn't touch her, but I sniffed her, and as I sniffed I realized that her smell changes depending on how I sniff. It's always essentially the same, but it moves, becomes more concentrated or more diffuse. If you sniff hard, the smell is overpowering, and if you sniff lightly you can hardly smell anything, as if there's nothing there, only scentless dead air.

I'm leaving next week. For a Scout camp in the Berkshires recommended by Maud's mother. Mary Jo is going to Illinois, to a camp her mother saw in *Vogue*. I wanted to go there, too, but Mom says I have to stop being so attached to Mary Jo—I have to spend time with my other friends, widen my social circle. At least she's not sticking me in another Holy Cow, where the cabins were practically rotting and the "social activities" were confined to Bible readings by that awful Stinkhorn, and there were no sports, no swimming, no canoeing, only walking in the woods. Constantly. I got such indigestion from the woods that by the end I hated them. Worst of all were the orphans with their pimply faces and greasy hair. The head girl in our cabin was always smearing her face with Acnomel, and every so often she'd kneel down and say her prayers. She claimed that the cream worked better combined with prayers. Meanwhile pimples were breaking out right before your eyes. Still, she never lost her faith; she was so dumb she couldn't even do two times two. She came with a group from an orphanage in Wellesley, and she was convinced that no one would adopt her because of her pus-yellow face. It was awful, the way her voice drawled. I stuck my fingers in my ears so I didn't have to hear her, which was really a pain when I was reading and had to turn the page. And she stank: she made the whole cabin stink of rotten wood, rotten pus, rotten prayer. On Sundays we had to put on white shorts and go to the chapel in the woods, which was a tent. The holy tent. On the last day they made us exchange addresses and give each other a hug goodbye. Stinkhorn even made me embrace the pimply girl, and for at least two months afterward I was afraid that I would break out in those same revolting pimples. If I had a pimply face like hers I think I would kill myself out of shame.

Dear diary, I'm sorry if I left you at home. Camp really wasn't bad, because there were lakes and hills where you could ride horses, and you could take tennis lessons, and the director was really loony and had fun with us. I learned tons, and we actually had a lot of free time. We slept in these really cool tents, with only two people, which was fantastic because I was alone with Maud. I had never realized how nice she is, because in class I was always with Mary Jo and she was with Maggie, but with the two of us together it was like being in paradise. I'd lie in my hammock and she'd caress me all over, she'd smooth my hair and then kiss me, just touching me with her lips and darting her tongue in the corners of my mouth, and do a lot of other things that made me tingle all over. I confess, dear diary, that I gave her the first kiss of my life, which is O.K. since Maud is convinced she's a boy and told me, in strict secrecy, that her real name is Charlie.

The last night at camp she burst out crying. I'm her ideal, she says, and next year they're sending her to a different school, where she has to stay overnight. It's a special very swanky school, where they learn a lot of foreign languages, even Russian and Japanese. We'll never see each other again, she said, sobbing, and I comforted her a little, but at the same time it didn't seem like such a big deal, because it would have been so incredibly weird to have a boyfriend named Maud. It could take her forever to become a real Charlie. Besides, Mary Jo is my best friend and to have two best friends is so complicated you could go nuts, and anyway it seems weird for her to be so in love with me.

2.

THIS SUMMER I so totally betrayed Mary Jo that I really have to spend a page of my diary on her. Mary Jo Hilton lives next door and she's my best friend. I tell her everything, but I didn't tell her about Maud because she might have gotten mad. Mary Jo is really jealous, but she helps me out whenever I have a problem. When I started middle school here in Goatscreek she asked if I wanted to be her best friend, since I didn't know anyone yet. I didn't appreciate her telling me I needed one, so I was vague, although I liked her right away, because she's pretty and I love people who are good-looking. I can't stand ugly people—I don't care if they're the sweetest people in the world, if they're ugly I just am repelled. Then Mary Jo asked me again, so after a while I gave in, O.K., let's be best friends, why not go for someone who's pretty and rich, and who can wear a different outfit every day if she wants. Her father owns the nicest hotel in Goatscreek, and her uncle owns a movie theater. But what I like most about being best friends with her is that we're the cutest girls in our class and when we go out everyone looks at us. Mary Jo has soft, curvy hips, just like a woman, and long, smooth dark hair that brushes her cheek when she turns her head. The boys are crazy about us—they call us the two little cross-eyed mermaids of Goatscreek. We always go around arm in arm, and a while ago we also started going "*prrrr*," just like Maud taught me. But I told Mary Jo that purring is my invention, *prrrrrrr prrrrrr prrrrr*, a gurgling in my throat as I push my head against her back, just like a cat rubbing against the edge of a chair. Mary Jo likes it so much that now she writes me letters on pale-green paper, sealed with red sealing wax, and she puts lots of *prrrr prrrr prrrrs* in them, decorated with swirls and drops of wax. Now we hardly say anything to each other except *prrrr, prrr, prrr,* and we spend days going *prrr* in front of her grandmother, and when she says we're nuts, then we do it to her, too, purring, rubbing our heads against her, vibrating with *prrrrrrrs*. She tells us to leave her alone, but it's obvious that she likes it a lot. She'd get down on all fours and purr herself if she weren't embarrassed. I go to Mary Jo's every day, but she never comes to my house, because there's always some problem like Mom is sick and wants quiet. Now I'm used to the sandwiches Mary Jo's grandmother makes, all kinds, butter and ham, cheese and cucumber, salami and radish, egg and mayonnaise. Grandmother Hilton is enormous, and her hair is very short, almost a crew cut. Her fingers look like sausages because her rings are too tight, and her nails are painted dark red, like scabs. The Hiltons have money coming out of their ears, really, compared to me, and Mary Jo also has an older brother, Bobby. Some time I'll have to write about my brother, who died.

O.K., my dead brother was younger than me and now that he's not here he'll always be small—he'll always be two, because when you die you stop growing, and though I should have always been two years older than him, after he died I got to be three years older, then four, then five, and now nine. His name was Nelson. Nelson G. Maze. In her room Mom only has one picture, and it's of Nelson, who died one day when there was a tornado, the serious kind. We're sitting in the house listening to the radio, to find out what that raging tornado is doing: it's already torn off roofs and broken windows and uprooted enough maples and oaks for a forest. And then it goes away. Nelson and I are dying to go out and look around: the street is beautiful, submerged in drowned leaves, black branches, and blue puddles. We turn to the right, toward the church. The tornado has downed a light pole, and the wires are on the ground, twisting, sizzling, throwing off sparks. They create so much heat that the asphalt on the street is melting. The air smells of tar, and we stand there watching. Suddenly Nelson runs toward the wires screaming with excitement. He wants to catch the sparks, he doesn't understand that exactly the opposite will happen. Nelson is completely contorted, his hair stands up straight, like Peter Porcupine, then it goes all wavy. I am stuck to the spot. I can't move. Not a sound, not a cry, only a suffocating silence, stink of tar, of hair and burned sausage. Then I feel myself shaking, I think the wires have grabbed me, but it's Mom shaking my shoulders. End of the silence. Daddy comes right afterward, he rushes toward Nelson to get him away, but Mom stops him, and I see him motionless against the sparks, arms stretching toward Nelson. For a moment that never ends there's my daddy with his arms out, held back by Mom clinging to him. I see them against the light in the orange-and-black striped air. Until the wires stop frying Nelson, and hurl him to the ground in front of us—a piece of toast popped out of the toaster. He's all puckered, his eyes wide open, no longer blue but coal-black. Age: two. I was four.

I didn't really want to write how Nelson died because I tell it every year when we have to write a paper on the most important event of our lives. Each time, I add something new. In Whiskey I always had to read it in class, but here in Goatscreek my homeroom teacher didn't like it: she said you shouldn't dramatize the ordinary facts of life, we all have someone close to us who died. She has a crooked nose and blond bangs, and looks at me as if I had made up the story and later asks Mom if it's true. Instead of getting angry at Crooked Nose, Mom tells me to stop using my brother's death to write the most sensational paper in the class. Stupid jerk. I don't write about it to make myself interesting, I write about it because it's the most important thing that ever happened to me. Mom says that here in Goatscreek it would be better to write about the death of my father. That had never occurred to me. I've always written about Nelson's death. How can you all of a sudden change something as big as the most important event in your life? If something is the most important and something else happens, the second can't take the place of the first. And if there are two things that could both be the most important, which is truly the most important? The first or the second? Which is more important, the death of a brother or the death of a father? And if a thing is used to being the most important, how can it not be offended if it becomes less important than before? I think I will keep writing that Nelson's death is the most important, because there were three of us to be upset about it—Daddy, Mom, and me—and there were only two of us left when Daddy died. In a democratic system that makes three against two. Besides, I don't know how Nelson would take it knowing that all of a sudden his death wasn't so important anymore because Daddy's death had replaced it.

I almost fainted. Leaving school today I saw a guy who is just my type. He was wearing faded jeans, a really cool leather jacket the color of cracked old wood, and dark sunglasses with metal frames, and he had a motorcycle so shiny you could see yourself in it, all distorted. He must be waiting for someone, so Mary Jo and I hang around for a while, trying to figure out how to approach him. We haven't really come up with a plan when Lilian comes out, all dressed up. She gets on the motorcycle and grabs him tight, and they take off with a roar, at top speed. Damn! Mary Jo and I hug each other in despair at having missed him. Then I feel someone tapping me on the shoulder, and I turn, idiotically hopeful, but it's only our private little monster, Ian, who takes advantage of the fact that there's no one around to make us look at his wiener, which is cherry-colored. Yuck.

·   ·   ·

PIA PERA

It turns out there's some hope, because the cool guy in the leather jacket isn't Lilian's boyfriend but her brother Ted. He's here visiting his family, but soon he's taking off to write a book about the U.S.A. He's going to hitchhike all around the country, and then write about the people who pick him up. It should be a huge success, because hitchhiking you get to travel free, and you meet really weird people to write about. Anyway, it all works out because you make pots of money without spending anything on the research. I haven't managed to speak to Ted myself. I heard all this from Lilian, who is wildly excited about her brother's plan—according to her he's a genius and will be famous someday. Which brings me back to my story, the death of Nelson, or rather the story of the time right after he died. Daddy was away a lot on business. Mom went to bed, and I developed this passion for sniffing her feet. I remember as clearly as if it were now how I inhale deeply through my nose: my eyes are closed, and when I open them I'm astonished that Mom is still lying there on the bed, because I'm sure I've sucked her up inside me, along with her smell. I am full of her smell, so full my head's bursting, and yet she's lying there motionless and whole, not an ounce less. I try to grasp how it's possible to steal pieces of her body from her, suck them in through my nose, without changing anything in her, without reducing her by even an ounce. Mom is lying there motionless, I am removing parts of her, which are in her, and yet she doesn't get any smaller. Inexhaustible. If thousands of noses started sniffing Mom, instead of just me alone, I wonder whether there would be enough to go around.

I was sniffing up Mom, but Dad's the one who died after Nelson, quite a few years later, in our old house in Whiskey. The only insurance agent who forgot to insure his own family, comments my witty mother right after the funeral. She says that with Dad gone—God must have sniffed him up with his cosmic nose, the biggest nose in creation—it's time for a change of scene. Time to get away from damned Whiskey, where too many people are dying. I ask her if she's afraid it'll happen again. "Nonsense," she says, shrugging her shoulders. "In this family only the males die." Would it have been better if after Nelson a female had died? Which leaves, as a definite possibility, either me or her. But when I ask if that's what she meant, she doesn't answer. Mom does this thing which infuriates me: she always forgets to answer when I ask her a question. Anyway, if Mom had died instead of Daddy, there would have been just the two of us; if I had died, the two of them would have become orphan parents. The fact is that the variation Mom liked least is the one she ended up with, that is, her and me left alone. Something else occurred to me later: maybe Mom wants to get married again and is afraid that Whiskey might bring her bad luck. After all, there are no other men in the family. In the end I agreed it was better to move, because when the kids in my class came back from vacation they had neat stuff to talk about and I didn't have anything—I had spent the whole summer sniffing my mother's feet and collecting spiders.

"What's new?"

"My father died."

"Oh! How did it happen?" Right, how did it happen. God sniffed and Dad's soul flew away in an instant.

Lilian's family's having a party for her brother. I absolutely have to be the coolest-looking, absolutely I have to have a really super outfit. I tell Mom I need a new dress, all my old clothes are revolting, they're too short and shabby and make me look ridiculous, like a snot-nosed kid. Who do you think you are, Mom says. I just want to make a good impression at the party, but she tells me to forget it—if I want luxuries like that I have to get them myself. Maybe I could win a subscription to *American Girl*, like Chloe, and not come asking her. Because I mustn't kid myself, we don't have a lot of money, like Mary Jo. Ever since that brownnoser Chloe won a stupid subscription to the stupidest magazine for stupid model girls, Mom has been throwing it in my face. I've never tried to win a single thing. To win anything you have to pretend to be different from what you are. The ones who win are the ones who just pretend they're better. The ones the teachers consider the best are only the best pretenders. The teachers hate the ones who really are the best. Anyway, I'm going to dress the way I want for Lilian's party, even if it costs me . . . whatever it costs.

Mom showed me a photo of President Truman's daughter: the first daughter. So what does that make me? The second or the hundred-and-twenty-one-thousandth? And what's Gitta, with her stick legs and breath so bad that even if she was stuffed with Sen-Sen you couldn't sit next to her without throwing up? The last daughter? On Thanksgiving you could have a banquet with the first and last daughters giving each other the kiss of sisterhood, even though one is the first and the other the last.

In the end Mom caved in and we went shopping: I got a new dress with a flared skirt, a pearl-gray top, and a lace collar. And patent-leather shoes with straps. I had to get shoes anyway, because last year's don't fit me, but I got them in my size, not one size larger, like Mom wanted, with an insole: I refuse to wear one, because when you take off your shoes everyone can see what a cheapskate she is. Mary Jo would never speak to me again. But maybe that wouldn't be such a tragedy. Lilian could be my best friend and then I'd see Ted whenever he comes to visit his family. With Mary Jo my only possibility is Bobby, who's a great carpenter, but to fall in love with—forget it. Too bad Lilian is nothing special—I like my friends to be really pretty.

Mom's birthday: she's thirty-five but I'm not supposed to tell anyone. I gave her a novel by Betty MacDonald. Mary Jo's mother read it and liked it a lot.

Rainy Sunday afternoon. At the movies with Mom and Chloe and her mother, who put on a hat so she wouldn't spoil her permanent. There was a fantastic actress with an endlessly long neck. She came down a wide, curving white marble staircase, wearing a long white sequinned dress that left her back completely bare. She walked very slowly and at every step a long narrow shoe peeked out from under her dress. She took her time, so she could be admired by these men, all captivated by her, and she was smiling as if she were made of pure light and not even standing on the ground. She had feathers on her shoulders, like wings, and it seemed as though at any moment she might float up into the air. She was holding a letter in her hand, but she didn't open it because first she wanted to give everyone the joy of seeing her at least for a moment. Yet still she seemed sad, maybe she felt sorry for all those men who were madly in love with her, who could have kissed the ground she walked on, but could never marry her because she loved someone else: they would be unhappy forever. I felt like I was dreaming, almost like I was in love with her myself. Afterward, we went out for hot chocolate, and right in front of everyone I started crying: because of that incredibly beautiful woman. It seemed terrible, unbearable, to think that I might never walk down a staircase and be looked at that way. I ran out, feeling like I was suffocating. Mom yelled at me to come right back, and then that stupid Chloe ran after me, and her mother (who asked *her*?) managed to grab me and asked me: won't you tell us what's the matter? Even if I were her daughter I wouldn't answer a question like that. Meanwhile my mother sits at the table with a very amused little smile: "Would you like to be a beautiful lady?"

I could kill her. She's always making fun of me. And in the midst of all this Chloe, attached to her mother's skirt—and she is the shortest and ugliest of all the mothers in my class—sits there with whipped cream on her nose and every so often lets out an idiotic giggle. I will be a gorgeous woman someday, and then she can laugh as much as she likes, but she will never never ever be one. I will be even more beautiful than my mother. Grandma always said, before she got senile, that Mom may be pretty but I'm prettier, because I take after my father, and the Mazes have been good-looking for at least four generations, while among the Tonguefishes only Mom is passable. The others are all little monsters with razor-sharp features. It's obvious that Mom adores the atomic bomb because she hopes it will change the Tonguefishes' DNA. But in the meantime I have to go to Lilian's party tomorrow in that stupid gray-on-gray dress. To really make an impression I'd need a grand marble staircase and a backless white sequinned dress.

Lilian's party would have been fun except that I barely got a minute with her cute brother. It was really crowded, and he spent most of the time standing in a corner with a drink and not talking to anyone. He's observing, Lilian explains. You know—a writer has to be alone with his thoughts, on the outside looking in. So he just observes. He wants to talk to people without really becoming friends—that's why he likes the idea of hitchhiking and talking to whoever picks him up, people who will be totally frank with him because they'll never see him again. He has a terrific memory—he remembers everything people tell him, and he has this idea to make a kind of collage with all these streams of conversation that are inside him. If he started talking here, with the same old people in Goatscreek, it would just be a social game, because nobody says what they really feel. Then they put on some boogie-woogie records. I was dancing with Bobby, and I was *really* good, and then: miracle of miracles! The great inaccessible Ted was dancing, with a super-tall, super-cool girl who looked tough and slinky. I looked at them and tried to be noticed. Not a chance. When they went out on the porch to have a drink, I sat down next to Bobby with a cherry coke and tried to hear what they were saying, Ted and the beanpole. She was fantastic— never once opened her mouth. When he started a conversation, telling her he was going away to write a book, she shrugged her shoulders and told him she hates reading, so then he said he loves girls who hate books, and they went back to dancing. It was a slow dance: he was holding her close and she was acting tough, and he didn't seem so heroic anymore, but he was still handsome. Then he was standing by himself again, so I went up to him but didn't know what to say exactly. He was looking sulky, smoking cigarette after cigarette, so I asked him to give me a drag, but he looked me up and down and said what did I take him for, a guy who gives kids a smoke? So I said I hate books but I like cigarettes, and he started laughing, but then the beanpole came back and took him off. All because of my stupid gray dress, while she had on tight jeans and boots with fringe, and she's got those long legs—she took him away just when I thought he might ask me to kiss him. The way he was looking at me it was pretty obvious how much he liked me. We'll probably never see each other again because he's leaving soon. Lilian says he picked up the beanpole in a bar before the party. She'd never seen her before and can't stand her. We all can't stand her.

Today out of the blue Mom decides I should think about my future instead of wasting time playing cards with Mary Jo. This business about the future started in Whiskey, right after Daddy died. I'd asked her to stay and talk to me, but she said she had things to do.

"What do you have to do?"

"I have to think."

"Think about what?"

"About our future." Said with a look of resentment. No one ever talked about the future before.

"Why are you worrying about the future?"

"Because your father died and left everything a mess." So my father was the one who put things in order. Since he's been gone we've had the future and the future is a dangerous thing. My father liked to talk. If he were still here I could ask him about the future. He also liked to invent things. After Nelson died he built a tiny electric chair in the garage for lizards. He'd watch while they jerked around, but it didn't last long, because lizards are small and the current was strong, and when it was over a thin thread of smoke came from the electric chair, along with a smell like burned fish. Daddy would pour himself a beer and sit watching quietly. He'd stay sitting still like that for a long time. Sometimes when I went to see him in the garage it was dark, and I'd go in and he'd hug me tight. I didn't like it when he kissed me because he made my mouth wet with beer, but I stayed anyway, to keep him company. I felt sadder for him than for the electrocuted lizards: they didn't feel anything anymore, while my dad was there with his lips wet and his eyes wet and his striped shirt wet, too, and he hugged me and didn't say anything. Quite a few times we sat around in the garage electrocuting lizards, but once Mom came in—which she almost never did—and flung everything on the floor. "It's time to stop this nonsense," she yelled. But she was wrong because she had no right to dump our electric chair on the floor. It would be like if I were to get angry now and throw Mom's vase that has Dad's ashes inside it at the wall. I think that vase is ridiculous. There's a photograph of him above it: what a really stupid idea. In the picture he's smiling, looking satisfied, the way people do when there's a photographer and out of politeness you have to look happy. So there he is smiling like an idiot, while in front of him, right under his nose, are the ashes of his own big, roasted lizard's body. I don't think I'd be smiling so much if I had to keep watch over my own ashes and could never forget that, after all, I'm dead. A person really does look like an idiot, always smiling no matter what happens. Even at the things we wouldn't like in the least if we were still alive. Every once in a while I go up to him and call him an idiot: You are really stupid, Daddy. But he goes on smiling. Poor Dad. I think Mom did it just to make him ridiculous. She did it out of spite.

3.

GITTA'S MOM INVITED mine to the book club next Thursday. There's going to be a lecture by a writer who's from Goatscreek but doesn't live here anymore, and even though he is "really I mean really famous," he's coming anyway because he promised his uncle the dentist. Mom is glowing. Ever since we've been here she's dreamed of getting invited to the book club, and I have to say that in this I turned out to be very useful to her: if she didn't have to take me to school, she wouldn't have anything to do all day and would never meet anyone. When I ask her who is this writer who's so important, she tells me his name is Gerry Sue Filthy and he's written some hugely successful plays, although she can't actually name one, since she's never seen one. She spent all day in the library doing research, poor old Mom.

School is in a big uproar because the horrible dentist's famous nephew is coming. Everybody wants to go and see him. The only one who doesn't care is Mary Jo. Her mother told her that before this guy became "Gerry Sue Filthy the famous writer," he wanted to go out with her aunt, but she told him to get lost because he was always broke. As soon as he kissed her—and he wasn't even much of a kisser—he tried to get money out of her to buy a motorcycle. So the Hiltons are unexcited and unimpressed by the success of "that cheap worthless Filthy," Mary Jo concludes, smug because she's the only one not making a fuss about this idiotic lecture. "The Hiltons are not the type to go wild for some writer." Unlike a certain Maze née Tonguefish.

Today in school Gitta announces proudly that she had a cavity filled by Dr. Ellis Filthy, "the uncle of the famous writer." It turns out that even having a cavity filled by Ellis Filthy is a sign of social distinction. Could he have gotten rid of her bad breath? Maybe the uncle of the famous writer fainted while he was digging around in her mouth? I wouldn't go near it. Anyway, I still have all my teeth. I've never had the pleasure of meeting Dr. Ellis Filthy, or any of his colleagues.

Mom went to the hairdresser for the occasion. Her old ponytail won't do anymore, and she comes home with a "Marlene Dietrich style" haircut. She wants to be sophisticated. Whenever she passes a mirror she practices little gestures, smiles, intense glances . . . The spectacle is unbearable. At least she can't do that in public, but she's not embarrassed about anything around me: it's all in the family, as she says whenever I have to put up with one of her disgusting habits, like hanging her stockings to dry in the bathroom.

Suddenly Mom decides she wants to take me to the book club with her. I had just promised Mary Jo not to be like all those stupid girls dying to go with their stupid mothers: Gitta the cripple, Chloe the brownnoser, her majesty Miss Keats, even fatso Carla, who never read a book in her life, like the rest of her family, even though they pricked her in the bottom with a fountain pen to try to inject a little love for culture. Now Mary Jo will never believe it was my mother who made me go.

I tricked them all, and Mary Jo can't accuse me of anything. The lecture wasn't bad, in the sense that it was a scream to see all those hens decked out in their so-called best clothes, with their hair waved on rollers, all oohs and ahs around the famous writer. Beside him at the lecture table was a spotted terrier he called Rimbaud, or something, and he petted him the whole time. He talked about the magic of little girls, and those thick-ankled former little girls made a tremendous effort not to appear offended that no one considers them enchanting anymore on account of their age. They had sugary smiles stuck to their faces anyway. Obviously they were all fishing for compliments, but they never got any, because the great writer talked the whole time about children in literature. Then he said he wanted to create "an American theater devoted to the feelings of childhood and early adolescence, because such a theater would be the most powerful means of bringing out what is inside every young American boy and girl." The moms nodded, and I started worrying about what to say to Mary Jo. Then there was a question period, and I took advantage of it to set things straight, to make it clear that I wasn't there to please the famous writer. I raise my hand and stand up: "Mr. Filthy, you said more or less the same things our teachers say, that stuff about personality and development and so forth. So if you have the same ideas, why don't you just become a teacher?" And

I sit down. Mom incinerates me with a look, she's about to make excuses for her daughter's "incredible bad manners." Her face pales at the thought that she'll never be invited to the book club again, but instead Gerry Sue Filthy compliments her on my frankness, and says I've behaved exactly the way every American child should—in fact better, because I have the courage of my convictions. I am the ideal adolescent of the glorious atomic age, and it is from "young persons" like me, "open and capable of expressing their thoughts," that great things can be expected for the nation's future. He says so many complimentary things that the other ladies look at Mom enviously, and she does her best to go from an expression of dismay to one of great pride in a daughter raised "in the best spirit of the American Constitution." I'm dying of embarrassment listening to all these pompous speeches—already I'm sorry, and when I look around to see these images of what I'm going to be, I meet the gaze of none other than dreamboat Ted. He obviously hasn't left yet and had nothing better to do than go to the book club with Lilian and his mother. He seems a little ridiculous with his tie and his clean-shaven cheeks—it doesn't look like him. He winks at me, and afterward when refreshments are served he says to me, sarcastically: "Aren't you the one who hates books and loves cigarettes?" So I go: "Aren't you the one who was supposed to be leaving?" I liked him better with his leather jacket and his chrome motorcycle. Then I am right in front of Gerry Sue Filthy, and he lets me play with Rimbaud, an amazing dog, who even calls his master by name. When Mom sends me to say goodbye he sits me on his knees and gives me a kiss, almost on the lips, and I want to sink into the ground because there's Ted and I look like a stupid kid who lets famous people pet her, but Mom is in heaven because Gerry Sue Filthy kissed me, and on the way home she doesn't say anything that makes any sense at all. She's fantasizing about how we're friends now, and how happy she is about this interesting connection, blah blah and blah blah and blah blah. From my point of view all she has to do is buy me a little dog like Rimbaud, who licked my nose when I picked him up.

Thank goodness she didn't realize it—she so dislikes dogs, she would have sent me right off to wash my face. She says dogs stink. I think she stinks worse, with that disgusting hairspray that she puts on to join "the best society of Goatscreek," where you're not supposed "to have a hair out of place." I'm going to ask Mom to get me a dog like Rimbaud for my birthday.

Mary Jo is furious that I went to the lecture and Gerry Sue Filthy kissed me. She said that if her mother knew she'd never let me in their house again. I couldn't care less. In my room I hung up a picture of a terrier exactly like Rimbaud. I'm dying to have a Rimbaud of my own, so I can take him to bed with me at night and hug him tight and make him nuzzle my cheek with his shaggy mustache.

I saw Ted leave. He was at the bus stop, with a knapsack and a guitar, alone, without the beanpole. He told me he's going to New York, and he's going to stay there with some friends and then start his real trip, to the West. I asked if he'd take me.

"You're too young."

"And if I were older?"

"But you're not older." Still, when I asked him to give me a kiss and come see me when he finishes the book, he took my head between his hands and held me tight and gave me a spectacular kiss. I'm sure that anyone who saw us must have thought of that scene with Rhett and Scarlett. It left me utterly transfixed, but then the bus came and he went off with a smug grin: "Listen, it's not everyone who can give such a romantic first kiss." How did he know it was my first kiss?

Mary Jo is truly ridiculous. Today she didn't say a word to me. She just looked offended. An insult to her dignity. That idiot doesn't come off it until Lilian tells her how I knocked out Gerry Sue Filthy during the question period. Still, she doesn't apologize, because she never wants to be wrong, but as a peace offering she invites me over after school. While we're having milk and cookies she admits that people change and maybe even that cheapskate of an aspiring gigolo writer is different from when he was going out with her aunt.

Mom invited Mary Jo, her brother, and her parents over: turkey and mashed potatoes and for dessert lemon meringue pie. Mary Jo and I start a conversation about animals to see if we can get something going, and Bobby gives us a boost. Mom smiles, wider and wider, which encourages Bobby and Mary Jo to tell her how happy it would make me to have a puppy all to myself, to hug and pet. Mary Jo's mother helps us out, saying how important it is for a child to have another creature to care for. She and I spend too much time by ourselves, we ought to have someone else in the house, if only to lessen the silence. Mom, furious but not wanting to show it, says that's why Celeste is there, and she is more than enough. Still, under the attack of the Hilton coalition she promises to get me a hamster, but it has to stay in its cage and I have to clean it myself. Great. I want a dog and all I manage is a hamster. Mary Jo says not to be mad, because hamsters are cute, she'll get one, too, a female, and then we can mate them and sell the babies.

Tonight Mom screamed. A terrible scream. I run to her bed, but she can't stop screaming. I struggle to wake her up, but when she sees me she shrieks louder than before. Like I was her nightmare. She says she had a horrible dream, but she won't describe it and sends me back to bed. I ask doesn't she want me to stay with her?

"Why, do you think you can protect me?" She must be absolutely furious because tomorrow she has to buy the hamster. She must have dreamed about it. She must have dreamed that the hamster was punishing her for her violent hatred. Maybe he was taking bites out of her until he'd stowed half of her in one cheek and the other half in the other. Which she would deserve, seeing how she hates animals.

.   .   .

The pet store is behind the church. It's got parrots, doves, kittens, the cutest cocker spaniel puppies, turtles, and canaries. It smells of animals and birdseed, and I close my eyes and breathe in, trying to lose myself in it, but Mom tells me to hurry up, the stench is disgusting and she's going to faint. I'd like to stay and look at the animals, but Mom is grossed out, she hates the place. The noise of the birds in their cages, their wings rustling, makes her nervous, and the parrots' cries give her a headache. So I choose a hamster quickly. The man in the store opens the cage for me and I feel around among those little light-brown bodies. I take one out without even seeing it, it's so deep down among the others. A really soft little thing, with closed eyes and groping pink paws, and I can't imagine how anyone could tell it's a boy.

"That mouse thing better stay locked up in his cage," Mom whispers as she pays, looking very annoyed. The cage isn't very big; it would have been better to get one with a divider, for when we have babies and Mary Jo and I can put the father in one half and the mother in the other. But Mom says the big one costs too much, and she doesn't see why a mouse needs all that space.

"To get some exercise," I say.

"You can buy a wheel for that," advises the man in the store.

"Maybe another time. First I want to see if she likes it: she's a fickle child, very capricious, today one thing, tomorrow another . . ." Today one thing, tomorrow another. The truth is I have always said I wanted a dog. She's the one who let herself be talked into "that mouse thing." It seems less troublesome to her. I put the cage under the window in my room and name the hamster Nelson, like my brother. Rather: Nelson the Second, so there's no confusion.

On a class trip, to a camp in the mountains. The leaves are already red, the sky is a weird gas-blue, the air is cool and nips your face. A perfect day for horseback riding. I think of Maud and whinny in her honor. Mary Jo asks if I've gone soft in the head, but I don't explain. Her grandmother made sandwiches for me, too. In my knapsack Mom packed a bottle of water and a bag of peanuts: on

the theory that I should get used to not eating much on hikes, otherwise I'll get fat and then the walking becomes pointless. She seems
to have got me and Nelson the Second mixed up. In the afternoon
we stop at a cabin. I'm taking a nap, I feel a tickle on my neck, and I
scratch myself, and then an itch on my shoulder, and I scratch myself
there, too. There's a straw sticking through a hole in the canvas deck
chair. It's Perry Maderna jabbing me. We squint at each other through
the hole. He laughs, hides. I put my eye to the hole and see him
squatting underneath it. He's covering his mouth with one hand so I
won't hear him. Then I move so he can't see me, and his eye appears
and looks for me, a huge black eye, which he rolls like a sea monster,
clicking his tongue. But as soon as I get close he stops and hides. I
take a blade of dry grass to stick him with, he cries out and runs away,
then comes back. I poke him again, until his twin sister, Carla, comes
over, tears the straw out of his hand, yells at him to cut this stuff out,
and then drags him off. She is so jealous you could throw up.
Everyone at school knows they've been sleeping in the same bed for
years because their parents are too stupid to realize that they play husband and wife.

When I get home I find Nelson the Second half dead from
hunger. Not even a peanut, nothing at all, barely any water. I run
down to the kitchen, to find Mom, the hamster starver.

"Nelson!"

"Nelson who?"

"My hamster!"

"You call it Nelson? *Nelson*?!"

"So what?" I say. "Why didn't you feed him?"

"I'm supposed to feed him?"

"I was on a trip!"

"Listen to me. Did I warn you or not that I do not wish to have
anything to do with any animals?"

"And you'd let my hamster die while I'm away?"

"You mean he starved to death?" she asks hopefully.

"No, but he could have."

"But he didn't die," she objects, irritated.

"But he could have!"

Loud snarly laugh from Mom, then: "Try to leave me out when it comes to that mouse thing: tell Celeste to feed the hamster next time you're gone. You're old enough to tell the maid what to do in your room. And you are not to call it Nelson."

"He's called Nelson the Second," but she insists that I change his name anyway. Interesting. I can give orders to the maid but not choose the name of my hamster. Next time she sticks her nose in my room and starts yelling about what a mess it is I'll tell her that I'm old enough by now to decide how my room should look. Poor Nelson, he was terribly weak when I took him out of the cage, light as a powder puff. I gave him some milk, a very little because you shouldn't give someone who's dying too much to eat. People in Europe died because they suddenly started stuffing themselves and weren't used to it. After an hour or so I gave him some of the peanuts that were left from the trip. His cheeks were so full they seemed about to burst, and then he just huddled in a corner. He must have been thinking of the risk he ran while I was away. Luckily I got back in time—my dear mother would be capable of murder to get rid of him. But I'm not going to change his name. Nelson the Second is the perfect name for a hamster who is the founder of a dynasty of hamsters. It's the name of the emperor of Hamstertown.

Today when I come home I hear Mom yelling and Celeste crying. I crouch under the living room window to find out what's going on. Celeste says she wants to have a baby, Mom says if she shows up with a baby she's fired, and then she goes out, slamming the door. Celeste, left alone, is making strange wailing sounds, like a coyote. She looks out the window, but her eyes are so swollen she doesn't realize I'm there, and she stares at the sun with tears dripping down her cheeks. Then she dries her eyes with her apron and goes to the kitchen, where Mom is making tea, and tells her that she's going to have a baby anyway, come what may. Mom tells her to do what she likes, as long as she never has to see it. And that's how the conversation ends. Celeste adjusts the scarf on her head, passes her hands over her eyes and cheeks, as if to make sure everything is still in the right place, and goes to the sink. Mom pours herself a cup of tea. I come in as she's offering Celeste a cup, but Celeste says no thank you and goes on washing the dishes. As soon as she sees me Mom yells: "Go right to your room and clean the hamster cage, it stinks so you could faint."

In this house, as far as children, animals, and living things in general go, we don't do very well. I would say that ever since I got Nelson the Second Mom hasn't been able to stand me. She dreams about how to get rid of the two of us, though we have never, ever done anything to her.

4.

*C*ELESTE DIDN'T COME today. Mom showed me how to wash the dishes and said that from now on I have to do the breakfast dishes before school. And when I complain, she brings out the *Manifesto for the Atomic Age*, and reads me the part where it says man has free will, meaning that God has given him the privilege of creating himself however he pleases—he can be happy or unhappy, good or bad, obedient or disobedient. So, she concludes triumphantly, if I complain it's because I'm too stupid to understand that it depends on me alone whether I'm good and happy or remain a stupid, disobedient, egotistical, and sulky child. Yuck. Apparently, I'm not her daughter anymore but my own: so then why should I wash the dishes, or rather, why should I wash her dishes, too?

Since it's Celeste's fault that I have to wash the dishes now, I ask her why she didn't show up the other day. It's better than what happened to me, she says, but she doesn't say exactly what, only that it was very bad and she hopes it never happens to me. I hug her tight to comfort her, but she just starts crying like a fountain, sobbing so her chest heaves. I give her a sugar cube, to take away the bitter taste, and go to my room to write a geography report, which is incredibly boring. Besides, I keep thinking of Celeste in tears, and although Grandma swore by it, a lump of sugar ultimately doesn't solve much. So I go back and find her ironing in her pink housedress, and she seems glad not to be alone. She sits me on her lap, and talks, then sings, and while she sings she rocks me, looking far away out the window. It's a really nice song, but her voice is so low I can hardly hear it. I stay still, with my head and hands on her chest, my nose stuck in the furrow between her bosoms. It's so dark inside there I can hardly see, but I can't take my eyes away. I don't know what it is that attracts me: there's a shadow between two chunks of flesh, and very softly, very gently I pull on her dress, so I can see better. But I can't see beyond some dark points, and I'm afraid she'll notice and then what would I do?

The whole class was at Mary Jo's party. Except Chloe, because she has never ever said a bad word, never ever disobeyed her mother, and she never ever ever does anything except exactly what she's told. And when the teacher praises her in class she gets such a goody-goody expression on her face it's disgusting. Even Perry Maderna was there. Mary Jo wanted him to dance with her, but he just said no and giggled. She kept shaking her hair in his face, doing her super-cool boogie-woogie, until finally he tried it, but he couldn't follow the beat. He started clowning because Carla was staring at him, and when he goofed she laughed. It seemed like he was having more fun making his sister laugh than dancing with Mary Jo. Then they put on something slow and dreamy and he left Mary Jo and Carla and asked me. We were dancing really close, but as soon as the record ended we ran off in opposite directions. Later I caught him stuffing a sandwich in his pocket and he told me that he's going to be a theology professor when he grows up and so he won't be able to go dancing much anyway.

. . .

The song Celeste was singing the other day is from her church. I'd like to go with her, but Celeste says Mom would get mad. I don't get it—after all, we don't have to tell her. It's not like she ever follows me when I go to my tennis lesson. Celeste smiled but she didn't look at me. I think she's glad I asked.

Mary Jo slapped Perry when he refused to kiss her. He was chicken, she says. It's unheard of, she told me. A true gentleman never lets a lady appear ridiculous—he should at least have kissed her. I can't believe I missed it—Mary Jo trying to make Perry kiss her and then getting mad. A lady shouldn't get to that point; in my view you have to keep a firm hand on a man, just like a horse.

At church with Celeste. Mine was the only white face. I've never seen so many black people all together. When we go in they're utterly still, concentrating, with solemn expressions on their faces, which seem even blacker than usual because no one's smiling. Suddenly the preacher is shouting terrible accusations, saying they are all sinners, from first to last, and that no one, not a single one of them, will escape the fires of hell. Celeste is crying, she tells me to think hard about all my sins, because now is the moment to confess them to God. I try to remember them all—I'm not sure if some are really sins but I include them just in case. All you really need is to say them to yourself in your mind. But everyone does it their own way: some, like me, are thinking about the bad things they've done; others are shouting because they're about to meet Jesus—they seem mad with excitement, shaking and jumping up and down. Even Celeste is crazy. She suddenly leaves me and trots off, and when she comes back she says she's exhausted but free, her sins and troubles don't weigh on her conscience anymore, she's shaken them all off. Finally everyone quiets down, and they go back to their seats look-ing calm. They sing, and it's lovely, like the time I sat in Celeste's lap and felt so warm and peaceful.

Today Mom tells me that:

1. I don't study enough,
2. I'm growing up to be bad,
3. I shouldn't play cards with Mary Jo all the time because then I'm not studying,
4. I should spend less time with Celeste, who is a Negro and has only Negro ideas,
5. I should stop flirting with boys because I am too young.

After which she drags me to church: gray-blue dress, gloves, umbrella "just in case." Mom is dressed more or less like me: my hair's in pigtails, she has tortoiseshell combs in hers and a lead-gray hat with a little veil. A great chill surrounds us. There are so many tall, bony people, with severe, mean, dull faces, all looking reproachful, though you can't tell why, and dressed so you can barely distinguish them from the dove-gray walls and the white columns. They hold black missals in their hands, and the sermon, read in a monotone, is deadly boring. There's organ music, too. Even the other kids look dull. Every face is expressionless—there's no desire to be reborn or to unload even one serious sin and begin happily all over again. All of them with their pathetic little sins, their thin lips, every hair perfectly in place, and their stiff clothes, not a wrinkle in sight. Stilted conversation on the way out: with one hand over their mouth, they complain about their maids. Awful. My mother is totally polite—like a governess, not a mother. This isn't a church, it's a refrigerator for keeping God in, and if possible he's never defrosted. Maybe I shouldn't have gone to Celeste's church, because now I can't stand Mom's.

That stupid Nelson bit me. I let him out of the cage to play and he bites me. I get mad and slap him. He makes a really nasty face, baring those long flat teeth—he's furious because he wants to hurt me but he can't, so he looks at me with those dumb eyes. I only wanted to pet him a little and hold him close, but he, God knows what's got into him: he bites me again and it hurts. I slap him again, so he knows who's in command, but instead of calming down and being reasonable he grabs me with his teeth and won't let go. I take him by the head and force him to open that stupid mouth, but he breaks the skin and now my finger's bleeding. He stares at me with his odious snout, all hunched up and mean. O.K., since he doesn't want to play like a good boy, I invent a new game: I take him by the scruff of his neck and put him on the light bulb, which is boiling hot, and he jumps. It's fun, better than the wheel, which is too squeaky. Nelson looks angry when he jumps: he'd bite all of me if he could, gnaw me to the bone and send me bloodless to the other world. But it so happens that I'm stronger, so he has to perform a cute comic number, because if he doesn't get busy he'll get burned. He pulls up his paws so fast it's a scream—he wants to run away, but he's stuck. My friend, I say, it's pointless to try and escape, because the enemy is under your feet—you can't escape until I say so. He makes me laugh: he looks like a sweaty cyclist who's using all his strength trying to win. He pedals like a lunatic, shaking his stupid whitish paws as fast as in a silent movie. Do you like this new game? I ask him. Now you'll learn to stay in my arms when I want you to. Next time I pick you up I'm sure you will, otherwise you'll run on the light bulb again, get it? He is silent, mute. I can't really tell if he's learned his lesson or not. Anyway I get tired of watching him after a while—as entertainment it's kind of limited. Every jump is the same; really, he's not very bright. That's enough for today. I hurl him in his cage, throwing him really hard so he'll remember that I'm angry and he must never ever dare to bite me, his master. He must have understood in the end, because he stayed in one corner, without moving. I want to see now if I've finally taught good manners to that rat creature. He has to understand, good or bad, that here the master is me. And that he must never ever try to bite me again. I had to get a Band-Aid without Mom knowing, otherwise she'd use it as an excuse to throw Nelson away.

· · ·

Disaster. Mary Jo came over after school to do her homework. Mom made ham-and-cheese sandwiches for us, naturally not as good as the ones Grandma Hilton makes. Then we went to my room and Mary Jo goes to pick up Nelson, and Nelson is stone-dead. She drops him in horror, and runs off to wash her hands because she's afraid of infection. While she's in the bathroom I pick up Nelson with a handkerchief. He's all cold and stiff, and has enormous blisters on his paws. His teeth are sticking out of his mouth and I can't shove them back in. I try to arrange him so Mary Jo can't see the blisters, and since I ought to cry I rub my eyes hard, but I can't. I am really sorry I hurt him on the light bulb, but what can I do. I close my eyes and pretend to cry, while Mary Jo tries to comfort me. After all, she says, he's only a hamster and I can always buy a new one. At that I sob as loud as I can and say that after Nelson I don't want another hamster, and besides we can't tell my mother: she hates Nelson so much she might put him in the garbage grinder. I want to bury him in the back yard. Mary Jo agrees, she's enthusiastic about having a real funeral, a full-dress ceremony. Her brother will make the coffin. But I'm going to sew the shroud myself, with gloves and shoes, so no one can see how swollen his paws are.

Mom is out, luckily, so I tell Celeste what happened. I hug her, and she sits me on her lap and rocks me, and now I really do cry. It must be all that warmth, that softness in Celeste's body, but there's something else. I've tried drawing Celeste when no one's looking: I make a big bottom and bosoms that go all the way to the edge of the page, and an enormous stomach, although she's not that fat, not compared to Mary Jo's grandmother, anyway, but that's the way I feel like drawing her. I want her to be so huge that I can sleep on her and live inside her. Once I made a drawing of her with a piece of chocolate and then I licked the whole thing. I nestle my head between her bosom and her stomach, crying, and finally I almost manage to get myself inside there. I feel good there, it's like paradise.

"Let me see Nelson," she says to me after a while. I get scared.

"Why?"

"So I can see how he died."

"You want to put him in alcohol in a jar? Do an autopsy on him?"

"What are you talking about jar, autopsy—you all say anything you like in this house." She glares at me, I shut up, and meanwhile she goes and opens Nelson's cage, takes him out, examines him. She immediately notices the swollen paws. "And how did this happen?"

I lower my eyes. "I don't know."

"What do you mean, you don't know? What did you do to him?" Then she explodes: "This is worse than kids on the street who torture cats—at least they're doing it to stray animals, animals they don't know. While you . . . " She rubs Nelson against my nose. It's gross, that piece of damp fur over cold flesh. Celeste is really angry, and I'm getting angry, too. How dare she? Then I try to explain that that idiot Nelson bit me. But she glares at me even harder, and right away I'm sorry I told her.

"And so what? What's wrong with that?"

"I'm his master and he has no right to bite me." Celeste is furious. "He hurt me."

"Oh, he hurt you . . . Let's see this terrible wound."

"Here," and I lift up the Band-Aid.

"And he deserves the death penalty for that?"

"See?" Barely visible are two tiny dark-red spots.

"Think about what you did to him. What would you say if you found yourself with blisters instead of feet?" She takes one of Nelson's paws, and the toes come off in her hand. "Would you like it if your toes were detached from your feet?" She shakes me: "You don't even have a scratch, and Nelson is dead. And if he were still alive he would have stumps instead of feet."

"That's not the point, it's the principle of the thing. I'm the master and he has no right to bite me, get it?"

"Principle! Master!" Celeste says scornfully.

"You don't understand because you're a stupid Negro with

Negro ideas, and you Negroes don't have principles and besides you can't stand not being the masters yourselves." Celeste turns into an icicle, worse than Mom.

"All right, then I'm going to call Mrs. Maze and we'll tell her what you've done."

"Mrs. Maze hates Nelson and she would have done even worse things to him," I shout, since Mom's not home.

"You think I don't know that? You think I don't know your mother is even more of a brute than you are? Who *can* I call?" Rage takes hold of me. I want to tear her to pieces, hearing her talk like that about my mother. How dare she? But there's no point in insulting her, since she's not listening to me anymore. She looks at Nelson again and starts crying very quietly, sitting on my bed, with her hands over her face. I feel mean for calling her all those horrible things. Finally she dries her eyes. "So, will you tell me what you did to reduce him to this state?" Hiding under her flowered skirt I tell her, very fast so she can't hear me clearly, that I made him jump on the light bulb.

"What? Say that again, I don't understand." She pulls me out from under her petticoat and says: "It doesn't matter how you did it, but on Sunday you come to church with me and repent, because a girl your age shouldn't keep such a terrible thing on her conscience. If it stays inside you it'll fester and turn gangrenous." I tell her I'm going to bury Nelson in the yard, but we have to let Mom think he escaped. Then I ask if she has a piece of black material.

"For what?"

"I'm going to make a shroud. Bobby's going to make a coffin."

"A shroud?"

"Yes, so no one can see that his paws are missing." Celeste gets Mom's sewing basket, and together we make a small black sack with a gray ribbon to tie it. Then we put Nelson inside: poor little creature, his head is sticking out, and I still can't get his mouth closed so the teeth won't show. They make him look mean and stupid: I wish that he'd at least have an intelligent expression now that he's dead. Celeste says to leave the cage in the attic, because Nelson might rot and start smelling bad in the heat.

"Bad how?" I ask, since all smells are interesting to me.

"A smell that's something between vanilla, vomit, diarrhea, and sweaty feet," Celeste explains, "and yet is different from all those smells, because it also has something . . . "

"Something between the sweat in your armpits and rotten flowers?"

"How do you know that?"

"When I grow up I'm going to write a book about the energy trapped in smells and I'm going to build a bomb so stinky that in comparison the atomic bomb will seem like the elixir of life." But she doesn't think much of this idea, because she gives me a push and sends me off with her favorite sentence: "Get a move on."

5.

I PASS A note to Mary Jo: "Shroud ready. Coffin?" She answers: "Coffin ready this afternoon. Coast clear?" "Coast clear." Mom's going to the movies with Chloe's mother and I'm staying home to do my homework.

Everything goes according to the script. Around four Mary Jo and Bobby come over. I let them in very quietly because Mom hasn't gone out yet, she's touching up her nail polish and putting on hairspray. As soon as she leaves I call them, and go up to the attic to get Nelson the Second's tiny corpse. Bobby takes the coffin out of his pants pocket: it's almost square, and made of pale veined wood. Mary Jo drew a picture of a hazelnut branch with a hamster wheel underneath, and her grandmother sewed a pink cotton lining.

"You didn't tell her about the hamster?"

"What do you think—I told her it was for a doll's funeral,

that's why she made it pink." It's really cold, so we have the funeral service first, in the living room. I put Nelson in the coffin, wrapped in his little black shroud, and we read the service for the dead from a prayerbook of Grandma Hilton's. Then we put some peanuts in the coffin, the way the ancient Egyptians did, so Nelson will find them when he wakes up in the next world. Beside him I put a lock of my hair tied with a ribbon so he'll remember me, because after all we did love each other. Celeste whispers in my ear to kneel and ask his forgiveness.

"Forgiveness?" Mary Jo is astonished.

"Forgiveness for not having protected him," Celeste says, unperturbed. I give her a dirty look, but I kneel down and I really do ask him to forgive me, inspired by Celeste, who is humming one of her hymns very softly. Something solemn is happening, because I burst into tears and I am sorry, truly, from my heart. I even give him a kiss, although he doesn't smell very good, but there Celeste says I'm overdoing it. O.K., Mary Jo says to Bobby, it's time to close the coffin. She hands him a hammer and nails, and we put it in the middle of the table, with a blue candle on top. Then we have milk and cookies and talk about important episodes in the life of Nelson the Second, from the moment I got him until we found him stone-dead. Celeste recalls how angry Mom was the day she had to go and buy him, Mary Jo expounds on our plans for intensive breeding and selling of hamsters; I tell how one time Nelson bit me, but instead of getting angry with a little animal incapable of understanding what he'd done I decided to be magnanimous and forgive him. They all applaud except Celeste, who always gets mad when I don't tell the exact truth. After the memorial snack, we go out to the yard, where it's already dark and the air is smoky. Bobby digs the hole in a corner sheltered by an elm-tree branch and then, with black ribbons, lowers Nelson down. I throw in a rose and the first handful of dirt, which is dark and icy cold, but I let Bobby do the rest, because it's the undertaker's job. I tell him to make the mound barely noticeable, so no one will see it's a grave, and afterward I cover it with the same grass that was there before, no stone or flowers. It turned out well—if you didn't know, you wouldn't notice anything. We make a cut in the bark of the elm tree so we'll be able to find the exact spot later. We stick a tiny wooden cross there, at least for the next few days—temporary but better than nothing. It's O.K., Mom never goes out in the garden in the winter. We say a final prayer, and the steam from our breath mingles over Nelson's grave and makes a nice effect, like incense. Afterward, we leave a piece of paper in the hiding place in my desk, with the distance from the tree trunk to the grave written on it, and also the date, so as the tree grows we can calculate how much wider the trunk is compared to now. This way, we can hold the annual memorial at the exact spot where Nelson is. Then Mary Jo and Bobby go home, and I stay with Celeste.

"You see, Celeste, now we're both left all alone, without our little ones, me without Nelson the Second, you without your baby," but she doesn't like this line at all. "Stop acting like an idiot," she yells. "You stupid Negro," I shout at her as she leaves the house, her bottom wiggling, her turquoise coat over her arm. I run after her, to apologize—after all, it's too bad to quarrel right after Nelson's funeral, which went so well, but she's already way down the street and she doesn't even hear me. The hell with it. The hell with everything. Even her.

Made peace with Celeste. But everything's kind of a drag now that it's over. I have the cage in my room, but it's empty, no more squeaking wheel. I'm sorry I didn't think about this before: I really didn't have to fry Nelson on the light bulb. Maybe there is a kind of curse in our family that makes all the males die. We might as well have stayed in Whiskey, which I liked better anyway, because of the garage with all my dad's equipment in it. I'd bring boys there to see it—they were in heaven, they sucked up to me so they'd get invited to see the electric chair. I knew as much as they did, because I learned all about everything from my father, but we don't have any of his stuff here. Mom sold it. She barely wanted to take anything from Whiskey, she was so desperate to shake off that house and all its bad memories. See, she hoped a change of scene would be enough to keep things like that from happening anymore. She believes the move has saved her. It's better that way, if you think about it; she's got such a short fuse, she explodes at practically anything, so it's better to let her be tranquillized by the idea of having escaped this whole business of how in our house male creatures die before their time. If she started thinking it had come with us she'd go crazy, like the time when she spent entire days staring at the fan blades. Celeste doesn't believe in the curse on our family. It's normal for the men to die earlier, she says. It's always happened that way—you see how many old ladies there are, and how few men. If it's a curse it's a curse on everyone, not only the Mazes. When we start talking about my father she explains that he never answered me in writing because he has become a spirit, and spirits are too thin to hold a pen in their hands. For the same reason, though, he can always read me, without my having to send him letters.

Dear Daddy, if I had realized it before, I wouldn't have written you all this stuff, but now you know, so I might as well keep going—besides, according to Celeste it's pointless to lie to you, since you would immediately know it: even if you can't hold a pen, you can read my thoughts and what's in my heart: spirits are so thin they can even get in there, and if I wrote something different you wouldn't have a very high opinion of me.

Probably you also read Mom's thoughts. I wonder what it's like to be a spirit and know everything, really everything about everyone. For example, Mom is going out with Mary Jo's uncle. Celeste says it can't bother you, because by now you've simply moved out of the body and all its passions, and you know that men have to live like men and women like women, and anyway when you're a spirit you have different feelings and emotions, which we here on the earth can't even imagine. Is that really true?

I let Mom think that Nelson escaped because I accidentally left the cage open. She wasn't at all sorry about it: "Finally—the mere thought of that toothy beast in your room made me ill." I don't understand why she hates animals so much. After all, I never made her do anything for Nelson, except when she had to go with me to buy him, and if she'd given me the money I could have gone by myself. When Celeste found out how happy Mom was about the death of Nelson the Second, she said that my mother hates all living things because they create complications, the same reason she buys plastic flowers instead of real ones. Since we were on the subject I tried to get her to tell me what happened with her lost baby.

"How do you know about that?" I heard her talking to Mom before she was sick, and I guessed. "Mrs. Maze was very nasty that day, very nasty. But she's made that way, she can't stand small living things, like your hamster or my baby ..." Then she was confused, because there she was, saying the same thing that when I said it made her furious.

"But with the baby you were expecting, what happened?"

"It's an ugly story: I got terribly frightened and I lost it."

"But where is it now?"

"With the spirits."

"So you have a spirit to talk to, Celeste?"

"Oh yes, I could have had one, only it's too bad I wasn't in time to teach my spirit to speak."

Dear Daddy, couldn't you find the spirit of Celeste's baby and teach it to speak, so she'll also have someone far away from here to talk to her and make her feel not alone? I can see that I was wrong to tell her that my losing Nelson the Second was the same as her losing her baby. If she were white, maybe she wouldn't have been offended, but people say that Negroes are apes, so it must have seemed awful when I compared her baby to a hamster. She was really glad when I apologized, her whole face lighted up and she said I have a good heart, deep down, even if I'm kind of domineering. We made peace, peace forever, and promised not to fight ever ever again. She picked me up and put me on her lap, then she dug in her pocket and gave me a kerchief that belonged to her mother, really pretty, red with brown and gold designs.

. . .

Mom is out, and Celeste uses the opportunity to take me to her church again.

"We have some weight on our heart, don't we?" she says to me, putting an arm around my shoulders. We get there late, in the middle of the story of the woman who turns into a pillar of salt while the city of sinners dissolves as if hit by the atomic bomb. The preacher reads very slowly, pronouncing his words syllable by syllable and pausing every so often to keep us all holding our breath. He rolls his eyes, and the congregation follows. He opens his mouth wide, and they do, too. When it's over, Celeste and I are completely captivated by the way he speaks and by his comments on the story, by the way he looks at us as if it had been written for each of us, without exception. When it's time to repent, Celeste kneels with me, then jumps to her feet and drags me, running. I'm a little embarrassed but what can I do—it's useless to protest when she's this excited. Finally I get used to it, because they're all doing weird things, worse than us: dozens and dozens of men and women are shaking with emotion, some are crying, and they're all gazing upward, at what I have no idea. The preacher has very long arms in very wide sleeves, and he joins his hands in front of the cross. There's so much shrieking that no one notices me. At first they did—impossible not to, mine's the only white face there—but with all the running and shouting no one's paying any attention to anyone else, we are all clinging to God, becoming more and more agitated. It no longer matters what I want to be forgiven for: at first it was for Nelson the Second, but then, as my voice is lost in all the others, I ask forgiveness for everything, even for the roasted lizards in the garage. On the way home, when I try to tell Celeste what I feel, she explains to me that at the end, when everyone asks forgiveness, and the voices are all mixed up together, each of us has forgotten the exact sin that brought us there, and the fact that we've forgotten is a sign that God is no longer angry, and we are now able to feel this immense joy of being forgiven all together, with no one excluded, and when this happens your heart can fly up all light and free, like at a dance when no one is left out and you feel happy. Then Celeste takes my gloved hands in hers and drags me in a ring-around-the-rosy of joy, on the street. We're still pretty far from my house, so there's no chance of being seen by one of our neighbors; otherwise, if someone found out that Celeste took me to church there would be real trouble. I love going there, being the only white, and seeing all the black people together. They're beautiful, moving so gracefully, with such excitement in their eyes; and they smell good, sort of spicy. I think that if being black didn't involve such a lot of practical disadvantages, like there being places you can't go, I would really like to have skin like theirs.

A red Shelby with nickel-plated handlebars and a basket: Christmas present from Mom. I can just reach the pedals. I go up to the top of the hill where the church is, and then down sharply, full speed, wind and cold stinging my cheeks. It had rained earlier, and the asphalt sparkled. Mom gave my old bicycle, the one we left in Whiskey, to the Association for Starving Europeans. I loved that bike. Daddy gave it to me, and I would have liked to keep it, to give to my children, but Mom says it's not at all certain that I'm going to have children, and anyway I'm too big for a tricycle. This red bike is really cool, with an elegant frame and a soft leather seat. Mary Jo has the same one, but blue. It will be fantastic to ride our bikes to school together when the weather gets better. There have been big storms and it's freezing cold.

Mom has the flu. She sends me to buy her a Nancy Bruff novel, but she's still bored. Mary Jo's uncle comes to see her. Even if he owned a ton of movie theaters and horses, I still wouldn't like him. He's greasy. It's not right for him to visit Mom while she's sick. To doll herself up Mom asks me to paint her nails red, but the fever makes her hand tremble, and nail polish drips on her ring finger. Result: she gets hysterical, shouts at me to take it all away immediately, get lost: "You will never learn to make yourself useful." Thanks. I do what she wants because she's sick and you have to be patient, but tough luck if her nails are even paler than before. I bring her her compact so she can put on some lipstick, and I hold the mirror while she sprays her hair. That gross spray stuff gets in my mouth and nearly poisons me, but then I look in her eyes, and they're so unhappy, it makes me miserable. So I advise her to put on her black lace gloves to hide those sad colorless nails—if you have a fever nothing is odd—and with her beautiful tapered fingers the gloves'll look good. She sends me to get them and her anger evaporates. All this uproar for that wretched uncle of Mary Jo's. When he arrives, I check him out: he has short legs, he's stocky, and his breath smells like exhaust fumes. Can't she see? Is it possible that a nice car and a movie theater are enough to make a woman happy? That a man is O.K. just because there aren't any others?

Mom is still sick, and she sends me to the Hiltons'. The whole family's there. They all ask how Mom is, so, to eliminate the possibility of ending up with Mary Jo's uncle for a father, who besides all his other defects is superstitious about death, I say: "Don't worry, in my house the women never die."

"What do you mean, they never die?"

"They don't die until they're at least a hundred, but in exchange there's a curse on the males in our house. Didn't you know?" They're all curious. Then I pretend to be sorry for what I've said.

"But don't spread it around, Mom doesn't want people to find out, or she'll be stuck by herself for the rest of her life." It worked: he's worried, as I expected; he won't look at me, but he pricks up his ears.

"Tell us all about it," Grandma Hilton orders, standing in front of the tree, that's sparkling with colored lights. She's taking command of the situation. I invent an elaborate story about the deaths in my house, first my brother and then my dad. I say that Dad escaped from a submarine in the Pacific, but he managed to make it home and within a month he was dead, curled up in a chair in the living room. Mom had just persuaded him to stop talking about the naval battles, because she had read in *Good Housekeeping* that a sure sign of mental instability was being unable to talk about anything but the war: it's

O.K. for the first two weeks at most, but then you have to get interested in civilian life, otherwise the war becomes an obsession and then how can a person become normal again. I go on like this for a while, just to hold their attention, but it's all a crock since my dad wasn't even a soldier. That wasn't too smart because the Hiltons could check, but on the spur of the moment it seemed like a very affecting story, the story of a man who escapes five hundred bombs and a thousand slant-eye ambushes and then, worn out by his wife's henpecking and his own unhappiness at not being able to tell her anything, dies. At that point Mary Jo's uncle unleashes a diatribe against women that goes on and on. When he calms down, no one knows how to get the conversation going again—like they're all made of stone—so I take up my subject that I won't let go of and make up wild stories about my female ancestors. I say that some of them lived until they were a hundred and ten or fifteen, and that my Norwegian great-grandmother had a child when she was seventy, by her sixth husband, who died a few months after the wedding—and they are on the edge of their seats listening. Even Mary Jo believes it all. If Mom finds out, I'm really in for it, but at least I've taken care of Mary Jo's uncle. We won't see him again.

Dear Daddy, Happy New Year. Mom will be in a really bad mood when she realizes that Mary Jo's uncle isn't going to show up anymore, just like you. But I'm sure you approve: it would have been awful to have a man in the house who's so ugly, so stupid and smelly and superstitious. If Mom gets married again I hope it will be someone you'd like, someone you could be friends with. For next year, I wish you'd send us someone like that, because Mom's hopeless, she absolutely has to get married, otherwise she'll be in a bad mood forever, and blame me for everything. It's true that even when you were here she wasn't exactly easygoing, but now—you must realize it even where you are—she's worse. Besides, I don't like being by ourselves all the time. There's not that much to talk about; all we do is fight. Sometimes there's a truce, but it's shaky. If Mom had a new husband we could do so many fun things. For instance, we're staying here for the whole vacation, while Mary Jo is going skiing, and everyone *everyone* in my class is doing something cool, and we're not doing anything. We're not even going to Grandma's, because what would we do there—by now she's turned into a complete idiot and wouldn't even realize we'd taken the trouble to visit her, so we're staying in Goatscreek. If there were three of us, though, maybe we'd do something or go somewhere, and Sunday lunch wouldn't be so stupid, and well, anyway, it would all be different. But you don't have to worry that the day Mom marries someone else I'll forget you, because you'll always be my only true father, and I'll always love you. Even if Mom got married eight more times, I'd always love you better than all her other husbands.

6.

MARY JO IS skiing at Pico Peak, and she calls on my birthday to invite me to come—she says I can sleep in her room with her. But Mom won't let me, because her best friend is arriving. How infuriating—it would have been so great to go on a ski trip with the Hiltons, and instead I have to stay home for stupid Nora. It must be the hundredth time she's been about to come and never does. This time, she actually does materialize, followed by a huge red trunk on wheels. "Why, she looks exactly like her father!" Nora cries in a soprano voice as soon as she sees me. Then she hugs me hard. Her perfume is so sweet my head spins. She's wearing a hat that's crammed with fake fruit, and almost as tall as she is; despite her spike heels she's barely an inch taller than me. But she's pretty: she has tiny features, like a porcelain statuette, and her skin is so pale and luminous that I just stand there staring at her, amazed. I can't believe she's as old as Mom.

"You recognize this, Isabel?"

Mom doesn't know what to say: "I don't know, it's lovely. . . of course it's not very wintry . . . "

"Oh I know, I wanted to surprise you. It comes from that Carmen Miranda film—it's the base of the hat with the cascade of fruit, the one that falls off the ship while she's singing . . . " Then she gives us Christmas presents: for me a chocolate Santa Claus, a night-cap with stars on it, and a jump rope. The prettiest package goes to Mom, who opens it, looks at it with one eyebrow raised, and then turns red. She wraps it up again and won't let me see it. Nora gives her a dazzling smile, dimples showing, and says: "Inspired, isn't it?" Mom pretends to threaten her, then starts laughing, but when I ask her what it is she tells me to clear out. But I'm not going to, because for once Mom is having fun and being nice, and I don't see why I should be left out. Luckily Nora pleads on my behalf, so I sit on her side of the sofa and she tells how she's organizing a collection of movie memorabilia and is going to found the Nora Elon Museum of Film Costumes. In the first room she'll display the hat she arrived in, which has an extension almost twelve feet long. Mom shakes her head, not convinced how successful this enterprise is going to be. Always eager to dampen spirits. Nora, however, is very sure she's going to make heaps of money: "This collection might not make me as rich as you, Isabel, but it will be enough to take some nice trips around the world." Mom lights a cigarette and corrects her: "Don't believe it. Gerald managed to lose quite a lot with his experiments." Oh God, if she gets off on the theme of financial hardship it's all over, so to change the subject I ask Nora what she does in Los Angeles. She's a makeup artist, she says, and tells me stories about all the actresses she knows: they really sound pretty amazing, with spicy per-sonalities and plenty of romantic adventures, practically two a day. Then she takes my face in her hands, looks me in the eyes, and goes: "With your pretty nose, your big smoky gray eyes, and especially your features, which seem to have been drawn with a hard pencil, you'd be a hit in Hollywood."

Mom doesn't appreciate that a bit: "Remember, you're going to study nuclear physics. I don't like thinking of you as an actress—the most that can happen is you end up on the poster of the atomic mushroom like that Spanish illiterate Hayworth."

"And nuclear physics?"

"You might still become the first woman to make a bomb so perfect that it would kill the enemy without destroying a single city. Wouldn't you like that? Winning a war without destroying works of art and ancient monuments?"

"I have never wanted to do anything else," I say in my dreamiest voice. Anyway I'm happy because after lunch Mom goes grocery shopping and Nora asks where her room is, so she can change, and then we go out together. It's snowing, and there's a cold wind that makes your eyes tear, so we just take a short walk, past my school, Mary Jo's house, and the church. Nora asks me a ton of questions about Mom: is she in a better mood, do we get along, do I try to understand her. When I tell her that I am truly unfortunate in having a mother who doesn't care about me at all, she says that someday I'll understand what a wonderful woman she is and be sorry for the mean things I'm saying. It may seem that way to her, because they're best friends, but not to me. Still, I must not be *so* horrible, because she told me that if she had a daughter she'd want one exactly like me. We have lots of nice talks, but at night they go out and leave me alone. They must want to talk on the sly.

Mom went to visit Grandma in the place for nutty old ladies. She didn't want to take me because I'd get upset, so she left me with Nora for a couple of days. We go ice skating, and run into some kids from school at the rink. They ask me who I'm with, and before I can answer Nora says she's my older sister. They look at each other in confusion and glide away.

"Why did you tell a lie?"

"It wasn't a lie. I was joking, and besides, right then you did seem like my little sister. Next time we'll just say I'm a friend of yours."

"But you're Mom's friend. Mary Jo is my friend. You shouldn't tell lies." Meanwhile Nora loses her balance.

"See what happens when you tell a lie?"

"Silly, you shouldn't pay attention to the people who want you to believe that we have problems because we deserve them. We have problems on their own account, whether we're good or bad, tell the truth or lie, do good or bad. So: see that you don't get confused. Besides, what makes you think your mother's friend can't be your friend, too?"

"But you came here for Mom."

"Are you jealous because we went out by ourselves last night?" she asks me, with her malicious dimples.

"No, I'm not jealous, but it's true that you came to see Mom, not me."

"Now, listen! You've got the wrong idea. It's not a lie when you confine yourself to telling a piece of the truth. Don't pay attention to Isabel, who is always so reliable, so absolutely precise. You're better off getting used to not blabbing about everything that happens to you. Not that you should tell lies, but as a rule it's better to confine yourself to part of the truth, because you never know, you may find yourself in a situation where you need a way out."

"Like what?"

"You'll see. Meanwhile, try not to become one of those spineless characters who can't keep things to themselves. But that's enough for now—I don't want you to forget the most important thing."

"Don't believe that you have problems because you've done something bad and don't ever tell more of the truth than is strictly necessary?" I ask, to check that I've understood.

"Bravo, Dolly, you're more intelligent than you seem."

"What do you mean, than I seem?" I ask, worried and a little insulted, but instead of answering she chases me around the rink, grabs me, and then goes, with a cackling laugh, "O.K., one other thing: go on pretending to be less intelligent than you are. It's the same sort of principle as not telling more of the truth than is strictly necessary." After which she launches into some spins: "Now I'll teach you." We do a lot of figures, and she holds my hand, but I keep falling just the same.

"It doesn't matter, the more times you fall the better—you gain confidence." We skated all afternoon, and we were exhausted. To revive we went to Betty's for a hot chocolate, where Nora told me a ton of things about when she and Mom became friends, and how my mother was much nicer than she is now. Too bad I didn't know her then.

Tonight Nora went out and, true to her principles, didn't tell me where she was going. She was wearing a black coat with a fur collar, also black, and she tottered on her heels. She really looked super, but I was in a bad mood because she wouldn't take me with her. She also told me not to tell Mom that she left me alone in the house. When she said goodbye at the front door, under the light, her eyes sparkled, and when she smiled she looked like a doll, with her dimples. I wanted to hug her and tell her how much I like her.

Nora and her lies: she told me she came here just to get to know me but I don't believe her. She's gone out a bunch of times by herself without telling me where she was going or who she was seeing.

"If you really wanted to get to know me you could have invited me to Los Angeles."

"And why should I invite someone I didn't know?"

"So why should you come and visit me when you've never seen me?"

"If you came and I didn't like you, I'd still have to put up with you; this way if I don't like you I could leave early or forget about you. Besides, you understand people better if you see where they live. When you see them in their own houses it's as if they had their clothes on; outside, it's like seeing them naked, and though you can learn some things about people when you see them naked, I wouldn't say that those are the important things."

"You think you've seen me wearing the type of clothes I'd wear if I had the choice? You know what it means to be a child? To wear clothes you'd never want to be caught dead in."

"I hadn't thought of that."

"Well, next time remember that you can perfectly well invite me to your house."

"And don't forget that I'm also your mother's best friend, and maybe I'd like to see her, too."

At the lake with Nora. We go for a walk among the pines, the sky is blue and the tops of the mountains are light gray, like on packages of Swiss chocolate.

"Did you know Mom named me Dolores for Dolores del Rio?"

"You certainly don't look like her, and anyway it's not true. Your father and mother named you Dolores after the owner of the hotel in Mexico where they went for their honeymoon."

"Do you know *everything* about Mom?"

"Let's not go overboard."

"But why would you choose someone like that for your best friend?"

"Like what?"

"Someone who's always telling you what you can and can't do."

"I didn't choose her for a mother."

"Me neither, for that matter."

"No? And did she choose you for a daughter?"

"Absolutely not. Did you know that for Christmas she got a psychology book, with a questionnaire about children, and she put an x next to all the bad things, without leaving out a single one?"

"Really? Are you so awful?"

"To listen to your beloved best friend you'd say that I'm going to be a depressed housewife with a tendency to alcoholism and kleptomania. From her description you'd say that I make her sick."

"That's an exaggeration—maybe she's only trying to be objective," she teases.

"Are you crazy? The way she describes me, it sounds like she hates me. Poor old Mom, she has to live with a hateful child. If I were her I'd be desperate, don't you think?"

"Not at all.—You're too sensitive."

Hell. In the end she's more Mom's friend than mine.

Mom came back from Miami and says Grandma is more nuts than ever. Besides staring at the marmalade jar she chatters, and when she pees she insists on having it saved for her in champagne bottles, and she spends hours and hours arguing with the clothes tree, convinced that it's her horse Peanut. But no one contradicts her, so she's in a good mood, which she's never been in her whole life.

Nora left this morning, and Mom drove her to the train, so I take the opportunity to look for Nora's present. After ransacking the whole house, I finally find it in the bathroom, high up on top of the toilet tank. It's a book—*How to Catch a Man: 101 Winning Strategies.* Juicy stuff. It explains how to bend any man to your will. It says that now that the war is over women have to go back to being total women. However, to catch a man they have to be energetic, too, because the war taught men to appreciate physical skill, strength, and agility above all. Thus to be attractive a woman should resemble a boy, with a husky voice and an athletic figure. Then there's a bunch of fairly dull psychological observations on relations with your mother, father, brothers and sisters, on the body, dreams, and sex organs, men's and women's timing. I skipped that since it wasn't very specific, but I only got through a little of the introduction, because Mom came back and nearly caught me.

I've been sick for a week. Bad sore throat and fever. Celeste brings me lemon juice and plays cards with me. I tell her about the book hidden in the bathroom and get her to bring it to my room. Rule No. 1: paint your lips deep red. Then pages and pages on fingernails, lingerie, perfume, all in a chapter on a woman's exterior appearance. Conclusion: devote more attention to your appearance than to anything else, because you will never have a second chance to make a first impression. Celeste acts out all ten of the rules: hilarious, she's a real comedian. She puts the book back just in time, but Mom scolds her for getting me excited when I'm sick. I try to convince her that I'm not at all excited.

"Quiet: you're sick and I'll tell you what's best for you." The same old story: she takes advantage of my being sick to control me, what I can read, how I should dress, how much I should sleep, who I can see. From the gleeful way she takes over, you might say the simple truth is that when I'm sick she's happy.

Mary Jo got so tan skiing that her face is the color of leather. She told me how one night they were playing a new game where you had to blow on the Ping-Pong balls to get them off the opponent's side. So she and her friends were all blowing on these balls, when a really cute guy started playing with them, and all of a sudden he looked her in the eyes, grabbed her hand, and asked her in front of everyone if she would marry him.

"He was sure I was eighteen. Look, Perry Maderna is just a kid and so he runs away. To him it's like I'm already a grownup."

"Perry's really in love with me, only he's shy. He looks at me from a distance, and doesn't say anything, but I know he's in love with me from that time when he was sticking the blades of grass through the hole in the deck chair."

Mary Jo doesn't appreciate this: "Oh well, sure, you don't scare him. After all, you're not a woman yet."

"And since when are you?"

"My breasts are growing."

"I don't believe you. Let's see." I look inside her shirt: there's a slight swelling, but otherwise pink nipples exactly like mine. "Doesn't look like much to me. Anyway, did you know that Teddy

Glass kissed me on the mouth before he left, at the bus stop? He also told me to wait for him, because he'd come back soon to get me."

"You know what?"

"What?"

"I got it."

"Got what?"

"My period. The day after I came back from Pico. Mom said: now we have another woman in the family." She tells me that this great privilege, which doesn't seem all that attractive to me, consists in this, that now she can have a baby.

"I wouldn't know what to do with a baby." Then I got out of bed and performed the rules for catching a man like Celeste, but not all of them, because right at the best part Mom brought us cups of warm milk.

7.

THE FEVER IS back. I dreamed that a really ugly old hag came down the chimney with a sack over her shoulder. She put it down and climbed back up by her cape, but first she took the salt shaker and dumped salt on the ashes in the fireplace, and spit on it, a yellow-purple saliva that sparkled like snail slime. I looked away in disgust, fell down, then crawled over to open the sack. It was full of coal, and among the lumps of coal was a straw doll that looked exactly like Mom, with the same hair and the same blue dress with the lace collar. While I was cleaning her off, blowing away the coal dust and brushing her, she bit me. I got really mad and tore off her arms, and then her head and legs. I dug out the eyes, and ripped the whole thing into tiny pieces. Then I piled them up and set them on fire. I sat in front of the fire to warm my hands, but though it was blazing it sent out puffs of cold air, and I was shivering. There were blisters on my hands and my fingers fell off. I tried to stick them back on, but I couldn't, and the old woman stuck her head out of the chimney again and told me she wanted to give my fingers to the poor children.

Expedition to see *It's a Wonderful Life*. If I'd known before what it was about I wouldn't have gone: it's one of those awful movies that make you cry buckets, a story about how everything turns out right because the father didn't die after all. I don't like to waste time thinking about what if things were different; those thoughts could drive you crazy, and wondering what my life would be like if my father hadn't died is torture. Obviously everything depends on the moment when the person disappears: if my father had died before he met my mother, I wouldn't even be born; if he'd died after he married her, maybe I'd still have been born but he might never have seen me. Then I could see him in photographs, or, rather, he'd be able to see me, but only from heaven, like now. But for him not to see me while I could see him—no, that would be impossible. If my father were still alive we would certainly still be living in Whiskey, Mom wouldn't have made a fool of herself with Mary Jo's horrible uncle, I would have a dog on a leash instead of a stupid hamster on my conscience, and who knows what else. As for me, if I died I don't think Mom's life would be any worse than it is: all she does is complain that having a daughter is making her old. So maybe her life would even change for the better. But what about the lives of people I don't know yet, like the man I'm going to marry, or the children I'm going to have, or new friends I'm going to meet. If I died now maybe their lives would be completely different and much less beautiful than if I'd been around. Or much more beautiful?

There's a weird smell in the air. I go downstairs, where Celeste is doing the wash, and tell her there's a nauseating smell in my room of rusting iron and rot. We look everywhere but we can't find anything. Nelson the Second's cage is clean and shiny, without a spot of rust, and inside is a picture of a happy hamster family. My iron bed doesn't look like it suddenly got rusty, and yet I keep getting whiffs of this smell that makes me choke and feel like there's all this mucus inside me. It smells like the butcher's, I say to Celeste. She wants me to show her my underpants. I'm not going to let anyone see my underpants, but suddenly I realize they're wet, and I feel like I'm going to die of embarrassment, thinking that that raw-meat smell is mine, so I lift my skirt myself. There's a red stain, I say to Celeste. You see, she explains, it was the smell of your blood. My blood smells like that because it's full of iron, which turns rusty when it gets wet; all those iron particles suspended in my blood clot, and it comes out of me like I'm disintegrating in tissues of blood. Smells make me sick, they're nauseating, all of them, and I'm not going to study them, I decide, because of all the things that exist on the face of the earth smells are the most repulsive, the most scary: they're everywhere, and there's no defense against them. With an ugly color you can close your eyes, with a loud noise you can plug up your ears, but with a smell there's nothing you can do, you can't stuff up your nose because you'd suffocate, or flies would get in your mouth. Smells penetrate everywhere. To hell with smells, I don't want to have anything to do with them. You exaggerate so, Celeste goes. I'm not exaggerating—I don't like blood, I say. But it happens to all women, she responds. To hell with women, what do I have to do with them, I say. But if it didn't happen you couldn't have children. I don't care about having children, I don't want to have children, I don't want to have smells, I want to be an actress and that's all. Oh really, Celeste goes. Yes, I want to be an actress. Well, the blood's going to come out of you just the same, even if you're an actress, thirteen times a year, not one less, and you can't do anything about it, she insists. O.K., O.K., I say, I'll sweat blood, but I have no intention of studying smells. But no one ever thought of making you study smells, she says. I know, I say, it's just that it was something I thought I'd like. Anyway, I get really mad, but Celeste doesn't pay much attention; she stands there and shrugs her shoulders, looking like she's just totally enjoying herself, like it's just a big joke. Then she calls Mom, who explains to me what to do and what to put there. It's a big nuisance, I don't see what Mary Jo found to brag about in this big blood-dripping success of hers.

Today, in Miss Andreas's class, Mary Stone is mesmerized by a photograph in a magazine of an ice cream sundae that costs a dollar. Eight different flavors, plus bananas, peaches, pistachios, raspberries, maraschino cherries, and pineapple, and whipped cream on top. There was a contest in San Francisco to eat one of these. An Irish girl won—she demolished the whole thing in fifteen minutes. Mary Stone is sitting openmouthed in front of the picture, and she doesn't even hear when Miss Andreas calls on her, so finally Andreas grabs the magazine from under the desk and gets mad: magazines are not to be brought to class, ever.

Scene with Mom because the school told her I am a disaster in math. She claims I'm doing it on purpose just to be bad, to spite her by not doing what I'm supposed to. I was doing well in Whiskey and she doesn't see why I shouldn't do well here. I can't stand it when she comes into my room and makes me take out my math book, then sits down beside me to go over the lesson, while she looks nervously at the book, afraid she can't remember anything anymore. Maybe it's true: maybe I am doing badly in math out of spite. Basically it's a good thing, it cuts the risk of having to study physics and perform all those dirty tricks scientists do: after all, they are paid for doing to mice more or less what I did to Nelson the Second. I saw a photograph of sixteen mice who were cut open while they were alive so the effect of atomic radiation could be studied. Some had grown up deformed, others were very weak: they're made to run on a wheel, but they're so limp they can barely manage to make it turn. Nelson the Second was lucky: he died immediately. But Mom keeps lecturing me about how the future belongs to the physicists, and if she hadn't had to stop studying when she got married and I was born, she would be at least at Los Alamos by now. She would be, she would be . . . if only she really were at Los Alamos!

Big announcement from Celeste: she's in love.
"With whom?"

"A man."

"Thank you, I would never have guessed." I insist, and drag the name out of her: Leslie Thomson, the counterman at the ice-cream parlor with the sign in front showing a cow dressed like a farmer's wife.

"Celeste, that's great! Think of all the ice cream you can eat free!"

"I'm hardly going to marry him for that."

"No, of course not, I only meant, it's a perk. Better than ending up with a shoeshine man, or a sailor, who'd never be home." The counterman at the ice-cream parlor is nice, but all the times Celeste brought me there I never realized anything. She kept it hidden, the sneak.

Mom has decided to rent the guest room. Mary Jo's grandmother says it's a pity for me not to have a living room of my own, like Mary Jo, who for her birthday is getting a new room with her own closet, a dressing table, and a love seat with pink-and-white stripes and matching armchairs for when she has friends over. In what's now her room she'll just have her bed and a table for doing homework. I'm not really interested in all that stuff. And maybe a boarder would be better than nothing. At least there wouldn't be just the two of us anymore.

"How do you know," says Mary Jo. "Someone really horrible might come, like Chloe's mother."

"Oh God, you'd want to shoot yourself. That voice!"

"Of course, someone fascinating might come, an unemployed actor, or a traveling painter."

"Oh yeah, Mary Jo, Prince Charming might come."

"I don't mean that, but a man would certainly be more fun. Your house is like a convent."

"If a man came Mom would immediately try to marry him."

"The first one?"

"Why? Isn't it always first come . . . ? My mother has that book just for learning how to seduce the first guy."

"Let me see—"

"Only when she's not home. You know where she keeps it?"

"In the bathroom on top of the toilet tank?"

"How did you know?"

"Because that's where my mother keeps the letters she got before she married my father."

"Have you read them?"

"Every single one."

"Are they good?"

"Incredible. When I look at my mother and think of some of the things he says to her I laugh. Actually, I've seen him. He came here once, without my father knowing: a small guy, with red hair and eyeglasses as thick as the bottom of a bottle."

"How did you know it was him?"

"I read about it later in a postcard on top of the toilet tank." In return I tell her that my father had another fiancée before marrying Mom.

"We have definitely run the risk of not existing."

Today I passed for a genius in science, all because of one of those discussions that Miss Andreas likes so much. She comes in with a folder of newspaper clippings and wants us to discuss how the world we live in will change as a result of things that have been invented or sooner or later will be invented, like chewing gum that makes perfectly spherical bubbles, airplanes that travel faster than sound, machines for drying your hair at home, devices with a siren to frighten robbers, television and frozen food to eat while you're watching TV, lawn mowers, movie cameras that take pictures by themselves, tape recorders, telephones where you can see the other person, even long-distance—anyway, all those things that people never even dreamed of having when she was little, Miss Andreas explains, waving her arms enthusiastically. Then she tells each of us to imagine what our life will be like, if it will be better or worse, if we'll be happier or unhappier. So everybody says something, and what makes the biggest impression is airplanes that go faster than the speed of sound.

Perry raises his hand and asks if the President could telephone the President of Russia and tell him that if he doesn't do what he wants he'll bomb him—blow up his country—but meanwhile, before the Russians can answer, the plane that goes faster than sound arrives, and the war has already broken out. Mary Jo, who's still mad at Perry for refusing to kiss her, declares that this idea is totally stupid. She says it couldn't happen because on the telephone a voice travels faster than a voice normally travels, and at least as fast as a supersonic airplane. This provokes an argument because Carla, Irving, and Walter claim that if the plane leaves right when the telephone call is made, then there's no way to stop it with an answer that would arrive seconds later; on the other hand, according to Gitta, Grace, Daisy, and Donald, no President would ever be so crazy as to let the plane go at the same time as the phone call, unless of course he wants a war to break out no matter what, and then one phone call is enough, along with sending the order to the supersonic airplane to take off. The discussion is endless—everybody has something to say. To me it seems pointless: after all, when you're on the phone it's like being in the same room, whereas even in a supersonic plane it's impossible to get from Moscow to Washington in the time it takes a voice to get from a mouth to an ear, or from a telephone receiver in Moscow to a telephone receiver in Washington. I raise my hand. On the telephone voices travel much faster than sounds in the natural state, I say. And who knows how long it would take a naked voice to get from Moscow to Washington: a plane that goes faster than this voice can't be that fast, not as fast as a voice that travels by telephone, so maybe also the speed of sounds varies, according to how they travel and what transports them; and so, I conclude, to say that an airplane is supersonic means nothing if you don't specify faster than what sound, and this idea of mine leaves everybody stunned. Miss Andreas applauds and says I'm a genius, and will surely be a great scientist, which throws me into black despair, because now Mom will have another excuse to make me study nuclear physics. From now on I won't say anything that might seem even just a little more intelligent than normal. Nora's right, you should keep your mouth shut in front of people, or they'll take advantage of you. I'm not going to talk in class anymore, so Andreas won't get so excited at the idea of my scientific future. Now that retard Mary Stone raises her hand to say she thinks the most important discovery of all is chewing gum that makes perfectly round bubbles, because the day everyone can make perfectly round bubbles no one will care about chewing gum anymore, and we'll find something else to do, which will radically change our daily life. Yikes! What a stupid idea. The only really important thing is this business of voices, sounds, and objects that travel faster than sound, sounds and voices that can't be heard or even felt. And yet the air must be full of voices that arrive from so far away that by now they're tired and can't make themselves heard by anyone, as if they were deafmutes. My father's voice must be among these: who knows where it comes from or how long it takes to reach my ears. Maybe it won't arrive till I'm already dead, so to find out what he has to say I'll have to wait for it to ricochet against some obstacle and come back to the point of departure, in the place where the dead live. Never mind, sooner or later I'll hear it. I'll have all the time I want, because, after all, the dead never die.

The unluckiest tortoises of all are the giant tortoises of the Caribbean. They weigh more than two hundred pounds and that's why it's so easy to kill them. They're brought to New York from the Caribbean, and are put in the back room of a restaurant specializing in turtle soup. When the owner of the restaurant falls asleep in the office, he hears the turtles groaning all night, making long- drawn-out sighs, as if they knew they were going to die. Then he has nightmares. The next day they're brought to the kitchen, and they don't even try to rebel. All they do is give the cooks dirty looks, annihilating them with contempt. But that's not enough to stop them.

Saw *The Big Sleep* with Mary Jo and the two Madernas. Next time I see a shooting star I'm going to wish I could be like Lauren

Bacall: she was fantastic, in her slinky shiny white silk dress, striding through the house of the crazy general in his wheelchair. Bogart realizes he's completely in love with her, but he doesn't want her to know it, even though she can see perfectly well that he would kiss the ground she walks on. He's angry that she's rich and spoiled and arrogant, while he's only a poor detective, with nothing but his brain and that sexy way of scrunching his eyebrows so they come together in the middle. She's mad about him, and she provokes him, so he'll do something, and he provokes her, but in the end no one does anything, because they're both proud, and he doesn't trust her. The fact remains that the two of them are flirting even when it doesn't seem like they are. Like when, trying to seduce him, she lets him see her leg, and since he's not stupid, and wants to let her know that the trick won't work, he gives her some contemptuous advice, from a man of the world: lady, go ahead and scratch. So then her face narrows, she's so mad she could kill him, furious that he's calm when she's showing off her beautiful legs. My legs are definitely not that long yet, but I'd love to look like Lauren Bacall when she puts on her lamé jacket, so thin and beautiful, and when she's in that shady guy's bar singing, in her white dress, with her hoarse voice and her incredibly perfect nostrils. When she sings she looks like her eyes are going right through you, a little trick that works with everyone except Bogart. I really don't have a voice like hers, and besides Miss Brown says I shouldn't imitate others' voices but make the most of my own. How idiotic. An actor has to be able to imitate whatever anyone else does, not be even more himself than he is in daily life. And I am sick and tired of the play about the farm with the piglets, and being the farmgirl in the patched apron who milks the cow and helps poor people's children. Yuck! If I don't change schools, with this stupid Brown and her idiotic idea that you have to be yourself, I will never become a great actress. The problem is to be someone else—anyone can be herself. I try to explain this to Celeste, who is happy today because the eye doctor told her she had to wear glasses. "You don't understand anything," she said. "Being yourself is so difficult that there are some people who go to a doctor just to figure out how to do it."

"And what are you when you're not yourself?"

"You're someone else."

"Someone else who?"

"Someone different, another person."

"You mean you imitate someone exactly?"

"No, you have another personality."

"And where does this other personality come from?"

"Oh, I don't really know. It's not easy to explain, but the personality that isn't your own isn't right, so you have to find the true one."

"And do you return the part of the personality that isn't your own to whoever sent it?"

"No, a personality that isn't your own isn't really anyone's, it's a personality that should never have existed, it's a mistake."

"You mean that that personality is killed? Like when you lose a baby?"

"No, it's different: when you lose a baby someone isn't born who otherwise would live like you and me; to be free of a false personality is to get rid of something that doesn't exist."

"But if it doesn't exist why do you have to be free of it?"

Celeste finishes ironing my checked dress, and she's quiet for a while, then she says: "It's hard to explain. There are things that don't exist but do more harm than those that do. Like nightmares: they're only dreams, and yet when you have them you scream and feel bad. If you have a personality that's not your own, it's like dreaming instead of living."

"But dreaming is nice. Not all dreams are nightmares."

"Dreaming is nice at night, but during the day you have to live."

"Why?"

"Because there is a God who has decided all these things, and has established that there's a time to live and a time to dream. If you have a false personality it's like you're dreaming day and night, so you never live and it's as if you were dead."

"Like my father?" "No, that's another thing. He's no longer

alive—he stopped living—but he wasn't a fantasy. He truly existed."

"And where is he now?"

"It depends."

"Depends on what?"

"On what he was like when he was alive. If he was a good man, he's in heaven now; if he was bad, he's in a bad place now."

"And if he's in a bad place, will he be able to read what I write to him?"

"No, it would be difficult, because it's like a harsh prison there, and you're not free to wander around."

Mustn't he have ended up in the bad place because of the electrocuted lizards?

8.

*M*OM HAD FORGOTTEN about her plan to rent the room. She hadn't run an ad in the paper, or even put up signs, when the tenant falls on us practically out of the blue. Or rather, out of the smoke and flames of the Turtles' house: Gitta's father bursts in, frantic because his house has just gone up in smoke. Mom looks really annoyed—she's picturing having to take in the whole Turtle family. To hide her annoyance she starts acting super-polite, practically offering to let them move into our house. Gitta's dad thanks her and says he's already sent his wife and kids to the country. Here's the problem: they were expecting some guy their cousin knows, a French guy who was supposed to stay with them for the summer to write a book, and they left him in the hotel practically hysterical. They absolutely have to find him a place to stay. Mom immediately perks up. "Oh, poor man, a European expatriate . . . " she sighs, wringing her hands and pretending not to hear Gitta's father explaining that this professor would certainly give me French lessons like he promised his daughter. Yuck, I'm thinking, what a drag—

school during vacation. On the other hand, speaking French is an extra advantage for an actress . . .

"I can't leave him out on the street, poor man. . . " Mom concludes after a complicated discussion in which she is basically trying to make it clear that she has never rented a room but in this case will make an exception. Having gotten her to agree, Turtle dashes off to ask the people across the street to lend him their car and chauffeur. He says the tenant will have to come by himself because he has to get back to his family—he's already late. In a rush Mom straightens the house, gives the sink a quick wipe, clears away the breakfast crumbs, then runs off to change. She asks me to put on something nice, but I don't want to. She can play the hostess. I mean, I just put on my bathing suit and I really don't want to change again. Besides, it's totally bizarre to think that the tenant's decision to take the room will depend on the way I'm dressed—he'll take it if the price is right. Anyway, how lucky, now it won't be just the two of us anymore. Let's hope he's not some jerk, or it will be out of the frying pan and into the fire. About an hour later, a car pulls up in front of the house. Celeste hurries to open the door, and then I hear this guy and Mom talking in low voices. I don't move—I don't want to seem too curious. It takes cool, lots of cool, not to show you're interested; if you do, a man's head swells and you can't unswell it. So when he and Mom come out to the porch I just peek at him over my magazine, which is open to a picture of a Humpty Dumpty costume. I have to say I'm really surprised. All winter she was making me eat everything on my plate because of the starving people in Europe, so hearing that a French guy was coming to our house I expected to see a skeleton, while the guy who's following Mom, looking kind of reluctant, is healthy, not at all undernourished, only in height sort of, well, medium, not especially tall, but tall enough, graceful. Not fat but not, like, skinny, and then he looks weirdly familiar. He's got a timetable in his hand, and he looks like he wants to beat it. Mom looks tense, or, to use her favorite word, "mortified." It's obvious that she's not going to convince him, that it's stupid for her to hover over him with her anxious voice. He's not listening to her, he's looking at me. I look at him—he's not bad for a professor, he's tan, broad shoulders. Must spend a lot of time outside. In fact he looks really nice, definitely a step above Mary Jo's uncle. Wow, I say to myself, to catch this as Daddy No. 2 wouldn't be something to sneeze at—already I can see us taking a walk in Goatscreek, my friends dying of envy because I've got the handsomest dad. I say this, dear Daddy in heaven, only because you're not here anymore, and I'm sure that when I asked you to send us someone you must have chosen this cool French guy, thinking he'd be best for me and for Mom, so thank you thank you thank you, Daddy. Because this guy is really cute. A super professor. He's like a cross between someone in a Hitchcock movie, all neat and respectable, and Gerry Sue Filthy, with his bad-guy stare. I'm peeking at him through my sunglasses: it works. The French guy immediately changes his expression and tone, and when Mom gestures at me, gaily announcing the name of M. Guibert, and then at the garden, he exclaims, totally captivated, "How lovely, how lovely!" But it's me he's looking at, not the garden or the lilies or the porch, just me. He turns to Mom, then throws me another quick glance, and continues to look through the timetable. He's trying to decide what to do, obviously, but his eyes keep running over me, not the timetable. I give him a big inviting smile, because you shouldn't take all hope away from a man, though you don't have to pour it down his throat, either. Anyway, I smile at him, not too long, maybe a second, and then I go back to reading my magazine, all cool and collected, pretending I couldn't care less if he stays or not, which is easy because I can look at him through my sunglasses as much as I like without him knowing. My lips are just slightly parted, because according to the how-to-catch-a-man book a woman should always appear half-open to a man. Then for a second, but really a flash so he can't swear he's seeing right, I let my sunglasses slide down my nose and give him the famous deep wink, but quick, so quick he doesn't know if I've done it or not, and now he has to stay because he has a dreadful need to know if I really looked at him like that or if it only seemed that way. (In the book this has a specific name—fluctuating seduction.) Now this poor French guy has a snapshot in his head, a flash of the second when I looked at him in that way to make him totally confused, and he's devoured by doubt: did she or didn't she? Poor guy! Then a final touch, because, if you ask me, it's not safe to count on curiosity alone: I suck in the bubble from my gum and show him the back of my tongue, which is pink, a perfect triangle, and right at that instant he says to Mom that he's changed his mind, he likes the house after all. I keep leafing through my magazine, so he can't see that I'm following the negotiations, and my eye falls on a photograph of the corpses of 188 workers burned in an explosion in Texas City. Really gruesome. I get up to go inside, and passing between him and Mom I brush against him and blow a minty breath up under his nose. In other words I combine two different sensations, a system that I would call multiple-reinforced seduction. Safest of all. Because, as my dear dad used to say, a woman doesn't have to be different to make a man go wild. She simply has to have more of what all other women have.

Dear Daddy who art in heaven, the man you sent us is really nice, I hope he falls in love with Mom. He is maybe a little too young for her: of course you were the right number of years older than her, but what do you want, it's not the end of the world. To me it seems that if they fell in love even Mom would improve—poor thing, happiness would really do her good after all the bad things that have happened, first Nelson and then you. Don't be mad if I entertain myself by trying out on him the tricks in Nora's instruction book—you can read my thoughts, so you know I'm only doing it for practice, and then, if I hadn't come up with that seduction routine, he obviously wouldn't have stayed at our house. I did it for Mom. To keep him here.

School's out because of a diarrhea epidemic. Even the Frenchman is taking it easy. He's always in the garden—maybe he hasn't really settled in yet and can't write. I might as well use him as a guinea pig for a new seduction technique (or else Mom, with her

methods from before the war, could easily let him get away).
Experiment in elusive-hypnotic attraction: throwing pebbles at a can
of beans. The guinea pig is frozen in his chair, ears perked up and eyes
staring, just like in the book: rhythmic sound and movement transfix
the male. Possible variants: swing a foot back and forth, flutter your
eyelids, fan yourself, snap your fingers to the music, blow a bubble
then suck the gum slowly back into your mouth. To start a conversation, he asks about the girl he would have taught French to if her
house hadn't burned down. He had a lucky escape, I tell him. Gitta is
the most boring and clingy girl in the class, and besides, her legs are
skinny because she had polio. This makes him laugh. It doesn't seem
that funny to me for a girl to end up with sticks instead of legs, but
these French must have a weird sense of humor, because once he
starts laughing he can't stop. While he's amusing himself behind
Gitta's back, Mom shows up, all in a twitter, exclaiming that we make
such a pretty picture it must be immortalized, and she goes inside to
get the camera. The French guy sits there staring like an idiot, but I'm
scowling. I don't like to smile for photos.

Mom announces that we're going to eat with M. Guibert every
day, it's politer than making him eat by himself. So tonight at the table
our source of additional income tells me I can call him Humbert. In
fact, he will be offended if I call him M. Guibert. Mom isn't very
enthusiastic: "M. Guibert, if my daughter calls you by your first name,
I don't see why I . . . " He frowns for a fraction of a second and then
with a sort of forced smile: "With pleasure! Such steps, after all, must
start with the ladies." Such steps! Maybe he doesn't realize what he's
saying when he speaks English. Mom lights up: "Such a delicate
thought, to propose it indirectly, through Dolly . . . " Humbert
Guibert raises his glass: "So, from today: Isabel!" "From today:
Humbert!" she answers, in a glow.

We got new bathing suits. You can't keep wearing the stupid
ones from last year, and besides I only had bottoms and a polka-dot
kerchief for a top.

"But you don't have any bosom yet," Mom objects.

"Mary Jo does, and I almost do."

"Let me see."

"No." Mom looks smug, but then she buys me a black two-piece just like hers. She read that the French philosophy of bathing suits is "less is more": given our new amorous circumstances, we have to abandon the politics of the old one-piece that was supposed to make the most of "long American legs." I put on my new suit right away to show Celeste: "It's ridiculous for a child to dress like that."

"Look: I have bosoms!"

"You call that a bosom?"

"Yes, I call it a bosom, anyway it's enough so that it wouldn't be right to go around just with bottoms, especially with a man in the house."

"Are you afraid it will bother him?"

"You don't think so?" Ever since she got engaged, Celeste has been acting very superior. In fact my breasts hardly show at all—my best feature is my back. It's tan, like a biscuit, and I have sharp shoulder blades that seem like they should have wings attached. Mom and I are sunbathing on the piazza, in our matching suits, and Humbert pretends to study but really he's looking at me while I'm reading *Barnaby*, winking, until Mom makes him listen to the plot of some novel that's being made into a movie. Humbert quickly opens his book again, saying he doesn't like American movies. He must have said it to shut Mom up: can he really not like the most fabulous thing in the world? Things aren't going too well: he looks at me more than at Mom. He ought to show a little interest in what she says. Not that she says anything interesting, but it's Humbert's duty to act like a gentleman. Oh well.

Today my idiot mother grabs me in the kitchen, sticks her nails in my arm, and hisses at me like a wildcat: I'd better stop acting like an imbecile with M. Guibert, because she's had enough of being treated like a governess and considered a nuisance in her own house.

It's ridiculous that M. Guibert, instead of writing his book and suggesting grownup activities to her, like going to a concert or a movie, finds nothing better to do than wander around the yard, always a step away from me. And then at night he goes right to his room instead of keeping her company—it's a scandal that he's in her house without showing the least interest in her, and . . . What do you expect, I say. After all, he's a paying boarder, not a friend staying for free. At that she bursts into tears like an infant and, thank goodness, lets go of my arm (the marks from her nails are still there), then falls on the floor sobbing. It's embarrassing. Poor Mom, I don't know what to do. I hug her and kiss her, tell her not to feel bad—I'm just trying to help her. I only joke around with Humbert to make him stay with us—thanks to me he's still here. She shouldn't get so mad, she should be grateful for all I've done. What's got into you? she hisses. Who do you think you are, you monster. At least I think that's what she said, because now she's having convulsions. So I tell her how things are, explaining that I'm just trying to put into practice the advice in her book. What book? she asks with a gasp. You know, the book you keep on top of the toilet tank. You little whore, she shouts, getting up, suddenly recovering all her energy. What makes you think you can spy on my life? Actually, I was spying on the toilet tank. You're an insolent little beast, she screams. Then the stupid hen calls me all sorts of things, when I'm just trying to make her see that I'm doing this for her, and if I apply the advice in Nora's book it's for her own good, so the field will be open, and the two of us can finally have a dad. But she doesn't hear me—she's kind of hysterical—and she punches the wall, then grabs the book from on top of the toilet tank and burns it page by page in the toilet. Then she takes me by the hair and tries to drown me in the toilet bowl. I'm all dirty, covered with ashes, half suffocated. This is how you repay me, I say, like this, instead of being a little grateful. Don't let it go to your head, she says. You'll pay, believe me, because I know the book by heart, you old hen. You're just as old and cuckoo as Grandmother and you couldn't take advantage of my help and advice. I push her out of the bathroom and lock the door while

I get cleaned up, because hell, I don't want Humbert to see me looking like a chimney sweep. And now, I'm so sorry, dear Daddy who art
in heaven, but I'm going to get this Humbert for myself. Let's face it,
there was a certain age difference between you and Mom, and here
it's more or less the same. Since I know how to seduce Humbert and
Mom couldn't do it in a million years, why should I leave him to her?
After all, there's the little matter of my allure, though she must have
had some once, to listen to Nora. But now she doesn't have a drop.

Mary Jo is teaching me to smoke. We do it in the attic because
her grandmother told her children shouldn't smoke—it stunts their
growth, although it's good for your lungs if you're a grownup. I don't
like smoking—I hate the way Mom takes out her cigarette holder,
puts the cigarette in, and stretches out on the sofa with that knowing, pained expression which seems meant to make you feel guilty
because she is so-beautiful-yet-so-alone. It's like she thinks she's the
heroine of a novel—she doesn't realize she's acting like some stupid
woman who has nothing to do but blow smoke rings up at the ceiling, one after another, nothing to do but be bored out of her mind
by the world. At least she can pass herself off as my mother. How else
would she justify the absurd rules she invents just to annoy us? I can't
imagine anything more pathetic or boring than a so-called handsome
woman who's no good for anything. Not even for Humbert, it looks
like, since he hardly ever seems to offer to keep her company. She's
always the one following him, with a scared look in her eyes that I
never saw before.

Celeste says I shouldn't smoke because smoking is for men, and
smoke is dirty. She puts my cigarette in a glass of water, then makes me
look at this kind of amber-colored stuff that's left on the wet paper.
"You see what happens to your lungs when you smoke?"
"They're not made of paper."
"Don't be stupid. If you don't believe me take a look at the fingers of the man at the newsstand the next time you go out with your

mother." We go out right away: it's true, his fingers are yellowish-brown, the nails are the same color as the wet cigarette. I ask Mom if her lungs are the same color as the newspaper man's nails.

"What's gotten into you? Are you turning into a complete idiot?"

"I'm asking because you always have a cigarette in your mouth."

"Nonsense, smoking is good for the throat and strengthens the lungs."

"Why are the newspaper man's fingers yellow and yours aren't?"

"Because I use a cigarette holder. He smokes non-filter cigarettes with his fingers, so they get dirty."

"And where does the dirt from your cigarettes end up?"

"First it stays in the cigarette filter, then in the cigarette-holder, and when it gets to the lungs there's only the part that's good for you."

"Good for you in what sense?"

"In the sense that when you feel a bit tired but you're not sleepy, it helps you think about things—you light a cigarette, pour yourself a drink, and think."

"And without a cigarette and a drink you can't think?"

"Do-nothings like Celeste can, but someone like me who is accustomed to being active can't sit idly, and having a cigarette stimulates your thoughts when you're tired and keeps your hands occupied."

"Why don't you knit instead?"

"Ohh!" End of the conversation. It's not true that Celeste does nothing. In fact, she's knitting a pile of little sweaters while she thinks—maybe that's why she doesn't smoke. Celeste and my mother have never seen eye to eye on anything.

No lake. What a drag. It's all arranged for us to go with Mary Jo, but as soon as Mom hears that her uncle's coming too, she doesn't want to know about it, because he "mortified" her and so she never wants to see him again. What a jerk: if you had to react like that every time a man changes his mind. I tell her, but she's in a rage: "You shut up, with your stories about the Tonguefish women who bury their men! A goddam Maze, that's what you are." How the hell did she find out? One of the Hiltons told on me. Maybe that slime of an uncle of Mary Jo's. The widow Maze really blows up at me. Her mania for shouting has been getting worse. Maybe she wants Humbert to hear her better. Certainly in the how-to book there was nothing about shouting to attract the male's attention. This must be her variation—shouting until she's hoarse, with Celeste trying to restrain her, calm her down. But Mom is really furious, and finally she grabs me and lets me have it. And then there's worse trouble: she hits me, and I slap her. She turns to stone, turns pale, then her face gets mean, so mean it scares me. She doesn't move, stops hitting me, takes me by the hair and forces my head toward the floor, by her feet. I'm kind of scared myself that I slapped her—I don't even try to escape.

"You will apologize immediately." This she says all calm, her voice cold, subdued, starchy. But suddenly she shouts: "You witch! You and your horrible Maze blood! You're a disgrace! A disgrace!" She keeps yelling at me that I'm a disgrace while she rubs my face against her loafers to the point that I get scratched by the buckle, and then she calms down. Or rather, she doesn't calm down, but she is so furious, she hates me so much that now she gets nasty, cutting, and she repeats—the sound is very faraway yet burning: "Apologize immediately for what you said to the Hiltons." I apologize, but she's still pulling my hair and twisting my neck. At one point her painted fingernails are so close to my eyes I think she's going to dig them out and I'll be blind. I'm beside myself, and if she weren't really hurting me I wouldn't apologize, because it's true I was wrong to invent the curse about the Tonguefish husbands and I shouldn't have slapped her, but she went after me—she hit me—so it's the only legitimate defense, and besides, if we fail yet again, she's the one who ought to apologize for her tirade against the Maze blood in me, which is a terrible thing to do to your own daughter, and also a terrible insult to your husband, who's dead and can't defend himself.

9.

RAIN RAIN RAIN. A sea of rain. No lake, as usual, no trips, I'm shut up in this prison of a house, this cage of a room whose walls let in all the noises from outside: as soon as I stick a foot out in the hall I catch sight of my dear mama, who hates me more and more; it's clear from the way she looks at me how furious she is that I exist at all, and she just dreams of getting rid of me. She puts me in such a state, I must be careful not to eat apples, a poisoned one can easily turn up in this type of situation. And I have to stay on my guard, because who knows what Mom might be plotting to get rid of her vile daughter with her vile blood. While she's out I raid her room to make sure she hasn't got hold of any strange powders or potions. With all the mysteries she reads she might get some not very nice ideas on how to dispose of me. I open the drawers, look in the closet—the usual stuff—and while I'm digging around something gets in my eye. Oh God, I think, I'll go blind, have I fallen into some sort of trap? I look in the mirror to try and see what the hell got in my eye. It's only an eyelash, luckily, but what a scare. Still, I can't get it out—it's incredibly hard to get a thing out of your eye. Then I hear the *shshshsh* of Humbert's slippers on the carpet. He's been wandering around the house for a while now: he's dying of boredom, too. What a crazy thing to do, to come and stay here. If I had a choice, I wouldn't stay if you paid me, not in in this house, for sure. Still the *shshshsh shshshsh shshshsh*, leather gliding on carpet, until Humbert opens the door softly, stops, looks at me. I pretend not to notice, and keep rubbing my eye, without getting anywhere. He comes over and takes me by the shoulders, which gives me a nice shiver. Shivers of love are nice when it's raining outside and you feel like you're melting inside. He takes my head in his hands. He's going to kiss me, I think, now it's happened, we'll be lovers, lying in each other's arms kissing all day long, while the rain streaks the windowpanes, until the hen comes back. Then we'll have to stop. So I stand there motionless, waiting for his lips, but nothing happens. He doesn't have the nerve, the big coward. To make him do *some*thing, I tell him I'm about to go blind in one eye.

"Let me see," he says. I let him: after all, the golden rule, the most golden, the only really important one, is to give the man the illusion of making himself useful. Humbert caresses my sharp shoulder blades, like an angel's in the making, and then, muttering something about what he saw a Swiss peasant do, cow-with-calf type, he sticks his tongue in my eye, licks me lightly on the mouth, barely grazing it . . . a kiss on the edge of the lips . . . and on his face there's a sweet little smile, like a timid dirty old man.

"O.K., keep going, you're getting it, I feel it," I say to encourage him. "But don't tickle me!"

"Stand still, I have to clean the other one!" Apparently he has a taste for licking my intimate parts: he pulls up my eyelids, and I see his super sexy mouth coming closer, that lower lip drives me wild, with the wider part all pink and smooth. I feel a wave of warmth from his wide-open mouth, and then I see his big tongue, a forest of bumps and furrows; it looks like it's going to sink me. I run away, so as not to ruin everything: never make the man feel ridiculous. Better for him to believe that he is formidable, intimidating. Better to escape and let him feel triumphant rather than laugh in his face, especially when you have him in front of you with his tongue hanging out. God, god, god, what wouldn't I give for an invisible Mary Jo, to see how silly Hummie is.

Mom bursts into my room while Mary Jo and I are smoking a cigarette. I barely manage to stick the ashtray in the desk drawer. The smoke goes right in my eyes, burning, and I pretend I'm crying.

"What's the matter, why are you crying?" stammers Mom, looking in alarm at Mary Jo, an inconvenient witness of her implacable hatred.

"I'm crying because you don't love me, you're always out, and even when you're home you never spend any time with me—you're always trying to get rid of me so you can be alone with that French guy." I follow up with a few artistic sobs and a theatrical wail, like a poor sad orphan. Mom hugs me tight, she even kisses me to show Mary Jo that it's not true she doesn't love me, the hypocrite. First she calls me despicable, then she kisses and hugs me in front of Mary Jo. It suits her to play the part of the adoring mother, in spite of her desire to eliminate me, because otherwise how's she going to arrange the perfect infanticide?

There's nothing more detestable than mom when she has a plan. Suddenly she gets all rigid, even less natural than usual—a kind of plastic mom. The stupid hen, she can't even want something grace-fully. The project this time, it seems, now that Mary Jo's uncle has been discarded, is to become a madame by marrying Monsieur Guibert. Too bad he doesn't smoke, because it means she can't resort to one of the simplest and most important seduction techniques (chapter 5, paragraph 2), the one on the strategic use of cigarettes: have him light your cigarette while you look him intensely in the eyes, but without blowing smoke at him: it would be rude, he'd start coughing, and coughing is lethal to the delicate web of seduction. No, the cigarette is supposed to function as the magical conjunction of the man and the woman.

Cute, Humbert. Whenever Plasticmom gets mad at me, he looks at me as if to say: I know perfectly well that you're right, but what can I do . . . Today I went into his study and he slipped a black notebook into a drawer. Too bad he locked it—I'd be curious to know what he's writing. I could always break it open and make him think it was Mom; all she ever does is ask him questions about his past. I'd like to know if he's in love with me or not. He'll never say it on his own: he's always buzzing around me, but he keeps his mouth sewed up tight. I think he makes up lots of things, because when he's talking his eyebrows move, one here, one there, which means that he's using part of his brain for what he's saying and part for what he's thinking up to say next. The other day I called him Hummie, and one eyebrow stayed almost stuck to the roots of his hair. That copycat Mom immediately started calling him Hummie, too. Mrs. Maze ought to behave with a little dignity, she ought to go on calling him Humbèrt, with that sophisticated French accent, instead of singing Hummie Hummie under her breath and fluttering around with her endless stupid little smiles. She should develop her own personality, not imitate mine, since she'll never succeed in being like me: it would be against nature. True beauty vanishes by the time a woman gets to be her age. The most she can have is style. That jerk doesn't get it. I ask her if Humbert doesn't maybe remind her of someone, but nothing comes to her—she doesn't see how much he looks like her adored Gerry Sue Filthy, the great love of the ladies of Goatscreek, their friendly dramaturge, demiurge, and rising star. It's odd how they look alike, those two, although I must say that Hummie is definitely handsomer than Filthy, who's a little pudgy. On the other hand Humbert is really graceful; he plays tennis, which is amazing, and he has fabulous legs. He is definitely the handsomest man I've ever seen. He doesn't at all seem the same age as Mom; but I found his passport and discovered that he's actually three years older; he was born in Paris in 1910, and he's been in the United States since 1940. He doesn't have even the slightest French accent, because when he was young he went to school in England, at one of those really chic places. In fact, everyone in Goatscreek thinks he's English, also because of these British-looking shirts he wears. Anyway, he's been here for six years, so all those fantasies of Plasticmom the Merciful about the hunger he must have endured during the war go up in smoke. Of course I should also say that he has never come close to letting her know the truth: I think he amuses himself by letting her stew in the juice of her wild imaginings—the widow with a heart of gold who welcomes the poor expatriate into her house and very generously offers him everything, especially herself.

· · ·

Mom finally decides to take me clothes shopping, and while we're out she asks me what I would think about having a new father.

"I like the one I have perfectly well."

"But he's dead."

"Didn't you tell me he only went to another place and I can write to him there? If he can read what I write, then he's alive, right?"

"Yes, of course, your first father is always your father, but I mean what would you think of having a new one here on earth, in Goatscreek, to be precise, at 231 Grassy Street, to be even more precise."

"Maybe in the guest room, to be even more precise?"

"What does the guest room have to do with it? A new father would sleep in my room with me." Purchases follow, aimed at the long-range matrimonial plan: Plasticmom gets a dress with a slit, a tight black skirt, just-below-the-knee length, with mother-of-pearl buttons. For me she buys an awful blue checked dress. It's so ugly I run out of the store before they can get it on me. I have no intention of dressing like a poor orphan.

At night she makes the grand gesture of inviting my future second dad to have a drink on the patio with her (in the dark!), so I throw myself between them, clinging to Hummie's side, and to distract Mom, me, and also himself from the fact that he is caressing my leg in a very voluptuous way, he launches into a lot of improbable stories about hunting reindeer, expeditions to the North Pole, fleeing on sleds from ferocious white bears, their jaws dripping with blood. Pretty entertaining. But right at the best part Mom (a poor reader of her handbook) sends me to bed. I confine myself to a snort, very successful to judge from Hummie's appreciative expression. Such an idiot! Doesn't she see that the only way for an older woman to get herself married is to get the absent-minded man to fall in love with the child first? That utter fool can't think of anything better than to send me to bed, and on top of that she throws my *Barnaby* after me, so I shout, You stinking witch!, and Hummie makes a little noise, a dry cough, by which I understand that he is behind me a hundred per cent. My "burning insult" forces the stupid hen to turn the conversation to the definitely boring subject of complaints about me, how disobedient and insolent and nasty I am . . . She is a birdbrain: before, Hummie couldn't distinguish between her rancid, rotting presence and the warmth of the inside of my thighs, but now her powder-smeared face and that horrible sprayed hair will only make him think of a petty woman who doesn't know how to grow old gracefully. She's even gotten to the point of asking him to give me lessons, like he was going to do with "the little Turtle girl." Stuff that would send even the most enamored man to sleep. In fact, at the first pause in the torrent of maternal lament, Hummie declares that he is overcome by exhaustion. Sooner or later the incompetent aspiring madame has to realize that, without the combination of two for the price of one, that man will not even think of marrying her. And here's the cherry on top: the grand master of the elusive arts goes and knocks on Hummie's door with the excuse of asking if he's finished with the *Reader's Digest*. I shout to her that I have it. My God, doesn't she remember that the role of knocking on doors is the exclusive province of the male?

Damn diarrhea epidemic, this forced vacation is worse than school: the consequence of yesterday's "burning insult," since I refuse to apologize, is no picnic with Mary Jo and Hummie by decision of Mrs. Pain in the Neck, who takes advantage of her monopoly on the car: you see, this is a free country but only if you don't have a family. Instead I go with Mary Jo & Co. to see *Great Expectations*. When I get home, I grab a Coke from the refrigerator, and sitting there on the kitchen stool I'm hypnotized by the disgusting spectacle of Plasticmom making lemon meringue pie (the ideal dessert for a hot summer day, she explains to Celeste, seized by one of her unbearable attacks of joviality).

She's wearing mules.

I hate mules.

The sight of her heels lifting up from the soles of the mules makes me puke. I wish I could purify my eyes from that disgusting sight, but they are riveted. Mom gets nervous feeling them fixed on her: "Don't you have anything better to do than stand there staring at my feet?"

"I'm thinking, Ma."

"Don't call me Ma."

"Don't call me, don't call me . . . "

"What do you mean?"

I stop answering her. I put on the inscrutable face of a fakir, I feel that face hardening on me, mud cracking as it dries, a mask pulled over my skin. I'm immobilized, I close my eyes but still I see opening before me the dark wet whirlpool of foot and slipper, the air enclosed between the thick skin of a female, a widow, and the sole of a shoe, pink pompom flopping, rotten with last year's sweat. All of Plasticmom is in that summer stink of feet. I'm choking, I can't believe that that is my mother and I came out of a hole between her legs. What lousy luck to come out of a hole like that. Something to be ashamed of your whole life. The pie is ready. Plasticmom puts it in the oven, sets the timer, turns to me with a mean, sharp face, a humanoid hen always ready to torture me, as if it were my fault that she's turned moldy and ugly, and that no one, and I mean no one, would ever dream of putting a hand between her thighs. I see a sudden quivering of colors and sounds, a wavering of outlines in the warm air of the oven, Plasticmom is staring at me, even without looking I feel her face coming at me in bursts, and when I turn I'm hypnotized by the sparkle of her smile, blotchy with cheap lipstick. Smiling, sinister, she gets close, with the nauseating stink of her moisturizer-smeared skin, the fake smell of hairspray mixed with the sweat of armpits, a stench that makes my head spin, it's so totally revolting. And she goes: "Tell me, are you falling for your new daddy?"

Triumphant at having packed me off last night, that stale nonentity punishes me for my scrap of rebellion. Not to give her the satisfaction I stay still, I don't react, but I feel a *crack crack* on my fakir's mask, a fissure opens around my mouth, a smile of disdain for the big filthy hen creeps over it. I'm standing still, but scorn for everything that revolts me about her vibrates in my face. If I were alone I would scream with pain and revulsion, but in front of her I won't, so, slowly, unperturbed, I get up. Not taking my eyes off her, I get to the door, stop, and say: "If you think you can do it without me. . ." Too bad I let go of the door—I wanted to be cold and distant, just like her when she makes me suffer, I wanted to make her bleed inside, the maternal bitch—but the door slams by itself, and this gives her an excuse to have a hysterical outburst. She follows me, infuriated by the noise, and sticks her head out into the hall: "You poisonous little witch! Damn worthless little bastard!" And then she slams the door, mean and violent as usual (what wouldn't I have given for Hummie to see her right then as she truly is). She must have wanted to hear a whole concert of slammed doors, because she sticks her head out again, wavy with pink plastic curlers, and yells at me: "I'll send you to a psychiatrist, I'll send you to college, you, you, you . . ." Another slammed door, and then, because her hands are burning with the desire to slam something endlessly, in the absence of being slammed herself: "And after college you will never come back here, not even dead." Not even dead. Nice, Plasticmom.

10.

I RUN TO Mom: "Sorry for yesterday, sorry for the other day, sorry for everything: Mary Jo's mother's on the phone. She says can I go to California with them." It would be fantastic, to see the Pacific before it turns the color of pee, see Nora's costume collection. Mom gives one of her nasty little laughs, as if she'd been lying in wait for me.

"What's all this hurry to apologize?" She goes to the telephone: "You are so kind, Claudia, to invite the child, but we've already made arrangements for this vacation." That pig! She hasn't arranged a single thing, she won't let me go with them as a punishment and she won't even admit it. Worse for her: she wished it on herself not to be staying here alone with Hummie. What her viciousness won't make her do. She'll be sorry, keeping me here to rot, while in Hollywood there's that snotty Liz Taylor. She's only three years older than me and has been on the cover of *Life*, and when she was two years younger than me she was in the *Lassie* movie, and now she's in a real studio. I'm already twelve, and I'm stuck in this damn Goatscreek where I have to put up with the ongoing spectacle of a middle-aged widow pathetically trying to seduce a French professor who thinks it's fun to stick his tongue in my eyes.

This prospect of severe punishment coming out of nowhere makes Mom all cheery. She's in the kitchen cooking a special dinner, from the "culinary seduction" chapter. It's the most pathetic seduction of all, when the only way you can agitate a man's insides is by stuffing them. Upon his long-awaited return, Monsieur the Model Tenant is welcomed with a real banquet: shrimp and peas, cherry-tomato salad, poached fish with mayonnaise, Wisconsin cheddar, almost as good as French cheese, and lemon sherbet for dessert. The whole thing (bad, atrocious, horrendous maternal taste!) inspired by the need to celebrate what "would have been Mr. Maze's fifty-fourth birthday, but unfortunately is the anniversary of his death." Not a very congenial seduction technique, I'd say. You might as well suggest a picnic at the cemetery. He already thinks of her as old, and yet she carries on so as to remind him that she's the widow of a man seventeen years older than he is, in other words the widow of a man old enough to be the father of the guy she wants to seduce, and that makes her someone who could be his mother, which is, so to speak, incest. Not very subtle. In fact definitely crude. Anyway, just as she's serving the fish, her dear monsieur says he's thinking of growing a mustache. He must have seen the one on Gerry Sue Filthy in my room and is racking his brains for some way to amuse me. Plasticmom, who still doesn't get who's trying to catch who, says that's not such a good idea, because someone here might lose her head. Winking, with a complicit-compassionate look, allusive and vulgar, she adds: "We'll have to put a brake on these jokes, or our little girl will end up falling for someone, and we can guess who that someone is without saying so out loud, right?" Our little girl? The coward. She doesn't dare say she's the one who's fallen, so she unloads it on me. I have never fallen for anyone. I simply have him at my feet, her dear no-good Monsieur Tenant, and if I feel like it I'll take him. Anyhow, if Plasticmom ever is granted the luxury of a second husband it will be thanks to my magic potions. He's a definite candidate in the ranks of sexually excited stepfathers, but Idiotmom doesn't see this. On the other hand, maybe she has this type of seduction in mind after all: maybe, by saying in front of Hummie that I'm the one who's fallen, Curlerhead intends to make me ridiculous (our little huntress of men, that's what the eyeshadowed glance at Hummie meant), but also to create the famous impalpable atmosphere of "multiple fascinations," from the chapter "Children as a Seductive Prothesis," where the author expands on the possibilities of diverting to one's own advantage the erotic vibrations emanating from the child's cutaneo-muscular complex.

Anyway, I'm not going to let that sarcastic remark pass unnoticed. I jump up from the table, tug hard on the tablecloth, sending Grandmother's Wedgwood plates flying (sorry, Grandma, I didn't do that on purpose, but you're too loony to care anyway), and then I crush my furious parent with a scornful look and slip out the door. The stupid goose, she can't contain herself and follows me to "give that girl a piece of her mind," as she explains to Hummie. She could have saved herself the trouble of all her fancy food, because I've removed all my special vibrations, and Monsieur the Unseduced is left alone at the table. He must have figured out by now that the husbands of these harpies don't last long and all you can expect from the Tonguefish-Maze family nest is hysterical scenes and slammed doors.

As if that weren't enough . . . What a hen! She can't think of any better punishment than to say no again to the lake trip, meaning that we'll go only if and when I apologize (again?). Apologize? I wouldn't dream of it. I just don't get it: she begins by making fun of me in front of Hummie, and then I'm supposed to apologize to her? Dear sweet Mama wants to make it plain at all costs that she's in charge: it's that primitive, blind desire of hers to crush me. She will be destroyed by her own hand, take my word for it. Because the basic equation is Mom = shit. Shitmom: the key to every mystery of the locked maternal lap. Mother full of shit, Mothershit overloaded with hatred. Mothershit inflated with rage against the disobedient dwarf. Mothershit desperate with the desire to bend everything to its will. Momshit, the bony cackling hen, domineering and clumsy. Momshit, Shitmom: and vice versa and vice versa and vice versa to infinity.

So no trip to the lake, fine, then I'll go to Hummie's study. For a while he goes on writing, pretending not to hear me, until I sit myself down on his knees and brush his face with my sun-warmed hair. We're just sitting there, not moving, I glance at the page, and he covers it with a book, as if by chance. Then slowly he leans closer to me, and I wait to see what he's going to do—maybe he'll kiss me, or something—but it's too soon, too soon for now; I feel a burning desire to press myself against him, feel his softness—his skin is smooth as silk—but no, I say to myself, that's not done, not by the woman who wants to enjoy her well-deserved triumph. What I wouldn't do to nestle against his chest . . . Don't give in, I repeat, don't give in, but I am giving in, I'm dying with longing, I'm almost gone, but luckily from downstairs Celeste shouts to Mom that she's found a dead mouse in the cellar. I scram, leaving Hummie sitting at his stupid desk full of unrealized desires, because he nearly made it! Now I'd like to know how he'll manage not to kiss the ground I walk on. His face is blurry with desire. I'm left with a mad wish to hug someone, so I jump on Celeste and sink into her neck, which is soft and smells of lavender. Celeste tries to free herself but I won't let go, so finally she pulls me down and says to me: "Gently! Don't you know I'm expecting a baby?" But I stay there just the same, clinging to her and thinking of Hummie, of his smell, of the tickle of his cheek, his hand on my shoulder (I still feel it). Hell. How long can my mother put off marrying him?

Plasticmom lying in the garden sunbathing looks exactly like Evita Peron on her visit to the Pope: sunglasses with two-inch-wide frames and a smile stuck on with hairspray.

We have to read Huck Finn for next year. Judging from the way he hates widows you'd think he knew my dear little mama in person. When we discuss it in class I'm going to say that now that we've entered the atomic age we should consider a policy of exterminating mothers right after they've given birth. Exterminate mothers and we'll eliminate everything that gets in the way of progress and happiness, truth, joy in life, and the spirit of adventure. Exterminate mothers and get rid of faded loveless creatures who have nothing more to give, all they can do is pollute the world with their envy, their resentment, their unhappiness. Creatures so repulsive that they can't even get a tan, because they have old skin that doesn't respond to the sun's caresses, or maybe it's that the sun won't touch them anymore because it's revolted by that grainy skin, just like a plucked, frozen chicken.

Mary Jo is twelve today. I gave her some charms for her bracelet: a miniature Pepsi Cola, a Mobil Oil, and a Campbell's Tomato Soup. She got a record player from her father, a record from Bobby, from her mother a jacket with a blue collar, from her grandmother a vanity case, from her uncle a horn for her bicycle, and lots of other presents from the millions of other relatives and friends who I can't even remember and who were all at her party. Mary Jo has an enormous family, while all I have is that excuse for a mother, with her poisonous little tyranny. If I didn't have Celeste, there wouldn't be anyone to understand how awful my life is. But if you want to be an actress maybe it's to your advantage to have nothing in your life to feel nostalgic about, nothing to hope for: that way, you're really eager for a taste of the lives of others, and soon it's like you have a lot of lives instead of just one. Even Nora said that while it may not seem that way now, in the end it's better to have nothing of your own, better to try on other people's feelings, because then it's like staying outside of everything, even yourself, which for performing is a good thing. Anyway, the unhappiness that comes from having a horrible mother like mine and having all the people who love you dead or far away can be useful, in fact indispensable: it's the condition of success, because how could you persuade a happy person to imagine herself in someone else's life? What advantage would there be? I try to explain this to Bobby, who calls it cynical. But then he doesn't explain what "cynical" means. To me it seems reasonable. Logical.

Mary Jo looked really cool at her party, with a pale-silver bell-shaped skirt and a dark-silver blouse with a low neck. Even so, Perry Maderna hung around me and not her. He is really cute. Hummie must have been something like Perry when he was young. Now he seems like his older brother. Perry is too young for me, a luxury I can't allow myself. Maybe the most sensible thing is this: for the moment I'll keep Hummie, then when I'm older and Hummie's too old for me I'll come back and get Perry. That way I'll have them both in one lifetime. I imagine he'll wait for me, because he won't get very far if he keeps looking at girls from behind a deck chair. The hen spent the whole time talking to Jasmine's mother, because Jasmine's going to the same camp where Mom wants to send me. After the cake there was dancing, boogie-woogie and fox-trot. I hooked Perry for practically every dance, and then, secretly, I brought him up to Mary Jo's room and kissed him. He turned as red as a lobster, but he gave in, even though afterward he ran away and didn't dare to come near me again. I think I stole his first kiss. They say you remember your first kiss for your whole life: he will always remember me and I will always remember Teddy Glass. Because a first kiss is like this: it's never two people giving each other that famous first kiss, it's not mutual, and afterward of course things are a mess and you're never really happy with anyone.

Sweet sweet Hummie. Really he is sweet, I like him a lot. He's like a movie star, he doesn't show his age: it's as if he'd always looked the way he looks now and will never get old. Other people his age look boring and fat, pain-in-the-neck fathers; he's like a boy but with something else, a low voice and a seductive, fascinating way of doing things. I could almost fall in love with him. Let's hope Mom doesn't ruin everything. She really doesn't see that without me she'll never get him to stay. He decided to stay the moment he saw me, obviously; otherwise what was he doing with the timetable in his hand? Plasticmom doesn't understand anything, it's like she can't see, she's suspended in a kind of fatal distraction; or maybe she's like a windup doll, which always does the same thing no matter what happens. She's deaf, more deaf than a deaf person, who may not hear voices but is aware of everything else. Plasticmom is impervious to me and to Hummie, and not even Nora's present did her any good—after all, it has a whole chapter on how a woman should be able to listen, see, and feel, meaning love. Plasticmom doesn't love anyone, not me, not Hummie, and she didn't even really love my dad or Nelson: she got married because a person is supposed to get married and she had children because it's normal for married people to have children. She follows two parallel tracks of body and soul that never meet, and you can see that whatever she does it's like she's doing it in front of a mirror, not with living people. She's a fossil: her bones creak when she moves. I really don't know why people continue to live when they're no longer able to live. They're there, hanging around, they go on moving, eating, sleeping, talking, and imitating others, but they do nothing on their own account, all they're capable of is interfering and making trouble. Like this morning she yelled at me because I swiped the bacon off Hummie's breakfast tray. What does she know about what's between us? Hummie wasn't at all sorry; besides he doesn't even like bacon, and I do. Plasticmom: "Don't you dare touch Monsieur Guibert's breakfast tray. Leave him alone."

"Don't disturb Monsieur while he's writing his book."

"Don't make noise, Monsieur is resting." And this nonsense of calling him Monsieur when she talks to me and Hummie when she talks to him . . . Putrefied old slipper. She has nothing to say to the world but Don't do this and Don't do that. She doesn't even know anymore if she's a woman or a landlady—she manages to make everyone feel like a guest, the object of careful hotel management. You can never feel free with her always getting underfoot. This afternoon she goes as far as trying one of those pathetic false maneuvers of hers. She doesn't know where to begin, so—she must have gotten the idea from an ad in one of those junky magazines she reads at the hairdresser's—she imagines that the right perfume will fix everything. But she's not sure of guessing right, so, looking totally unnatural, she clumsily grabs Hummie when he's coming out of the bath—he's still got shaving cream on his face—and, since he once worked in a cosmetics factory, practically orders him to help her choose a perfume for a friend of a friend of a friend of a friend. One of those lies you can smell from a thousand miles away. Hummie's got zero desire to go shopping with the widow Maze: the outing will be torture, it's written on his face. It's heart-breaking—if Mom does this he'll run away at the first opportunity. So I bring in reinforcements. I make a run for it, block them as they're leaving. Hey, where are you going? I shout. The old hen, with her delusion of omnipotence, wants to get rid of me, leave me in the dust. She tries frantically to accelerate, but luckily she's not in gear, so I open the door and squeeze in next to Hummie, who goes immediately from pale to bright, while Plasticmom is red with rage, a boiled lobster, and tightens her lips in a sulk. She is really ridiculous; at her age she shouldn't make these bratty scenes. And to get so mad just because your dear little daughter wants to come along isn't a very nice reaction in a mother, either. Her face should light up at the sight of me, too: it would make a different impression on Hummie—like, here we are, mother and daughter so happy to be together, we don't need anybody else, in fact we radiate happiness and joy in life. Also, the book says—and besides, everyone knows it—that men have no maternal instinct, so the way to make yourself interesting is not to seem needy but like you have a lot to offer. Naturally this is in the realm of feelings and happiness in life, because when it comes to material things you want to let it be understood that you maybe *are* a little needy: women are wonderful but unfortunately we don't have everything we ought to have. So here they come, and maybe they don't have the joy in life but they know how to take care of the material aspect, and in return we soak them with all that happy emotion we have inside; it squirts from our eyes, as if in place of a brain there were a cake with candles. That's how it goes, though I must say, in criticism of Nora's book, Hummie seems to be more sparkling with life than Plasticmom, but of course the ones who are most of all would be me, Mary Jo, and Celeste.

Anyway: the hen's face doesn't light up a bit when she sees me swinging into the car: she has the sulky expression of someone who's just bought a carton of broken eggs; her eyebrows are as ugly as spider legs. It's hard to be touched by such shortsighted egoism. Plasticmom just won't see that I'm her own, ingratiating little Eros. Here's a real problem: she knows perfectly well that she's not Venus—*she* came out of the water back in the mists of time, so by now she's really dry, dried out, not a drop of seawater on her. If she were Venus she'd realize that her child preserves the memory of her former beauty, but she's blocked by her regret for Nelson. You can see that the role of Cupid, with bow and arrow and little wings on his shoulders, was meant for him, whereas if only Plasticmom would touch my back she'd feel my sharp shoulder blades under her fingers, she'd realize that wings could grow on me, too. She wants to go by herself in the car with Hummie to buy that stupid perfume, but I'm going to save her from herself, and meanwhile if Hummie isn't furious and hasn't already packed his bags it's only because I'm here to sweeten things. In the car I secretly take his hand, and he holds it tight, smiles with half-closed eyes, happy to have me beside him; thanks to me the terrible bore of Mom shopping passes without too much suffering. Dreamily he sniffs the perfumes and winks at me, then he chases me with the sprayers until I've got all the scents on me. Plasticmom gives me her usual dirty looks; by now not even her nasty expressions are alive, she's a fossil through and through.

"Come on, Dolly, leave Monsieur Guibert in peace, let's hurry up and buy the perfume, so he can get back to his book . . . " All because no one pays any attention to her. Plasticmom stands there so dried up and mean, the jerk, when all she has to do is be natural, natural like us, and she'd be one of us, we'd be together, me and Hummie and her. But no, she has to be in charge, give orders, arrange, judge everything. Oh the trouble, oh mothers, really there is no way to save them, they should all be wiped out, from first to last, because there is just no way to reform them. And then the stupidity! The amazing stupidity! First she contrives this scene with Hummie, to help her choose a present, which is a delicate, personal thing, for this friend of a friend of a friend, blah blah, blah, and then as soon as he says which one he likes—in other words, the perfume that's going to attract him—she forgets her original excuse for dragging him to the store, and, totally practical, just taking care of business, says to the clerk: "All right, I'll take this one, no need to wrap it." What a show! She doesn't even have the sense to buy two bottles, one wrapped as a gift and one for herself, which would be a delicate way of letting Hummie know that she appreciates his taste in perfume, but all Plasticmom knows is how to be cheap . . . That moment marks the start of the disaster, and there's not much to be done about it: Hummie is disgusted by his landlady's clumsiness. It's as if she'd told him she intended to seduce him, and, as if that weren't enough, she makes me sit in the back seat on the way home, so she has Hummie next to her, all to herself. What does she think she can do while she's driving? She tells one of her usual incredibly tedious stories, like a well-brought-up lady, a lady who goes to the book club, who speaks very clearly and correctly, she makes some allusive smiles, but meanwhile Hummie's getting exhausted beside her, you can just see him fading. As soon as we get home, to escape from the perfumed woman, he takes off, complaining of bad back pain, and doesn't even come down for dinner. Now it's over for sure, he's going to leave, and the worst thing is she has no idea. When he goes up to his room she follows him to give him a tube of Musterole. From the chapter "Seduction Nurse-Style."

11.

𝒯HERE'S A HELLISH storm, the wind bends trees to the ground, and hail pounds the windowpanes. Might as well forget about the trip to the lake. I read about a five-year-old boy who derailed a train: he put some stones on the track so the train would cut them in half. The train flipped over on its side instead.

Hummie is practically mine. I really know what it takes with men.

1. subtlety

2. elusiveness.

It has to feel like an irresistible distraction, something you accidentally dropped. Not like my heavy-handed mother with her cellophane-wrapped seduction, presented on a tray along with yesterday's cold leftovers. Yes, it takes something else.

It's still raining, so hard you can't even stick your nose outside. I'm dying of boredom. Humbert wanders around the house looking unhappy, poor guy, here he is all alone, in a situation crazy enough to make anyone else jump out the window: he doesn't know anyone here, doesn't have a lover or school friends or parents or a wife or children, he is as lonely as a dog in this house of strangers, with a hen who's trying to seduce him and a book that's got to be written. I can hear the tap-tap of the typewriter keys, tap-tap of the rain on the windowpanes. It must be terrible to be alone in the world, far from home, far from everything, while in front of you is a stupid book you don't care about writing. He taps the keys for a while and then he stops. He must be looking at the ceiling, like my idiot mother when she was staring blankly at the fan blades. Something bad must have happened to Hummie, too, something he hasn't told us about—what train he fell off of, and why he seems like someone waiting for a train, with no idea when it will come. So to pass the time he does something like writing a book that's of no use to anyone, and doesn't even amuse him. I can't think of anything to cheer him up; this house certainly doesn't offer any resources. Just to keep him company I show him the drawings in my school album, the illustrated history of the Maze dynasty, when there were still four of us; Grandma's house, where we live now, but when Grandma was still fine, making apple pie; then Grandma on a horse, Grandma with the prize cup for steeplechase riding, my dad in the garage with his special machine for mixing sauces, Mom in the hospital the day Nelson was born, then all of us on a trip, then the day of Nelson's funeral, with Mom's veil stuck to her face because she's crying so much, and Daddy holding her so she won't fall even though he's crying, too. Finally there's the drawing of my friends at school, which didn't come out too well, because I'm not very good at faces. Hummie looks at everything, holding me close, with his head leaning on mine, and a melancholy, dreamy look. Then, for kicks, I take out my secret album, with the giant women whose boobs go out to the margin of the page and their bellies stick out, too, overflowing the edge, and you can't tell where they end or if they go on to infinity, and their bottoms protrude in the opposite direction. They are really big, really indecent, but Humbert doesn't find them funny at all. He doesn't smile, and makes a squeamish face, like he's disgusted. I'm sorry he doesn't understand my fat asses and big bosoms and bellies; it comes out that my drawing should be more refined. Refined like those French poets who make him terminally sad on rainy days? No thanks. My gigantic bottoms are magnificent and if you don't see it you must have a stunted brain.

Poor Humbert, he no longer knows which fish to catch. While I'm leaning out the window talking to Kenny, he comes up behind me on tiptoe but then gets scared—scared of being unrefined?—and gives me a stupid little shake. So I tell him to get lost, especially after his fuss about my big overflowing women, but he looks so pathetic that I'm sorry I was mean, and after Kenny leaves I go up behind *him* on tiptoe and cover his eyes with my hands, to show him how to be a little smoother, because, goodness, he's as clumsy as a bear. I can tell he'd die happily patting my legs as he tries to guess who's there; and he keeps not guessing right so he won't have to stop. Too bad that just at the best moment, of course, the hen shows up, alarmed by our laughter and worried that, every so often, in spite of everything, there may be flashes of life in her house. Anyway, she shows up and encourages the tenant to slap me. Great, encouraging a stranger to hit me. Fuck you, I say to her in a voice low enough so that she doesn't really hear me but she hears something, after which I go to my room.

A small revolution and Mom doesn't even realize it: she decided—obviously her own idea—to put off the picnic, because Mary Jo has a temperature. Seize the opportunity: no picnic, no church. Eye for an eye. I've had enough of being the little orphan who goes to church with her checked pinafore and white patent leather purse. So Plasticmom goes by herself to pray for divine aid in her dubious undertakings, while I stay home with Hummie.

A perfect chance to put on lipstick. I choose the color myself— I certainly don't go and ask what his favorite is. Dear Hummie, which color seems most exciting to you? That's what the attentive hen would have said, and he would have responded: Dear Isabel, I am past the age where the color of lipstick can arouse me, I am an old scholar of French literature and what little ardor remains to me is devoted to prewar France—that's more or less his line of defense when he scents danger.

When Mom paints her lips, she draws an outline with a pencil first, very carefully puts on the lipstick, and then starts wandering around the house: her lips look like they were cut out of cardboard, like they're detached from the rest of her body, like she's trying to impersonate "the lady with painted lips"—which usually goes along with "the lady with painted nails," waving her hands in the air so the polish will dry, or "the lady with her hair in curlers," who with her freshly polished nails and her painted lips stuck out like a fish goes around the house as if she's a kind of walking prayer: want me, want me, want me.

I do it all the opposite: I put on the lipstick *almost* carefully, I say almost, and not *completely*, on purpose, because the guy's eyes should be hooked by uncertainty: was it put on well or badly? Does it need touching up or not? So his thoughts go around and around until he forgets why he was curious in the first place and is simply lost in contemplation of the mouth, the blinding-white teeth, the red tongue darting between the teeth, redder than the lipstick, until, without meaning to, he gets closer and closer, and suddenly he's stunned by the blood-hot breath, and doesn't have the strength to pull back . . . That's how it's done. What possible interest can Mom's lips ever have had—they're so precisely painted they look like an advertisement.

My lips are *almost* impeccably painted: it's like a piece of me has been peeled away, a tiny lip muscle laid bare, red blood just veiled by skin too fine to hide the flesh, so in reality two pairs of lips can be seen, superimposed, *almost* superimposed . . . a dizzying, out-of-focus effect. But lipstick by itself isn't enough: the attack has to come from multiple directions, otherwise the defense can concentrate on a single point. So a red apple, red plus red, two red spheres in perpetual motion. The principle of hypnosis. Anyway, the apple is essential. How come these hens don't get it? They go to church year after year, they read the Bible, or at least they keep it on their bedside table, and then they forget how the first seduction of the first man occurred? With an apple, that's how. No man can resist a woman who has an apple in her hand. It's theological. A woman with an apple in her hand is the first woman, the only woman in the world, and he's the first man—he stumbles on love and he can't shake it, never ever ever. This isn't in Nora's book; the truth is, a lot of stuff isn't in it. I'm going to write a new one someday. Anyway, armed with my two red patches, lips and apple, and wearing my dress with dark and light pink checks, I go and sit on the sofa next to Hummie, who, poor guy, tries not to notice me for a while. And I seem to be there for reasons having nothing to do with him. Eventually I get tired of that, and start throwing the apple up in the air and catching it, concentrating so it's like I'm not even aware of Hummie sitting there next to me. The apple flies up in the air, and I catch it with a thwack, skin against peel. Finally he grabs it out of my hand, and I yell at him to give it back. Give it back right now, I yell, hurling myself at him. Give it back: I open my fire-colored mouth and blow my blood-scented breath on him. The action begins! Battle! I grab the apple, being more alert than he is, and stronger and a hundred times more agile. I bite it, and it's like breaking a jar containing a love potion. The air is pierced with fragrance—acidic apple and blood-scented throat warmth. But to conceal the main frontal attack from him I take his hand off the magazine (diversionary tactic), and while I'm looking around for something or other for him to look at—to see better I stretch across him—my fragrance stuns him completely. I find a dumb but funny photograph of a naked lady, in marble, so then Hummie, who seems stupid yet very happy to keep playing the game, throws the magazine aside. With new protests, I fling myself away to get it back, but he holds on to me, trying to think up something, anything, just to keep my sunburned legs from escaping. It's obvious with every move of the struggle that he's trying to position them against him, on his lap. Under the thin silk bathrobe he's all on edge. His cheeks are fiery, he mutters a pile of nonsense so that I'll stay, he wants me there, whatever the cost. He'd have a heart attack if I stopped right there. He even starts humming my favorite song, without ever getting to the end—all this so he can keep rubbing against my legs. I feel that trunk of his swelling, bigger and bigger. He goes on singing, endlessly, now slow, now fast, very fast, then he turns red and, fighting for breath, mangles the words. It's a waste of time to try to correct him by singing along—by now he's out of time, in the sense that he's all in my power. He looks at me as if he hoped to keep me there forever, comes closer and closer but doesn't dare. Then, so he can touch me right at the edge of my underpants, he remembers the bruise I got when I stumbled against the chest of drawers: another hypocritical trick, like the day he stuck his tongue in my eye. But what can you do except put up with these big cowards who want to act refined. I just wish I could get him to be a little less phony. Anyway, he searches for the bruise, making tremendous faces so that I won't guess how excited he is, while he keeps letting my knees roll so they rub against him. I'm all hot inside, I'd like to hug him and kiss him without all these pretenses, but I'm going to wait till the next move; for now I pretend nothing's happening, and go on biting my apple. With every bite I get under his nose so the whiffs of acidic apple get stronger and stronger, and at every crunch he rocks more quickly, throwing his head back as if he's on a swing, and then tries to act normal so I can't tell how excited he is, until only the core is left, and since I feel sorry for him for not being able to just take what he so desperately wants—to hold me tight against him, crush me—I throw the core in the fireplace and end up right on top of him, against that hard little stick, and then I start humming along with him again. We're hand in hand, our arms coming close and then moving apart; I fling my head back, and for a second feel his mouth on my throat. I press against him, until he holds me still, interrupts the nursery rhyme, and, all trembling, forgets to keep up his pretense. I feel weird, too, I melt, and something goes by without my really seeing it, a whir of swift wings, it disappears in an instant and we sit there looking at each other, all blushing, not knowing what to do. I'd like to curl up and wrap myself in his arms. It would be nice but then he'd get scared; I'll put off the courage lesson till another time—you can't insist on everything all at once. Luckily the telephone rings, and I run to answer it. He takes advantage of this to get up and go to the bathroom, and when he finally comes back I'm in the garden. He looks around confused and satisfied, maybe he hasn't yet realized what happened to him: that I seduced him. That now he's mine. Too bad it was the hen on the phone, who, in spite of being so obtuse, must have guessed something, because she orders me to meet her at the Clarks' for dinner, and there she tells me a bunch of horrible things: that she wants me to get braces and she's sending me to camp with

Chloe and Jasmine. I don't need braces, and I wouldn't dream of closing up the slit between my teeth: it's clear she just wants to disfigure me. As for camp, it's a last-minute invention to get rid of me. I tell her—there at the Clarks', because it's not my fault if she wanted to talk to me in front of them—that if I have to go somewhere I'd rather go with Mary Jo, to which her response is that I have to quit seeing only Mary Jo all the time, and play with other girls from good families—Chloe, for example, who can be my friend at camp. I'll show her what sort of friends we'll be, she and I. Then the nasty hen sends me to the movies with the Clarks, so she can stay alone with her adored tenant.

The hen's bossier than ever. She's furious that I put her lipstick to better use: she says I broke it off and now she'll have to buy a new one, how dare I, etc. etc.

"Who do you think you are? How old do you think you are?" Yelling these stupid remarks, she bursts into my room and grabs my only decent nightgown. "I want to see how sexy you'll be with braces on your teeth next fall! Let's see if that won't calm you down." All this she says in a hiss, revealing her true nature as a viper, which she is so careful to conceal from her adored monsieur.

"How are you feeling, Humbert? Send the child away if she's bothering you. Oh, you are truly too kind to let her stay there with you, you should be more severe . . . Are your teeth troubling you?" Oh what a phony she is, always speaking in that flat, toneless voice. But when she yells at me, her voice turns into a kind of storm-tossed sea that goes in all directions, an earthquake of shouts. With Hummie, a completely different voice. The voice of Plasticmom. With me: the voice of Shitmom.

That stinker Hummie. Mom announces the plan of sending me to camp and he doesn't say a word. Not a single word. First, while she's in church nibbling at the host and admiring the new windows bought with contributions from the congregation, he plays all these cute little games with me, and then he turns chicken. Bad enough that she decides to clear the way for her pathetic attempt at seduction, and that he, vile-weak-spineless coward, lets her. Even worse: he approves. At the table Shitmom says with a triumphant look how good it will be for my character to spend the whole summer at camp. Hummie nods, then with a meek, wavering, sheepish smile he objects: "I only hope the child will be all right away from home for such a long time." When I see him in the hall I don't let him get away: he tries to get close and caress me and all the rest, but I hit him so hard with one of my father's shoe trees that he falls down. And while he's sitting there, with the dopey expression of a person flat on his ass, I tell him off, tell him he's a really dirty double-crosser. He stands up looking like he just doesn't get it, like he fell out of the sky, the revolting coward. First, happy as a clam, he rocks me on his stomach, then he pretends it was nothing, and it's obvious from his empty gaze and his evasive-polite smile that he would give anything for me not to have realized anything, and for Mom not to have realized anything, and even him. With his grayish worn-out face, he doesn't have the guts to be alive, that jerk, that relic from the former kingdom of France, who shows us invitations to Masses in memory of Marie Antoinette, with his ridiculous books, and his quotations that Mom tries to learn by heart so she can repeat them in her awful, nasal pronunciation, and those revolting I-am-a-man-and-so-I-am-superior looks. Disgusting.

Tonight, to make me really furious, Plasticmom tells him how I bullied her into getting the now confiscated nightgown, and Monsieur the hypocrite has the nerve to raise his eyebrows, dismayed at the idea that a little girl "should have clothes like that." When once I found him rummaging through my things. He doesn't even deserve to be spit on.

I'm paging through *American Girl*. Humbert comes over and runs his hands nervously through his hair.

"What awful little girls! And here I was thinking that all American girls were as seductive as you!" Ass-licker Humbert, but those girls are wearing really gross outfits, with full skirts and smocking, and their fat legs look like squished bread—they're not at all sexy. "Their flesh is like butter," he goes on. "There's nothing exciting about them, do you think?" He smiles while I continue to ignore him, and then he makes a last attempt, touching the inside of my thigh: "Not like certain slender sunburned girls I know."

"Cut it out," I yell. If he thinks he can get me back that way. . .

I'm leaving tomorrow. I'm glad. I can't take Plasticmom's making up to Hummie anymore. The hen is exiling me. Good. She doesn't like what's happening between me and her planned madame-maker. It annoys her that he has eyes only for me.

Great! Fabulous! Do they think I can't get along without them? I want to see what Madame Maman manages in my absence. But of course anything is possible, that boiled fish of a Hummie might even get himself seduced by the widow Maze while I'm away: now that he's installed, and writing who the hell knows what scholarly crap, it will be hard for that lazy jerk to detach himself from a woman who serves him something different every day and, to please him, is trying to "perfect" her French cooking. For that reason alone, besides not having to pay the rent, he's capable of getting married. Let them both croak, I don't give a damn. I dumped my spider collection in Plasticmom's bed: so she'll have company to sleep with in case the conquest of Humbert Guibert drags on.

12.

*I*NCREDIBLE. NOT THE thing as such but the timing: less than twenty-four hours. Early morning, Thursday: the hen gets me in the car to take me to camp. I'm still angry with Hummie, because he's such a revolting coward. But just as we're leaving I can't help glancing at his window: his nose is pressed against the glass, the tip turning white. You can see he's pretty down, in despair at having to stay by himself in Goatscreek. I get kind of a lump in my throat. My anger evaporates—it's sad to leave without even a goodbye. Mom's already at the wheel, a whole bright halo of crow's feet around her eyes. As I'm about to close the car door, I slip away, running, while she shouts at me to get back in my seat. I run really fast, and Hummie opens the window with an incredulous look—flash!—a snapshot, if I close my eyes I see him in front of me. He comes down the stairs in his narrow-striped pajamas and his leather slippers, still smelling of his bath, a loose-limbed doll with bushy eyebrows. I jump on his neck, I touch his mouth, caressing again, for the last time, that smooth pink lip, he hugs me tight, so tight my bones crack, and he whispers I'm sorry, or maybe remember me, or something like that, it's all too emotional to distinguish the words clearly. During the whole trip, sitting beside Plasticmom, who's furious at my ultimate disobedience, I try to recall what exactly he could have said to me, but all I remember is how soft his chest is, still warm from his bath, and my bones cracking, mine and his, as he holds me away to see me better, with a tragic-emotional look (he's always getting that look, because of the gutless poetry he studies), and I bring my lips close to his. End of film. Hummie has such an intensely painful expression at seeing me leave that I expect him to come downstairs and announce to the hen that we're getting married, that he's going away but will come back to get me, and we'll never leave each other, we'll buy a ranch in Wyoming and have thirteen children.

The whole way I'm thinking about the cracking bones and the kiss, and I feel so faint and languid. Trying to avoid turning to my left, I really concentrate on the landscape on my right. Otherwise my picture would be obstructed by Plasticmom, who is driving nervously, her lips curled with joy at the thought of being free of me for the whole summer and maybe more. She drops me off as quickly as she can, twitters a greeting to Chloe and Jasmine, congratulates the director, Mrs. Watson, on her book about girls' camps, proposes a meeting at the book club, and takes off, stripping her gears, toward Hummie, who is finally hers.

They call me to the phone while I'm still unpacking my suit-case: it's Hummie. My heart skips a beat, a big beat, so he's come to his senses, thinks Dolly the halfwit, he finally understands, he's com-ing to get me, he'll take me away and we'll get married, because as soon as I left he realized that without me there is no life for him . . . because he had to lose me to find me . . .

What the hell. Not a chance. I take the telephone, still panting from running, and what do I hear?

"Hi, Dolly, how was the trip?"

"You can imagine, with that . . . " He doesn't let me finish.

"I want to tell you something: your mother and I are getting married." My arms drop, I stand stricken, the receiver dangling by my side. Marry who?

"Sorry, a stupid puppy just pulled my sock down. What did you say?"

"That your mother and I are getting married." This time the tone is less convincing. You won't get me, you piece of shit: with the greatest nonchalance, in an even falser tone than his—not even the hen could make it more plastic-sounding—I tell him: "That's swell news! When?" I hope he's upset that I couldn't care less who he mar-ries. I feel a burning sensation in my throat, but I ignore it: rather, I'm dying, but I'm certainly not going to give him the satisfaction of bursting into tears.

"Wait a second, here comes that stupid pup again!" and I shout at my fantasy dog because at the very least I have to let out some-thing, otherwise . . . But it's not enough, so I press the receiver against my stomach and yell even louder, while outside the booth people start running toward me. I give a big smile along with a gesture brushing them away, and then I breathe deep in my abdomen, the way Celeste taught me to do when everything, really everything, is a complete mess. I feel like I'm being mocked, but I let out a big laugh and pick up the phone. "That dog must be crazy." Then I add: "You know, it's kind of a nice place here, not such a bad idea after all." Hummie doesn't utter a word. We say goodbye like old bored relatives, I leave the phone booth, I tell a group of the girls standing there that I screamed because of a cramp in my stomach. I must have eaten too much watermelon yesterday, I have diarrhea, I say, so I can go to bed alone, since I have a box of cookies from Leslie's store, a present from Celeste for the vacation.

The witch! What a witch, spawn of the Tonguefish! She got rid of me so she could be married in peace, although I would like to know when they managed to come to an agreement, those two. I see her, Isabel Maze at night going to Hummie on tiptoe, on the fat callused pads of her feet, with her ugly red painted nails. And to think that during the day they looked at each other as if there were nothing, those two, while really they were squalid accomplices, a criminal association. Worse than Al Capone. Thieves.

Those two monsters were having fun behind my back. Every night, I'll bet, Hummie described to the widow Maze how he was seducing me—I've always suspected that old people who can't get excited themselves use their children. They beat them or cheat them to prove something and then they stay together, as if it were nothing, as if they were still attracted to each other in spite of their wrinkled faces . . . Old impotent Hummie, he got excited with me so he could go to bed with the hen, because if he couldn't do that then she couldn't marry him and then no free room and board in the Maze house. Everyone knows how these good-for-nothings manage to survive for more than thirty years running: self-interest is how. Money, sex, steak. That's it. And respectability, of course. A fine façade. There are plenty of displaced people who come here to get themselves back in the money. With all those Siberias they have over there. . . I should never have told him that Plasticmom is stingy but rich: now he will never let go, not until he's sucked up everything there is to suck up. He could even steal my inheritance.

Not to mention their amazing deviousness: first they use me to seduce each other, then they don't even invite me to the wedding— they don't even want me to carry a bouquet . . . They send me into exile so they can get married with some conviction that they're doing it because they actually want to. Use it and throw it away. I'll show them—see if I can't join them and even beat them in their pathetic selfishness. I think about the hen's odious little conversations with Hummie, about how I had fallen for him. What she wouldn't do! Vicious conversations at my expense the better to enjoy her conquest. As for Hummie, he's obviously been playing both sides the whole time, pretending to seduce me to please Madame Maman and her mad thirst to humiliate me, and then seriously petting me to have some fun on the sly, while, like the big fat coward he is, happily screwing the bossy hen, who thinks she has everything—everything—under control.

I decided to have a glorious and deep sleep. The next morning I say I still have a stomachache, so I can stay in bed all day, because in this situation the only cure is to snore as loud as you can, and then after hours and hours closed in the world of dreams you wake up and everything seems far away, on some other planet. In the evening I finally get up and have dinner with the others, but again today I stay here by myself, dozing. Tomorrow I'll be cured, I'll consider myself purged of that revolting Goatscreek shit, and then I'll begin to look around and see what the possibilities are. This famous Maple Camp is really a sort of tent city for war refugees, with a single small white red-roofed building, where the head of the camp, Mrs. Watson, lives with her son Roger, who is the handyman. In front of the director's house there are some long tables with just a roof over them: the gathering place for meals. We have four in our cabin: Nina and Sarah, the German twins, and Rowe and me—she's tall, with long blond hair down to her waist and bosoms almost as big as Celeste's. We're in the cabin called Donald Duck, between Snow White and Pegleg, across from Daisy Duck, where Chloe is with three other plain girls. Donald and Daisy are "engaged," which means that the eight of us have to do group activities together, under the leadership of our head girl, who is Rowe. Jasmine is in a different cabin, Mickey Mouse, along with Rowe's sister, Lucy; she's older than Rowe, and it's her second year here; she's in charge of water sports, although Rowe is beginning to beat her in swimming races. Watson is a big lady with red hair and enormous thighs, and she always wears lipstick. Roger looks just like her—I wouldn't say ugly, but his shoulders are kind of narrow.

First expedition with Rowe and the others: near the camp there are some woods, and in the woods are two tiny lakes. Rowe and Lucy have divided up the lakes—Rowe has a little island with a willow on it for her swimming team—so they don't bother each other and don't quarrel. Back in Boston, where they live with their grandmother, who is secretary to a biology professor at Harvard, they do nothing but fight. Rowe tells me how once her mother threw a watermelon at Lucy but it hit the wall right above her head and broke into a thousand pieces, green, white, and pink, and the seeds flew all over the place, like cockroaches. Lucy didn't bat an eye, so as not to give her the satisfaction. That's nerve. She wants to keep her canoe team all to herself, without younger sisters underfoot, so she didn't mind giving Rowe the island. It's no use to her, and then it's an island only in a manner of speaking—you can see what happens there perfectly clearly from land. You can get there by canoe, but really it's almost faster to swim.

I investigate the situation here: Watson's husband was very small, and when they argued she'd pick him up off the ground and carry him away under one arm, and if he was drunk she'd give him hell. This henpecked husband passed the time wandering among the tents; he didn't do anything in particular. Every so often he'd start a conversation with the girls, but he was really boring, so she sent him away, and now it's not clear if she's with this sort of hunchbacked deaf guy or a blond guy who comes in an old Ford to sell eggs. There's a bunch of special activities you can do here if you want: riding, tennis, ham radio, sewing. I'm not going to do any of them—that way I'm free to train with Rowe to win the swimming race. I'd like to go riding, only I'd have to join Jasmine's group with an odious girl who's stuck up because she won a steeplechase race. Chloe wants me to do sewing, which is taught by Watson herself, but when I said no she gave it up, too, so she could do whatever I'm doing. Well, what a fine idea. How flattered I am . . .

The hen calls. She says Hummie is delightful. I can't tell if they're already married. She's not very precise—she kind of beats around the bush. I hope she chokes on it. I hope she suffocates.

First practice race. A tiny red-headed girl wins, Nina's second and Rowe's third. Jasmine's fifth. I come in fifteenth. I'm out of practice because Plasticmom only brought me to the lake once and never to the pool: too busy with her matrimonial intrigues. Chloe finished last.

Second practice race. Rowe is first, I'm fourth. The hen calls me.
"Hummie and I are married."
"I know."
"Are you pleased?"
"Does it matter?"
"Don't be impossible."
"What would you rather?"
"What do you mean?"
"Nothing. Happy second."
"Second what?"
"Husband."
"Call when you feel a little less nasty."
"Then let's say we'll talk when I get home."
I hang up. Not even a hello from Hummie.

Chloe and the other dummies from Daisy Duck are jealous of me and Rowe. Every day we take the canoe out to practice. As soon as we're on the island Nina and Sarah jump in the water to swim laps around the island: Rowe makes them do ten a day; Chloe and her three drips on the other hand don't do more than five laps, then they sit on the pebbled beach and sunbathe. We've given them the assignment of picking out the most beautiful pebbles so they can make a mosaic to present to Mrs. Watson as a monument to the spirit of the willow. This should keep them out of our way till the end of the month. After the twins do their laps, Rowe and I go to the other side of the lake and check on the girls from there. They can't see us, because we hide behind a mulberry bush. Every other night Rowe has to make a report to the head of the camp on the group's activities: if something bad happened she'd be demoted to cleaning toilets for the whole summer, which would be really awful because the jobs here, although they're all revolting, at least are done in rotation: cleaning the cabin, refilling the water tanks, cleaning out the toilets, peeling potatoes. The only thing we have to do every single day is make our cots and wash our things. Watson says that next year she'll have a Bendix for the sheets, but for now you have to manage with a washtub beside a stream. The water is so cold you get chilblains even in summer.

Rowe tells me she's done it with Roger Watson.

"That stringy-haired fatass with all the freckles?"

"You can't be too picky, he's the only male around."

"Undoubtedly an advantage."

"Have you ever done it?"

"More or less."

"With?"

"With my mother's husband, ten days ago: he started singing a nursery rhyme as an excuse for rubbing against my legs, and then he made me sit on top of him, but his bathrobe was in between us, and the idea was that I wouldn't notice."

"But did he put it in or not?"

"No, how could he, I might have noticed."

"If it doesn't go in, it doesn't count. Pretty bold move, though."

"Europeans have the courage of lions."

"Your stepfather is European?"

"Yes, Humbert Guibert, professor of French literature and our former tenant."

"Is he handsome?"

"Passable. He looks like Gerry Sue Filthy, but his eyebrows are thicker and his accent's more sophisticated."

"Filthy who?—the one in the cigarette ads?"

"Yes, that's him. I have a couple of photographs of him at home. One he gave me and the other I cut out."

"Does your stepfather always sing nursery rhymes?"

"Yes, even to my mother."

"How do you know?"

"I don't. No, here's how I think he does it with my mother: he goes into the bathroom and puts on his aftershave humming *ta ta ta ta ta ta ta,* and then he turns out the lights so it's not too obvious that he has to go to bed with that revolting excuse for a mother, and then he makes monstrous efforts to imagine he's with me, so while he's making Plasticmom rock he hums 'Three Blind Mice'. . . otherwise it wouldn't work at all."

"Mom what?"

"Plasticmom, Shitmom. Whatever. My mother. He sings three blind mice who were making love, then he closes his eyes and . . . "

"Comes."

"Definitely. Do you come with Roger?"

"We come. You want to come?"

"All together?"

"No, one at a time. First me, then you, or rather: first you and then me."

"But where?"

"On the island."

"Tomorrow?"

"Tomorrow."

"And today?"

"Today?"

Today, on the island, Rowe sticks her tongue in the corners of my mouth, Maud Greyhound style, not bad. She takes my hands and puts them on her tits, and I like that, too, it's what I wished I could do with Celeste, but I get nervous when she takes my head and forces it under her t-shirt. I wriggle free and later I make up a dream with her in it, or rather the two of us in my house in Goatscreek: she says she wants to make love with me, and asks if I want to. I say I'm attracted to her, that when you're friends it's important to like each other physically, too, but we don't have to actually do it. It's great to just say it—more would be creepy. I hope she understands that doing it with a girl is not for me. The same with Maud: a little was nice but it got to be a mess when she was jealous of boys. Evidently there are situations where leaving things out isn't enough, sometimes you also have to invent.

The hen called: they're putting off their honeymoon.
"Why aren't you going?"
"Humbert says that first he has to finish his book."
"And when will that be?"
"In the autumn."
Yellowbelly Hummie. He wants to delay our meeting as long as possible. He's afraid to look me in the eyes.

Rowe decides that today we'll go with Roger. As I understand it, Roger will loom over me and I'll find myself under his melon-colored face.
"All you have to do is close your eyes," says Rowe.
"Impossible. I'm sure I'd keep seeing him in front of me anyway and I'd burst out laughing. Then he'd be insulted."
"Laughing at what?"
"When you kiss it's like being transported to a marvelous land, to a kind of paradise where the two of you become one, you forget you're on earth, but the idea of becoming one with Roger makes me want to laugh, or cry."
"Cut out the romantic stuff. Where did you read that?"
"I don't know, movies, songs . . . "
"You idiot—in movies and songs they're talking about kissing, I didn't say you have to kiss Roger, I said making love, in the sense of going, you know, going and coming: you won't go to another place, but you'll have great skin."

"You don't kiss Roger?"

"Does he seem like the kissing type? It's good just for staying in shape. But there's one really funny thing about him, you know, when he comes? He puts his hand on the visor of his cap and shouts 'Kilroy was here.' " Yikes!

Mrs. Watson sends Roger off to do some shopping, so Rowe's plan comes to nothing. I'm a little scared of going with Roger. Because of something the hen told me, and I can't seem to get it out of my mind. I ask Rowe if it's true that it hurts the first time, that you bleed and you can start hemorrhaging and end up in the hospital, but she says that's all nonsense, nothing but nothing happened to her, she barely even noticed it. "That's the sort of thing they say to make you afraid."

"What about diseases?"

"Same thing, silly." In effect: what got into me to pay attention to the hen?

"And babies?"

"As for that, don't worry. Roger collects condoms—he's a genius at stretching them like a slingshot to make sure they hold."

With Roger on the other bank of the Willow island. I try to do it, but I feel like laughing: I'll never manage with that smiling melon face. Rowe starts getting annoyed—if I can't make up my mind she'll get a new friend, she's had enough of my childishness. I wish, at least, she hadn't told me about Kilroy, because when I try all I can think about is that at the end he'll shout Kilroy was here, and I can't do it. Anyway it's better this way, because Chloe and her three jerks had the nerve to come over to our side of the lake without permission, and they might have caught us. Rowe made a scene and told them that they mustn't dare do anything other than what she tells them, because she's the one who has to make the report. They slunk away and went back to picking out their stupid colored pebbles.

· · ·

Rowe is furious with me for putting off Roger. I am furious with myself for getting into this situation where if I don't do what Rowe says I seem like a halfwit. Roger came back to Willow bank B again today. I was under a tree reading *Nancy*, and Rowe walked up to me with a carrot in her mouth looking like a rabbit: "I'm Roger and this time you won't escape." Then she tackles me. I get really angry at being treated like this, and in front of Roger besides, which is outrageous, so I jump on top of her before she can get me under her, and hit her hard. Rowe yelps and kicks, then she kind of gets a taste for it, and I also start feeling good, having her under me with those enormous tits, that sea of swaying flesh. I plant my feet solidly on the ground, with one hand I pull her hair, and with the other I crush one of her arms to the ground; she still has the other free and gives me some trouble, but she's too much at a disadvantage to turn the tables. I hit her harder and harder. She's getting weaker under me, hotter, breathing quickly. I slap her face and just sit on top of her, hitting her, until I feel something curling inside me, a boomerang current, a kind of flash of light, and suddenly I stop hitting her and find myself stretched out on top of her, and she's heaving like a tidal wave. While we're lying there, exhausted, peanut shells start raining on us: it's Roger, he climbed the tree to get a better view of the fighting.

"Get lost, she's a lot better than you," Rowe shouts at him. Roger stays on the branch sulking. What a bitch to treat him like that, she's taking advantage of the fact that he likes her, and he looks so sad that I tell him to come down and kiss me, since she's acting so superior. He jumps down from the tree, caresses my hair very gently, and I feel like I'm all gurgling inside, with little jets piercing me here and there. He goes on kissing me and stretches me out beside him with his hand under my neck, and then he pulls at my neck, the way you do with a cat. Then he starts going inside me, slowly, very slowly, it feels like a stick of fire that pushes wet and hot. I like it, there's no pain at all, only the sensation that I am made of a thousand layers that he is unfolding one after another. I don't feel like laughing anymore, I only want to keep lying here while he digs inside me and makes me rock back and forth, and when that thing happens like a current that passes through you suddenly and makes you feel sort of like a lightning rod, it's not a boomerang but bubbles of light, little spheres of fire and then nothing. No one had been anywhere, it was a coming without arriving, without staying, and then nothing, nothing, nothing, just the wish to stay still, eyes closed, to see where the bubbles of light and fire disappeared, with my hand on the big stalklike eye between Roger's legs, soft like a sponge of fur and skin, that every so often jolts as if to flutter its eyelids and start looking inside me again. Eye in an eye. Eyes that rub against each other in the dark, ignite so many sparks of light, a sizzling and then again the blind darkness. We're lying there, quiet, Rowe turns her back to me, I tear blades of grass and still feel little flames and hot rivulets darting inside me and making shivers up and down my back. Then Roger kisses me, and, hell, he's a good kisser, he holds my hands behind me and I feel like I'm all dissolving, then he dives into the lake. You come too, he calls, and as we swim toward the island Rowe reaches us, swimming faster, and touches land before us: "This is the only way I can forgive you." Forgive what?

13.

NOW EVERYONE'S GETTING married. I got a letter from Celeste overflowing with marriage: hers to Leslie next month, then a very detailed report on Plasticmom's wedding to Hummie, with a clipping from the paper, which calls Humbert "a representative of that extraordinary group of Europeans who arrived in the United States along with Albert Einstein, Thomas Mann, Bertolt Brecht, Aldous Huxley, Stephan Zweig," as well as Auden, Stravinsky, Bartók, and Chagall. It goes on to say that Isabel Tonguefish, then Maze, and Professor Guibert were acquainted many years ago, that he is a distant relative of my dad's, an explorer and the author of books on poets who have never been heard of before. But explorer of what? I am speechless. I show the letter to Rowe. It's monstrous that Plasticmom didn't tell me she knew Hummie before I was born, and then all that ridiculous pretense of formality: M. Guibert. And that he was a relative of my father's and also of mine. Don't I have the right to know who my relatives are? Celeste includes a list of the guests: everyone who's anyone in Goatscreek except the Hiltons, who are in California—Mary Jo wouldn't have gone without me anyway. Celeste says Mom has a more spontaneous smile: could she be less plasticky? Could she be more like she was when she and Nora got to be friends?

Camp director Watson doesn't want Roger in the canoe with us all the time: he's supposed to look after all the girls, not just our group. Now, what could she possibly mean?

Chloe complains: her mother writes that the two of us should do more together, that it's not good for her to spend all her time picking up pebbles.

"Sure, come with us," I tell her. Then we tell Roger what to do, so Chloe turns flirty and brags that the only male in the camp is making up to her. She even tries acting superior toward us, but when things get serious she starts shrieking. Meanwhile we're swimming, not paying any attention, and Roger's chasing her. Then she bursts out crying and threatens to get even more hysterical, so we decide enough for now and go back to the mulberry beach. Chloe comes over in tears: "Roger jumped on me all naked and he wanted . . . he wanted . . . " She can't go on, she's suffocating in sobs.

"Naked?"

"Yes, naked," she whimpers, barely getting out the words.

"But what do you mean, can't you see he's wearing shorts?"

"It's not true, he's naked and . . . "

"Didn't he get it up?" I ask abruptly.

"He followed me and said that . . . that . . . " between sobs.

Rowe and I exchange a victorious glance, but to stay out of

trouble I tell Chloe that she suffers from a serious hereditary illness; she's never been told, so that she won't get any ideas. We persuade her not to say anything at home or she'll end up in an institution and never come out, because with that sort of stuff they'll at least do a lobotomy, which means they open up your skull and take out a big slice of the gray matter. Even if the operation goes O.K. there's the risk of being an idiot for your whole life. So when she imagines she's seeing things, she'd better keep quiet. Chloe listens, blowing her nose, then with her handkerchief she cleans her glasses, which must be an inch thick: to keep away the hallucinations, I suppose.

Celeste calls. To construct her love nest, Mom is making a revolution in the house. Good. One benefit of this matrimonial fervor is that she'll finally let go of the purse strings and get the house in decent shape.

Today a lesson in how to light a fire without matches. Only Nina, Rowe, and I were successful. Lucy said that when we go on hikes Rowe's group will have the job of lighting fires for everyone. Lucy is really boring. I don't know how Rowe can stand her. In fact, that's one piece of good luck—not having an older sister.

Chloe keeps whining about how we're supposed to be friends or her mother will be disappointed. O.K., if she really wants to. She must be feeling nostalgic for Roger's ripe-melon-colored nakedness. We invite her under our tree, and Roger starts by sticking out his tongue and making obscene gestures. Chloe shrieks like the simpering goose she is, but as soon as Rowe gives her an elbow she composes herself and pretends not to see anything. After Roger dives into the lake with Rowe, I ask her if the hallucinations have returned.

"Yes, it was horrible."

"You were really good—you didn't give yourself away. You should do that all the time, or people will think you have a dirty mind."

"Why?"

"They'll think you're imagining all that smut because you want it so much. What exactly did you see?"

"Roger was taking a watersnake out of his pants. I was dying of fright but I didn't run away; after all, I knew it was a hallucination. Still, I really wanted to scream . . . " Not bad. I find Rowe and Roger and report. We decide to continue, and go back to the shore. We ask Chloe if she wants to play steal the bundle: "O.K." We deal the cards and start playing, but at a prearranged signal Rowe and Roger get up, with exaggerated movements, like you'd only see in a hallucination. Rowe does a belly dance, then she takes a stick and pretends to play it, like a snake charmer, while Roger shimmies like a cobra, half naked under Chloe's nose—we've hidden her glasses—and Rowe starts swooning over Roger, who's lying on the ground making little cries, then she throws herself on the ground as if she's dead. Through it all, Chloe, not to give herself away, keeps playing. I'm playing the other two hands, keeping track of the points, and Roger and Rowe return just in time for the second game. Chloe thinks she has her hereditary illness under control but she starts looking worried when Roger gets up again and I lie on the grass with my feet in the air and Roger trots back and forth over me making whinnying sounds. I also start whinnying, to keep from laughing at Chloe, or later she might realize that it's a joke, and then we rush back to the cards. The amazing thing is that Chloe still can't win. She loses both games, and we don't have to play a deciding hand. On the way back to camp Chloe says it's been a perfect day.

"You didn't see anything strange?"

"What do you mean?" feigning amazement in order not to let Roger know about her illness.

"Oh, there were flying fish leaping in the lake . . . "

"It wasn't a hallucination?"

"I saw them, too," says Roger.

"So did I," says Rowe. "They were beautiful, silver with red stripes and blue heads."

"Oh wow, you could have told me."

"But we did tell you. I don't know where your mind was," I tell her, rolling my eyes toward the sky.

Mom calls, sounding less pompous than usual, I guess this husband business is good for her personality. In a very jolly voice, she tells me about going to the lake with Hummie, and she wants to know if I'd like to go to private school and then college, to study whatever I want, even if it's not physics. As long as there's a good theater department, I say, and instead of getting mad Mom says that she read about a college on Long Island that is the best on the whole East Coast. Fantastic. I'll miss Mary Jo, but the idea of not having to live at home makes me feel like sprouting wings. I love these places where everyone lives together and you never have to go home to people who are suffocating you because they're dying of boredom. I must write to Nora that her how-to-catch-a-man book has been a resounding success, and although at first Mom seemed too stupid to figure it out, she has put it into practice and has finally become a human being.

That stupid stupid hen: it turns out that it's too late to enroll me in a private school, and for now the only place she can send me is that horrible institution run by old maid Stinkhorn. That means more time wasted in another stupid school for no reason. It slips out that she wants to go to England with Hummie.

Afternoon naptime, Chloe comes to confess the hallucinations she had while she was playing cards.

"You know, we didn't notice anything? You were terrific. And what did you see?"

"Horrible things. First Rowe turned into a witch, she was puffing her stomach in and out, and it rolled and rolled, then she sat on top of Roger, no, first she played a flute and Roger just stood there, while the usual cobra came out of his pants but purple. Rowe played the flute to charm him, then, all in a mess, she sat on Roger: she didn't even realize that the snake was going inside her and it gnawed its way through until it came out of her mouth. Finally, though, she realized she had a poisonous snake inside her, and she let out some terrible cries and threw herself on top of him, half dead."

"This is very worrying. Do you mean to say you suffer from hearing hallucinations, too?"

"Yes, I heard cries that gave me goose bumps."

"Maybe you do need treatment."

"But what if they lock me up for life?"

"True. Did you see anything else?"

"Yes, you and Roger turned into horses, and you nuzzled one another, until you fell on the ground and Roger kicked you, whinnying, and in the end you both died. Then the hallucination went away and you were playing cards like before."

"There are a lot of animals in your hallucinations. Have you had some trauma?"

"Once a dog bit me."

"That explains everything."

I call home to talk to Plasticmom and tell her that I'll die before I go to old maid Stinkhorn's school. Mr. and Mrs. Guibert are out, Celeste answers with a perfect imitation of a butler: they are not going to England because Hummie has no intention of seeing Europe again, and besides he doesn't think it's right to leave me alone in Goatscreek while they're traveling. Aha!

Willow bank B, urgent consultation with poor Chloe. We decide the only thing to do is group-psychoanalyze her. We make her lie down under the tree, and we sit behind her and make her tell us about her childhood. But we stop her almost immediately because it's such an unbelievably boring childhood. The only event worth noting is that once she went into her parents' room by mistake and saw her father on top of her mother and asked if he was winning. She is really hopeless.

· · ·

Tomorrow we leave on a three-day hike in the hills. They handed out green Army knapsacks, the ones Roger bought for us in town, and sleeping bags. We also have foldable rain jackets and survival kits: matches, a knife, a pencil, a compass, some sugar cubes, and a bar of chocolate. Rowe is in charge of our group, and this time we have four tents for two people each. Lucy is in charge of the older girls. Roger sleeps in a tent by himself.

I'm exhausted. We walk from morning till night, up and down, up and down. Shade sun, shade sun, sun, sun, sun. Not a moment's peace. Miss Tennisball is always on our backs. She drills us on the names of trees, birds, and plants, urging us to appreciate the beauty of nature, with the result that not a particle remains for us to enjoy on our own. The black-and-white spotted cows move her incomprehensibly. Cows, cows, cows: we can't stand to be told to admire the cows anymore, so Rowe explains to Miss Tennisball that she considers herself a friend to animals but only to male animals. She looks at her blankly. "They're all the same to me." (Just as you'd expect.)

At night we take off our knapsacks, put up our tents, and make a fire. To wash we use water from our canteens, which we refill whenever we can. We wipe ourselves down with a small sponge but don't get very clean. We camped at a lake today, and finally got rid of the sticky coating of sweat and dust. After we got settled, Miss Tennisball called us all together, Lucy's big girls and Rowe's little ones, and made us sit around the fire to say a prayer that she must have thought up herself, where she thanks the mountains, the woods, and the animals, and even God for welcoming us into their territory. Then we eat: bread and cheese, bread and Spam, apples. Every day the knapsacks get lighter, every day one less full can to carry, and that's the only progress on this stupid hike. You could die of boredom—you can never be by yourself, you can never ever have fun on your own. Miss Tennisball is obsessed with our knowing what to do if we get lost. She has already repeated fifty times that moss doesn't grow on the north side of the trees, it grows on the shadowed side. And to figure out what direction we're heading in we have to look at the sun or the stars; if it's cloudy we're in big trouble, but in any case trusting the moss is a waste of time. The worst thing, absolutely the worst of all, is the songs Miss Tennisball makes us sing around the fire before we go to bed. Even now they are shouting one of those revolting things. I managed to sneak off and get some peace. But if Miss Tennisball finds out I'll have to take down her tent, too, in the morning.

We'll finally be back in camp tomorrow. I miss our island. That stupid Miss Tennisball twisted her ankle, which has slowed us down.

End of torture. Director Watson comes in person to the Donald Duck bunk to tell me that my stepfather called, and is coming to get me tomorrow because my mother is sick. I'm very curious to lay eyes on the old double-crosser again, but it's irritating to leave the day before the party. That stupid hen could have chosen a different time to get sick. She specializes in doing just the right thing at just the wrong moment.

Professor Guibert comes to get me around three. I find him with Mrs. Watson, signing the release papers. I put on my dress with the little red apples, in memory of our nice up and down, just to remind him of his life when he was still a happy bachelor. As soon as I see him: "Hi, Dad." Dazzling smile. Classy, on my part, after a betrayal like his: I'm jaunty, casual, suntanned, while he's confused, embarrassed, his eyes evasive, he's ashamed of having gone over to the enemy. Rowe and Roger are at the window in order not to miss the unique performance of the meeting with the former tenant. I bombard him with "Daddy" every three words. Irreproachable conduct in the car: low, controlled voice, short, cynical remarks, that's to say, sexy ones, to make him slobber at my feet. Vague allusions to my activities at camp, while the old traitor, worried, knits his bushy eyebrows. He says we'll have to stay one night at a hotel on the way to the hospital. It's worth a snapshot, his look of terror when I tell him the hen will have a fit as soon as she discovers we're lovers. He's suffering, the poor beast, and he won't look at me. It's the same as being in the car with my mom. The tense, tight-lipped profile, innocent face, hands gripping the steering wheel—like he's the one who just left camp. The whole way, he's playing the role of father, very pompous—he pontificates just right, pretends indifference to my references to life in the wild, ignores my declarations of friendship for male animals.

"But what a lot of escapades!"

Good lord, he really is a wimp. All that shit-faced snottiness, the expression of a complete imbecile. I take him down for good: "You were sure quick to forget me."

"What on earth do you mean?"

"Well, you haven't even given me a kiss." Immediately he brakes on the shoulder of the road, thinks he can get away with a little kiss on the cheek, but I open my mouth and give him a real movie kiss: firm and vigorous, while his is trembly, wet, kind of piggy. He immediately corrects it to a tight-lipped grimace, frightened at realizing so quickly that he doesn't care for the hen in the slightest. Half a second more and I'd have cleared out all the nonsense invented by the easily consolable widow Maze. But a police car pulls up: have we seen a car going over the speed limit? More genius: he doesn't realize it's ours, or maybe he's deep: a parked car is not a moving car. We get back on the road, I return him to his fatherly role, because if I've learned anything it's that you should never let them stay too long in the same position, these gutless males.

"How's Mom?"

The rumble of a truck drowns out the answer.

"What did you say? Stomach?"

"No: I said she has a stomach problem."

"Oh, stomach."

Mrs. Guibert is in a hospital near here, and tomorrow we'll go see her. But it sounds fishy to me. My mother has always had an iron stomach, she's a steamroller hen. She must have said a crock to Hummie so she could go and get herself put back in shape in a clinic for rich widows overflowing with life. After all, Nora's book says you can't always let the man see you with moisturizer on your face and curlers in your hair. At her age, screwing isn't enough to maintain her complexion.

"And how is it that you fell for Mom?"

"One day you will understand the beauty of a spiritual relationships." Oh wow. We're reduced to spiritual beauty. But not a bad euphemism for the subspiritual body of the widow Maze, her thighs lumpy with cellulite, her arms mottled with goose bumps. Anyway, my less elevated attractions are enough for Hummie, who (immediately after buying me an ice cream) tries to suck on my neck, which gives me a chance to tell him what he is: a dirty old man. A dirty old man at a convention of priests: in this absurd hotel there are few truly male animals, apart from the marble swan in the lobby and a gray-and-black spotted cocker spaniel owned by a witch wrapped in purple veils. Otherwise there's a horde of old ministers with shriveled wives, their faces wrinkled like rotten potatoes, lipstick smeared on thin lips, veils instead of makeup. A detail worth noting: we're in Room 231. I look forward to telling the hen, especially about the big bed with its pink chenille bedspread, while I wonder if Hummie will say that two separate rooms for the whole time of her recovery would cost too much. What he says is that now that he's my father there's nothing wrong if we sleep together.

"It's called incest," I explain, just to scare the shit out of him him. He turns white. Brutal to call things by their name, isn't it? Indelicate, very indelicate. He takes out a suitcase loaded with presents for me. Not bad stuff, a sexy shirt, perfect for going to see Mom in the hospital: low-necked, of copper-colored silk, like my skin, more or less, which makes a super effect of nakedness, diamond (fake) belt. She'll be lying in an iron bed in that ugly nightgown of hers with the beehives on it that goes right up to her chin, a hospital band on her wrist, and maybe a couple of needles in the crook of her elbow, the kissing corner . . . I'll walk in dazzling next to Hummie, who's tan, like me, I'll bring her a bouquet of forget-me-nots and a box of exotic fruit, and she'll have to stay there in the hospital, choking on her rage while we have fun telling her about the fabulous movies we've seen, the moonlight walks we've taken. Hummie will do his best to act the "good stepfather" and play down how happy he is to be alone with me, trying to convince her that he's doing it for her, taking care of her daughter. At the high point of this matrimonial performance I will let it slip, "en passant," as those two say when they want to appear united, that we are sleeping in the same room, same bed (king size). Then Plasticmom will let out a shriek that will be heard through the whole hospital, she'll tear off the IV, look for a scalpel to slash Hummie with, try to strangle me. Or maybe she'll play the grande dame and say very coldly that she wants a divorce immediately, now. I wonder if that idiot realizes that for her that would be the best solution after all, to be paid rent without having Hummie in the house as a tenant—but she'll never get to that point, because the older they get the more sentimental they get, those hens who are so desperate for affection they've forgotten the art of keeping male animals well trained . . . What a big coward Hummie is. Afraid of what might happen, he goes down to the bar and leaves me alone. If he thinks he can get away with this . . . When he comes back I'll get him, before he turns completely moldy. He must be terrified of getting old, the dirty old man: he takes enormous blue vitamin capsules to stay young.

I was almost asleep when I heard the door creak: it was Rimbaud, Gerry Sue Filthy's terrier. He wags his tail, jumps on the bed, then runs away down the corridor and comes back and sits in front of the room next to ours, 233. Gerry Sue himself opens it! He invites me in, and with him is a kind of Cleopatra, very tall and thin, painting her nails green. She gives me a long look, then starts combing her hair. She is mute, Gerry Sue Filthy explains, because he couldn't bear a woman who talks, and anyway in an ideal couple either the husband or the wife should be mute. Of course, I say. Our camp director's lover was deaf. Filthy is writing a comedy that has the same name as the hotel, *The Enchanted Forest*, and he couldn't resist the temptation to spend a night here. Just for something to say I tell him that I had to leave camp because my mother is sick and that when I grow up I'm going to be an actress. He had already heard about Mom's marriage from his uncle in Goatscreek. He gives me the address of his ranch in New Mexico—he's always there when he doesn't have a play on. He tells me to keep him informed on my theatrical progress: maybe there will be a part for me in his new comedy. He makes me promise not to say anything to Humbert, because he knows how men are about these things.

"But at least I can tell Mom, Mr. Filthy?"

"Oh, whether you say anything or not to your mother doesn't matter," he answers with a little smile. Then he tells me to go back: "My friends call me Filthy Sue."

"Bye, Filthy Sue."

14.

*T*HAT'S THAT. HUMMIE'S definitely a bore in bed. He doesn't know anything interesting. In spite of his vast "experience" he's way below Roger. He lies there like a straw man. A real sexual parasite. Aside from stammering some French poetry, he brings nothing of himself. And that's only quotations anyway. Nevertheless, a truly historic night: Miss Dolores Maze possessed Monsieur Humbert Guibert. Now I'll return him to Plasticmom, all tied up with ribbon and bows, a good hospital present. I'll deliver her adored monsieur with a bunch of flowers and the sweetest card in the world, the sentimental syrupy kind that the hen loves, especially now she's at death's door. At last, our interests coincide: let Hummie go back to his nice little house in Goatscreek with his devoted little wife. It's time for him to return to spiritual relationships: he's too inept for the body-to-body. After my endless fantasies about him, all he made me feel was acute nostalgia for Rowe and Roger. I dreamed that the three of us were in a canoe, under a blazing sun. Roger was kissing my hair, Rowe was paddling and was stringing together one dirty word after another, all the ones we know, wonderful dirty words, the sounds so beautiful they drive you wild. Roger and I repeated them with her, singsonging them clearly, syllable by syllable, and we were so moved by this music of divine obscenities that we burst into tears. The tears flowed down our cheeks, we didn't have the breath to continue, and the words failed us, as if they had run away: in fact we saw them up in the sky, "cock" written all in black, "blow job" in blue, "cunt" in red, "asshole" in emerald green, all those filthy words were suspended in the sky like clouds. Then the three of us held each other tight, sad because the dirty words had abandoned us and gone up to heaven without us, and we were alone, mute, left motionless in the silence of the lake. We kept hoping that the words would pour down on us again, but instead Chloe showed up to spy on us: she wanted to denounce us all to director Watson, and we ran away in three different directions. I found myself at Mary Jo's, and the hen brought me a present: a rag doll full of sawdust with Chloe's dumb face. "This will be your best friend," she said to me, and Mary Jo and I bowed to the ground: "Thank you, Mrs. Maze, it's very nice of you to give us this lovely doll, we promise to obey all the orders that come out of its belly, whatever they are." When the hen left, Mary Jo punched the doll in the belly and in a slow, drawn-out voice it wailed its order: "Cut me open, hurry up and cut me open." We obeyed, the sawdust poured out of the wound, and we were in a sand dune. The tiny windblown grains issued order upon order, a buzz of voices that followed us as we ran to the lake and dived into the water. It was cool there until the hen came to take me out of camp. She shut me up in her house, and put me in the arms of her husband, Humbert Guibert; but I wasn't me anymore, I had become Rowe, and I spit in his face, just like that time when I told him he had acted like a coward. I spit in his face and then I asked for something to drink: I'm thirsty, I'm thirsty, I said, give me something to drink . . .

Now I feel all bruised. It was so absurd. I am in the lobby of a stupid hotel with a convention of ministers, moldy unsexual types, except for Gerry Sue Filthy, who told me to sit in this chair while he looks at me, and that way he'll be inspired and write about me. It's really weird and exciting, to feel his eyes as if they were touching me, otherwise I'd be suffocating from boredom with these walls and their stupid murals showing scenes of hunters and trembling rabbits. Humbert stayed in the room to clean up. He doesn't want to leave a trace. He's afraid of the hen. With the hen around we'll never really have fun. The same routine as yesterday, when he went down to the bar first so that it wouldn't seem like we were staying in bed together. He even found the nerve to say to the waiter: "I don't know if my wife will be able to join us." Hypocrite! I left him alone because I was exhausted and just wanted to go to sleep. When I woke up, at first light, with all the toilets flushing, more or less at the same time we had to get up at camp, I found him in the bed instead of on the cot. O.K., it's time to seduce him, I thought, now or never, time for him to see how much I learned without him. In spite of him. I felt very happy at the idea of teaching him a lesson. I put my arms around his neck to give him a good-morning kiss, a kiss like a breath of wind, light as light can be, then I whispered in his ear: "You want to be with me?" The only response a dazed look. "Come on, let's have fun . . . " He has a dopey expression, like a sleepy man who doesn't know where he is or what's happening to him. "Are you for real or what?" Blank. "You're not going to make me believe you've never ever ever . . . " No, it's not possible—after all, Celeste gave me a detailed report on the humanization of Plasticmom at the hands of her dear Hummie, it's not possible that they never did it. He must think I'm too small, I say to myself. Now I'll show him. Of course he wants to do it but he doesn't dare—he's afraid of the hen, enslaved by his wife, like all spineless husbands. With frightened eyes he lies stretched out on the bed, then he moves his head toward me, but not even an embrace, only dirty, quivery, drooly kisses sticky on my back. I won't let him get away with this, I think, a thing done and not done. I move him over, I check that it's all O.K., surprisingly it is, everything's O.K., then I kiss him, just to encourage him. Meanwhile he lies there, not moving a muscle, that skunk, he has no idea, just lies still the whole time and leaves me to take care of everything by myself. I even have to put the rubber on. The whole time he's pretending not to realize what the two of us are doing. Well, now I'll show you what sort of games I learned when I was out from under your retarded influence, you old jerk, I'll show you what we can do "at our age." He keeps his eyes closed so he doesn't have to see anything, but finally he can't help giving some sign of life, and even then he tries not to let me hear. He bites his lips, knits his forehead, suppresses his cries, and then goes rigid, like a plaster cast, and smiles at me idiotically, mumbling a few words in French that don't have anything to do with anything: in rhyme, of course. Kilroy was here, I shout. Kilroy was here, here, here! Now he'll tell the hen I raped him. Here it is, our great longed-for freedom, our magical moment together. It was almost better when the hen was lying in wait. More exciting. I climb off him while outside they knock with the breakfast tray. "Pass the potatoes," I say, "I'm starving." He hands them to me with a look of disgust (for the fries), then goes into the bathroom, comes back wrapped in his bathrobe and says to me: "Look what you've done, the bed is full of crumbs." Crumbs . . . Well, we're having breakfast, he's drinking his coffee, and he must have gotten used to the idea, because suddenly he gets all perked up and wants to do it again and again and again, and in the end it hurts. Really revolting, this morning seemed to start off well, but I have to say that the more he holds on the more deflating it is for me. And besides this day is so gray you could die, it's like there's a cover over the sky. He's a lousy lover, really lousy, either from too much or not enough, but always and in every way bad, the extremely boring Professor Humbert Guibert. And when he stops screwing he puts on his deputy-hen tone: "Get dressed and wait for me while I straighten up." What a pig. He wants to go swimming but he won't get his feet wet, he won't stop playing the fake father who tidies up: he won't take the risk. An idiot. A creep. Phony from head

P I A   P E R A

to toe. Well, why am I surprised, I already knew he was a double-crosser. Maybe I'm the fool. That's it, I don't know what got into me to deceive myself. It's only that once I saw him again I liked him, like the first time I saw him, and he looked handsome, and handsome is handsome, but I still didn't know how revolting he was inside. Besides, you always think that people can improve; instead, not a chance—Humbert totally hardened into Humbert, rather, double Humbert, Humbert Guibert, whose soul is even more plastic than the hen's. Well, it's not so surprising, after all he's even more decrepit than Plasticmom, although with his suntanned face he manages to cover up his real age, the age of his heart. On the way to the lobby I see Filthy Sue paying his bill, and I pretend not to recognize him, as I promised, but Rimbaud starts playing with me, biting my wrists and licking me on the nose.

"Leave that stupid dog alone," Humbert rages. "All we need is for you to get rabies, and then you'll both be in the hospital." What a jerk. He's got to be more contagious than any dog. Meanwhile, Filthy Sue makes a face behind his back. I yell at him, You're a shit just like Plasticmom, who'll never get me a dog. All the emaciated ministers and their skinny wives look at me horrified, a bunch of bony hands covering a bunch of toothless mouths. Only Filthy Sue winks and gives me a thumbs up.

I'm not sorry I screwed Humbert Guibert if only because:
1. At least it's good for my skin.
2. Now I know he's absolutely worthless and I won't waste any more time on him.

I don't ever want to waste my time again on this type of swindler who's only good for the hen. I don't want to waste time, that's it. You don't get a thing from an imbecile like that, sperm by the gallon, but truth—not a drop. To me it was obvious what he wanted, only he didn't want to admit it, above all he didn't want me to know, the big fat hypocrite. He doesn't have the nerve to say what he wants, he doesn't know that we all have the right to our own happiness: the Constitution says so. So he's under me and I'm kissing him, I'm licking the edges of his lips, I'm touching him lightly with my tongue, stuff to make a mummy come to life, and he can't not get excited, in fact he is excited, but he tries not to look into my eyes, he keeps averting his; still, he has no escape, because right under him is my hand, and there's no way to deny what's happening, no way at all, yet he runs away from me and chases me both at the same time. He'll go on like that to the end of his days, without admitting a damn thing. He thinks he's superior because the mere idea of eating french fries in the morning makes him sick. I suppose now he'll be in a hurry to escape from the scene of the crime and join his hen wife in the hospital.

He must have had his fingers crossed behind his back when he pledged to be faithful to her. He can go to bed with me, but in fact it's only a game and Plasticmom is still the one in control, still the one to decide how we live and who sees who, and Hummie will never be brave enough to do anything against her will, he'll never dare to challenge her, he's so scared. He allows himself all these great liberties because Madame Guibert is in the hospital and out of the running.

For me to have fun with Hummie, the hen would have to croak in the hospital: it happens, once in a while, a mistake, the wrong anesthetic, whatever . . .

Hummie promised that tomorrow when we go to the hospital he will tell her he is in love with me and it was a mistake to marry her and they must leave each other, and if she threatens to go to the police he's ready to face anything, even prison, even the electric chair. But I don't want you to go to prison, I tell him, I don't want you to die. I also explained to him that we can arrange things so it's the hen who dies and can't hurt us anymore. She's so mean and nasty that if he were so bold, so cool, as to tell the truth she'd persecute us, punish us. All we can do is kill her, pull out the IV, give her the wrong medicine, whatever, since a shit like her for sure doesn't deserve to go on living. Does she give anything to the world, anything good? Nothing at all, nothing, she grabs everything for herself and keeps us from being happy. Hummie began cackling like a madman and said: You really want her to die? Yes, I said. O.K., he said, that's it. O.K., baby, it will be done—winking an eye. Wow! What happened to him? Did he become someone else? A snap of the fingers: "O.K., abra-cadabra, the hen is dead, do you believe it now?" Wow wow wow!!! And then we'll be like Bonnie and Clyde, the two of us, adventuring through the world.

But maybe we don't actually have to murder her: when I show up in all these sexy clothes that her second and last husband bought me, she'll die in a burst of rage. She'll choke on it. Definitely.

15.

*T*HE HEN IS dead. I was too late to make her drop dead by showing up in a copper-colored silk blouse and a dia-mond belt. While I was with her Hummie, she was already dead. Stone-dead like her husband, who was stone-dead under me. Maybe she saw us. Even if she's in paradise, seeing us must have made her feel like she was in hell. I mean, if paradise exists it's a place where you don't get any information about what's happening on earth.

The big news was communicated like this: Humbert's driving. I notice a squirrel squashed on the road, which reminds me of Nelson the Second. I point out the squirrel to Hummie, but he pays no attention, only a sort of distracted "Oh, really?" What can a dead squirrel matter to him? Nothing, absolutely nothing. He's still licking his mustache after his multiple thrills and kisses of the morning, and he looks at the squirrel squashed in the road with the most absolute indifference, like it's a pretty red decal burned into the gray-blue of the asphalt. Of absolutely no importance. Seeing how he doesn't give a damn about anything at all makes my blood boil. I tell him to stop.

He parks in front of some bushes, gets a piggy romantic look, like he wants to try it there. Revolting. He wants to squeeze me dry, down to the last drop, before handing me over to the hen, I think, still knowing nothing. I have to pee, I yell at him, take me to a gas station. When I pee I bite my lips it burns so much, then I think of calling Mom, to tell her we're coming and give her some idea about how her dear husband's behaving. She can get me away from him. She's my mother, after all, and should take care of me, me and herself. I go and ask him for money for the phone and the number of the hospital.

"You can't call now. Get back in the car."

"What do you mean, I can't call?" I ask, thinking he's in a panic about what I might tell his wife. He doesn't answer right away, then, as we're passing a truck, he goes: "You can't call your mother because your mother is dead." Logical, right? And this, of course, changes everything. If he'd told me right away, back at Maple Camp, that the hen was dead, I wouldn't have gone in for that wild screwing, I would have taken it more slowly, much more slowly. Today all day it's been hurting, because this morning he made me do it three times in a row. I still didn't know anything—O.K., then, three times if you want, or five, or ten, even a billion, without pausing for a breath, so he understands that with me you don't play around, I am resistant, unbreakable, stainless steel. Afterward, when I tell some juicy stories about my adventures at camp, his eyes are glistening at the idea of what we dared to do. Part of what I tell him is true, part is made up, but it doesn't make any difference to him—by now it's clear he's just like Plasticmom, not interested in the difference between what's true and what's not. He needs to get excited just to feel he's alive at all. He must be really dead to need so desperately to feel alive. Anyway, I took all that trouble to make him look like shit with all that screwing he never could have dreamed of, but now it burns, and the worst thing is I keep having to go. What a mess. Far from being good for my skin: I have such a worn-out greenish look I feel like hiding. Moral: screwing is good only in small doses. Don't overdo it. That burning sensation could last forever. Damn Humbert. He put off telling me that the hen was dead to make me do what he wanted. The fact that the hen is dead opens up interesting prospects. Totally new prospects. Hummie, whether I like it or not, is mine now. So we don't have to be secretive anymore. And surely I've inherited something, between the house in Goatscreek and all the money Mom piled up in the bank. Why didn't he tell me right away: the hen is dead, the way is clear. What was he scared of? That I would burst into tears of sorrow? Jerk. I know some people who would die of envy knowing that it's me who lost her mom and not them. But he's a brute, and he hurt me. Tonight I want to sleep by myself.

Humbert lets me sleep alone at first but he hides my purse: so I can't call Goatscreek. The idiot's afraid I'll run away. All the same I find a nice man who gives me some change, but no one answers at home. Of course. The hen is dead, I keep forgetting, and Celeste must be at Leslie's house, so there's no way to call her. I try Nora's number, but the line gets disconnected and my money is all gone. There's Grandma, but what's the point, she's senile. I'd like to know how the hen died, exactly, but there's no way. Humbert doesn't want to talk about it. Of course he doesn't, he already knows how it went, so what does he gain by telling me about it? I feel weird inside, alone in this bed. I saw a cute waiter in the bar who looks like Teddy Glass. I wish he were here, I'd like to talk to him. But when I go down to look for him he's not there. Later I hear footsteps and I open the door a few times, but no luck. First a woman with glasses, wearing men's hiking boots, then a bald guy with a potbelly, who winks as he goes by. I'm so miserable. Because in the end that's how things turned out: I'm completely alone. I don't know what to do. Take a train and go to Nora's? Stay with M. Guibert? Go back to Goatscreek? What would I do there by myself? The poor little orphan. Get myself adopted by Celeste? It's all shit, so I go and deal with the enemy. Hummie, dear Hummie, I'm lonely, I'm scared of the dark, open the door, hold me tight. He opens to me, with a look of satisfaction: first he holds me in his arms, then he starts with caresses, finally he comes back in and he doesn't give a god damn that I don't want him to, that he's hurting me. He pins my hands down and he says, See, you're all wet, you want it; and he holds me still and I don't have the strength to kick. I don't care about anything anymore, nothing in the world.

He certainly doesn't seem upset by the death of his wife. All it took was the sight of me for an instant to remember what he was and should have remained, the bachelor tenant of Isabel Maze, née Tonguefish. I wouldn't be surprised if he'd murdered her. Like in that movie about the sneaky Frenchman who marries all these horrible rich neurotic widows so he can murder them in peace. But this guy murders the widows so he can inherit the money and bring it to his real wife, who he adores; Hummie murdered the hen so he could inherit me without even marrying me. Now he's making good use of his inheritance. The most awful part is that Mom's dead but I'm not free.

Humbert catches me trying to telephone and slaps me. Tough guy. A real man. Why aren't I happy? Shouldn't I be, having him all to myself, with no hen in the way, and him doing everything, really everything, that would send Plasticmom into raptures? Like tonight, after we made up, as a reward he bought me a prix-fixe dinner, the works, including candlelight and dancing. We're the only father-daughter couple, and Humbert smiles understandingly, pretends to be teaching me the fox trot. I have the hen's jade necklace, the result of ransacking the widow Maze's drawers in Goatscreek before leaving for Maple Camp. People smile at us indulgently, revolting. It's like they're sugar-coated. The whole time I have this sensation that I stink of incest, and I feel the blurred smiles of the other women, who nod at Humbert and then say something encouraging to me. I don't care one bit about a stupid dance with a stupid Frenchman in a jacket and bow tie who is pretending to be my father, and as soon as we get back to the room, in a fury at this ridiculous scene acted out in front of the exclusive clientele of the hotel with dinner and dancing, prix-fixe all-inclusive, I start crying hysterically and in my frenzy beat my head against the wall. He tells me to stop—the walls are thin and someone might hear. And then, taking me by the shoulders and shaking me, his face twisted in triumph, he tells me that if I don't stop immediately he will turn around and take me to the Appalachians to that horrible old maid Stinkhorn's farm. Take me there, I scream, what's the difference, anything's better than this comedy with you, you piece of shit, but then I remember how bony Stinkhorn is, how she walks around the classroom sticking a finger in her ear and then in her mouth, poking way back to her wisdom tooth, and then she sticks it in her nose and then in her mouth again. Seeing her rooting around like that is so gross it makes me want to vomit, and there is absolutely nothing at all in that place, only mud and swampy fields and wind. Imagining myself there with Stinkhorn and maybe even Humbert I feel like I'm suffocating with horror, so finally I say O.K., O.K., let's go on with the hotels and the prix-fixe menus and lots of screwing. What's the difference, in the end? Isn't it as good a way as any of passing this shitty time from now till I'm eighteen? Isn't it obvious that ultimately all of us are born into the prison of childhood, and freedom doesn't come till later, after we've sweated our way to it?

Heading north. New Hampshire. I leaf through the atlas, a present from Hummie for the start of our trip (after all, a man who just got married should take a honeymoon, and if his wife is dead, well, what's the difference? he can go with his daughter). I'm given the job of map reader, "so I don't get bored." Ha ha. He believes in model prisons, with mobile cells, to keep the inmates amused, and he gives them varied occupations, so that, since they can't escape themselves, their will to live can't escape, either.

I don't feel like talking, I hate talking to the person who's got control of the wheel. Humbert tries to make conversation, but I order him to be quiet. I'm reading the newspaper, getting absorbed in it, but after a while he starts on the business of French lessons, because it makes him nervous when I'm quiet. He starts rattling off French phrases, describing everything we see, and for a while I go along with it but then I change the subject and ask how the hen died. He mentions "*une voiture blanche*" but no other details, then he remembers that he hasn't offered his condolences, but I give him a dirty look just in time. I think I would throw up if I heard condolences in French. If he goes on like this I won't sleep with him anymore. I don't get it: the hen is dead and we're supposed to be having grieving, mournful conversations? Is it possible that he doesn't have a crumb of courage? This is what he longed for, to be alone with me, and now the mouse doesn't dare to be free and happy through and through, he wants to soothe his conscience. Maybe he'd like it if I cried on his shoulder. The enemy's dead and you cry? Since when?

"Live Free or Die": it's the motto of New Hampshire. We read this as we reenter our state, the first to declare independence. But we're not going to Goatscreek. Live free or die: not bad for the start of my journey as the sex slave of a French creep. In school when I get assigned the usual essay on how the history of America would have been different if the French had won instead of the English I'll be able to suggest a new perspective. If the French had won instead of the Pilgrims . . . Meanwhile at the diner I order an Adam and Eve on a raft and make him fork out some money for the jukebox. Music at top volume. A tremendous high. Music music music and Humbert can open his mouth as much as he likes, since I can't hear him. Humbert the fish, Humbert the mute. Meanwhile I'm dancing and everyone's looking at me. Because I am super sexy, and I know it.

Humbert sneaks into a bookstore and buys a book about dealing with girls my age. He studies me on the printed page. What a grind. In the afternoon, sitting in the room, I don't feel like reading, so I make him put a quarter in the radio. I close my eyes and listen to the music, sink into my chair, deeper and deeper, darker and darker, humming inside, until I hear the didactic voice of Humbert holding forth from his book: "The normal girl is always eager to please her father." You could say that he madly enjoys imagining himself as my father. That I am flesh of his flesh, blood of his blood. If he weren't a raving lunatic he wouldn't enjoy playing my dad. Not like this, at least. Mary Jo and I used to play this game, but she always insisted on being the mother, which she used as an excuse to slap and pinch me, which wasn't any fun, so I stopped playing. Professor Humbert acts like a ten-year-old playing his favorite game. It's exciting for him to call me "little" and "child," instead of doing the logical thing, which is to remember that he is not my father and that if he hadn't committed the vile act of marrying my mother he wouldn't even be my stepfather, but he's bored by the variation of so-called normal reality.

Also, he enjoyed trying to convince the Gazebos that I was his natural daughter—claiming that he met the hen sometime when she was quarreling with my father, and although he says it so that the Gazebos won't interfere, it's obvious that his real interest is different. It's the excitement of imagining that he's entering the "fruit of his loins." As if I had come out of him and he were entering me, and this coming out and going in were ultimately the entire world, with no escape. Dear Daddy in heaven, did you also imagine doing this when you sat in the dark in the garage with the incinerated lizards? And tell me something else, dear Daddy in heaven, assuming it was you who granted my prayer and not someone else that time when I asked for someone nice for Mom, doesn't it seem like you went a little overboard?

You could say that motels were invented for just this sort of thing: a separate entrance for every room, only a few yards between the parking space and the door, no common rooms, no conversation from armchair to armchair. And the ones we go to are budget motels. There were a bunch of places that I wanted to see in this country, but now I can't remember what they were. It's all confused in my head. And besides I am furious. Like today, when we passed a movie theater showing *Life with Father*, with that stupid Elizabeth Taylor who's not even fifteen. They're calling her the new star of the future. I wonder if she also studied while wandering around the country with her mother's widower. In *Movie Love* they throw a pious veil over that whole side of things. "They've made a film about us," says Humbert, winking. "Yes, dear Daddy." God, how he loves to hear himself called Daddy.

Like all couples, we have our routine. We sit in the car, we drive through changing landscapes, and every so often we get out and visit some worthy sight that absolutely cannot be missed. As soon as we're in the room Hummie sticks his hands under my shirt: I like it when he touches me there, I feel relaxed and tingly. He began as such a disaster of a lover but he's been quick to learn. Technique, I mean. Always before dinner, because you're too exhausted then to do anything anyway—when you've been in the car all day you need to unwind. After miles and miles of asphalt the only thing you want to do is throw yourself on the bed and push, push, one against the other, enter one another, get all stirred up, and then have a good shower and go and eat. It's so hygienic. And he, he's so paternal . . . There's always a dance band or a jukebox or a radio turned on, you can dance alone or with other people, or throw yourself in a chair with your eyes closed and think. It's still a long time before all this will be over, but every day is one day less, a small step toward freedom.

Old Shaker village. We drive through it in the car.
"You want to stop?"
"No, thanks. I'm not interested in old German religions."
"You know why they're called that?"
"They were the first to mix cocktails?"
He stretches out his arms (without taking his hands off the wheel—easy with monkey arms like his). "No, it's because they get all worked up in order to shake their sins off."
Wow. Why doesn't he stop giving me history lessons? Oh yeah, it's normal, this will be an educational trip after all! Can't that dope Hummie figure out that I don't feel like thinking about Shakers and

all that stuff? Anyway, I once did a research project with Mary Jo. Boring to the third degree. Meanwhile they stare at us from the fields, their heads wrapped in kerchiefs. But Humbert wants to stop anyway. We find a place to get something to drink, and when he asks for the bill they tell him to pay what he can, according to his means. He leaves the smallest coin he has. I'm dying of embarrassment. A tightwad pig.

"How boring, all those long skirts." Hummie shrugs his shoulders, I put my arms around his neck. It's fun to give him a hug in the car in front of all those devout people. He pulls away—afraid they'll see us. In my opinion they already understood the whole thing anyway. They're not so dumb. There was a woman with a basket full of strawberries, and I wanted to buy some, but Humbert accelerated. What a drag he is—why don't we enjoy this freedom that descended on us out of the blue?

If I were Humbert I'd have more style: if nothing else I'd get another car. It kind of revolts me to take this trip in the same old blue sedan. When I open my eyes after being asleep for a while, it's like I'm seeing the hen at the wheel. Why the hell doesn't he get a new one? Costs too much? I'm trying to find out how we're set for money. After all, I'm the heir, I think, unless my farsighted mommy committed the folly of leaving everything to him. With the good feeling there was between us, I suppose even that is possible, a will to M. Guibert's advantage. When I try to find out about my financial situation I never get anything straight out of him. "These are not matters for a child like you. Too complicated." Oh? Then what the hell are things for a child like me? At this point my only hope is my senile grandmother in the old people's home. Yesterday I saw a really cute guy hitchhiking, my heart skipped a beat and I thought I'd die—for a second I thought it was Teddy Glass. It looked just like him, and he had an Army backpack and a guitar. I begged Humbert to pick him up, but he drove past at full speed. I'm furious that he can't understand how picking up hitchhikers would make a lot of sense, because

it means having someone to talk to on this trip that I see will practically never end, and also we'd have someone to talk about later,
because by now we really don't know what to say to each other,
everything sayable has already been said. The advantages of hitchhiking are obvious; not only do you save money but also you're not
always alone and you have someone to talk to. It's all more interesting, but Humbert has a one-track mind: how to guard his possessions,
with me at the top of the list.

Fight with my dadfriend. Fight about the route. I miss the sea
air, the ocean is nearby. Smooth sea, shells, and lobsters: that's what I
want. Instead: mountains. Granite. Rock. Stop at a big lake. Cows.
Angus. Angus. Angus.

"What dumb black faces those cows have," Humbert remarks.

"Weren't those the animals so intelligent that they lick the eyes
of their calves?" You see, now the cows are no use to him anymore.
Stupid animals on stupid hills. Far away the gray of the mountains. In
the fall it will be beautiful, but now it's all green green green.
Boredom painted green. Then we go down to a smaller lake, and
there's a rock where the river begins, the Merrimack, which we
passed before. I've been to this lake, with little Nelson. We stopped at
the same place, coming back from a visit to Grandmother. We were
supposed to go to the top of a mountain that's the windiest in the
whole area, but Mom refused to because the wind makes her nervous. Odd that no one thought of calling me about her funeral;
among other things she seems to have been done in by the Stones'
father. A piece of paper with a fresh stamp and I pass to the jurisdic-
tion of her second husband. Mom could have gotten a divorce, but
I can't get divorced from her widower. Weird. So many restrictions
on having fun and then there are these absurd laws made by people
with no imagination. A girl can't live with a stranger, but if this
stranger marries her mother it's all O.K., because this Mr. So-and-So
suddenly becomes her father, or stepfather, or whatever he wants to
call himself. In a certain sense, it's the law's fault if Hummie had to

kill the hen. What the hell am I saying. Professor Guibert who kills the hen . . . it takes guts, for a thing like that. He never would. Anyway, even if he had killed the hen, it would still be the stupid law's fault because it keeps people from being free and doing what they want. Because when I wanted to be with Hummie there was a law prohibiting it, and now that I would like not to be with him there's a law that says I have to stay or I'll end up in a reformatory.

He buys me presents when we fight. Since he controls the finances it's to my advantage to fight as often as possible. Presents, lots of them, for the poor orphan—bought at the big department stores in the capital, Concord, as a matter of fact. While he's paying he looks at me as if he expected me to be moved by his generosity. It's so moving for him to be separated from his money. A manicure set, comic books, candy, a travel clock, a ring with a real topaz, a tennis racquet (a sign that we won't be going back to Goatscreek), roller skates with high white boots, binoculars, a portable Motorola, a clear-plastic raincoat, summer clothes: perfect for a long vacation. Mary Jo must be about to get back from California. She'll go to my house, find it empty, they'll tell her about Mom, how she was crushed on the asphalt under Mr. Stone's tires.

I am sick of always being in the car, sick sick sick of it. I get carsick in the White Mountains. It's raining, and the road is endless, and I'm cold. I put on a sweater, but I'm still cold. There's a cog railway that carries you up the mountain with the wind. Kisses for Hummie to get him to take me. I really want to see this wind that the hen was so scared of. A train with a green engine and a gray car, bridges that are like the ones for a model railroad, and wooden ties, gray rocks and green pine branches. Clouds rush across the sky, pushed by the wind. We get off the train, and Humbert loses his white cap. Train full of kids and mothers and fathers. Crying babies, mothers all "My goodness, why, the scenery is marvelous," fathers looking satisfied but silent. There are two old men who have only one arm each: one holds the guidebook open with his left arm, the other turns the pages with his right arm. Everyone seeks shelter from the wind, pretending to be scared. One stupid kid really is afraid, and starts crying. Her mother holds her in her arms. There's not as much wind as I expected, no tremendous gusts, two hundred miles an hour, that can hurl people off the mountain. When the wind dies down you can breathe, and then you smell a resiny perfume, so much perfume, nearly more perfume than air. Humbert takes out the map. I want to go to Maine, to the ocean; he has already decided on Maine, but the mountains. He's obsessed with mountains. We can go to the ocean later, he says, we'll do the mountains now, before it gets cold. Mountains later, I say, ocean now. I want to go swimming in the ocean, I'm tired of swimming in lakes. But he wants to show who's in charge, so it's the mountains. I ask the guy at the refreshment stand: Has the wind ever blown anybody off? It happened once. This is what old Isabel Maze was afraid of. Egoist as always. If the wind had blown her off I would have stayed with my dad, and Nelson wouldn't have died, because his death truly was an accident. If one day in the succession of our stupid days could be changed, then everything that happened afterward would be different. Nelson wouldn't have died, not like that, at least; my dad wouldn't have taken to drinking his own brains out, and wouldn't have had all those electrocuted lizards on his conscience; we would have stayed in Whiskey, and even if we'd moved to Goatscreek he would have rented the guest room and maybe a different tenant would have come, and even if a Humbert came I could at least have married him and gone on seeing my friends, instead of doing everything in secret and everything halfway, and we would have come to the windy mountain on our honeymoon. She had such a fear of dying, old Isabel Guibert widow Maze née Tonguefish, but no matter how carefully that idiot tried to protect herself from one sort of death, she never realized that she was only leaving herself open to another.

16.

*W*E GO THIS direction, that direction. Still in New England. I want to go to Nora's in Los Angeles. Here all it does is rain, we're pursued by rain. Driving when there's lightning scares me to death. Humbert says there's no danger, but it's scary to me just the same. As if that weren't enough, here we are in Mom's old heap of a car, with the roof leaking, *plop, plop, plop,* right on my shoulder, the sky all streaked with silver, rivulets of black water washing the windshield, as if there were no windshield wipers, and that dope Humbert decides it's time to tell me how his mother died: she was struck by lightning on a mountaintop wrapped in a cloud, when he was tiny. Poor little orphan! And ever since, he's had this mania for doing in the mamas of others. So much for settling accounts.

The sky's finally clear, and the air, freshened by the rain, has a wonderful smell. We leave the highway to get to the river: there's swift white water, *glu glu gargl glu glu,* then patches of dark smooth water. Trees are reflected in it, big black birds screech but as soon as they stop you hear a strange cry, of swallows with downy feathers. They seem too small to cry so loud, like kittens. It's a good place for a walk, but Humbert immediately slips on a smooth round mossy rock, more slippery than ice. On purpose I didn't tell him to watch out for the green rocks, and he ends up like an idiot: *splat!* As soon as he tries to get up he goes down again—it's impossible to get a grip on those green rocks. Hummie struggles, falls, waves his arms in all directions and gets mad when I won't help him. He's cursing in French, *merde, merde, merde,* he wants to go back, but I leave him there slipping and sliding on the rocks, since I know that sooner or later he'll get up. The world would be too simple if a slippery rock were enough to trip an ogre. I get to the lake I saw on the map. I wanted to see it because it has a great name, Umbagog. Gog. Umba. Gog. Umba. Gog gog. African music. Humbagog. Humbert Umbagog. Name of a tribal chieftain. It's too beautiful not to take a swim. The sun is burning. I dive off a rock head first, it's cold, then I'm burning inside, and when Humbert Umbagog arrives, limping slightly, cursing the grass seeds that stick to his socks and prickle his ankles, I tell him to stop complaining, hurry up and get in the water. But no, he doesn't like cold water, he's susceptible to sore throats—he really is a drag. Rowe and Roger wouldn't have made a fuss, with them swimming was a serious sport, but Humbert Umbagog only does one sport: the rest is distraction, free time between one ring and the next. He acts the gallant gentleman, anyway, old Humbertgog: he takes off his shirt to dry me when I get out of the water, what cold skin you have, and a tic appears in his jaw, the little muscle under his lip twitches. He looks around, it's obvious what he has in mind, and why not, it's nice here in the open, with the trout splashing in the water, the leaves rustling like parchment paper—less oppressive than the usual motel sheets and electric light. If it weren't that sex is a good thing in itself and at worst you can always close your eyes, it's really like shooting yourself doing it in motels. Hot and cold form a fiery crystal inside me, a burning that doesn't burn, and then I get the giggles, a non-stop gurgling. I never laughed so much after sex, and later, seeing Humbert sleepy at the wheel, I feel a little tickle of flames darting across my skin.

We are north of the Androscoggin, of the magical lake Umbagog, but we can't cross the border: I'm not on Hummie's passport. There's always some stupid law getting in the way, but if the law is truly interested in my not having sex with Hummie, well, there it has failed; all it's done is keep me from seeing Canada. Assuming that this is not the law's real intent, and that its real, secret intent is not simply to keep people from doing what they want, it must be to get them used to the fact that the law is always there, with or without a reason; the reasons get stuck on afterward, to make a good show, to invent an excuse, but the true purpose of the law is simply to be a nuisance, just like the hen.

Indian territory: Penobscot, like the river.

"You know why it's called that?"

"No."

"Because it was the name of the Indian tribe that lived there, like the Appalachians." Pathetic. When he plays the professor he really does become pathetic. Hopeless. Giving me geography lessons! He makes himself useful. I always pretend not to know anything: he is so pleased when he can explain, and it costs me so little to listen to him. Why not let him speak, let him feel important; it's better for me to keep my dear daddy in a good mood. Because the fact is that inside— though you wouldn't notice at first glance—he's old. He's old because he wants to be old, because in some way my mother and all the other hens he's slept with must have transmitted their decay. Sometimes it seems like if you scratch the surface he's exactly like Plasticmom. You can see from the way he acts, always fearful, always careful, that he has the same brain. I can't bear it when he looks at me to gauge the effect he's having on me, just like the hen, who also had this passion for staring. Staring and teaching. They all have this passion for teaching. To stick some burrs of knowledge on you.

Farther and farther north. We stop for apple pie and ice cream. Some workmen are playing cards at the next table. One is very cute, he's wearing yellow boots with fringe and a checked shirt like mine. As he passes he puts a hand on my shoulder: "On vacation with Dad?"

"Yes, with my adorable dadfriend." Hummie doesn't appreciate that, he makes a face like an outraged father, while the other guy dances out, making a V sign. Terrible scene with jealous Humbert: he says that from the way I looked at the guy it was clear I'd a hundred times rather be with him. Jerk. I'd like to know why the hell he's so jealous. We could be a little less unhappy: we're alone together traveling, no hen in the way, but that idiot has to keep an eye on me for fear I'll run away. By treating me like someone who wants to escape, he really will make me. What does he want, proof of my love? Did I walk over the corpse of my mother to be with him, or not?

I'm trying to explain to him what kind of shoes I need, and not long afterward we pass a car crash, and I see a woman's beige moccasin on the ground, all bloody. Humbert makes a suitable face, prudent in a murderer of widows.

"Look, on the ground there, that's the kind I was trying to describe to that dumb guy in the store." Scandalized face of Daddy Humbert: cynics can't stand cynicism.

Baxter State Park, you can't get any farther north. We head back south. Usual menu of woods, lakes, woods, lakes, more rivers, tree trunks floating down the rivers, slow on black water, fast on white water. We make a detour to see a waterfall; there's a clearing in the woods, and the waterfall isn't very high, but the rocks are beautiful colors. It would be a good place for a shower in the open and then a little amorous fling, like at Umbagog, but there's a group of stupid picnickers and we have to give up. Damn! I hate sex indoors, day after day, every day. Dear Daddy in heaven, why don't you try to instill in your successor a true liking for screwing out in the open, which invigorates your lungs and is good for your skin tone?

We pass a school. Mama Humbert parks in the shade of an elm and orders me to let him touch my knees while he watches the girls filing out. I tell him he's disgusting, and he says brazenly: "Don't be so selfish. Try to understand what might please others, instead of thinking only of what you want." Then, with the idea that he's going to make me happy, he picks up a hitchhiker: totally of the female sex and of an unsexual age anyway, a lady whose batteries are dead and who as soon as she realizes that Humbert is French chat ters for the whole time about her honeymoon in Burgundy forty years ago.

How nice it would be to be a couple in love instead of a stupid widowed stepfather with a child who's not his. After all, if he had more guts we could be something else.

"Do you feel guilty that you murdered the hen?"

"What hen?" Like an alien from another planet.

"Come on . . ."

"What's got into you? I've never murdered anyone."

"I don't mind if you murdered her."

"Be quiet."

"Really, you can tell me, you can tell me everything, really everything, dear."

"Will you stop it? What ideas you get in your head. Do you take me for someone who murders women?"

"Sorry, I guess I was mistaken."

"Mistaken about what?"

"O.K., let's say you didn't murder her. But then how would you have managed to be with me, with her in the way?"

"If your mother hadn't died we wouldn't be together."

"Oh, so that's it."

"That's what?"

"I mean, it turns out you could just as well be with me or not, it doesn't make much difference? I mean: it wouldn't make a really big difference, like life or death, right?"

"Dolly, one cannot kill."

"Why not? What if there hadn't been any other way?"

"We would have had to give each other up," he says with a virtuous sigh. It's been a while since his mouth drove me wild. He uses it to say such crap.

"It would have been easy to give up. So then I don't matter that much to you."

"But I'm always with you!"

"But you could also do without me."

"It doesn't depend entirely on us, and anyway I came and got you as soon as I could."

"And what if you never could have? What would you have done, gone on fucking the hen?"

"Stop speaking like that."

"Hen, hen, hen."

"Stop it!"

"Stop it like hell. You mean in the end it would have been all the same, with me or without me."

"But it's not at all the same, in fact . . . "

"In fact what?"

"Once I did think of drowning her, but I realized I couldn't do it, and luckily I didn't try because a friend of hers was at the top of the hill and from there she could see everything, even the make of my watch."

"You mean that one mustn't kill but you did have a kind of thought, and then at the crucial moment you got the jitters. And is this a little crumb thrown out so I'll think you would have killed the hen or is it a lie to convince me that you didn't? One thing is obvious, you don't trust me."

"Stop it."

"You don't trust me at all: you won't tell me the truth about Mom's death and you think I want to run away with boys." Why does he create all these problems if he doesn't feel guilty for murdering the hen? Why doesn't he trust me? Why don't we go places we'd both like, instead of going nuts with boredom in these mountains? Why is he so complicated and evasive? Why, when out of the kindness of his heart we picked up a soldier going home on leave, did he do everything he could to humiliate him and make him feel like an imbecile with that stupid superior tone of his that makes him immediately hateful? Why did he marry the hen and not me? Why does he make me call him Daddy? He only would have had to wait a little while, a nothing . . . But he is that way and always will be: you can't, you can't, you can't. All he can say is You can't. But how is it that all of a sudden he became such a creep? So hateful? So . . . so . . . so I don't know what. Anyway, he's not the same Humbert who chased me with spray bottles in the perfume store, he is absolutely not the same, and the only explanation is that when he married the hen that stupid marriage ceremony must have changed who he was, and now I want to know how I can make him go back to what he was before, because even though he has the same body it's as if somebody else had sneaked inside.

That pig of a Humbert. I didn't want to, but he sees one of those mountain scenes that according to him are romantic, and he insists. I give in, I tell him, but in exchange you have to promise to stop this nonsense about being my dad, stop saying I'm your daughter—it's all right in the hotels, but otherwise no. He says O.K., really O.K., the way I'd say it, parks the car, takes out the blanket, and we follow a trail. He chooses a place near some bushes with blue flowers that scent the air, and spreads the blanket on the grass and strokes me all over to arouse me, but he hurries because he can see that I don't have much patience today even if we are outside, and the result is I don't have time to come. I lie there half stunned and naked and dirty and wet and irritated, and while I'm still filled with disgust all he can do is make the most treacly face in the world and traitorously say, Give Daddy a little kiss. Dirty pig, he went right back on his O.K.: now that he got what he wanted the old habits return exactly the same as before. What did I do to find myself in a fake incest with a fake father, I wonder, and everything I might have done passes before my eyes, from Nelson the Second to fights with the hen, but it's too much, I have a fit of violent crying, of sobbing that makes me shake all over. Humbert holds me in his arms, hugs me, smiles paternally; he likes to feel me all warm from crying. I lean my cheek on his chest, because in spite of everything he has a good warm smell. It makes me furious that he can always attract me, with his smooth skin, his body that I want to hug tight and at the same time sink into.

I remember in Goatscreek how I seduced him with the apple and the smudged lipstick, and it was like a dream, going up and down without realizing it, everything seemed possible then: I thought he would understand, would find a way to take me away from there, but not like this, like a secret slave. I couldn't imagine that he would marry the hen, that he would be incapable of opposing the implacable unstoppable will of Shitmom the Tank. Humbert had to be mine and mine alone, because he's only alive when he's with me, but she managed to paralyze him with her mortal poison, she seized him, bewitched him, I don't know what she did exactly, I think, sobbing. I don't know what she could have done with him when I wasn't there, taking advantage of my absence, when I couldn't keep her from hurting him. In any case she must have cast some black-magic spell over him, so he's no longer himself, no longer my ally. He's still in her power, now more than before. Dead, Shitmom managed to cheat me for real; like the witch she's always been, she transformed Humbert into the dummy of my father and our love into incest. We could only have been safe if she'd never seen us, never breathed her poisonous acid breath on us. Instead she married him, and from the outside it must have looked like an ordinary marriage, but in reality it was evil, because for sure he is not the same person I left in Goatscreek when I went to Maple Camp. He only has the appearance of the old Humbert of before; buried inside is the soul of Plasticmom, it's her, the damn dirty hen, who's pulling the strings, and we can't do anything about it. This trip isn't a trip, it's like tossing in bed when you can't sleep. There's no point in holding Humbert tight, or trying to bite into him, I'll never get to his heart; there's no point in beating my head against his chest, to try to get inside: he is lost, gone, and Shitmom succeeded in what she wanted, murdering me, taking away from me all the freedom and joy I had, and she did it in the most treacherous way, with a fake Humbert she manipulated from a distance. I fell for it because I never imagined the depths of her evil and her power: if I'd realized that though he seemed the same as before, he wasn't at all, that he had the body of Humbert but the soul of the dead hen, I would have run the hell away, shouting with horror when I saw him at Maple Camp. I would have been saved by Roger and Rowe, and I, I . . . I don't know, but I would never let them shut me up in a reformatory—we would have barricaded ourselves on the Willow island, better to die than surrender, and we would have started a riot to amend the Constitution, and ended the dictatorship of pigs over children, and made a new American revolution. Instead, here I am naked and wet and angry, crying and praying that somehow he'll get a clue about what I'm feeling, that somehow his eyes will be opened and he'll do something, be released from the spell of Shitmom. Then I hear his automaton voice ordering me: "Get up, quick, get going!" Naked though I am, I stand up, not getting it, and abruptly he tells me to pick up everything, drags me by the arm, hurting me. I turn and catch a glimpse of two boys looking at me openmouthed and behind them a fat woman wearing a hat wider than she is; she must be nearsighted because—thank heaven—she didn't know she had ended up on the perfect set for a horror movie.

17.

I WILL NEVER understand people who like the mountains better than the ocean. You've seen one mountain, you've seen them all. We go back to the Penobscot. Humbert wants to stay on the main road, but by threatening him with various denials I make him take a back road that heads toward the coast. After a while, I see a sign for Mount Desert Island, and I make him go that way. We arrive under a leaden sky, and stop on some gray cliffs whose surface is rough with black shells. Long gray waves spray our faces, air spewing drops of ocean; it goes in your nostrils and makes you feel light and happy.

Then we see a theater where some decent movies are playing. Humbert makes a face, so I say, if you don't want to go I'll go by myself, but that idea he likes even less. The people here are beautiful—they're thin, they have golden skin, and their eyes sparkle like the sea. Tomorrow we'll be on the island. Meanwhile Humbert remembers that I know a few tennis strokes and he takes me to the courts at the hotel to improve my style. He's a huge pain, always on me with his instructions. It's only a game, but he gets furious when I miss, storming me with absurd terms like forehand, backhand, passing shot, lob, backspin, topspin, double fault, triple fault, hundredfold fault, and I don't remember what else: anyway it brings on an agony so deep that I don't care if I hit the ball or not. He rages and rages, I've never seen him so angry. This tennis thing brings out these attacks of, I don't know, perfectionism, and he insists I do my best to win, to hit the ball precisely. It makes me nervous, and it's so boring, and then it seems like work and not play; it's so much more fun when you do what you feel like and even let the other person score some points. Because I don't see what's so important about winning—winning at tennis doesn't change a thing in your life, what's important is to let the ball make a nice arc and take off on its own. It's more natural that way, and then why should all the shots be accurate? Then it's not a game anymore, because if you take this business of accurate shots to an extreme, it could end up that the person who's better hits everything perfectly and the other poor person always misses and that's it for any sort of game. The idea should be to have fun, not for one person to be triumphant and the other humiliated. I get so angry I can't sleep: it's like there's a strange whining beast scratching inside me. I'm so furious after playing that, not knowing what to beat my head against, I look through Humbert's stuff. In the inside pocket of his jacket I find that old black notebook, which makes it plain that he has always been after me. From the moment he walked in with the timetable in his hand at the beginning of the summer. He is a great strategist; in life, as in tennis, he never misses a shot. Who knows if the idea of murdering the hen occurred to him right away or came to him later.

· · ·

Humbert says that Mount Desert reminds him of Norway, with its fiords and rocks and the mosaic of waters so that you can't tell which are fresh and which are salt. When the ocean recedes, sparkling stripes are left on the ground, silvery like tinfoil. There are white-and-gray birds called sandpipers, which hop on these remnants of ocean and dig for worms. The sun sets, and the beach turns a feathery gray. There's a big frayed cloud that looks like a jellyfish stretched motion-less in the sky. Two guys go by on horses, the sandpipers hide behind a dune. We go, too, and seeing a telephone I feel like calling Nora: it's my aunt's birthday, I tell Humbert. She'll be worried if she doesn't get my usual telephone call, I add, to confuse him. Who is this aunt, he asks, suspicious. Aunt Nora. To frighten him with a more concrete authority than a reformatory, I make up an energetic aunt, my father's sister, who is a lawyer in Los Angeles and who if she doesn't hear from me today could start a search for me through the entire United States and beyond: she's a real ball-buster, I add, to assure him that I am completely on his side, while he gives in and, for the first, the absolute first, time since we've been together, lets me use a telephone and even gives me the money for it. But he doesn't leave me alone for a sec-ond while I'm talking. The telephone rings, rings, oh God, she's not answering, I think, then finally there's Nora with an incredibly sleepy voice: "Oh, Dolly, yesterday I was at a party, late, really late, a wild party, but where are you? I've called Goatscreek a hundred thousand times and no one answers, I thought you'd all gone to England."

"No, Aunt Nora, we didn't go to England, I'm sorry, I should have told you before. But I wanted to wish you happy birthday. I'm at the ocean with my stepfather—we're taking a trip to help us get over Mom's death, a really nice trip, you know?"

"Dolly, what's this about Isabel being dead and I'm your aunt? Have you gone mad?"

"Sorry, it's nothing. I don't have time to tell you the details, but it was a car accident, she was run over—you really didn't know?"

"Oh heavens! No, I didn't know a thing. She was so happy!"

"Don't cry, Aunt Nora, Mother died instantly—at least she didn't suffer. I didn't mean to ruin your birthday, I thought someone would have told you about the accident . . . " Humbert looks at me as if to say, see why you couldn't make this phone call?

"Why are you calling me aunt?"

"No, I'll go back to school next year. You see, it's a wonderful trip, and I really needed something like this, because it was horrible how Mom died so suddenly." This said so that Humbert can see that I'm gazing up to the sky, having fun playing the poor little orphan, and that I'm doing it for him, so no one suspects. "And you, how are you?"

"Fine, or rather, terrible, terrible now that you tell me Isabel is dead. I thought she was traveling with her husband, and instead you phone and confuse me by calling me aunt, and I don't know what to think. If it weren't that you sound so calm, I'd think you'd been kidnapped or I don't know what, but you don't need me to come and rescue you, do you?"

"No, Aunt Nora, there's no need, you keep them, you'll give them to me when we come to see you. Humbert says we'll go through California. Mom really wanted him to know you, you were her favorite in-law, you know."

"What a disaster. But don't despair, Dolly, even though your mother isn't there anymore, just think about your trip and what you'll do when you grow up. You know, I've always thought you should act, so if nothing else try to gather impressions, ways of speaking, ways of moving, learn to see everything with your own eyes. You know, school is useless that way, because all they teach you is how to be exactly like everyone else. Only, tell me if you're in danger."

"No, I'm at Mount Desert."

"But you couldn't tell him that I'm a friend of your mother's?"

"I don't know, the Hiltons are still in Goatscreek; of all Mom's friends they are the least sympathetic to Humbert." Humbert threatens me with a fist.

"But how can I find you?"

"No, Aunt Nora, I don't think you can phone me, we're always in a different place, but I'll call you often, if you like." Nervous look from Humbert.

"Is he treating you badly?"

"No, the East Coast is so beautiful right now that I think it will be a few months before we see you. You want to say hello to Humbert?" Humbert coughs as he takes the receiver, has a long conversation with Nora on the "agony" of losing the woman of his dreams as soon as he's found her, and what a consolation it is for him to be looking after me as he's thinking of her, and blah blah blah blah blah. Then he gives Nora back to me: "Poor thing, if nothing else take advantage of the opportunity—it's a nice free trip around the country. I know it's not a normal life, without a mother and far from home and your friends, but it doesn't matter—it's better, really, and at least it's not like anyone else's life, it's an original life, like all famous people have. And then traveling like this, you can observe so many people. Don't waste time being sad, take advantage of the situation, since what happens happens," and she sobs.

"Come on, Aunt Nora, please don't cry!"

"Poor Isabel, she was so in love with Humbert, she was so . . ." Oh good heavens! She is the last person in the world I can tell the truth to about how things are. "At any rate, you'll come and see me soon?"

"Yes, Auntie, happy birthday, don't be sad. Yes, of course I'll send you lots of postcards." Revolting. She didn't understand a thing, even calling her aunt didn't click, and she's supposed to be so intelligent. Always keep part of the truth for yourself. Don't tell everything . . . Even if I were to tell her everything, at most she'd only understand a teeny tiny little part.

Nora's so full of fine speeches about my extraordinary good fortune in not having a dull life like my friends, and all the things I can learn. It's true that what you do in school is pretty predictable, but at least there's us, I mean kids my age, while on this trip the only serious observations to be made are of Humbert Guibert, the occasional waitress, gas-station attendants on the highway, and the hitchhikers he picks up when he forgets to be Humbert the Jailer. But there's not enough time to get to know anyone, so I don't see that there's much to gain professionally, and then I'd like to know how Nora thinks she can call this a free trip. What's so free about it? I'm fed up with these practical types who only appreciate stuff that's useful for something else: Humbert with his tennis balls that are supposed to score points, Nora with her theory that travel is supposed to broaden my mind—everything is useful for something else and never interesting on its own, in the present, as if my life right now had no value, might as well be eliminated, and if it's not that's only because it's useful for getting to another, more important part of my life that I might not even get to see anyway, because, who knows, I could die tomorrow. And since I could die tomorrow or even today, what's the point of all these speeches about what I should do for my work in the future, because after all, if you think about it, I'm already working: I'm a little concubine who doesn't even have the right to quit.

This Aunt Nora gives Humbert anxiety attacks. He has an uncontrollable fear of busybodies. Humbert the Doctor of Laws jumps out. He gives me a lesson. The law, he says, is totally on his side: "You realize you are an orphan and a minor?" He makes it clear as we're going up to the top of the mountain. "You know what would happen if you tried to tell your dear aunt Nora about me and you?" (Said with an oily smile.) "Well, better not try." (Furrowing his brow.) "You could end up with a guardian. You wouldn't have any freedom, and you're not used to having someone tell you what to do anymore." (No?)

"Don't be ridiculous, I wouldn't end up in a reformatory, I would simply be handed over to my aunt," I say, challenging him, but then like an idiot I burst into tears, because I remember that I made up the aunt who is a lawyer, and the fact is I don't really know what would happen. I'm choking with sobs. Humbert plays the protector, but then he's infected by gloomy thoughts, too, because he goes, "You know, at some point our trip is going to have to end." (Good news!) "But let me give you some advice: don't tell anything to your aunt or your future best friend, when you go back to school. In fact, it would be much better if you can avoid this silly best-friend business."

"And why does our trip have to end?"

"Because you are much younger than me and one day you'll leave me." There he goes again. And it's a lie, because one time I told him I wanted to go to Alaska in an airplane, and he said we can't travel forever: he'll have to go back to work eventually, since he's not Uncle Scrooge McDuck, and so we had to keep to routes we could take in my mother's car. Skinflint! "And above all, when this aunt of yours asks you what we're doing, see that you don't act the innocent child, you have nothing to gain by it."

"Don't worry, Hummie-Dummie, I have no intention of speaking out, and I've never had any illusions about escaping."

"Stop calling me Hummie-Dummie, could you try?"

"How much?" Seeing how he treats me, I don't see why he shouldn't pay me. But he never says exactly how much. He shrugs his shoulders, sits down on a tree trunk, and opens a little book of poetry. I sit on a rock with my comic book, a little higher up than he is, where I have a good view of the coast: between here and the ocean is a big patch of fall, green cooked by the cold and the first splashes of raspberry syrup on the maples. Soon all the leaves will be candied. A whole forest of lollipops.

It's the first anniversary of the death of Nelson the second. We should have marked it all together, Mary Jo, Bobby, Celeste, and I, with commemorative songs under the tree. Instead the house is empty and the elm tree's probably been knocked down.

I got a fever after I went swimming. The sea was beautiful, smooth as a lake. I entered the water slowly: it was cold, but I wanted to sink in gently, slow motion, as if there were no difference between me and the ocean, and then I didn't want to give Mama Humbert the satisfaction: "You'll catch cold, be careful, you're crazy." It's because he's so sensitive to the cold. I like cold water. It makes me tingle all over. But then I got this fever. I'm sure that my slow swim in the slow water of that slow evening at Mount Desert has nothing to do with it, but Humbert has it in his head that it did. More than anything else, he's terrified of my getting sick, because then he has to find a doctor, fill a prescription—he has to be seen, father-stepfather with little girl. A late vacation, school is about to begin, what's he doing alone with me on an island? Why isn't he at work? Why am I not at school? He claims that one afternoon when the fever was at its height I was delirious, and if anyone had been there he would have ended up in jail. That's how things are, the risk of prison for him is at least as great as the reformatory for me.

No more coast road, Mama Humbert decides, because of my "natatorial follies." I can recuperate in the mountains, but no more diving into lakes. The great educator at the wheel: "You know why it's called Vermont?"

"No."

"It means green mountain in French, and it's a place full of green mountains." Fascinating.

"You see, the French managed to keep it for spring and summer, but in the fall they had to give it up to the English. Luckily the English won. Think how awful it would be to hear salutations and felicitations in French right in the middle of the American forest." Mama Humbert isn't listening to me.

"Close your jacket. Cover your throat." Yuck. It's so annoying when he plays the normal dad. Almost worse than the morbid dad. And this whole scene takes place in front of a snot-nosed kid with a satchel whom Humbert made the grand gesture of picking up, and who didn't open his mouth the whole time, he was so timid, or maybe he was ashamed of his stupid chinless albino face. Letting the hitchhiker out in front of a wooden cabin, we settle in a motel in the middle of the woods. Here fall arrives early. The sugar maples are all red, orange, and candied yellow. Old people come to admire the leaves. Every so often they stop where the colors are flaming, and get out and look with binoculars to see the leaves full size. What's there to watch so much? It's only sap, sap oversaturated with glucose, sap trapped by the cold. It's as if the trees had varicose veins: the sap runs slowly, like poor blood, only instead of varicose blue it's red, because the trees have opposite colors from us, in reverse. If it were all uniformly green like summer you'd shoot yourself, being trapped in the car with nothing but trees, trees and mountains all around you. I propose to Mama Humbert that we take a horseback ride through the woods. No. "You're still too weak." Help! His real calling is to be a nurse.

I could still adore Hummie, but sometimes he really makes me mad. That irritating habit of interrupting me when I'm reading. I'm sitting on the couch with a book, not even aware he's in the room, and he can't find anything to do except rub against me. Or yesterday evening I was reading *Life*, for lack of anything better; the road had been horribly boring, and I was minding my own business, peacefully, and at one point I laughed. "What are you laughing at? Tell me." Travel is fine, it's good to see the country where you live, sex is great, for your skin and general tone, but this business of bothering me even when I'm reading, really, I don't get it. And then he is so repetitious, so incredibly repetitious.

Vermont is the most boring place in the world.

"Let's stay a little longer, the air is good for you."

"I'm dying of boredom. I want to go back to school, I want to see my friends."

"You'll do what I tell you."

"I'll turn you in. For kidnapping a minor."

"Go ahead, but you won't return to Goatscreek—you'll end up in a reformatory and none of your friends will want to see you again."

"Why?"

"Because you are the consenting lover of your mother's widower."

"I'm not consenting to be dragged to the mountains. And why would my friends refuse to see me?"

"The word is incest." He's stealing my lines, my retarded dad.

Humbert keeps bugging me about tennis lessons. It's like doing homework. I'm outside playing happily with Carmen, the daughter of the waitress in the restaurant, and it's going so smoothly, it's fantastic, one point to me, one to her, no problem, we're running in the sun and really feeling good. Then Mama Humbert shows up and decides that we're not playing properly, he's going to give us a lesson. He takes advantage of it to pet Carmen a little—she's not bad-looking, she flits here and there and has a lilting voice. No doubt if the ineffable Professor Guibert had landed here instead of at our house, it wouldn't have been too much trouble to marry the waitress. Why not? It's a pretty spot, with a tennis court, tree-covered mountains all around, and the wife of the owner has a passion for French cooking. Humbert's paradise. I, however, can't stand it anymore. I'd like to see a real city. New York. This is death. The car, the motels, the roads, the trees, the clouds, the cows, the same frogs and the same squirrels. Today he buys me *Archie*, and I read it straight through from beginning to end. Then when I'm finished: "Now give a kiss to your dad who buys you so many nice things." Revolting! As if a comic book were enough to make a person happy; and besides I don't like it when he pretends to be my father. My father was Gerald Maze. Humbert is my lover and stepfather. No need for confusion.

It's really long, the road to New York. Humbert makes it even longer. He wants to go through the Adirondacks: "Let's go see where the Hudson begins."

"I couldn't care less about where the Hudson begins."

"It goes all the way to New York, don't you want to see where it starts?"

"No."

"But I do." Too bad we're not married, then we could get divorced.

I'm so sick of dragging my suitcase from one motel to the next. We never stay more than two nights in the same place. And with the same variations on the theme of what to say to Mrs. Guibert when she telephones. The only thing that happens is that we're always about to see the hen. Really fun. Today we stop in a place that's half inn, half farm. There's a really cute boy in a red-and-blue sweater, Tom, and as soon as Humbert locked himself in the toilet, which he does only when he's shitting because it doesn't bother him if I see the rest (but it does bother me), I go to look for him. I find him downstairs, drawing in an album, and at first he doesn't even look at me, he's got an expression like I really disturbed him, but when he finishes the drawing, which is of a parachutist jumping from a propeller plane, he smiles and asks if I want to draw with him. I draw the blue sedan with Humbert and me in it, and he asks me how I happen to be in that area. I don't really know what to say, because no matter what anyone asks about my present life there's nothing to say, no way to explain how it happened, and especially not to someone who looks so nice. How do I tell him the revolting truth, aside from the fact that I couldn't anyway. So I make up a story about how we're going to see my grandmother in a nursing home for senile old idiots. How do I know she's senile, he asks me. All she does is stare at the marmalade jar, I tell him. He shrugs his shoulders: that's what his grandfather does, but they wouldn't dream of shutting him up in an asylum just for that, he explains. I feel very ashamed, and promise that I'll try to convince my father to let my grandmother come back to us. He's pleased by this, and tells me that when he grows up he's going to go into politics, and he asks me what I think of black people, so I tell him about Celeste, who is practically my best grownup friend. Just then Humbert comes down and gives me a close, dark look. Fuck you, I think, and sit there talking to Tom, but Humbert sits down at our table, without even asking. And then Tom does something absolutely fantastic, and I'll remember it for the rest of my life: he simply asks Humbert if he wants to make a drawing. And my incomparable second dad, without realizing how ridiculous he is, takes a piece of paper and a pencil and makes a gray leaning tower of Pisa with butterflies all around it. Meanwhile Tom is explaining to me that when he finishes school he will start a campaign to give black people the same rights we have: to ride on buses, go to restaurants and movies and everything, just like us; he'll have enemies, but he couldn't care less, he's going to be like Gandhi. Then, since I don't know who Gandhi is and Humbert confines himself to raising an eyebrow while he's drawing his butterflies, Tom explains that Gandhi is a genius, because he won independence for his country without a war. He wants to do the same for black people. But why are you drawing an airplane with a parachute jumper? I ask. He explains that his parachute jumper is on a peace mission, to liberate a friend. He wanted to tell me more, but he couldn't because Humbert made me leave, saying that it was dinnertime, which threw me into a fury. The one time I meet someone decent to talk to and we're having an interesting conversation, he shows up and puts an end to my fun. Not only that: later, in the car, he tortures me with a bunch of nauseating questions about what we were doing before he came down.

I finally managed my escape from the Adirondacks. I had to go on strike. No sex. When he comes close to me, I scream. Loud, so I can be heard from here to the ocean. Humbert pale as death. "Shut up! Someone will hear you."

"Exactly."

"Do you want to end up in the reformatory?"

"Are you afraid of ending up in jail?"

"No one has anything to gain from this, is that clear?"

"But I do. I gain this, that If I don't feel like it, I'm not going to be forced."

"What makes you think these things don't happen in a reformatory?"

"Don't be stupid, this is a free country." And what if they did happen? And you found yourself locked up in a reformatory and forced to make so-called love with a warden? Someone even worse than Mama Humbert?

"Well, I don't want to go to the mountains, I want to go to New York."

"O.K., New York. Now be a good girl."

"I won't do a thing until we go in the direction I say." I did do something, but later I got him to buy me a gold pin to keep my pocketbook strap from falling off my shoulder. I won't tell you what it cost me, dear Dolores Maze of the future, or you'd have a fit.

All day I've had this scene in my head: I'm in the ocean, and a shark appears. Instead of running away I stay still, and when the shark opens his mouth I quickly grab him by the fin and climb on his back. Then I gouge out his eyes and eat them: first the right eye, which tastes disgusting, like a bad oyster, and I spit it out, and then the left, also disgusting. The shark is blind, and blood is dripping from the sockets, and he's writhing with me on his back, and I open his mouth to dislocate his jaw, so he can't open or close it anymore. He can't stop the air from entering his stomach, and with all that air going in he suffocates, dies, sinks under me, slides between my legs, while I keep floating, and when the shark finally sinks to the bottom I go back to the beach and lie in the sun. No one saw the struggle, and I won't tell anyone about it. I don't care about being admired. I don't want anyone to know that I am so incredibly strong I can murder a shark in the ocean, without a weapon, just with my hands and my teeth. It's my secret, and besides no one would believe it.

18.

NEW YORK!!! I'M so out of practice for walking in a real city that my head is spinning with all there is to see in every direction. In the morning we go to the aquarium in Battery Park, which is round like a big box of cheese. Inside, wall after wall is covered with water behind glass. The most interesting fish is a kind of electric eel called a torpedo, which looks like a gray tube. A light goes on every time it touches some electrical wires that were put in the water just for that purpose. A fish that turns on the lights. There should be a torpedo in every house to save electricity. There's a guy explaining to a group of kids that these electric eels live in the Amazon and give other fish shocks. They carry enough current to kill a horse. I told Humbert that my brother died more or less like that, killed by a power line that suddenly turned into a giant torpedo fish. Then it occurred to me how odd it is that Humbert, given his age, has never had a child.

"I hate children."

"Really?" Even worse than Plasticmom, as far as children and animals go. He makes an exception only for girls, and only if they're pretty and slender. I make him promise to get me goggles for next summer, so I can look at fish enjoying their freedom. After the aquarium we take a ferry to the Statue of Liberty. It doesn't bother me in the slightest that Humbert's miserable because he's been there before. It's my first time, and I wouldn't give it up for any reason in the world. There's another school group in the elevator, and the teacher's explaining how the French gave us the statue. It had to be a trick if it came from the French: when you reach the top, after the hundred and sixty-eight steps that take you up inside the crown, you're in a cage: you see New Jersey, the skyscrapers, the islands, the boats all perfectly clearly, bright and shining, but your hands are holding on to the bars . . . you're shut up there spying on liberty from behind bars. That is truly a French joke.

I still haven't been to the movies; instead, this afternoon I watch myself and Humbert on a TV screen, which is even better than going to the movies to look at someone else. It's at a show of electronic inventions. There's a banner over the entrance saying that television is the first daughter of radio, and below it are some movie cameras that film you while you're looking at yourself on a screen mounted on a kind of big box. It's incredible: you see yourself at exactly the same instant you're being filmed, like in the mirror, except that instead of having a mirror in front of you it's a television screen, and instead of seeing yourself from the front you see yourself from a different point. I look much more grownup on the screen. At least eighteen. I see what Nora meant, I have much more presence in the movies than in the mirror. Even Humbert comes out O.K. He bought a radio for the car, and it's really great—to have music when you're driving changes everything; you don't have to make conversation all the time, or suffer through horrible silences that make you want to strangle each other.

In a bar where we went for a drink there was a slot machine that really inspired me. I concentrated hard and said all the prayers I know, because I only had two nickels and ran the risk of losing them immediately. I also put in a prayer to you, dear Daddy, but not to the hen, because the less she thinks about me the better; in fact I said a special prayer so that she wouldn't remember to look down in my direction just then, since she always screws up everything. Well, I had incredible luck—I quintupled the first time and got ten the second, so I had a purse full of coins, and I went to the telephone in the ladies' room and called Nora. "Nora, you know I've just been filmed?"

"Already? How?"

"For television."

"How did that happen?"

"They saw me with Humbert and they filmed us: we put on a good show. They told me I'm enviably photogenic. We looked like Humphrey Bogart and Lauren Bacall." I go on for a while. Nora listens, amazed, but after a while she realizes it's only a joke and tells me not to make up such nonsense. Then she asks me what's the story with the last time I phoned and called her aunt, so I told her that Humbert is very miserly and lets me phone relatives but not friends, because once I called Mary Jo from the hotel and I was on the phone for two hours.

"But does he make you go hungry? Cold?" Nora asks, worried.

"No, nothing like that. It's just that he has this obsession about wasting money on phone calls. He's kind of stingy, but it's nothing to worry about." She went for it, she's convinced. She tells me she didn't expect me to become a liar so quickly. I laugh, and she does, too, but then she returns to the subject of Mom's death and gets gloomy. Forget it. As long as I'm here I figure I'll call Mary Jo. If I come back with too much money Humbert will take it away anyway, so I might as well spend it.

"What have you been doing?" Said in an offended tone.

"I was sick after Mom died" (lie).

"It must have been terrible, they told me about the accident. So what are you doing now?"

"Humbert took a vacation to take care of me, and now I'm better. He's making me go on a trip to get over the trauma."

"Do you miss her a lot?"

"Terribly."

"I don't know what I'd do if my mother died. I'd kill myself" (typical exaggeration).

"I was so desperate I did try to kill myself, that's why Humbert's making me travel, to distract me" (said with appropriate sobs).

"Come on, Dolly, don't cry."

"Oh, I miss everyone so much" (almost true).

"Send me a postcard."

"I'm not very good at writing, but I'll try. Now I've used up my money."

"But I wanted to tell you about Perry Maderna, you know, he ..."

"My money's all used up, Mary Jo. A kiss, ten thousand kisses, a hive buzzing with kisses ..."

Click ... click ... Damn. What's the deal with Perry Maderna, I wonder.

New York: screw and go and no movies. Mama Humbert really didn't like the trick I played. We're at the Empire State Building and I decide to make fun of those jerks whose job it is to keep people from killing themselves when they want to. So, standing at the window where you buy tickets for the highest floor from a big-chested red-haired woman, I make a tense, upset face, chin quivering, and she falls for it and calls the ticket-taker on the eighty-sixth floor to keep an eye on a man with an upset child. In front of the ticket-taker at the top, I pretend my arms are trembling, so when we get to the terrace two undercover guards are ready. I wander around making sad faces, then I lean over the parapet like I want to climb over it. They are immediately on me, and they drag me over to Mama Humbert, who's waiting near the door to the elevator.

"Is this your child?"

"Yes, she's my daughter."

"What's she doing there alone?"

"I have vertigo, so I told her I would wait here." Look of utter contempt from the guards.

"She was trying to climb over the parapet. What's going on?"

"What?" He looks at me with the tragic expression of an outraged father. "It's not possible. Really?"

"I was fooling," I say with a perfectly straight face, no trembling, not upset.

"See?" says Mama Humbert, triumphant.

"Children must be accompanied by an adult," the guard insists. Then I start worrying that they might really call the police, so I make a sly face—like an enfant terrible, as Humbert would say—and he seizes the opportunity to play the role of the "poor widower with an uncontrollable daughter." The guards give me a talking-to, and while they're lecturing me on taking things seriously and not wasting the time of working people, we hear a shout. A real one. *Aaaaaaaa! Tum. Patapum.* More shouting. A siren. The guards stand frozen, faces frightened, then they dart toward the parapet. We take advantage of the confusion to get away before they start again with us. We walk down all eighty-six floors because Humbert has it fixed in his mind that otherwise they'll arrest us as accomplices in a suicide.

"Accomplices in a suicide? Don't be an idiot."

"Be quiet and hurry up." Hard labor: at least three hundred million steps. My legs hurt like crazy. A hundred times worse than the mountains. And there was absolutely no one following us. Obviously the guards couldn't admit that a little girl made fools of them. Anyway, goodbye New York, no theaters, no movies, no Metropolitan Museum. If nothing else, I got a little acting practice. My audition wasn't bad. I made them all look stupid. When we get to the car Humbert is so exhausted by going down all those steps that he can't even press the accelerator, and the old sedan stalls every so often, or moves with a jolt, like a drunk. Luckily there's the radio, and we keep it on the pop station at full volume, otherwise we would have smashed against a wall by now.

Humbert says that we shouldn't buy any newspapers for a while because it's better not to know who the person was who was able to kill himself because of me, better not to ever know the name or face, because I'd get nightmares. How sensitive! As if it were my fault that someone decided to kill himself. In fact, I was helpful, because it stinks to be forced to live when you have absolutely no desire to.

Mama Humbert outwitted: I was talking in the hotel garden to two cute boys from Milwaukee, Pete and Bob, and we were telling each other about our trips. I was holding forth about the suicide on the Empire State Building, and they were very impressed with my performance. Then their mother came by and invited me to go with them to the movies. If it's O.K. with my dad, I said, so she went to find Humbert, and I don't know how she convinced him to let me go. That her husband is a judge is not completely irrelevant, it seems to me. Anyway, we went to the movies, and I sat in the middle, and Pete and Bob each held one hand, without the other knowing. Pete even kissed me and whispered in my ear that I am the most beautiful girl he's ever seen in his life.

We can't leave because we're in the tail of a hurricane that arrived from the Carolinas. Our windows shake all night, the wind

beats on the foamy water and the sand, and we're wide-awake discussing whether to take the northern or the southern route to the
Pacific. Southern, I say, so we'll get to Los Angeles first. Today must
have been the first day of school. Mary Jo will try to sit next to Perry
Maderna. To start a conversation she will tell him how my dear mom
died, under the car of Mary and Jack Stone's father, according to
Humbert, and that I am traveling with my stepfather. Maybe to ingra-
tiate herself she'll hint that there's something romantic between us.
And Perry will think that a future theology professor certainly can't
have a scandalous wife. Unless he means to make his career by boast-
ing how he led me back to the straight and narrow.

Humbert the educator: worried because I'm not talking, and
the French conversation lessons do almost nothing for me, and
besides, this portion of the trip has been overcast, and you see
absolutely nothing of interest out the window, only the dirty colors
of a landscape without any light—anyway, because of all this he
decides to give me a course in culture. Wherever we go he takes me
to the local museum, no matter what it has on display (mammoth
bones, dried-flower collages, butter molds, the history of local battles
with the Indians, the Wright brothers' twelve seconds of flight at
Kitty Hawk), and then I have to write a short composition in a notebook on which he pasted a label saying "Travel Log."

"You can show it to your aunt when we go and visit her, so
she'll see everything you're learning." I wish he'd relax for a minute—
he's always agitated, as if someone were following us. So now I also
have to keep an official notebook, for the use of Mama Humbert.

"Should I keep notes on every blow job, every cunnilingus, and
every new position you teach me?"

"Don't be foolish, you know perfectly well what I mean." I
know perfectly well. On the first page of the journal I write a nice
little summary, from the day we left till today, of each state, with area,
towns, populations, characteristic plants and animals, motto, industrial
and agricultural products, and culinary traditions, all more or less

copied out of the atlas and various books that Humbert stuffed into the suitcases. He makes me write in the motel, then he makes me read it out loud while he's driving, and in the background he has on the classical music station, his favorite. Every so often he checks my spelling: "How did you spell Susquehanna?"

"S-u-s-q-u-e-h-a-double-n-a."

"Why is it called that?"

"From the name of the Indian tribe that lived beside it, boss."

"Did you write about the countryside, the course of the river, and the vegetation?"

"No, boss."

"You should, it's a good exercise."

"I don't want to write books, I want to be an actress, boss."

"If you learn to write well you'll be able to propose your own subjects."

"So what." We don't stay anywhere long enough to really observe people. The only character study possible is Humbert. I think I could play him with my eyes closed. Accent, walk, everything. We stop in Ligonier: it's the anniversary of the French defeat. Serves them right. It was raining, and people were wearing eighteenth-century soldiers' costumes. Humbert the pedant criticized the accents of the fake French soldiers. Musket smoke, cannon shots, in the end the French are crushed. Hurrah!

We head back to the ocean. The air is warm, outlines are clearer and colors are more intense, like temperas, but also dirty, like temperas on a rough surface. There are even palm trees. Long stretches of low-lands. Interminable straight roads with a white line in the middle. At a gas station I see a dog wearing sunglasses. The gas-station man explains that he's a terrible, lazy dog, he put the glasses on him two hours ago as a joke and the dog didn't even notice it. What a stupid man: the sun is beating down, of course the dog would rather have the sunglasses on, that's why he didn't take them off. He's a big terrier with a very intelligent face. I'd really love to have a dog to travel with—it would be so nice. I ask Humbert to get me one, but he says no, no, and no again: he hates animals. We go inside to get drinks from the vending machine, and when we come out the sky has become the color of wine. You can still see, but the gas-station man turns on the sign. And suddenly it's dark, and the dog slides the sunglasses off his nose with one paw: which shows that he is much smarter than his master.

The days seem long, even longer than usual. Maybe it's because they're getting shorter. Humbert is in bed with an attack of back pain. Immobilized. Reduced to impotence. I don't know what to do, so I go to the library across the street. I get a book on dinosaurs, sit down and put my feet up on the chair in front of me. I am so immersed in prehistory that I don't notice anything around me, until suddenly I feel a little tickle: it's a boy with red hair on the other side of the table, and he's grabbed one of my feet and is trying to take off my sock: "Hey, what do you think you're doing?"

"You want to have a Coke with me?" I get up and go with him to the drink machine.

"Where are you from?"

"From the North."

"What's your name?"

"Dolly. Yours?"

"Madison Cox. You like it here?"

"Very nice," I say just to be polite.

"I hate it. I'm leaving as soon as I can."

"What's wrong with it?"

"My house."

"Why?"

"Forget it." He glares at me. It's not my fault. "Do you like animals?"

"I love them. My father hates them, though, just like my mother."

"I'd get rid of all animals. What are you doing tonight?"

"Nothing, but . . . "

"Me neither." And he leaves. Completely idiotic.

In Goatscreek it must be winter, here it's like something got jammed. The sky can't jell, it seems too big and exhausted, drained by the summer heat; it dangles like an empty condom. It's not cold enough, it's not truly summer but it's not really fall, either, just something dragging on. The fields are dusty green. I'm dying to talk to someone, someone different. Yesterday, in Savannah, we stopped at an ice cream stand with stools that look like poisonous mushrooms. These two girls have ordered huge sundaes, with syrup, bananas, nuts, and all the rest. I sit down at their table.

"On vacation?" the one whose nose is covered with black spots asks me.

"Mmm . . . "

"Who's that?"

"My stepfather."

"Does he beat you?"

"No."

"Does he give you food?"

"Yes."

"So what sort of stepfather is he? Does he have other children?"

"No."

"And where's your mother?"

"She's dead."

"So why doesn't your stepfather get married again?" asks the one with braids. I put on an expression that I think should clarify the situation, but no, zero imagination, all they ask is if he gives me lots of presents and then they say enviously how lucky I am not to have homework.

"But I do have homework. I have to write essays on everything we see."

"Does he give you grades?" asks the one with the blackheads.

"No."

"See? Then you don't have to worry about flunking, and you can do whatever you like." Whatever I like! Meanwhile Humbert comes over to the table, and the idiot with the acne leans her chin on his shoulder and says, kittenish, "Will you take me on a trip, too?" Then silly laughs and challenging looks. Revolting. I don't know why, the whole thing gives Humbert the idea of grading me on my daily and nightly performances, and making purchases in proportion to grades. A horrible suspicion: Humbert misses his college, and I'm beginning to miss school. School? Me miss school? I can't believe it. But I miss something, and a lot.

In the morning a desire for movement seizes me. I *seem* to be going somewhere. I'm seeing new things. But then I think of past falls, when the days were getting shorter and we were practically numb with cold before Mom decided to turn on the heat. And now in the evening I realize that all we've done is get to another bed. And these motel beds are not very different from each other. We seem to be moving, but really it's always the same thing. We're not going to Florida, because Humbert doesn't want to run into the Greyhounds. Florida's not that small, but anyway Humbert is convinced that as soon as we get there we'll end up under the eyes of the fearful Greyhounds, which to me would not be at all unpleasant, because if Maud were around I'm sure the two of us could come up with some plan of rebellion, and finally I would get what I'm missing.

19.

I CUT A picture out of a Camel ad of Filthy Sue dressed like an Arab and pasted it on the car door on my side, to spite Mama Humbert. So when I want to imagine that I'm somewhere else I look at Filthy Sue in the turban with the cigarette in his hand and I have a little breathing room. I remember that there are other men in the world.

New Orleans is damp and moldy. The Mississippi is a river of coffee. Humbert says it's brown because of waste. We go to see the delta, part of the way in the car, walking the rest. People look at me, which makes Humbert intensely annoyed. I like feeling eyes on me. It keeps me warm. But Humbert gets in a rage. We stop to eat and the boy who serves my Abbott & Costello sits down at the table to tell me the story of the ants and the rats, which goes like this: the delta is full of anthills, and the ants reproduce excessively and threaten everything else, especially the muskrats. When there are too many ants, the muskrats die of fright because the ants go into their dens and eat them all up, leaving only the bones, cleaned sparkling white. Luckily, hurricanes come and destroy the anthills. But the ants are clever, and they don't all drown. When they feel a storm coming, they form a big ball, holding on to one another by their six legs, and this ball of ants floats for however long the hurricane lasts. Some ants are underneath and some are on top, out of the water, and they keep changing positions so that none are submerged the whole time. As soon as good weather returns, they land in a dry place, and this ball of ants holding on to one another by their six legs, like acrobats in the circus, comes apart, and the ants build a new anthill, and start multiplying again and threatening the muskrats. And so on, to infinity. It's a great relief to Mama Humbert when the ant boy is called back to the counter. He hates how much I enjoy these stories about the animals of the Mississippi delta and the struggles between fresh water and salt water. That boy is really cute, too, and as soon as Humbert feels the call of the toilet I go and ask him what he's doing in such an out-of-the-way place. He says he's working here because he studies hurricanes: he wants to write a book demonstrating that natural disasters for man are not always disasters for other species—mice, for example—and if men would stop thinking only of their own interests they would realize that everything that happens is not all good or all bad: it's good for one species and bad for another. He explains that you have to learn to imagine things with eyes different from man's, but at that point Humbert comes back and angrily drags me away: "You touched his watch as if to tell him that you would prefer to be with him."

"Yes. He had a lot of interesting ideas."

"The waiter?"

"He's a scientist—he's working as a waiter to make a living."

"And what is he studying?"

"Mice and ants, to show that natural disasters are not disasters for everyone, they're only relative." Humbert unfurls his cynical-contemptuous smile: "What is he, one of those Buddhists who are sprouting like mushrooms?" But when I ask him to explain what Buddhists are, not a word. It's always like that: when we stop somewhere, even just for ten minutes, people are interested in me, they tell me things, and I like to listen. But there's the usual Humbert bow-wow who frightens them off, and then they leave me alone. He never says anything interesting, or else he hauls me off, so I always get taken away in the middle of a story. He is sickeningly jealous. His jealousy makes me so angry I can't sleep. The other night I had a horrible attack, and I went out and was walking for a while under the trees drooling with moss, which in the light of the full moon looked like long beards. Suddenly I realized I wasn't alone. Someone was calling me. I turned. I didn't see anything. Then I heard the scratchy sound of a car engine behind me. I ran away, really frightened.

In *Life* there's a photographic essay about some dumb fourteen-year-old girl from Virginia who on safari in Africa killed an elephant, a lion, a rhinoceros, and a bunch of other animals all more beautiful and nicer than she is. She was with her father. They asked her what she was going to do with the elephant: stuff the head and use the paws as wastepaper baskets. She deserves to have that done to her.

In a hobby museum there's a picture of Humbert's father's hotel in the south of France, with the striped awning, and such a lot of blue sky. He has an attack of nostalgia for his lost childhood. He insists that I should feel moved, too. What's there to be moved by? He at least had a childhood to lose. I don't care in the slightest about his post-card childhood, a childhood as the hotel pet, spoiled by all the ladies, penniless émigrée countesses who were mad about him, and their husbands, the counts, who taught him to play chess, and a famous actress who was his first tennis teacher, cousins who came from Switzerland, and trips to the mountains. I don't care at all, it's just plain nothing to me, this childhood of his which gives him the right to look at me condescendingly because I am smaller and in my shred of life I've seen a hundred thousand billion times less than what he's seen. Revolting. A not too bad-looking guy in the museum is staring at me the whole time, and when we come out he follows us, at a safe distance, in his big black-and-chrome car. We stop for gas, and while Humbert's paying he walks by my window and drops a note in my lap: thank you very much, he gives me his phone number and if I want he'll carry me off, he's in love with my gray eyes and long legs and the fed-up faces I made "behind that clown's back," faces that touched him to the bottom of his heart. As if I could telephone when I want. Idiot. And anyway speeches that come from the bottom of the heart are not my favorite.

I'm beginning to like this city. It's the paradise of the blind. When I close my eyes I see better than with my eyes open. The smell of the river after rain swells the air and makes it all foamy, the smell of breath runs behind the voices, the smell of mud fills your nostrils with a phantom of earth. At night we leave the window open and hear so many voices and so much music, and with that confusion of smells and sounds from outside I no longer seem to be with Humbert but inside all those fragrant waves; I close my eyes and I'm transported far away. The only smell I don't smell is my own. I imagine I feel what blind people and dead people feel, scattered in the air and in the water, or in the clouds: there are big clouds in the sky, all on differ-ent planes, wide swollen waving clouds, and under these are clouds as big as prairies advancing on the city, which becomes a strip of houses crushed against the earth.

Humbert has decided to drive up the Mississippi. He gives me big lectures on the Frenchmen who traced the course of the river in the eighteenth century and were better than the English at dealing with the Indians. We see Tennessee again, Kentucky, Illinois. Cairo: completely flat, barges. No more smells, neither mountains nor sea. I feel like I'm dying inside. I have no desire for anything. There's something so oppressive as the days get shorter, and we spend hours and hours in the car going upstream in the dark. The river never ends, and Humbert wants to go all the way to Lake Itasca. It was better before: time had stopped, but at least there were strong smells everywhere and even dying was more like life than life. Here there's nothing. Only two drifters traveling against the current.

Lake Itasca, the end of the Mississippi. It's about time, after all that prairie and all that mud, and the boring house where Lincoln lived, in Springfield, after all those barrels of muddy water going the opposite way from us. The cold is terrific. It's snowing, and it seems like Christmas. I put on three sweaters and two pairs of socks. The lake is almost all frozen, but you have to be careful because in one place there's black water moving in concentric circles. And there, with that dark sucking, the river starts. Humbert finally shuts up. We sit looking for a while and then I tell him I saw a skating rink nearby and I want to go. You can't come with me, I say, threatening, because it's the time reserved for kids and you'd just be a pain. But he won't leave me completely on my own; he waits in the car and spies on me from there, especially after he sees me talking to some boys—three boys from Minneapolis, Bill, Joe, and Dick, who are spending the weekend at a friend's house. While we're skating together a stupid girl comes over who thinks she's a star: she's wearing microscopic red shorts, and all she does is clumsy turns, she has no style. We take off toward her and she falls, legs in the air. She's furious. Too bad for her, she's by herself and can't get even. The boys invite me to spend the afternoon at their place, they're having a party. But how can I manage it, I say, my father won't let me. What do you mean, they say. So I pretend he's crazy and I can't leave him alone. They insist on knowing what's wrong with him. It's a secret, I explain, and I can tell each of you separately, but you better not talk about it to each other. One by one I lead them behind the Coca-Cola stand, out of the binocular range of Humbert, and one by one I kiss them, which is what they wanted to do anyway. After that they stop asking about my father, they're in heaven. Well, what can you do, *c'est la vie*. Certainly if I were going to the party I wouldn't have had to kiss all three in such a hurry, but when time's pressing you have to take what you can. Because, at the end of my allotted hour of skating, I have to go back to my steady, who, since he couldn't fail to notice Bill, Joe, and Dick, is in a black rage. He claims that he has rights, too, and yet all he can do is ruin my life. He yells that I am not to see those dirty boys. But what if they're the sweetest boys in the world, I say. And they were, really; in fact they were kind of stupefied when I kissed them like that, all of a sudden. Yes, but they don't really know what my father is like, what I have to invent to keep him at bay.

The first information from the Bikinis has been published. To determine the effect of the bomb, they cut up living animals. I saw pictures of a goat, or rather of his flesh, with the dilated blood vessels. Goat No. 63, which is still alive but might prefer not to be. On the other hand, sow No. 311, the one that's famous for being saved swimming after the cruiser Sakawa sank, became sterile, which is an advantage since otherwise she might have produced dangerous offspring, populating the whole earth with enormous pigs who would eat men instead of acorns. An old man, sixty-six, who raped a girl of fourteen was imprisoned in San Quentin, but that is independent of the effect of the radiation. That was a plain old preatomic pig.

South again. Following the natural flow of the river. The year is almost over. A memorable year: the spell under which only men died in our house was broken. Certainly Humbert shows no sign of illness.

Missouri. Culture stop in Hannibal, visit to Mark Twain's house. Humbert assigns me a paper on the adventures of Tom Sawyer in relation to the places I've visited. I'd like to know why mothers don't act like mothers, lovers like lovers, and so on. I hate Humbert when he's teaching. He gets so pompous, and then so pedantic, it's worse than school. At least in school there's lots of us. Here it's an uninterrupted tête-à-tête with the professor. I miss having someone to badmouth him with, a friend to make fun of him with. I have to imitate Humbert in front of Humbert. And he doesn't even smile a little.

Arkansas. Humbert suddenly changes plans: we'll spend the winter in the desert. Deserts. America is the biggest and richest country in the world, and has an almost infinite number of deserts, Mama Humbert lectures from a book. I look at the map. Until now we were in the green zone, striped with blue rivers. Now we'll move into the light-brown area. After that we'll do the slightly darker brown. Then to the area that's the color of frozen earth, with white spots. To me the map is more fascinating than the reality. In reality you can't understand where you are. Who can say why Humbert suddenly decided not to go to the end of the river. Weren't we supposed to see it from beginning to end, I ask him, and he says we've already been to the end and he's not interested in going back.

"But I'd like to see the spot where it mixes with the sea."

"You've already seen it."

"I want to see it in order, after the source."

"There's no reason to see the mouth after seeing the source." He must be afraid of running into the guy with the ants. So we head west. Mississippi interruptus. We've interrupted the only river in the world with four "i"s, four "s"s and two "p"s. We've cut off its head. On the map the Mississippi is like an enormous tree that grows out of the Gulf of Mexico, with the crown branching out in all directions. But you can also see it as the opposite: an upended tree, all leafy, as in summer, with branches that go down to the ground and roots that go up to where it starts, up, up, up to where it swallows the other rivers, up to the mouths of these poor rivers destined to be devoured by another.

The desert isn't what I expected: it isn't brown, the way it is on the map. The ground is white, and sometimes there are denser patches of a pale color. A huge abandoned cemetery that spits up bone dust. Bone dust, shell dust, salt dust left by the retreating sea. An expanse of limestone. Grandma could cure her osteoporosis here, get down on all fours and lick the ground. We come to a valley that has a strange smell, like rotten eggs, a changing, undefinable odor. It's a valley without edges, you can't really see where earth and sky touch, and the sky is the same color as my faded jeans. We get to the Sangre de Cristo Mountains, and go down again into the valley. A floury sand runs over us, and when the wind dies down it falls on the ground like flakes of sunburned skin. Lower down there's grass, in scattered tufts, like the hair under your arms.

Then we go north. Hard work: the sky is blue, the sun is an enormous bright round torch, and at sunset it's like entering a tunnel of glass that goes straight down. The colors don't look the way they should: we're outside the orbit of the earth, and the sun is the color of fire because it's made of fire, the sky is reddish blue because there is nothing but layer upon layer of air, window upon window. The names are all foreign because we're no longer in the United States of America, we're in the Kingdom of Heaven, and the places are all God's places. And that's where we're going, literally: to the city of Los Angeles, on the edge of the Pacific Ocean, which is paradise. If I put the map with Goatscreek below, it all becomes clear: the real earth, with the normal colors of earth, is the one at the bottom, with normal seasons and the colors sort of dirty, like faded, worn-out objects. Then come these places where we've just been, before the Mississippi, with that very deliberate, motionless atmosphere, where it seems like all the wheels, of the brain, of time, are stopped. And then the place that's white with pulverized bones and evaporated seas, and after that is the blood of Christ, Death Valley, and finally the angels

. . . the flight of the angels . . . and at the very top, above everything, the Pacific, which is made of condensed air, and so it's paradise, because condensed air is like water, and everything in it can fly, even creatures without wings: everyone becomes an angel in the condensed air of the Pacific, which is way above everything, and so it takes more time to get there. My father must have come to live here. In heaven, Plasticmom would have said. But with the map in the right position I can see that he ended up around here; maybe we'll meet him. "Hey you, take this and this and this for murdering Isabel," he'll say to Humbert, and he'll take the beating without protest. Or: "Bravo, my friend, that was a good deed you did getting rid of our wife: now let's go on together." Dear Daddy who art in heaven, maybe the first version is better: so you and I can go on together, without Mama Humbert, and if you are too ethereal to hold on to the steering wheel, I can drive the car: by now I should know how, I haven't looked at anything else for months.

Today Humbert outdid himself. I wanted to have coffee in bed. First do your duty, he orders me. Maybe if I considered it my right and Humbert's duty I'd start having fun? I hate repetitions on a theme.

I wake up before Humbert, and go out for a walk. Absolutely forbidden, but who cares? Since death doesn't exist anyway. It was invented to frighten us, but in reality all you have to do is turn over the map, and here it is, the country of the dead—you can get here easily by car. The desert is so beautiful at dawn it seems worth the trouble of getting here. It's freezing cold, and the sand is rough, like sandpaper, and you can see the prints of animals that passed by in the night. As soon as the sun comes out the sand warms up and a wind rises, sweeping away every trace of nocturnal life. The desert is only alive at night; during the day, when the false living are there, the true life hides.

New Year's in the desert. Birthday in the desert. My first desert birthday. The fourth leap year of my life: 1936, 1940, 1944, 1948. Humbert says now that I've completed four leap years, which corresponds to an age between thirteen and sixteen normal years, I'm the right age to be with him—he is ten leap years old, only six more than me. He does acrobatics on this theme, to soothe his conscience. I no longer remember what I did on my last birthday. The guy who rented us the cabin hears Humbert singing "Happy Birthday" to me, and he comes to the door and says: "What are you, a horse, counting your age on January 1st?" He hadn't opened his mouth before and didn't again. Only a little smile when I say I'm not a horse but a Capricorn. Oh no. Pathetic present from Mama Humbert: *The Little Mermaid* in a deluxe edition. This kind of goop would have been more successful with the widow Maze. He should have given me Bluebeard, it would be more appropriate. I tell him I've already read it.

"But look at the illustrations, they're lovely."

"I've seen them."

"Do you like the story of the little mermaid?"

"I like the moral."

"What's that?"

"Never save a man."

20.

THIRTEEN IS ALREADY an advanced age. If all goes well, soon I won't be interesting to him anymore. I wonder if he'll try to eliminate me, too, or if he'll find it more convenient to keep me so I can bring home the younger sisters of my school-friends. There will be a home, sooner or later. Meanwhile, if I'm going to play the part of the private, domesticated little mermaid well, he ought to get me some better clothes. I'd like a long skirt with a layered petticoat and fringe that rustles like snakes when I walk: *hiss! hisssss! shshshshshshshsh!* I'm desperate to have one. Mama Humbert promises to buy me everything I want as soon as we're in a place that has really cool stuff. Which means not tomorrow, since we're spending the winter here.

So many things move in the desert: the wind blows the sand and the grass, which can grow anywhere, because it doesn't have roots; it nestles in the shelter of the dunes, which have such short lives, swept away by the first contrary wind. Because there's no shelter, the earth has been scraped away like flesh from bone. A strong gust and the soil vanishes; the rocks and the sand remain in so many little boomerang-shaped curves, but these go, too, at the first breath of wind, and the rock that was underneath remains, polished like wax. When there's a storm the air is a tumult of amaranth and scrub that pricks like barbed wire.

Some people really are lucky. I am where I am, whereas the Oppenheimer children go for a walk on Sunday with Dad and Mom and find so many of these four-leaf clovers that Mrs. Oppenheimer makes the children eat them immediately so there aren't too many in the house. Not a bad diet. Maybe the hen wasn't completely wrong in wanting me to make atomic bombs. But I don't like that Oppenheimer: he's perched at his lectern like a vulture, and with that angular face he looks like a devil. Dolores Maze of the future who will read these pages: you've never found a single four-leaf clover, at least until now, but whether your life has been richer or not, remember to compare it to the lives of others your age, and consider: not bad, not bad for a thirteen-year-old.

Morbid gray hills, with the endless gray highway like a pinpoint on the wax tablet of the hills. It's an infinite gray; every so often gusts of wind and trash attack us, and you can't figure out where it comes from because you haven't seen anything for miles. In the middle of these fleshless rocks it's strange to touch bones clothed in flesh. I run a finger over Humbert's ribs, he's lying so his stomach's in, and I caress the depression that goes from his breastbone to his belly button, touching scrublike hairs: there's always too much for these places where everything should be fleshless, and on him I should feel only waxy-smooth bones, and his breath should be like the wind spiraling with grains of sand—there's nothing else around here. Sand, wind, and thorns. Sex in the desert is different from when you're in places full of people, body heat is hotter here, and when you take a bath it's like feeling a rush of blood that immediately evaporates it's so dry: you have to keep it gushing, because it's like there's a brushpile of twigs inside scraping and scratching against your stomach.

Out in the civilized world they are inventing millions of things that my father already invented. Except that he had to do it secretly because there was the war and people were only supposed to think about that, and concentrate on things that would help win it, like the bomb. My dad had invented a cool thing, a magnetic mixer: you put a piece of iron in a pan, and on top, instead of the cover, you put an electric wheel with a magnet attached, so when the wheel turned, whatever was cooking in the pot also turned. Sauces could be stirred long distance, as if by magic. But he didn't have time to patent anything, and now no one will ever be grateful to him. I tried to explain to Humbert how the magnetic mixer works, but he laughed contemptuously, like the one-dimensional literary snob he is. He's always acting superior, so I make him read the story of an American journalist who went to Europe to see why it took them so long to recover from the war. In Paris he had to wash in an enamel basin because there was no bathtub. There wasn't even hot water: "In your snotty Paris you have to wash in a basin of cold water." He doesn't react, M. Guibert. He's always so fussy about our bathrooms, he complains about the plastic shower hoses, but where he was it's even worse.

"In my father's hotel there were fabulous bathrooms." An ostentatious sigh of regret follows. His father's hotel!!! Ever since we went to that hobby museum all he does is mourn the hotel of his dear father and some little bastard named Annabel who was his first great love. Bleah!

·   ·   ·

Dawn in the desert is so short that it's hardly worth getting up for. It only makes you sorry. It's incredibly beautiful, but you never have time to take it in. I try to see it just the same, even for a second, because the world at dawn is fantastic, and even if you get mad that you can't look at it as long as you want, you might give up hope altogether if you missed all that pink and gold before the day's oppressive whiteness begins. In this skeletonlike part of the planet everything changes quickly because there's no earth to restrain it: in other places, normal ones like Goatscreek, the world is alive, it has its seasons, grass, trees, earth, flesh, skin, blood, and lungs. Here it's only a skeleton. The rocks are hard as bones, the color of bones, and there's a sort of glaze on them that has the neutral taste of time if you lick it. The desert has a strange effect on the widower Maze: his eyes seem sunk into his face in this dry air, and there's something lugubrious about him. I don't like his expression when he's on top of me, I don't like it when he suddenly turns on the light to see if I come. He studies me, making my eyes burn in the lamplight. I hate his nervous gaze. How can I come with him watching me. I tell him he's hurting me staring like that; but he doesn't care, he goes on staring, paralyzing me with his greedy eyes. He's on top of me muttering stuff that doesn't make sense, in an obscene ecstasy.

There's no grass in Arizona. Only scrub, ugly, formless, prickly.

Professor Guibert explains that it's called Arizona because there's no water.

"You could get in an airplane and throw ice cubes in the clouds, so instead of making water over the ocean the clouds would let rain fall where it's needed," I tell him.

"Don't make up stories."

"I'm not making it up, I read it: it's a system called seeding the clouds."

"And what are they seeded with?"

"With seeds of rain, or cubes of dry ice thrown out of a flying plane. But you have to be careful to get out of the seeded cloud quickly, otherwise you'll find yourself in the middle of a snowstorm, and a small plane might not make it."

"You should read fewer comics and more serious books." What an idiot. I read this in the newspaper, not a comic book. He's the one who doesn't keep himself informed. His sphere of interest is becoming more and more narrow. So narrow that even the idea of going to see Nora seems unimaginable to him. I have never been so close to Los Angeles and so far from home. I open the glove compartment of the car and behind a rag for cleaning the windowshield I find a pistol with the initials G.M. on the butt. Priceless, Mama Humbert: travels in my mother's blue sedan and carries my father's pistol. Has he decided to become the distilled essence of my dear dead parents?

Here in Arizona the cactuses are so tall they're scary. They can be thirty-five feet tall, as tall as a building, and it's scary to pass close to them when the wind's blowing—it would be no fun if they blew over. These saguaro are stupid trees: their height isn't good for anything—they're too thorny to climb, and they don't even make shade. But from a distance they're pretty.

Mama Humbert makes the grand concession of letting me go horseback riding with a nice girl called Maria. She's never been anywhere and has no desire to go. Humbert doesn't mind if I talk to her because he thinks she's dumb, he thinks she's a retard. I don't think so, it's only that she speaks Spanish better than English, and she taught me a lot of cool swear words that I'd never heard: *cagadero*, which means toilet; *chiquitero*, which means someone who likes to screw women from behind; *pendejo*, pubic hair but also someone stupid. We decide to baptize my dear father: Umberto the Big Pendejo, which fits him perfectly. When we get back we call him that, but he doesn't get it; he smiles like the big incurable pendejo that he is. He thinks it's a compliment. That "big" appeals to him so much that later he interrupts us playing tennis to say we're playing badly, in the sense that we're not scoring points. So what, we're having fun, but for him that's irrelevant. He's critical because Maria doesn't hit anything, but I don't mind winning that way, even though in general I don't care if I win or lose, and I was having fun hitting one ball after another without missing a single one. It's exhilarating to hit them all, playing them randomly, but Umberto the Big Pendejo shows up right at the best part and makes us start all over again. *Cinga a tu madre*, I shout at him, stick your head in the *cagadero*, you're nothing but a *chiquitero*, you big *pendejo* . . . then maybe he understood that it wasn't exactly a compliment.

Studying the map I find the Chocolate Mountains.

"Excellent, if those mountains are really chocolate, maybe they'll taste good. Maybe afterward we'll find a river of Coca-Cola." How clever he is. We end up arguing for at least four hours on this absurd question of whether America is true or false. I don't even know how we got started. The fact is, I look up and suddenly see that the desert has ended, and I'm so exhausted I'm hoarse. We stop for something to drink. I sit on a wall with Mama Humbert, somewhere behind us are the Chocolate Mountains, which I will never taste, and my hair is mussed by a fresh breeze. The air blows differently here, no more desert gusts that arise mysteriously out of nowhere and disappear for no reason. This is the breath of the great Pacific Ocean, which I am about to see because it's still alive and no one has transformed it yet into a bowl of water the color of pee.

I've touched the other edge and seen the other ocean. First, from a distance, it's like a more luminous piece of sky, lit from below, with the outlines of rocks drawn in silver, and then, as we round a curve, comes the blue of the sea. Mama Humbert parks; I run out on the sand, among the rocks. Inside me warm tears rise, because suddenly I feel so tired, with all those miles of road behind me, all those days of arguments, petty disputes, blackmail. Now that I have before me a beach with long lines of foamy waves and seagulls squawking, my eyes fill with tears, and they dig hot furrows inside me. I'm bursting with love for the sea, I want to detach myself from everything that ties me to land, Mama Humbert, the blue sedan, the run-over hen, the two fried Nelsons, my father sniffed up by God—it's all totally insignificant beside the sea. I sit on a rock and close my eyes to engrave in my mind the foamy layered pastry of the waves, that ocean of condensed air that seems like water, where everyone can fly with the angels; it's so peaceful I seem already to be part of that world of water, air, and fine earth of fine sand, world of tears and streams of sorrow and peace all at once. Then pathetic Humbert arrives, and says something incredibly stupid, I don't even remember what. He sits beside me and I feel tremendously depressed; yet somehow with those waves before me depression is transformed into a promise of good to come, of infinite patience and expectation, a gentle erosion until everything is smoothed out by the ocean's caress, every memory will lose its thorns, and Humbert Guibert will be forgotten.

We missed the the gray whales. We would have had to rush here, instead of letting ourselves be hypnotized by the desert and all its weirdness. The whales passed by around Christmas. They migrate south from the Arctic; they're underwater but every so often they come up to breathe, three times in a row, and since it's cold the air comes out of their lungs like smoke. It's a huge amount of air—it would take more than a thousand men to breathe out so much air. On a boat you can follow closely enough to see that the reason they're gray is that little craterlike shells are encrusted on their skin, which otherwise would be smooth and dark. The older the whale, the more densely covered it is with these little craters, becoming an all-white Moby Dick. It must be wonderful to live underwater and come out only now and again for air, to make love underwater, give birth underwater, and have a baby whale to nurse underwater. It must be wonderful to be as big as a whale and be protected by the ocean, which is even bigger, and not be seen by anyone; to be suspended, swimming, and never feel anything solid but the mouth of the baby whale and the stomach of the male whale when you're making love, nothing else, because there's no one bigger in the whole sea that can bother you.

North. I call Nora from a phone on a street with huge, tall palm trees to tell her we're here, but some woman with an incomprehensible accent answers, and says Nora is away working, and she doesn't know when she's coming back. Mama Humbert smiles with satisfaction at escaping the confrontation. I am furious. As a consolation (for himself) Humbert arranges tennis lessons for me with a former champion, Ned, a nice man who turns out to be a much better teacher than Humbert. I have to say that thanks to him I've finally learned all those tricks of drives, volleys, dropshots, passing shots, baseline strokes, smashes, cut serves, and scoring. Which are very simple things—you just have to know how to explain them and not have a fit if someone doesn't understand them right away. Mama Humbert, of course, is present at every lesson and wants to have his say. It's not bad here. The motel is just a step from the ocean and we take long walks along the water. There's almost no one here, only occasional drifters like us who have come to be consoled by the sea. It's very peaceful, except suddenly one day there's a big uproar, and we find ourselves right in the middle of an absurd race: hundreds of women running through the park, each with an egg on a spoon, climbing over picnic tables and benches. The one who gets to the finish line first without dropping the egg wins.

Mama Humbert has had a seizure of chicness: we go to Bel Air, and he takes me to Rodeo Drive to buy me all the rustling dresses he promised, plus a whole new tennis outfit, and today, to make up for all those tennis things I learned without him, he taught me the Continental method of picking up the ball: you trap it between your foot and the racquet. Mama Humbert also spruces up his own wardrobe, he got a swell polka-dot bow tie, a cream-colored jacket with tiny blue stripes, and cream-colored pants. It's nice here, you can sunbathe at the pool and drink cocktails at the hotel bar; everyone looks at me with great interest, and there're a lot of incredibly rich people. Too bad Mama Humbert has already informed me that we can't stay more than two nights. What a pain. I wouldn't mind waiting here for Nora, but he says forget it.

Humbert is extremely unhappy with our arrangements: he hadn't anticipated the infinite entertainment possibilities here, with all these shady streets and tropical plants and people so beautiful they take your breath away. I've had some success on the tennis court—I don't really win that much but everyone admires my style. Yesterday a guy with a red beard came up and asked if he could put me in a film with a mute tennis player whose movements are like a celestial melody, and because of that she's killed by someone who's not as successful. He says I'm perfect for it. Result: Humbert decides to pack up and flee this horrendous city where they can snatch his precious nymphet like nothing. He bursts into a vulgar, revolting invective against the falsest city in the falsest country in the world: "Everyone comes here hoping to make it in the movies; even the policemen, even the milkmen are aspiring actors."

"Does it bother you so much that they're good-looking?"

"No, I'm only trying to make you realize that they're all failures."

"Why failures?"

"Because they didn't get what they wanted."

"What about you, did you get what you wanted?"

Satisfaction on the face of Mama Humbert. You could say that he has achieved exactly what he wanted. Terrific, really terrific.

"But they're as good-looking as actors."

"And that's the trouble: they're as good-looking as someone else, but as themselves they're nothing."

"You're just jealous because they're taller and have a better tan than you and mainly they're younger." But Humbert pays no attention and keeps his perfectly satisfied expression. He doesn't consider himself a failure—he's managed to get a sex slave for himself, which is not for everyone, I hope.

I thought that finally I would get to see a movie studio. The usual bust. Smug look from Mama Humbert when I do what he wants, but then he doesn't keep his promises: the excuse this time is that the tickets are all gone. Next time he'll pay first. I trust myself but not him. In the end, as if following a script, we leave Los Angeles and all its waving palm trees, without having seen anything, not even the footprints at the Chinese Theatre. I wanted to stay here by myself: even if we're together I don't see why we have to stay so attached to each other.

"By yourself? What would you use for money?"

"There's the money from my inheritance."

"I am the executor. Remember that you're a minor. And not only a minor, but consenting. There would be no extenuating circumstances for you."

Extenuating for what? Who are all these people showing up to tell me what I can do? Why should I need extenuating circumstances?

"What's all this about my being consenting?" I ask for explanations: it annoys me that I can't stay in Los Angeles. Not to be the mute tennis player in that bearded guy's movie, not even to have seen the studios, like any other tourist.

"If you didn't like it you could always run away and go to the police. If you really didn't want to, you wouldn't stay with me all night." What does that have to do with it? You have to stay in shape. At camp, there was Roger, now there's him. But he can't say that I consent to everything. He can't say that I consent to become a vegetable. Yes, I could run away. But then what? Maybe Mama Humbert is right.

You could die of cold, here in Death Valley. The names are not exactly inviting: Desolation Mountains, Canyon of Hunger, Funeral

Peak, Bad Water . . . It's all logical: before the Pacific, which is the place of the angels, there has to be a stretch of hell, and it makes sense that hell is below sea level, and has all these nasty places around it, although I must say that they are not as dangerous as they sound: people searching for gold made up the names to keep other people away. The fact remains that Death Valley is the ideal vacation place for a cactus.

The Grand Canyon tricks you in the sense that you don't see it until you're practically on top of it, and then the effect is fantastic, because it opens up without warning in the rock, which is all different-colored stripes, a stone rainbow. We descend by mule. Humbert insists on using the reins like a steering wheel, he can't admit that the mules know the way better than someone who was born in Paris. The river at the bottom is still excavating, a continuous hydraulic file. Sooner or later it will reach the center of the earth. If it passes the center, the earth will break in two like an apricot. The rocks are every color, every single one: light brown, gray, delicate greens and pinks, opaque reds, chocolate brown, slate-colored. As the river digs down, new ones appear, which no one has ever seen because they were buried in the earth before the river dug them out. We stay overnight in a cabin on the South Rim. We leave the next day, and at the gas station a poor crazy man comes over, shouting about God. He wants my bottle of Coke, and I give it to him, since God has forgotten to provide one for him.

"What an idiot," Humbert bursts out. "So who created God?"

"Humbert, who created you?"

"My father and mother."

"And your father, who created him?"

"His father and mother."

"And your mother?"

"Her father and mother."

"And their fathers and mothers?"

"That's enough, obviously their fathers and mothers."

"And all the fathers and mothers of all the fathers and mothers of all the fathers and mothers?"

"Apes."

"And the apes?"

"The apes were born from the first fish that came on land."

"And the first fish?"

"Before the fish there were amoebas."

"And who created the amoebas?"

"Leave me alone, Lo."

"Wouldn't it be nice if this was enough to prove that even you don't exist, Humbert?"

21.

I FEEL A hole inside me, a suction, from all this zigzagging back and forth. Also it's cold, and the occasional burst of warmth doesn't last. Nothing holds anything around here: there's not enough earth to hold the water, and the warmth comes and goes in a flash. I stole a pack of Camels, and I go out on the terrace and smoke. God what a relief to throw my head back and feel this consoling thought pass through me: fuck fuck fuck. Fuck the whole world and especially Mama Humbert.

Last night I dreamed that I was traveling not in the Western desert but in our old kitchen in Goatscreek, with a very tiny Humbert driving a very tiny sedan, among the blue ceramic cups and the breakfast plates and the toaster, and while we were walking in a big lake of sand the color of oatmeal we felt a shadow on us, but it wasn't a cloud, it was the hen's spoon, and she was about to eat us along with the cornflakes . . . Look, here I am among hills the color of toast and brass mountains and a varnished blue sky, in a kind of giant-size kitchen, so it makes sense that it's all desert and that there's no water: there wasn't any in the kitchen except from the tap at the sink. It was all polished and shiny, just like the rocks here, and the colors were all the same—china, the linoleum, formica, and colored glass.

Everything can become a fossil, even water. You walk and walk, until you see a cloud, and under it some black poplars, then creosote bushes twisted like stiff tongues of fire, and yucca palms, something halfway between pineapples and the blades of kids' scissors, standing around a puddle the color of pearls which hasn't frozen but is about to: it's water that rained down more than twelve thousand years ago, penetrating deep into the earth, and now it gushes from a subterranean spring, but it's fossil water because for all this time it stood still, separated from all the other water in the world, and so it's not even real water anymore, water like all the other water, but the fossil of water that was alive twelve thousand years ago. Until it's used up, there will be a little fossil oasis here. I didn't drink it because there could be all sorts of microbes in it, germs of diseases from thousands and thousands of years ago.

Sermon from Mama Humbert because I am capricious, I am never content: any other girl in my situation would be happy to skip a year of school and go on a wonderful trip. To put me in my place he explains that I am only the facsimile of a marvelous creature he loved when he was small. Annabel, as usual? I ask him, ha-ha, but then I really get mad. I'm jealous, though I don't know of what, exactly, and it's a raving, crazy jealousy: because it's not right for him to love me only for what I remind him of rather than for myself. He likes to put me down like this, but now, thinking it over again, I don't care whether he loves me or not. He's a fossil, too, because he's had the same petrified desire for years—he can never come up with a new idea. He is just nuts, and his craziness is this fossilized desire of his that has nothing at all to do with me. It's something totally different from the living desires of all other living people, it's a desire that has lost touch with every other desire in the world. A relic of desire. And whether he loves me or not, who gives a shit, and anyway can a fossil love?

The radio is broken and Humbert is even quieter than me. The desert has a strange effect on him. At least if he picked up hitchhikers we'd have someone to talk to. He never does, not since we ran into one who looked like Teddy Glass. For a moment I imagined that it really was him and that I had finally succeeded in meeting him on his hitchhiking trip. After he got out and I realized that I would never ever ever meet him, that we were lost to each other forever, I burst into tears and couldn't stop.

Incredible: a guy we meet at a gas station told me that even rocks decay when they get really old, like the Precambrian granite around here, which is more than five hundred and seventy million years old, or rather between five hundred and seventy million and a distant point in time that is called infinite. These rocks are the oldest things to be found in the world: no one knows what there was before them, maybe nothing, apart from God, who doesn't count, though, because you can't touch him or see him or hear him, and so he's not much different from nothing. They are the most skeletal skeleton in the world, these rocks, earth's oldest bones. Old rusty bones, dark red, which decompose into a kind of gravel, made of little cubes. And so even the earth began to suffer from osteoporosis, and after a while— at some point between now and infinity in relation to when these rocks were born—there will be death. The earth will breathe its last breath, its skeleton, a single round bone of rock, will break into splinters of rust, and everything on earth will break down, crumble and disappear like the dust of dead mushrooms.

Mama Humbert gets mad when I have conversations with tramps, drifters, people in gas stations. They're all crazy, he says; in these places where there's nothing, where anything can come into your mind, people's heads fill up with nonsense. Drifters. What's so despicable? We're drifters ourselves. Humbert isn't really a drifter, because a drifter is someone who is looking for something, while he will never be anything because all he needs is to get between my legs, spout off a little French poetry, turn up his nose at a hamburger and a Coke. He doesn't know anything about life. He doesn't want to. He wants to break me down and that's all. Satisfy his fossil desire, get back in the car, and satisfy that fossil again, which has nothing to with me and maybe not even with him. With the him of now. As if I could possibly care if I'm stuck by his side. If only he knew how far away I am when I seem close to him. I could even come to feel that heat inside and that hunger that makes me writhe. Then I close my eyes so I don't have to see where I am, so I can imagine where I'll be soon, although it's hard, it gets harder and harder, waiting for this time to pass, this time that theoretically I wouldn't want to waste, but that in fact I'm throwing away as fast as I can because it's time that was stolen from me, and if I treated it as something precious and dear to me all that would happen is that more would be stolen, and Humbert would take all of my time for himself, even the time that he hasn't managed to steal yet, the wonderful time when he won't be around anymore.

With Humbert by my side it's like I'm a great actress. He doesn't have the slightest idea of what I feel. He feels desire, he satisfies the desire, he rests from the desire, the desire returns. Between one desire and the next he drives, he eats, he takes me from one point in the desert to the next, with the expression of a martyr he buys me what he has to buy me to keep me behaving. He got me a dress with the Dior New Look, but the $8.95 version, the cheapest of all, because the real one, the one in all the newspapers, costs forty dollars, and at least in one thing Mama Humbert is precisely identical to Madame the Hen, in his incredible stinginess.

Fossil shit. We were in a place full of fossil shit. Big shit: it's called Bechan, to be exact. It's shit from a mammoth from I don't know how many thousands of years ago. The creatures all went to the bathroom in this cave, and the shit just sat there, layer upon layer. The shitters are all dead, but first they stuffed the cave with their shit. The creatures die, but their shit lasts century upon century, into eternity.

Mama Humbert catches me smoking, gets mad, throws away my cigarettes, even slaps me.

"I detest women who smoke."

"So why'd you marry one?"

"Because when you detest a woman the only thing to do is marry her." What a wit! One night I dreamed that I was trying to tell him what I thought of him, but I didn't have enough breath, the words stuck in my throat, and I choked. Just like when I used to dream about Plasticmom: Whore, I yelled at her, you whore, but since I could never say it loud enough I'd wake up with the sensation of suffocating. Because I'm always suffocating, whether awake or dreaming, because a person who is an orphan and a minor is a person the law has decided not to protect. You could say that in order to be protected by the law you have to be strong already, autonomous, and know exactly who to turn to. If I hadn't decided to be an actress when I grow up I would be a politician and get the Constitution changed so that minors would be citizens of the United States; in fact I would completely abolish the concept of minor. There was a war to abolish slavery for adult black people, but who will wage the war to abolish slavery for children?

There is no escape, none, and it's lucky that there are toilets, because at least there you can be left in peace. I now understand why God created shit and pee: to give even the desperate like me the possibility of refuge. If shit and pee and *cagaderos* that can be closed with a latch didn't exist, I wouldn't be able to write a line for myself. Only my assignments in Humbert's travel log. The journal to show to everybody when we settle down somewhere. The journal to show

Nora when finally she condescends to be found. The journal to show next year when I go to school. The book that will serve as Humbert's defense.

Gandhi was murdered. He was interviewed when he felt that he was about to die, in the sense that it no longer mattered to him whether he lived to be a hundred and twenty-five, as he easily might have. That would be almost to the end of the century, 1994, to be exact, the year when, assuming I don't croak first, I will be fifty-nine, which would make the right difference in age for us to get married. Gandhi said that he didn't care about living to such an old age because he saw no light, he'd lost all hope because of the terrible things that were happening, and the only possible action against the atomic bomb was prayer. When he was asked how he would react if he saw a bomber taking aim at him, he said this: "I would come into the open and show the pilot that I am not turning to him the face of malice. From that height the pilot wouldn't see my face, but he would feel the overwhelming desire of my heart asking him not to hurt me, and then his eyes would be opened. If all those who were killed in Hiroshima by the bombs had died in this state of active prayer, the war would not have ended in such a terrible way. Now the question is whether the winners are indeed the winners or, rather, the victims. The world is not at peace. It is even more frightening than before." Gandhi died because he was no longer interested in living, so he let himself be murdered. He didn't address any prayer to the hearts of the men who were killing him; he didn't oppose them, because he had nothing against them, and maybe he even encouraged them. He is immortal just the same, because they burned his body on an enormous funeral pyre made of twelve hundred pounds of sandalwood, three hundred and twenty of a special butter called ghee, a hundred and sixty of incense, and thirty of camphor. Afterward his followers each carried away a handful of ashes. Holy ashes.

We continue north through the Rocky Mountains. What a stupid idea, to call mountains rocky. Rocky Mountains is as stupid as saying Wet Lake, Sandy Beach, Cavernous Cave, Earthly Earth.

Shit, shit, shit. I saw the Glass family, all four of them, including Ted, who must have come back from his hitchhiking trip. They were admiring the view at Dillon. And I was a retard. Instead of finding an excuse to stop, that I had to go, that I was carsick, that I wanted to see the tops of the mountains, I don't know, anything, I was seized by this sudden absurd happiness at seeing Ted, and so like a first-rate simpleton I said, "Look, it's the Glass family, stop, please please pretty please . . . " It goes without saying that Humbert accelerated. Depressing; I felt a cramp in my stomach, an enormous lump in my throat. To find Ted right there, to go by and say nothing, not a word—it's like being muzzled, unable to cry for help. If he'd heard me, surely he would have found a way to save me from Humbert, even at the cost of marrying me: I know he's always dreamed of it, and if he hasn't said so it's because he's shy. Well, anyway, it will never happen. I saw him behind me, and if only he'd turned and seen me at that moment, my life would have been completely different from then on, and maybe even before that, because if the purpose of everything that had happened up to now had been to find Ted, then even all that had been bad before would suddenly become wonderful, perfect, totally perfect.

22.

ALL WE DO is look at big trees. The ones we saw today were two hundred and seventy feet high and twenty-seven feet around, and if they were hollowed out you could live there. Some are real old: four thousand years. Which makes a thousand leap years. I can't stand any more of these pilgrimages to see weird things. I couldn't care less about a plant four millenniums old. I don't see why it should matter to me. Since I will never live a thousand leap years. In theory, yes, I'm accumulating impressions. But the fact is that I don't feel anything anymore. I see so many things, one after another. I am becoming a kind of illustrated catalogue of the United States of America. I am a good girl who does her homework, who writes down everything she sees, hoping that it will be useful to the Dolores Maze of the future who will read these pages. But the Dolores Maze of now, of this exact instant, of this whole interminable series of instants, no longer feels anything. No, it's not that she doesn't feel anything: the Dolores Maze of now has a strange little pain in her wrists. A very strange sort of pain. Something that I would like to scratch away with razor strokes.

A short stay in Central City. We are in a small hotel in the town, triple-strength controls to make sure I don't talk to people too much. After a few days of this rest, and after a morning when I let him do whatever he wants, I have permission to go to the library across the street with an ugly kid named Mary. We find two snot-nosed students—how about a little diversion, I say to myself. Too bad they've got pimples, I've always had a fear of pimples. Anyway, I work out a plan. I start a conversation, one thing leads to another, it's clear that they're totally interested, so I tell them that if they pay some attention to Mary first, who is ugly and full of complexes and needs a hand, they can hang out with me afterward. They immediately act like idiots with Mary. She's kind of afraid but also flattered. They're all the same, in the end, girls without experience. I decide: waste of time. That's enough, I tell her, follow me. I drag them all hopeful and daring back to the hotel and there's Humbert, looking nasty, and he makes the two pimply guys take off. For once his despicable jealousy was useful.

We go back to the Pacific, and in the afternoon we take a walk on a foggy beach and find a little cave, near some stupid Girl Scouts, who are shouting, all excited by the waves. In the grip of his usual obsession, Humbert commands me to take off my clothes. It's cold, I say, and it's dirty, the sand sticks to me, it's all so bleak, but he insists. O.K., I say, but you'll pay for this, I mean you'll pay me and pay me well. He pushes me against the wall, not to actually make love, but he touches my legs, between my legs, he wants me to touch the corners of his mouth and nothing else. Shiver again, he tells me, I like it when you shiver. He makes me sit on an outcropping of rock in the cave, then moves away to get a better look at me. He comes back and licks my knees, cleans the sand off my feet, sucks my toes one by one, while close by the Scouts are still shouting. How come you're not afraid they'll see you, I ask, and he says, Did you know that only a few months later Annabel died of typhus, and you have goose bumps, and none of this makes sense. No, it doesn't make sense, I say, have you finally realized that? It's absurd to be in this cave with only fog outside, and you don't want me and no one wants anyone. What's this, I say, the grotto of truth? This, no, what truth, he goes, frightened. No truth at all, I say, only this gray sea has made me melancholy. Let's go back to the hotel. While I get dressed wondering what the hell is this typhus business that came into his mind out of nowhere, and thinking he must be even more nuts, he mutters some nonsense in French, but in the hotel he calms down and talks again about Annabel, and how he never saw her again after that time. Poor Humbert. Annabel is dead, but he's dead, too, and has been for a while, too, him and his evasive eyes. But the one who's in the most trouble is me, because later when I open my purse I find it empty.

It doesn't seem right that it's practically summer and I haven't been to school. My wheel of time has lost a spoke. And somewhere there are forty classmates of mine who I will never know. All we could have done together that will never be done. Forty possible friends who aren't aware of my absence. As if I had never been born. No one to realize that I am missing and that someone should come and find me. And some bitch will have stolen the boy who should have been with me. She thinks she did it all on her own, but it's only because I was kidnapped and the way was clear.

. . .

We are north of Death Valley, at twelve thousand feet, in the White Mountains. There are trees older than the land. One is called Methuselah and is four thousand seven hundred years old. It's all twisted because of the wind; in some places it's almost scraping the ground, flattened against the gravel. There's so little water that it has to make that little last: the water's trapped in needles that stay attached to the branches for a long time, like thirty years. I take one as a souvenir, a needle that will be the age of my mother when she died. Methuselah is even older than the big trees in California. These trees will outlive us all. These trees have already outlived us. I can't calculate exactly how many men can have died in all the time that the trees have been standing tranquilly in their spot putting on plant weight. Anyway, a tree of four thousand seven hundred years ago equals the life of a hundred and thirty-eight hens, or twenty-three hundred and fifty Nelsons, ninety Dads, seventy-five Grandmas, three hundred and sixty-one Dolores Mazes of now and twenty-eight thousand two hundred Nelson the Seconds.

We are the only people staying in the motel. Humbert feels like he's being watched, and he's nervous. I haven't been able to sleep these days, I keep getting insomnia. While he's snoring I go outside for a little walk. The earth is so blue it seems made of condensed sky, and the sky is pink like the sand at dawn. Everything is the opposite of day, which proves that at night everything is reversed. But Humbert will never realize it because at night he has the last fuck of his twenty-four hours as an illegal fucker, and afterward he falls asleep, and while he sleeps he sometimes mumbles phrases in French, *sans pitié du sanglot dont j'étais encore ivre* is his favorite nonsense. Poor guy, even when he's sleeping he can't forget that he is Mr. Émigré Professor. A little scholarly cog. My Daddy No. 1 also wanted to take me on a tour of America—a big country, he always added. As a country it's not bad, but the fathers leave something to be desired. My Daddy No. 1 did the tour on his own, my Daddy No. 2 would have done well to follow his example.

I feel this pain in my wrists. It's getting stronger and stronger. It only goes away if I press it down. But I must not, I must not, I must not cut myself with the razor: I don't want to lose my right to survive Humbert. The day someone comes to tell me that a certain Humbert Guibert, retired professor of French literature, is dead will just be too amusing, and I will have to make an effort to remember who the hell he was.

This country is full of parks. People live in normal places, and the big parks were invented to hold all the living conditions that aren't the normal ones, which I imagine must be deadly boring, and in this sense maybe I've been lucky. People who live a normal life come to the parks and go: wow! wow! wow! And then they go home. We don't have a normal life, we are bored and we screw, and we come to these revolting parks to kill time. Because it's a long way to go, but the road we're traveling on is time. You start out not wanting to waste time, then you reach the point where you'd like to do it in. Because your wrists itch and you want to cut them, but you can't cut your wrists because blood makes a mess, and you'd die die, so we go to the parks to listen to the people going wow! wow! wow!

We have a goal again. A French friend has found a job and a house in Ithaca, New York. Humbert will teach literature at a women's college. I, obviously, will go to school. Humbert starts instructing me in what I should say when we live again among people we'll have to see every day, people who aren't running and fleeing like the ones we see and yet don't see now. People who will have to think that Humbert Guibert is a model stepfather. A blessing from heaven for the poor little American orphan. And while he's lecturing I feel a huge anger at being in his hands, and I think it wouldn't be so bad to cut my wrists in Ithaca, these wrists of mine that are so yearning to be cut, to spite the model stepfather, but then I think I shouldn't: because he's capable of enjoying the idea of getting a brand-new twelve-year-old for himself, to replace this grumpy old thirteen-year-old whose repertory is used up. Although I'd like to see if he can find someone as good as I am for certain tricks.

If I'm not mistaken, the hen croaked just a year ago, more or less.

Dear Dolores Maze of the future, if I manage to resist the urge to cut these wrists which are so yearning to be penetrated, you will have to excuse me for keeping you so in the dark about what the Dolores Maze of now is experiencing: the fact is, this summer is really hot, or maybe summers are all like this, the metal of the car is burning, and, you know, this blue sedan of old Isabel Maze's has a real talent for absorbing the sun's rays. And since it's monstrously hot, I've even lost the desire to find a hiding place where I can write in peace, and I confine myself to making mental notes for you. It's not enough, I realize: it's so hot they evaporate. And then, I know, it's not too nice of me to have such a desire to cut my wrists: What did Dolores Maze of the future ever do to me that I should want so badly to kill her? The Dolores Maze of the future has done nothing to me, and I'll try to hold on in her interest, but sometimes I imagine the face of Professor Guibert when he wakes up and finds the corpse of his step-daughter beside him. My back is turned, he throws his hairy paw on me for the morning fuck, the one he uses to say let's start the day off right, and my still warm body falls on its back, and he finds himself with a big pool of blood. He makes an anxious face while his brain is working at supersonic speed to come up with answers to a pile of questions he would prefer never to hear: What is my body doing in his bed? Why is there a body to begin with? Why was I with him? Why did I skip a year of school? Why did Professor Guibert think that this was the best way to distract me from the tragic death of my mother? Well, Dolores Maze of the future, it's fun to imagine Humbert Guibert in the grip of these urgent problems of a judicial nature. It's so much fun that sometimes I forget that to enjoy the spectacle I'd have to pay for it with gallons and gallons of my own blood.

· · ·

In a couple of weeks the trip will be over. And what have I done in this moving jail? I should make a list of the highlights. But there weren't very many interesting sights, when I think back on it—only the singsong of the waitress with the potato-yellow hair after we went to the toy museum, and the gas-station guy who could flip cigarettes in the air and catch them in his mouth. Otherwise I didn't see much that deserved attention. There are really too many people traveling, and there's practically nothing original about any of them, not even a gesture. In the end there is more to study in things than in people. In the sequoia park I thought: if you could stand still with these trees, which are motionless, anyone who looked would be struck dumb. Even standing still is a gesture; it's the most difficult gesture of all; and if all these people who have nothing original about them would learn not to move around, at least they'd have something—a form. But they move too much, and so they're all the same, and they'll all be forgotten, from first to last.

School fashions in *Vogue*: shirt with cufflinks and big bow at the neck, skirt with a pleat in the back, low-heeled shoes, nylon stockings obligatory. I must make Humbert buy me a plastic raincoat and some nylons. Best to attack with a request for a velvet-trimmed mink jacket, and then tell him that if he doesn't want to fork out the money I'll settle for a plastic raincoat.

And yet some of the things I've seen are stuck inside me, like snapshots: the expressions of the hitchhikers not picked up, who I looked at from the window as we drove by. I stopped asking Humbert to pick them up, since he never really softened on hitchhikers, and when he did stop it was always for the ones who weren't worth the trouble: they were ugly or boring; if there was a cute or sexy one he'd step on the gas. I looked at them and waved from the window and they understood that I wanted to pick them up, and then I turned and kept waving until they disappeared. Now they are a little repertory of images that go flash-flash-flash inside me, as if all those interesting people I'll never know were alive, each with his own style, his way of standing with his pack on one side and the raised thumb on the other. I've collected their looks in my head, and they won't stop staring at me. With all these looks that came through my eyes from the edge of the road, I'll have the experience of a woman of ninety and the body of an eighteen-year-old when I finally get to the stage. I'm going on a journey for real; Mama Humbert on the other hand has only one place to go: between my legs.

More national parks. There's an inexhaustible number of them. I'm beginning to think that people all seem the same to me because there's a certain type that spends time in parks. The people who aren't exactly like all the other people must be at home or if they're traveling are traveling far from organized entertainment; they don't feel a need to rush around from place to place, and the places are always the same. It's the people who stay safe at home who must have something to protect. Or those who travel to places where Humbert never lets me go, places where things really happen. When I'm in Ithaca I'll track down all the people who have something original about them that I can steal for myself.

Today we were in these really cold caves, very wet and dark, with pools in the middle. Humbert gives me a lesson. He asks if I know how stalactites are formed.

"When the rocks ejaculate?" I ask him loud enough so that a woman with yellow eyes hears me clearly. Humbert looks at her embarrassed and says how difficult it is for a father alone to control a juvenile delinquent like me. To win her sympathy he makes up a story about his wife running away with an orchestra conductor. He feels appropriately pitied. The lady gives me a piece of candy to induce me to behave better with my father.

"I should do my duty?"

"Yes, always try to do your duty, young lady," urges the yellow-eyed lady, and meanwhile she farts. "Oh, pardon!" The hen also used to say pardon: it seemed genteel to her. More genteel than simply not farting.

Humbert decided that in Ithaca I will go to a really exclusive private girls' school, no more coed classes and other such modern inventions. That's the last straw, to end up in a school with only girls, I get in a rage, a total fury, then I say to myself, O.K., I'm going to make him hear the whole repertory of insults I've learned this year, including the Mexican ones, which he makes me translate because he can't get them by himself, and I spit out everything I've been keeping inside since we started our trip, I explain to him that he can't dispose of my life like this, that not even dead would I go to a girls' school. I'm yelling so loud that even I am amazed at the volume of my voice, Humbert is terrified, he presses on the gas pedal thinking he can escape from me, and in the racket we don't realize that two cops on motorcycles are pointing their headlights at us and they make us pull over while we're fighting worse than anything. I realize that maybe things are just this way, get rid of one Humbert and you find two more, so I might as well put on a good face, and I do, a big smile for the cops, who decide to let us go without arresting us, and we get back on our ridiculous road to a girls' school. But I'm glad I got mad. For once.

23.

*E*ND OF THE nomadic life. Miss Dolores Maze and Professor Humbert Guibert set up house together in Ithaca. From now on Miss Maze will attend a very exclusive private school for girls from good families. She will keep company exclusively with creatures of her own sex. The only male in her life, at least until her majority, will be her mother's widower. Xavier, a fat man with a long tuft of shiny black hair on one side combed over to cover the other side, found us a house at 28 Mayer Street. When we get there a boy with curly red hair and an insolent look gives us the keys and a note from Xavier welcoming us and inviting us to come and see him tomorrow. It's a dull cloudy day, with a low aluminum-gray sky. The house is gray, with gray wooden shingles, exactly like the one in Goatscreek. A new henhouse, without the old hen. A revolting house with green velvet curtains and glass cases everywhere, and a little room for me and a big one for Humbert, who also has a study, lined with chemistry books. The blue sedan broke down as soon as we got to the gate: Mom's machine held up until the last moment. How good of it not to get sick until the mission was completed. But what sort of mission? What did we experience, finally, in a year of traveling? What's the conclusion? It was a kind of whirligig through the United States of America, from east to north to south to west and then north and then south and then west again, high low up down, right diagonal, left diagonal, curves, ascents, descents, hotels, motels, national parks, boring hitchhikers because the interesting ones were left behind, some men in passing and in secret, wagging like puppies with pleasure at my caresses, and only a few snarling like guard dogs, some moralistic pain-in-the-ass types who refused, I don't know why—in order to save something in my life as a corrupted girl, I guess, and yet it's obvious that those bad-tempered puritans have no desire to see and understand, having only the textbook twelve-and then thirteen-year-old before their eyes, the legendary untouched child. They didn't give a damn who I am, Dolores Maze, born in Whiskey, 1935, time and date of my death still to be determined. All they cared about was not getting their hands dirty, and they left me in my same old shit, because in the end, with all their principles, they didn't lift a finger to save me and give me the freedom that surely I had a right to, according to the Constitution. Much better were the ordinary people, simple and spontaneous and without all that junk in their heads, who when I felt like being with them didn't lecture, and if I asked for something gave it to me without acting superior. They'd stay with me for the little time allowed by the ever watchful Mama Humbert, and we shared an instant of warmth. I remember them by the sensation of being in their arms, and if I'm still alive it's thanks to the ones who with that breath of freedom allowed me to hold firm, to go on day after day without cutting my wrists. Because, Dolores Maze of the future, it was no small thing to drag along this body which will one day be yours and not give in, no, never ever, to the mad wish to blow it up along with Humbert and the blue sedan and all those shitpile motels and diners and national parks. I say, Dolores Maze of the future, although this academic year wasn't very academic and next year I will be in a class with idiots who because they're a year younger will think it's their right to look down on me as if I were a repeater or handicapped or a retard—well, excuse me, but you know they're little shits and nothing, not a thing, has ever happened to them, everything has always gone smoothly and they've never had to rack their brains to understand something—while you, Dolores Maze of the future who will one day exist, you, for the single fact of being alive and staying in dazzling form, deserve a real hand.

Of course, Dolores Maze of the future, you will wonder where I was, what I saw in a year, and about this I have written very little to you personally. I had to keep the travel log for Humbert, which was a real pain since there wasn't that much time. But, you see, with you I unburdened myself on scraps of paper when I had a chance: I wrote to you when I went to the toilet, or at night when he was snoring and I was too angry to sleep, and I'd lock myself in the bathroom and write. Then I stuck all the scraps of paper in hiding places in my suitcase, and I hid some of them so well that I couldn't even find them. That was how I unburdened myself with my only friend, who is you, and since I was unburdening myself I may have left some curiosity unsatisfied. But anyway, what do you want, apart from Alaska and Florida, we went practically everywhere, and by the end I couldn't even look anymore, I had indigestion of the eyes—one more landscape and I would have gone completely blind.

. . .

Our landlord, Mr. Panzee, a professor of anthropology who is as hairy as an ape, came over to tell us how to use the lawn mower. He didn't even give us time to unpack our bags, he cares so deeply about the grass looking as well-kept as the neighbors'. Fine, says Humbert, but he wants a rolltop desk with a lock for his study—obviously he's going to start his secret diary again: it's my turn to be done away with. As a nymphet I leave something to be desired by now. Anyway, as soon as Panzee leaves, Mama Humbert drags me into his room, turns on the radio, an old wooden thing on a tottery table, and throws himself on me with all the fury of someone repossessing his goods. Clearly, in Ithaca, though I will have time for myself as a student at a girls' high school, our relations will remain basically the same, but with the radio at full volume. Because here, hemmed in by neighbors with their beautiful emerald-green lawns, it's better that certain facts not come to light. It wouldn't be so easy to get back in the car and leave this great security that we've barely won. On this Mama Humbert is crystal-clear: if they discover us, it's the end for him but also and above all for me, and so we have to be careful because we are a stone's throw from school, so close in fact that Mama Humbert was hoping to indulge in some forbidden fantasies by means of binoculars aimed at the playing fields, but he was disappointed because on the first day of school they put up a wall that blocked his view. So he missed seeing the electronic atomic supersonic orgasm that, to my extreme amazement, stunned me when I was sliding down the pole at recess: I suppose that's what that brown stringbean Liza Webster meant when she said that climbing the pole is fantastic, a "metaphysical" pleasure.

Seventeen advises: bra and girdle to make a good impression the first day of school. How idiotic. A girdle! Leave it for all those chubby girls who eat chocolate bars instead of screwing. I have a concave stomach, and wearing a girdle would only make me feel fatter. But I would like a bra.

Humbert had the old sedan fixed. If he'd been as attached to my mother as he is to that car, we'd still be in Goatscreek with me playing the great seductress and the hen shouting at me to keep my hands off husband No. 2. He has given me an allowance of twenty-one cents. Bravo, Mama Humbert: exactly what the hen would have done. The stingy hen.

Incredible! I read in *Teens in the News* that that retard Chloe became the national quiz champion because she guessed the roots of "oligarchy" and "psychiatry," and as a prize she got five hundred dollars and a trip to New York. I just imagine the faces of Rowe and Mary Jo. Five hundred dollars all for herself! It would take me two thousand five hundred weeks to earn five hundred dollars, unless I wanted to accelerate the process and do a hundred and sixty special tricks, which is a lot more work than coming up with two stupid etymologies in a stupid quiz, isn't it?

This school is revolting: it's all women except for the Reverend Stiffbone, who despite his name has less virility than a woman. It's full of little shits who pretend not to see me and spend the whole time talking to each other about their vacations. They're divided into four very exclusive and inaccessible cliques. Since I am the only new girl in my class, and besides am a year older than the others, the head-mistress, the giant Miss Short who will be Miss forever because her big head is covered with a bush of white hair and she wears horrible fuzzy sweaters, announces my arrival to the others. She explains, twisting her tortoiseshell eyeglasses, that my mother died last year, that I live alone with my stepfather (luckily she doesn't know anything about Nelson the first or second, or she would stick me with a full memorial service, complete with hymns and all the rest), and they should make me feel at home. So, all obedient, they come over, and a big fat girl with crooked legs invites me to have tea at her house in the afternoon—she says it in a loud voice for Miss Short to hear. I answer, also in a loud voice, that I'm very sorry but I can't because my aunt and uncle are coming from Los Angeles today. Then a girl with glasses and bangs that cover her face, who's been giving me this adoring-dog look but hasn't been able to say anything except some sort of hi that sticks in her mouth, asks me if my aunt and uncle are in the movies. I confine myself to nodding in a kind of distracted, bored way. I mutter that my mother died in an airplane crash, and I hear them falling into whispered speculation about it. I'm not worried, because I understand their type, they'll never ask me because they all want to show they have class and good manners—they want to pretend they've understood everything immediately, and those who don't will trust the pack leader.

It costs me three special effects to buy a sweater with a square collar like the one that little shit Kerlaw has. But mine is different, cherry red. Hers is a stupid color, canary yellow.

Dancing lesson with Miss Komar. But first Miss Short lectures us on being practical, learning things that will be useful in life: the goal of young ladies, she says, is to become perfect wives and mothers, to go out with boys from other schools, be respected, enjoy healthy amusements, and other crap. Humbert turns purple when I tell him he's sent me to a school where I will specialize in the art of going out with boys my age.

Saw *The Lady from Shanghai* with Liza, who is madly in love with Orson Welles. She says he's a genius.

"He doesn't seem like much to me. He's too big."

"Oh, but he's metaphysical. What movies do you like?"

"Musicals and gangster movies." I leave out Westerns because you never know, maybe Liza thinks they're stupid.

"Musicals? Which?" *The Wizard of Oz*, I tell her, which is also the only one I could get Humbert to see, because he hadn't read the book and wanted to know what it was about.

"A little old but not bad, not bad," Liza comments, taking a drag on her cigarette. "That one scene in particular, not bad. I went back twice just for that," she adds, jingling the charms on her bracelet. Who knows what she means.

"Listen, did you make up that story about your mother?" Well, pointless to put it off, I admit the truth in exchange for total secrecy. Liza snickers: "You did a good job—they're all just a bunch of shits, they don't deserve anything else." Then she offers me her pack of Lucky Strikes, and I knock one out, Robert Mitchum style.

"You know, last year I went with a marine who took them out just like that. Cigarettes."

"Did you screw?"

"Did we . . . " she sneers, blowing smoke out of the corners of her mouth. She looks like Bette Davis, with big, slightly pop-eyed dark eyes, and a too big mouth. She wears lipstick because she says that when you have a defect the thing to do is accentuate it, so it has a real impact. I reported this in my last postcard to Nora, to see if she agrees.

Horrible Miss Bluedick organized a trip to make us admire the autumn foliage. I hate women who are sensitive to nature. We all get on a bus driven by a guy who she makes eyes at in a truly revolting way, then, as we're going through the woods, she's flirting with him, right there: sugar maples, ta-t ta-t ta-t, elms, ta-t ta-t, and then, turning to Idelette, who's from Paris: "In Europe you don't have these trees because the great glaciation killed them. These glorious colors that light up our autumn like a great fire have been preserved only here, in America . . ." and quotations from Thoreau, Emerson, and blah blah and blah blah and blah blah, meanwhile wide-open-dreamy eyes at the guy at the wheel, who seems much younger than her. What a pig.

At the Country Club with Babe Ballard, our school tennis champion. Blond, taller than me, square jaw. She concedes that I play well, with style, and she appreciates my half volley: "Where'd you learn that?"

"My mother's sister sent me to take lessons with a tennis champion in San Diego, what's his name, you know, the one who beat Gobbert at Cannes, Ned something . . ."

"Oh, of course, he's really famous." Famous like hell, that stuff's all from ages ago, from Humbert's prehistoric childhood—she can't have known him—but Miss Champion can't lose face, with all the airs she gives herself. But the absolutely most stuck-up girl in the whole school is Holbrook, because of her uncle the president. She wears starched white shirts and a string of pearls around her neck, skirts and pants with large checks. She dresses totally like her mother. When they go out together you can't tell them apart from behind, except that her mother has a much bigger ass.

At first they thought I was in their class because I was stupid and retarded, but now that they know about my year traveling they're envious. I've seen more places than all of them put together. I never tell them anything specific, but occasionally I drop vague hints about a nervous breakdown after my mother's death. It seems very original to them to make a Grand Tour of the United States rather than of Europe. Miss Bluedick is the most enthusiastic of all—according to her, it's time to stop going abroad. I seem to have introduced a new fashion. They are wild to imitate my trip—the whole year, not a day less. They can't imagine how deathly boring it can be to wander for four seasons in a row without a shred of freedom. When I think back, it's all confused in my mind—names, places . . . For something to tell I have to reread my travel log; lucky there's that little book of Mama Humbert's defense, with all the details of our routes and the places we visited, otherwise I wouldn't remember a thing, and it wouldn't do to tell the class what I do remember. Because when I think of the past year it seems like the whole time I was shut up in a car with a Frenchman who was digging around inside me for reasons known only to him and in my purse with the more understandable purpose of swiping my dishonest earnings.

•   •   •

Miss Blumenau tells us we're going to put on *The Taming of the Shrew*; we're supposed to read it at home and then parts will be assigned according to what we liked best. That jerk Humbert sneers at the idea that we're doing Shakespeare ("Not that!"). Miss Blumenau makes us do lots of fun exercises. We have to think of something that isn't there, and try to imagine that it's actually right in front of our eyes, re-created through the power of our thoughts: for example, you imagine pushing a wheelbarrow, then you have to convince your body that the wheelbarrow is there, it's loaded and you have to make a big effort to push it, or convince yourself that there's a dog wagging its tail, or you eat something that's disgusting but you're polite and try not to let anyone realize it, or discover that someone you love is dead, or you've had too much to drink and can't stand straight on your feet—all kinds of things like this. It's fun to act as if reality were totally different than it is! And this technique is really useful with Mama Humbert because now I can convince myself I'm with Teddy Glass instead of with that maniacal old carcass stinking of talcum powder and mothballs.

Party at Liza's house, while Humbert's teaching. We play the game of temptation: every girl sits opposite a boy and looks him in the eyes, and the one who resists the desire to kiss longest wins. Needless to say, first prize goes to that bitch Kerlaw, with her diluted blood, who you discover is capable of lasting an entire millennium even with John Derek. For the boys the one who's kissed first wins, in the sense that he is the most irresistible. In other words, the most irresistible boy and the most resistant girl win. Liza's mother said this game reinforces stereotypes and we shouldn't play it. She must not have liked it that Liza lost immediately: opposite her she had Roy who she's crazy about because he sort of looks like Orson Welles. I was fourth to be beaten: for a while I was steady, but I had Freddy, with his faint apricot odor, and I said to myself, Well, if I wait till the game is over and unluckily manage to win, when will I get another chance to kiss him?

This raging Bluedick, who is extremely enterprising, distributed a booklet for our "hygienic education," with advice on underwear, intimate washing, menstruation and how to dispose of its "appurtenances," written in language so antiseptic that I couldn't resist the temptation to touch it up, so all the toilets became crappers, and when I show it to Liza she bursts out laughing, attracting the attention of Miss Bluedick. When she sees how I debased her beloved hygienic booklet, she gets furious and threatens to have me expelled from the school, which is a school for girls of good family, not street girls. She drags me by the ears to Miss Short, who doesn't seem too upset and makes a little speech to Bluedick about how there's no need to make a big deal of these jokes, which are perfectly normal in the tumultuous period of adolescence—the worst thing is to give them too much weight. But, she continues, turning to me, I must show a little more respect for the feelings of others, so I should apologize to Bluedick, which obviously I do, because so what, who gives a damn?

Liza drags me to see *The Lady from Shanghai* again. She claims I didn't pay attention to the ending, with the sharks, and the sailor saying that you conquer evil only by going toward the good, and leaving Rita Hayworth to die because she deceived him and never thought about anything but money. The sailor seems stupid, but in fact he's the only one who knows that what counts is love, even though the others seem much stronger than him because they're smarter. But in the end those smarty-pants tear each other to pieces like so many sharks, while he remains free and strong, and can love without deceit.

"Was he like that, your marine?"

"No. But he was a force of nature."

"Were you disappointed?"

"How can I put it, what can I say . . . " but she doesn't explain further. Liza never says anything precise about her marine. Every so often she gives a hint, then lights a cigarette and gazes into the distance. I make her read the interview with Gandhi, and she agrees: "Yes, on two different levels but they are the same person."

"The sailor in *The Lady from Shanghai* and Gandhi?"

"Yes . . . Gandhi also had something inside that sensed what was right even if he didn't know for certain," she concludes, putting out her cigarette. Who knows. I hope that at least they didn't look too much alike. Then Roy comes to pick her up (yesterday they had their first kiss, and that means they're going steady), but I go straight home, where Humbert is waiting at the door. He can't stand the slightest lateness. He's getting a hooked nose: sign of old age or increasing rapaciousness?

Birthday party for the Kerlaws, but I wasn't invited. Of our class only Holbrook, Idelette, Babe, and Liza go, and afterward Liza says I didn't miss anything, not even a decent boy, and the mothers were there the whole time.

"Shitmom," I say.

"Clever, a metaphysical concept. Although mine is different." She says I have to meet her mother because she's really fantastic, she looks half her age, when they go out together people take them for sisters, and they are, in a way. It's just the two of them living alone, which changes the atmosphere. This is because Liza's father is in China doing research on ancient porcelains; she and her mother stayed in Ithaca so that Liza wouldn't be uprooted to live in a community of foreigners, and besides it didn't seem worth the trouble of moving for just a year. Liza says that apart from hers the moms are disgusting and are all shitmoms, although it's true that no shit is exactly like another.

"Metaphysical," I say. But I bet her mother didn't know about her going out with the marine.

. . .

I sent my address to Filthy Sue. I wonder if he really put a part for me in *The Enchanted Forest*. If he did, I will crush those stupid Kerlaws and their stupid parties.

I tell Humbert about Liza's extraordinary experiences. His eyes get shiny and he hovers, wanting to know more. O.K., how much? We start with fifty cents for the general situation and settle on a dollar for the details. By inventing other intimate stuff I earn another six, which means that for a couple of weeks I can spare myself the afternoon extras and still buy some nylon stockings. A good investment, collecting secrets from your school friends. My weekly allowance has gone up to fifty cents, an incentive to regularly provide bits of sexually exciting gossip, but it has a strange effect on Mama Humbert: he got a monstrous toothache and was awake all night with an ice pack, groaning. Poor old sickie.

Filthy Sue answered me! His comedy is opening in New York, and there really is a part inspired by me. He writes how sorry he is about Mom's death—he recalls her sophisticated, Marlene Dietrich looks, such beautiful brown hair and deep-green eyes. He doesn't want me to say anything about the part, and he will arrange for Ithaca to have the exclusive school première. Fantastic!!!

I wrote a story about Nelson the Second's funeral, but I didn't say I was the one who killed him. I put in someone else's name, crippled Gitta, then I sent it to the *Seventeen* contest. If you win you get five hundred dollars, but it's hard because anyone between thirteen and nineteen can enter, and it's also unfair: there's a gap between thirteen and nineteen, and the nineteen-year-olds are already grown up, much more than the thirteen-year-olds. Hardest of all was to type it without Humbert knowing. He hates it when I touch his precious things, hates it when I get myself noticed. I didn't show it to anyone, not even Liza. Anyway, since she's seriously going with Roy, I hardly ever see her anymore.

24.

*L*IZA AND I spend two days reading the *Shrew* together. It's the story of two couples: one's boring, and the other's not. In the unboring couple the man gets together with the woman because of a bet he made with his friends, and the woman just does it out of spite, but it becomes true love: Petruchio doesn't care a bit that Katherina's nasty, since at least she's rich and he knows how to put women in their place, and Katherina hates everyone. Petruchio isn't frightened, and by the end she's crazy about him, while it's crystal-clear that he loves her although he won't admit it. He likes Katherina's odd personality a lot, because he's a rebel at heart, a daredevil; he thinks he's chasing a woman just for her money but he ends up falling in love with her . . . I absolutely have to play Katherina and Liza Petruchio. The parts of goody-goody Bianca and her fiancé, who she takes for granted, aren't worth the trouble. Miss Blumenau has scheduled a lesson all for me, a makeup class, on how to breathe so that you're always in control, and how to capture the entire audience in an imaginary funnel that starts from your chest. My diction isn't good enough yet: you have to open your lips an instant before pronouncing the sounds, to make the syllables more distinct. I have to repeat to infinity this sentence to improve my dentals: I did not want to pet the dear soft cat. Then Liza and I read some parts together, but I didn't do very well. It's weird to hear my voice as if it's coming from someone else, and then those ridiculous insults, like donkey, footstool, leech, and boor, sound false to me, although according to Blumenau it's O.K. that they didn't come naturally, because Katherina is already in love with Petruchio, and so it's hard for her to insult him convincingly. In fact, I could accentuate the false tone, just to make it true, and not worry about mistakes, they'll be taken for something original, which distinguishes me: "Work on this idea." O.K., it will be a principle like Liza's lipstick, but in the meantime I practice insulting Humbert, which does come to me naturally. I wish I could do it that way on the stage. That jerk doesn't even realize I'm reciting Shakespeare, he and his "Not that!" All he knows is his silly, revolting, boring, and false French poets, and then, because he's taking painkillers for his teeth, his eyes turn opaque, like a rotten fish.

We rehearse: I'm Katherina, Liza's Petruchio. Liza is out of this world in the part where she makes all those excessive compliments. I'm charmed, imagining it's all true, and I have a dreamy expression; but as soon as she stops, my expression changes, like someone who's suddenly facing reality, and I get angry at the idea that she's making fun of me, that it's not true; compliments and love have always gone to my younger sister, that bitch. My face is contorted, I lock my lips, I explode in insults for Liza-Petruchio, but they're not very convincing, since I'm already in love and am afraid it's all a deception, afraid of having believed it and then finding it's not true. In my view Petruchio wants Katherina only for the money, and so she's right to feel made fun of. Liza says no, in the beginning it's out of self-interest, because he's disappointed and no longer believes in love, but then he falls in love because he realizes that she is like him, she has rejected love only in despair at ever finding it and she defends herself like a fierce beast in order not to be disappointed. Miss Blumenau says that Petruchio and Katherina are like two people who fall in love at first sight but are unwilling to admit it, out of fear.

"And why are they afraid of love?"

"Because it would change their lives." Lucky them. I don't know what I wouldn't give to change my life. I wouldn't be at all afraid of falling in love, not a bit.

I tell Liza about me and Humbert on condition that she tell absolutely no one—otherwise I'll end up in the reformatory or in the hands of the horrible Dr. Sharp. Liza says that Humbert is the most revolting person she has ever met. As soon as he saw her he made eyes at her like a slime. Disgusting. Liza tells me some of her problems with Roy: she likes him but her marine is still on her mind, and she doesn't know which of the two she likes better. But she hasn't heard from the marine. Her mother says not to worry, it will happen in time, but she would like to know now. Roy is nice for talking to and she likes him physically, though he's not exactly like Orson Welles—he looks like him and that's about it. Sometimes she is nervous and there are moments when she'd just rather stay with her mom.

That traitor Blumenau assigns the parts, she and her no-good promises: I have to be Bianca! Even Liza won't say I'm right—basically she says that for someone who has never performed with the group before even the part of Bianca is too much. Not that she was so lucky: the parts of Katherina and Petruchio went to the Holbrook bitch and the taller of the Kerlaws (all because their families give a lot of money to the school), and Liza is Lucentio, which isn't so bad since at least we stay together. But our characters are much less interesting: we start out with the idea of having to fall in love and get married, having to do the right thing, what everyone does, and the result is that love doesn't change us in any way, for the simple reason that we've never opposed it, we've never fought hand to hand. In the end, with the wedding over, Bianca throws off her mask and you see she has no intention of complying with her husband, because she hasn't married him, she's married the position of wife. Miss Blumenau is right, theirs is not true love, it's a conformist marriage conducted with the minimum of good manners. Totally inane. Jade gets the part of the Hostess, Audrey's Christopher Sly, Babe will be Baptista, Bianca and Katherina's father, and Idelette is Hortensio. Jade is hopeless as the Hostess, but Miss Blumenau says it will help her overcome her pathological shyness. Audrey had to have the part of that lout Sly because a male part fits her perfectly: her hairy legs and her stomach will work perfectly with a beard, and then she has so few lines that even if she's terrible it won't be the end of the world.

I tell Liza my idea about being in the movies when I grow up, but she turns up her nose.

"What for? The money?"

"No, for the movies. Don't you like the movies?"

"Yes, I like movies, but I wouldn't want to be an actress. If anything a director. As an actress I'd like to work in the theater. Because there you really make things happen."

"And you don't in the movies?"

"In the movies it's like being cut out of cardboard, they take you and paste you on the film, more or less."

Maybe. But so many people would see me in the movies, I like the idea of being so large that my face fills the whole screen.

"On the stage you have this incredible sensation of being able to fill a whole theater with your voice, with something that comes from inside you; you don't need special effects, it's your own power, and your voice is so enormous that people going home still hear it echoing inside themselves."

"And when you die?"

"What do you mean when you die?"

"When you die, if you've made a movie people can still see you and never stop seeing you. In the theater, you die and no one sees you anymore."

"You think it's a good idea that after you die someone who maybe treated you badly or made you suffer can earn a living by selling films with you in them still seeming alive?"

"But the people who go to the movies never think about that, they see you and that's it."

"But the money goes to other people. And meanwhile you're underground, more alone than ever, and while they're watching you and thinking how beautiful you are and great and fascinating, they won't remember that you're full of worms, rotting in the ground. They're having fun but you're dead, you don't stop dying, you can't do anything but be dead."

I've thought about it, but I can't see how it matters. I like the idea of being admired even when I'm no longer around. I like it when people look at me. What's the difference if I'm among the worms? I'd be there anyway. To hell with Liza and her obsession with life-life and love-love. Between her and her mother you could say there's a contest for who is more coherent. Who is more metaphysical. I ask Humbert what "metaphysical" means, he says it's too difficult for me to understand, and is in a hurry to have his evening pleasure.

I go to Idelette's to get a scarf I left at rehearsal. She offers me a glass of water from the tap and then shows me her box of recycled gum: after she chews it she covers it with sugar and sprinkles cinnamon on it for flavor, puts it in a box, and after a while chews it again, over and over again, in an endless chew. She claims it's as good as new. Her allowance is too small for her to throw away her used gum.

While that bitch Holbrook is practicing with the scrawny Kerlaw, Liza and I filch a pocket diary from her purse and go to the bathroom to read it. What an idiot, a real snot. There were two pages of rules for how to act superior. In conversation: Be bold, aim at brilliance, don't utter banalities, express unusual opinions, use unusual words, have unusual ideas . . . A list of goals follows: Be sophisticated and show a strong personality, appear indifferent but alluring. Then there's a list of the means of achieving all these grand objectives: personal appearance (elegant clothes, exclusively tailor-made), conversation (bursting with uncommon and cutting words), manners (perfect, with a rakish touch). But the most revolting of all her rules, an addition to the paragraph on "Manners," is one that explains everything: When it's impossible to be interesting, act bored and superior. There she is. In fact she's never interesting, and so she's been sitting at her desk all year looking bored and superior. Her Katherina is painful. A real waste.

Audrey comes to my house to practice her part, so I can give her advice. I listen with as much patience as I can; it's such a short part you'd have to be a retard to have trouble learning it. There's nothing special about the way she does it, but she gets a little better as she practices. Her fatso father and mother come to pick her up, and Mama Humbert invites them in for a glass of port, just to be friendly and show that even we, in our mutilated little family, do all we can to be like others, and believe in hospitality between neighbors. While the two dads are talking about stupid things, Audrey climbs in her mother's lap and brags about her wonderful collies and then about her little brother and her new baby sister. She pets her mother like a baby, and she clings to her neck in a really disgusting way, pink flesh on pink flesh. Ick. Gross. Why doesn't she just stay home with her dogs and brothers and sisters and her mom who's always pregnant, and not come here to show off with the excuse of asking me for help, the little shit. I swear she'll pay for it.

First read-through all together. Miss Blumenau doubles over with laughter—she's never seen a Bianca so on the mark. Even she hates that phony goody-goody. Miss Ravensea is purple with rage, she says we have completely travestied Shakespeare. She's so bitter, what does she know about Shakespeare? She must be angry at having imitated Bianca her whole life without anyone ever marrying her: around here that type is out of date. Bianca is a total phony. Like the hen. First she pretends to hold her tongue, in fact she pretends she doesn't even have one; but as soon as she's married her character goes right back on like a glove. Katherina changes through love. Bianca is always the same piece of virtuous stale flesh, and as soon as she gets married she changes only in the sense that she no longer tries to hide her true nature, which is nasty and insensitive. Katherina is good at heart but pretends to be bad out of self-defense. Bianca is a person who's bad at heart but for her own advantage pretends to be good. It's really revolting the way Bianca shows off her humility. To do it well I'm inspired by little Kerlaw, with her eyes always wide-open to look innocent, and her singsong voice, and I do it so well that they all burst out laughing. Miss Blumenau pretends not to notice in order to maintain her "impartiality." She showers Audrey with praise for her improvement in the microscopic part of Christopher Sly, and does that little shit even thank me for helping her? Screw her. Why the hell did I take the trouble? Since she won't help me and won't ever understand me. She and her stupid fat freckled family, with their stupid collies. Miss Blumenau liked my Bianca so much that later she gave me a copy of *Wuthering Heights* so I could see how these turbulent love stories go, from one Katherina to the next.

I go to hide my allowance in *Treasure Island* and find it empty: now it's useless as a hiding place. All gone. All eight dollars flown away. Sixteen allowances up in smoke. I make a scene with Humbert and say that if he doesn't want me to accuse that simpering Halibut, who by my reckoning converted my eight dollars to gin, he'd better increase my allowance to seventy cents. He forks it over. What a drag, not being able to lock anything.

Liza plays Lucentio as if he were a drudge of a college boy, with his head in his books, and that's why he's totally unprepared and is seduced by Bianca's falseness. She puts on eyeglasses and speaks with a slight stutter, like a real student. And she says all those pretentious things. Ultimately it's good for him to end up married to a shrew who rules the household with an iron rod. And since there's hardly any sexual satisfaction with someone like Lucentio, you have to let it be understood that after the marriage Bianca will amuse herself with her husband's servant, who after all is more savvy. Katherina is right to despise Bianca: she's a sly fox who schemes in silence and has no true feelings for anyone. As Liza says: in this comedy no one is what they seem to be. As soon as she's settled, horrible Bianca shows everyone that she's the real shrew. She has studied her future part at Katherina's knee. How revolting, to reveal your true character only when there's nothing left to lose.

That bitch Ravensea gave me the worst grades of all, I got weird comments from Miss Bluedick, and those geese Root and Slaw made grudging remarks; the only ones who had something good to say are Miss Komar, on my aptitude for dance, and Miss Blumenau, who says my theatrical future is assured and I have an uncommon capacity to sink into a character. Despite Ravensea.

Miss Blumenau announces that at the end of the year we will do a new comedy that has been hugely successful in New York, *The Enchanted Forest*. I pretend not to know anything about it, as Filthy Sue asked me. If the hen were still alive, vigorous and squawking, and knew about my role in a play by Gerry Sue Filthy, she would go around telling all her friends. I called Nora from a pay phone and she burst into tears, she was so overcome.

Short meets with Mama Humbert to discuss my low grades, and to complain about all the toilet cubicles I've decorated with Miss Bluedick's hygienic booklet; she is still terribly offended. Afterward he comes to get me in the library, and there's that stupid Holbrook with her stupid potato-colored hair, which according to Mama Humbert is platinum blond. He promises me sixty-five cents in exchange for touching him under the desk while he's looking at her. This is what's scattered along the road to recovery of my eight dollars. Sly old Humbert.

Incredible! He doesn't want me to do Filthy's comedy! He hasn't even read it, but he's decided that it's a stupid waste of time, as long as it was Shakespeare it was tolerable, but this "bad comedy" full of sexy little scenes (sexy where, seeing he hasn't even taken the trouble to read it?), this joke of the Bewitched Forest, as he calls it—this he will not allow. I write to Filthy and he telephones me: "Don't despair." But I hang up immediately because Humbert's barking voice is descending on me, determined to know who I'm talking to. Who does this Humbert Guibert think he is, King Kong, to keep me in his grip?

. . .

Another yucky sermon from Mama Humbert because I don't study enough and am too involved in dramatics. Miss Blumenau's praise is going to my head, and I'll be sorry when I find myself an unemployed actress in New York, who, hoping for a bit part, works as a cigarette girl in restaurants where she can't even order an appetizer because she doesn't have a cent. To which I say that's better than being the slave of a swine. What do swine have to do with it, he says. Swine have to do with it because pigs are nice, intelligent animals, but swine are bristly and fierce and they grunt and all the rest. After which the plates fly, and we do in the Panzees' entire collection of blue porcelain. The next day when that stupid Halibut comes to clean up, Humbert tells her it was all the fault of a spiteful monkey who came home with a cousin of his from the French Antilles. What an imagination! He even invents monkeys, my dear, adorable, unique, and inimitable King Kong!

Last day of school before Christmas vacation: we do the *Shrew* in the afternoon, not the whole thing but with Miss Blumenau's cuts; in the end she decided that retard Audrey is such a desperate case that we can do without her completely. Her useless Christopher Sly makes you tear your hair. Of course Audrey is incredibly disappointed, and sits in the audience whining through the whole performance, while her stupid parents console her and tell her it's nothing. She cries so much that afterward Pat Ballard, Babe's brother, goes over to comfort her and takes her for a ride on his motorcycle. Revolting, even she can manage to get boys to take her out, in spite of her hairy legs. But who cares, I had my moment of glory, in front of the young ladies in the front row with the radiant Miss Short and the worried Miss Blumenau. My moment of true, authentic, shining, unobscurable glory came when, at the point where Holbrook-Katherina gives me a beating, I exit saying the line "When it's impossible to be interesting, one should act bored and superior," simultaneously flashing her an extremely mocking look. This causes massive confusion, but how can you resist the temptation to add a joke. And that jerk, instead of getting madder, which would be normal, turns all rigid, suddenly stops beating me, and literally starts acting superior and bored, exactly according to her rules. Miss Ravensea, sitting next to Humbert, who is alarmed by her big beaky nose, flies into a rage. During intermission, I have to apologize to Blumenau and convince her that I made up the remark to cover a memory lapse and I don't know how in the world it came to me. Miss Blumenau ends up reproaching Holbrook for not having a feel for improvisation, and then she describes a lot of situations in which actors managed brilliantly in the face of even worse disasters. And meanwhile that bitch Holbrook stands there livid and can't say that that sentence was written in her diary, because if she admits it then everybody will be laughing at her, from today till the end of the year.

25.

I'VE DEFINITELY GOT bronchitis. With a fever. Humbert climbs in bed to enjoy my heat and stays all day, taking advantage of the fact that Halibut didn't come and I'm in too much of a daze to protest. At least I could have given him something. No. Not even a cough. And he's happy as a clam, touching me where I'm burning and absorbing the heat from me as if I'm a hot-water bottle, like the multiple, complex, diversified parasite he is. He gets out of bed only when the doctor comes, a horsey type who must be a lesbian because she pokes me everywhere with her bony fingers, even where there's no reason for it, and every so often she taps my chest, for appearances' sake. That was Christmas Eve. On Christmas Day I'm better. Xavier comes and stays all afternoon playing chess with Mama Humbert, thank goodness, so I can read and write and listen to the radio. When I come down in my bathrobe, Xavier detaches his fat flabby butt from the sofa but barely looks at me.

· · ·

Since I still can't go out, Mama Humbert relents and lets me have people over. I write invitations on cards and make Humbert deliver them by hand two days before, with nice RSVPs. The responses come by telephone, and not everyone can make it, but the day of the great party (so to speak) Liza and Audrey come early to help me put up a tree with colored lights, while Halibut is in the kitchen spreading sandwiches with anchovy paste and butter. Almost none got eaten, because so few people came. Babe doesn't show up, and out of all the boys only Tim, Mark, and Roy and his cousin Sebastian, luckily those two know how to dance, because Tim and Mark are a disaster. We end up playing cards. It's impossible to have fun. As soon as things get going Humbert, worried by how lively it is—a real rarity in our house—comes downstairs, relentless, with some excuse. It would almost have been simpler to have him with us and invite the other parents—at least they'd neutralize each other, without all those stupid interruptions. I was getting nervous, with those two dopes who didn't even know how to dance, so out of desperation we played the game of Botticelli. But Audrey isn't very good at inventing, so we ended up playing cards until Liza came up with a clever way to get rid of Humbert: she sits at the table with Roy and starts talking about predestination and the laws of probability, so Humbert stops worrying about any hot prospects for the evening and leaves us alone for a good hour. At one point Audrey, who never knows what to say and just babbles, goes, with her most pimply dumb expression: "Your dad must really love you. Look how concerned he is that we should have fun." I explode and throw a porcelain stag against the wall. It breaks into a thousand pieces, horns and all. "What's the matter? Did I say the wrong thing?" Audrey asks. Then Liza whispers: "Listen, Dolly, after we leave you throw yourself in a chair looking exhausted and say that boys make you sick. Make him feel secure as the man of the house—it's an investment that always gives a return."

As a reward for the fact that boys make me sick, Mama Humbert gives me a new tennis racquet. I could sell it. Maybe to

Audrey. That idiot is capable of paying twice the price just to have something of mine. She's even started talking like me. Which, with her round yellowish face, looks really ridiculous. She imitates the way I speak, and then looks at me adoringly. I can't stand it when she acts like that. People who force me to be mean to them drive me crazy.

For my fourteenth birthday Nurse Humbert lets me stick my nose outside. In the morning while I'm still in bed he brings me a huge book about American painting, one of those stupid, incredibly heavy volumes that you leave on the coffee table in the living room. Then he takes me out to the garage. Surprise! he exclaims cheerfully, all fresh with aftershave. The surprise is a blue Schwinn, not as pretty as Babe's, which is a Monark with a crossbar made like a little gas tank on a motorcycle, but it's better than nothing; in fact, maybe it's cooler without the fake gas tank. Anyway, it was about time he decided to get me a bike. I was the only one in school who didn't have one. Before handing it over he inflicts a little lecture on the dangers of cars—I mustn't end up like the hen—and not going too far from home, not using it at night, be careful of boys on motorcycles because they could follow you, don't go too fast when you're going downhill, et cetera, et cetera. By what grace of God did he not think of getting a bike for himself? It would have been horrible to ride along the streets of Ithaca in a cycling duo with Dad.

My money was stolen again. Twenty-four dollars and seventy cents, all my savings plus the price of the racquet. I'm broke again. I can't understand why I am so stupid about working and saving when every time, regularly, it evaporates, so I don't accumulate anything but a tremendous rage. I no longer think it's that stupid drunk Halibut. Here the hairy hand of Humbert kills the classic two birds: he retrieves his badly spent money, and at the same time keeps me from having any money of my own at my disposal. From now on I'll spend it all immediately on candy bars, records, and lipstick.

Liza calls about the dance Saturday at the Academy. Humbert

makes his usual nasty face, wrinkles all up and down, and then with a threatening look: "You will not go to that dance." Liza asks her mother to call him, and really I don't know what she said, but the fact is that Mama Humbert came out of the conversation with the formidable Mrs. Webster utterly humiliated. In the afternoon he tells me to get in the car, and without a word, and the most henlike face I've ever seen on him, gripping the wheel in utter fury, a perfect copy of Plasticmom, he takes me to get a dress for the dance. He's so angry he's speechless and he lets me choose what I want, a low-cut dress, hourglass-shaped, but instead of black—by now everyone has a black one, even Audrey, in the $7.50 version—I get pale-orange chiffon. In front of the mute Mama Humbert I also choose dark-orange satin shoes with matching heels. Liza says they're gorgeous, she'll get a dress like mine, but yellow, so when we go in together, me in orange and her in yellow, my chestnut and her brunette, gray eyes and amber eyes, we'll make a sensation.

Poor, poor Mama Humbert, he had to give in on *The Enchanted Forest*, too. This afternoon the bell rings, I open the door and there's a guy with a black beard and glasses. He comes in and says, winking, "I would like to speak with Professor Guibert." I have the feeling that I know him, he must be the school psychologist. At the word "psychologist" Humbert darkens, but he has to invite this guy with the glasses to come into his "private room," that is, his study. They shut themselves in and confer for quite a while. Eventually I hear the door open, and I peer down the stairs and see the guy going out and Humbert promising him not to interfere ever again with my theatrical activities. Then I run down at breakneck speed so as not to miss the decisive moment, and embrace Mama Humbert, shouting an ecstatic thank you to his pale face, and then giving him a smacking kiss to seal the promise. The bearded guy smiles at me like the family doctor, shakes my hand and wishes me good luck in my undertakings. I look out the door as he heads for his car, a red convertible, and when he opens the door I see Rimbaud's grayish snout opening in a rosy smile . . . Oh holy shit!!! Dear Daddy who are in heaven, you really did send Filthy Sue as my guardian angel, because, let me tell you, isn't it super that he came right into the dragon's lair so I could be in the play? Isn't it generous that someone so famous goes to the trouble to save an orphan abandoned by everyone? Meanwhile the dragon Humbert has a violent toothache, the pain woke him up and he's seeing stars, poor Dad.

It was too good to be true. My dear dad may have given in on the play, but, in a delayed reaction, doesn't let me off the hook from the fright the psychologist gave him, the toothache, the dance he had to swallow, and my imminent success in *The Enchanted Forest*: he quickly balances the accounts by lowering the price for oral services, prized because of the softness and elasticity of my mouth with its hot-blooded, fragrant breath, and assigning the highest value to a new and never dreamed-of procedure. Where I had never let him go even with a finger. To frighten him I try saying that I could get a hemorrhage and then he'll be found out, but he is immovable, curiously bold. That or nothing, he insists, and I will pay a good price. I don't care about money, I yell. Very well, you won't get any, he says. And you won't have me anymore, I shout. Then my dear dad does something that he has never dared to do before: with a sudden burst of energy he jumps on me and holds me down and does what he wants, the muscular old shit. He practically breaks off my wrists, leaves me aching on the bed. I am plunged into such disgust that I say to myself, What difference does it make in the end, isn't it all the same horror, and then, what do I care, maybe something will change, maybe it's more advantageous to know how to do even that, rather than not to know, because you never can tell in life, anything can happen, better to practice, to be used to everything, as Rowe said. Well, I have to make the best of it, so I begin to bargain, not that I get much—ten lousy dollars—but it's a question of maintaining the price at a certain level rather than allowing it to sink sharply, like the blow jobs which I let him devalue. It's useless to cry over spilled milk, I have to climb back up with exercises from behind, but not too often, so I can reconstitute my little capital for basic survival, which is always a good thing to have, in case one of those moods suddenly descends on me where the only option is to cut the cord in order not to cut the veins. So I go to Humbert, who is buzzing with satisfaction at his exploit of male violence, and say, O.K., dear Daddy, ten dollars, not one dollar less, but do it right and don't hurt me. He yawns with a look of superiority. And give it to me now, that ten dollars. He does, and I run away to hide it, but I have to say I don't at all like this sensation of being impaled and stuffed and shitting backward, and when I'm alone in my bed, curled into a ball and biting my knees, I feel empty and excited, and my heart goes *pum pum pum*. And I'd like to know what I earned that ten dollars for, as if I didn't know I'll never get rich this way.

The dance was fantastic—Liza and I had the most invitations of all, more even than the Kerlaws. Holbrook was absent: she got that cold, which obviously knows how to strike the right people at the right time. Liza came to my house before the dance so we could get dressed together. I tell her about my last penetrating experience and it makes quite an impression, because she hasn't tried that yet. Roy has no desire to experiment. Every so often they quarrel about this. Humbert wanders back and forth in the hall, without daring to come in, because he has a providential fear of Liza. We put on Mrs. Webster's transparent powder, lipstick the color of black cherry, and even Chanel; we do our hair with the part on one side and an ivory hair-clip in the back. Mrs. Webster arrives in the car and gives me a little package: "Happy Birthday, sorry for the delay." I open it, and there's a stupendous string of pearls. I put them on right away. Mrs. Webster is wonderful, if I'd had her for my mother my life would be com-pletely different; a mother like this is a dream, though maybe if I'd waited mine would have improved. The fact is she died before she had time to understand anything. I say this because I can't believe she was as rotten as she seemed, such a witch. Who knows, dear Dad in heaven, the only thing would be for you to come and tell me in a dream, because I don't understand anything anymore. Anyway, back to the dance: we didn't sit down a single minute, we danced every dance. Some of the boys were drinking, in secret; Freddy, the cute guy I saw at Liza's party, drags me out onto the terrace, still dancing, and when I complain that I'm cold he holds me in his arms and kisses me so hard that I forget the cold, and when he brings me back inside he makes me drink something from a leather-covered flask, the kind you take hunting, and then we dance again, my head is spinning more and more and I seem to be in the sky gliding among the stars, until a waiter comes to get me. Mr. Guibert is waiting. It's exactly eleven, that pain-in-the-ass killjoy. I find Liza. What's happening? she asks. What's happening is I have to go. So I go and she stays because she has a mom who comes to get her when she wants, while I have to say goodbye to Freddy, and I don't know if I'll ever see him again, because he's leaving to go to school in England and is going to stay there for college. Quick down the stairs, into the car with Humbert, in dark coat and bow tie, soft cheeks, stink of red wine; he was eating out with Xavier and other professors from his pompous college. As soon as we go in, he hauls me up to the bedroom and throws me on the bed. Don't tear my dress, I shout. You're drunk, he says accusingly. In fact my head is whirling, and I have a burning sensation in my stomach, and because of that stuff I drank my head is spinning too fast to tell Humbert to go to hell. How sad that all that chiffon does is to turn me into an orange lollipop. I hate feeling excited in spite of hating him, I feel wet and dirty, slimy with saliva and sucking, I have no desire for anything and there's nothing to do but clean off all that slime. So I tell him to come inside me. You want it, he asks, the pig always wants to hear me say I want it. I want twenty dollars, twenty dollars is what I want, I shout. I'll give you twenty dollars but you have to tell me you want me. I want you, I want you, but first give me my twenty dollars. He gives it to me but wants to have it both ways. Who cares, really at that moment I feel like I might as well be fucked dry, because it's a shit life when you go out to a dance and right at the best part some Professor Guibert arrives and you discover that the powder and the pearls and the lipstick and the chiffon are only for him and for me there's nothing nothing nothing. I am right where I was before, penetrated by my revolting father, and I don't even get anything, because afterward he twists my wrist and takes away what he promised, leaving me only ten, and even that's too much, according to him. So the next morning I look like a hairdresser on Saturday night, I am dead tired and have such fury in my body that I'm almost happy when Humbert goes back inside me. By now it's just fine not to have a drop of energy, to feel myself beaten, feel myself disappear and not think anymore about anything. Fuck me but don't lick me, if you lick me I'll murder you, I tell him, and he does it, but he's so grim, and that's it and he goes away. Well, who gives a damn, the dance could have been fantastic.

The dance could have been fantastic, but Humbert is the usual shit because besides cheating me of half of my twenty dollars and taking me away at the best part of the party, today he pretends not to remember his promise to let me have the nicest boys from the dance over. He takes it all back. But am I not an idiot, a total, patented idiot, to have imagined that for once in my life I could do something normal?

Audrey's parents bought a television set, and they organize an uninterrupted day of television, with sandwiches, Cokes, nuts, apple and banana milkshakes. Audrey invites some friends, including me, though I don't know why since I'm not really her friend. Still, I'm always curious about that ridiculous Hawk family; they're so gross that they're kind of fascinating. We all sit in front of the TV, including the two dogs, who don't miss a scene, one on each side of Audrey. First there's a sort of babysitter who tells stories for children so they'll be good while Mommy and Daddy are busy with other things, and then this self-important babysitter draws a pigeon and recounts his adventures, which are not very adventurous; then there's a religious program that's really dumb, until a person called Amanda comes on, and sits down at the piano and sings some fabulous blues, which is torture, making me miss Celeste. I have no idea where she ended up or whether she has children or if she's happy with Leslie. It seems centuries since I last saw her. Then two hens come on full of advice about shopping, mainly for underwear. At one point they're interrupted by a boy in uniform who does an ad for Philip Morris, then the two hens are back, with their shopping advice, while trays of cookies are handed around by Audrey and her mother, and placid Mr. Hawk carries Cokes and milkshakes, all smiling and enthusiastic about his acquisition for family entertainment. Then we get the horrible "flaxen-haired girl" with her nauseating love songs. It lasts a while, this junk, until cartoons come on, with a story about giant mice who follow a poor little terrorized kitty, then a boxing match, greeted with great enthusiasm by Mr. Hawk and his daughter, who, I discover, has a passion for punching. The most fun thing of all is *The Amateur Hour,* a program with really absurd people imitating famous actors and singers. One lady tries to sing "Put the Blame on Mame," but they're all painful to watch, and don't realize how bad they are; in fact they seem extremely satisfied just to be seen on television by relatives and friends who have gotten together for that purpose, to hear them give a "special greeting"; and at this point—ha ha ha—we all understand why they decided to invite us on this particular day: an uncle of Audrey's is performing opera arias in the style of Caruso. He sends a special greeting to her, and she looks all radiant and blushes, while Pat holds her hand. They are really revolting, those two, Audrey buttons a button at his wrist, he makes a bunch of goopy faces at her, and then Audrey acts even more like a baby, a little with her dad, a little with Pat. Yuck. They are really obscene, these fat, sentimental Hawks, so disgustingly pleasant and happy when you can't see what the hell there is to be so good-humored about. A mystery. And then this ridiculous idea of having a television party, this marathon of programs coming on one after another. Finally there's a super-platinum blonde who teaches shooting, and a political discussion, and then that's the end. Mama Humbert comes to get me. I must tell Liza that she didn't miss anything by staying at her house with Roy—that had to be more interesting. But then, as Liza and I have said a hundred times, going to the theater or the movies is even better, obviously. I would never perform on TV: I don't see what's so great about being reduced to smaller than normal dimensions, and besides you can be switched off from one moment to the next by any imbecile; it's not like the movies or a theater where people look at you with respect if not actual adoration for the simple reason that they can't pull the plug and make you disappear when they like.

26.

I GOT THE lead role in *The Enchanted Forest*: I'm a farmer's daughter who knows how to hypnotize people, and since she's very successful—she studied a manual from beginning to end—she eventually overdoes it and hypnotizes herself, in the sense that she convinces herself she really has magic powers. This farmer's daughter is very pretty, with chestnut hair and smoky gray eyes just like me, and Miss Blumenau must have understood from this that I had to have the part. I wander alone in the woods imagining I'm a fairy, a goddess, or something like that, whatever, a non-earthly nymph-type creature, and when I meet men who are hunting in the woods, I whisper my spells from behind a tree, very softly, so softly that at first these hunters—who are easily recognizable because they all wear red caps—take me for the voice of the wind. Then they begin to fantasize, and all of them, while they're waiting for their prey, call to me, a little differently according to whether it's the banker (Holbrook), the plumber (older Kerlaw), the policeman (Idelette), the undertaker (Audrey, of course), the failed writer (Kerlaw junior), or the escaped convict (Jade). Then this girl, I mean me, shows herself at a distance, and they think it's a hallucination, because with my whispery voice I hypnotize them to the core, so when I appear they're prepared to see me, and when I run away they follow, because I've bewitched them first with my voice and then with my ethereal appearance, and as a result they forget the hunt and everything they did before. I devise various stratagems, and something funny always happens, because I'm kind of contemptuous and I laugh at the hunters' misadventures. I make them stumble (they're not looking where they're going, because they have eyes only for me), and they become the prey, until they find themselves in my cave, and there they kneel at my feet to tell me that their life is a nightmare and only I can make them happy, or save them, whatever. Each in his own way makes these grand declarations. I listen haughtily, then I make them scatter, and they are left to wander in the woods like inexperienced hunters, searching for me. When they actually see me for the first time—on a small hill in a clearing—I stand still in profile, and then start moving, sort of in dance steps, but very slowly, almost slow motion. As soon as I realize that a hunter is about to reach me I don't simply run away, but give the impression of disappearing without noticing him, that is, I run so that it looks like I'm still dancing. Otherwise he'd realize that I'm a real, flesh-and-blood girl. I'm escaping in order not to be found out. I do different little maneuvers, until eventually I find a poet, and you know it's a poet because his cap is green rather than red. Liza plays the poet. I do my tricks, but he stands there reciting something. Instead of being enchanted by my whispers, he makes gestures as if brushing away flies, but he looks bewitched and I think it's because of me. I whisper a little at him, then move to a place where I can play the apparition, and start my dance steps, but I realize that he doesn't even see me: he seems to be looking at me but in fact he's looking at something within himself, a woman he imagines, who has nothing to do with me. He's bewitched not by me but by his muse; I will never see his muse because I'm not a poet, only an apprentice fairy. The moment when I realize I have utterly failed to make him see me has to be funny. I'm really annoyed that I haven't enchanted this guy, so I get closer and closer, hoping to be noticed, and my dance steps keep getting more and more uncertain and awkward, since I'm feeling insecure, and he's going off in the opposite direction, not because he's seen me but by chance. So the situation is reversed, and I'm following him and my running dance steps become more and more like normal running in a race. Then the poet turns around, because my steps, feather-light at first, become more and more hammerlike, and, seeing me dressed as a nymph and running so oafishly, he stops, bursts out laughing, and says: You seem to have come out of one of my poems. But instead of following me, he goes away; I'm furious, and the next time I see him I lead him near my house and kiss him, so he has to admit that I really exist, I'm not some fantasy of his. Afterward we go to a tavern, and there we find all the enchanted hunters—the banker, the plumber, the cop, the undertaker, the failed writer, and the escaped convict—who, when they see me come in like an ordinary woman with an ordinary man, are left openmouthed and rubbing their eyes. And there the story ends, Miss Blumenau concludes, because if it went on . . .

Humbert went to the dentist. He has to have an operation that will leave him with hardly any teeth, just a few here and there to support the bridges. Revolting. The widower Maze has fallen apart quickly, poor man; just over a year of love with his dear Dolly and already he's losing his teeth. But he asked for it, didn't he?

Unbelievable! Miss Bluedick explains to us how babies are made. She comes to class all ladylike, with the same old Tim from the bus, who sets up the projector.

"Today you'll see a film." Glance at the class to enjoy the expected enthusiastic reaction. "How nice!" Kerlaw and Hawk twitter in unison.

"It's rather a special film . . . " in a tone of suspense. "Today you will see how you came into the world." Oh wow! Great expectation in the classroom. Pinch from Liza: "Don't laugh."

"I won't say anymore. The film speaks for itself." She turns out the lights. "Tim, let's begin." And we see another Bluedick in front of a class like ours, with a stick in her hand to explain what's happening on the screen, and then she disappears, and you just hear her voice explaining how babies are made: first you have to mature; then men produce seeds like little fish and women produce eggs, and all these fish that make up the sperm end up in the large "vagina of the mother." From there they go to the great "uterus of the mother," until just one succeeds in getting into an egg, and then a new cell is created, which begins to divide and double, and by dividing and doubling becomes a child, et cetera, et cetera. Occasional laughs from Holbrook, Kerlaw, Hawk, and friends when the baby comes out of "the mother's belly." Happy parents with the infant in their arms (at that point the generous donor of the sperm, who had been kept in the shadows, emerges, with his hanging pond of tadpoles), dissolve, END, the lights are turned on, radiant faces of Bluedick and Tim. Suggestion for an immediate class discussion. Exchange of glances with Liza. That pimply spectacled sack of potatoes Audrey looks at me, offering herself—her family is a baby factory.

"Ask why they called it 'the mother's' uterus." Audrey performs. Miss Bluedick awkwardly extends her arms. Audrey, on my cue: "How can you be a mother before having a baby?"

"She is a mother because she is one in her heart of hearts," fumes Miss Bluedick.

"Ask how the sperm gets to the mother's uterus." Bluedick turns red: "The father and mother love each other and they embrace."

"Yes, but where was the sperm before?" Bluedick gets furious at Audrey, Liza and I give her a superior look. At the end of class Tim takes down the projector, singing, "Oh, little fish, don't cry anymore." What a jerk. Made for Miss Bluedick.

Miss Komar says I should take piano lessons to improve my sense of rhythm. I report to Mama Humbert, who is so eager to make peace that immediately, looking like a whipped dog, he telephones a Miss Vicompte and then calls the tuner to tune our stupid cream-colored piano. I'll ride my bike to the lessons, since winter doesn't seem to want to come this year. Never before have crocuses flowered in January and the seagulls screeched so in the sky. You might say that Humbert has stolen winter from me forever. Last year in the south I stopped in autumn; here, too, a spoke in the cycle of the seasons is broken, and the cold has fled into all the other states, even California. In Wyoming a calf was caught unawares by an ice storm so sudden that the creature died standing, frozen, it didn't even have time to throw its hoofs in the air.

What a fright Miss Vicompte is! Not so much her incredible, unimaginable decrepitude but the fact that she wears some kind of white greasepaint on her face and has awful nails half an inch thick painted oxblood. It makes a macabre effect when she presses the keys of Baby, which is her piano. Every so often she gazes at it with a look of love and eyeshadow, and purrs, "Baby is all my joy." Her eyebrows are painted so they go up to where her hair starts, which is black with a layer of whitish hair underneath, *brrrr!* Her house is like Miss Havisham's, full of prize cups and photographs and diplomas, piles of records, and an old gramophone with a trumpet. She asks if I know the staff. They taught me in Sunday school, I say, but when she sits me in front of the piano I don't know where to start. So she explains it from the beginning, which keys correspond to which notes, then she gives me exercises to understand whole and half steps, a fourth, an octave, and all that stuff. I'm always going to ride my bike to Miss Vicompte's, it's a good distance, and I bought a speedometer, like Babe's, for training, so I can get my time down by summer, and then I'll be the fastest of all.

In June Miss Bluedick is going to marry Tim. She announces this herself all beaming. Revolting, I think, now the uterus of Mother Blue Dick will welcome the fish from Father Tim Timass, alias Oh-little-fish-don't-cry-anymore. Really gross, enough to make you puke. I go to the toilet with a very definite plan, but I'm caught in the act as I'm writing with lipstick on the mirror: "Hey, motherfucker! Tim Timass and Miss Blue Dick are man and wife today." Miss Blumenau intercedes with Miss Short, but still I have to apologize to Bluedick who's all puffed up, with her nose in the air, as she listens to me. Then I have to endure the horrible Dr. Sharp, who tries to find out if I have "problems linked to my emotional life," and insists that I have some sessions with her. I'll think about it, I say to get rid of her, because what a bunch of crap to be examined by a joke of a psychoanalyst and have to tell her everything blow by blow and then listen to her illuminating opinion. I know perfectly well how it would end—I'd be shut in a reformatory, and some shit of a doctor would examine what's going on in my mind, with the result that I might as well forget my play with Filthy, and my life will go down the drain once and for all thanks to the combined forces of this mass of shits. As you like, Dr. Sharp says, but I'm here if you change your mind, and she gives me a book, *A Mother's Heart*, with a horrible pink-and-pea-green cover.

Poor Mama Humbert! The dentist pulled out all his upper teeth, and when he tries to kiss me it's frightening, he can't control his mouth, his jaw is slack, it's revolting. Forget it, I say, but he insists. He's lost his sense of shame. He's showing the first signs of senile incontinence.

Liza is totally preoccupied because she's late. She wonders if she should tell Roy, we talk about it all afternoon, and really she doesn't know what to do. Certainly if there's going to be an operation you might as well keep the baby, because later maybe you'd regret it, thinking about how it would have been, and you'd get depressed dreaming about it every night or something like that. It's certainly a mess, but Liza thinks her mother will find a solution, she always has, after all. If I found myself with a baby inside that I didn't ask for, I'd feel like I had cancer.

First snow! I had given up hope. After school we find Roy and Freddy, in a white sweater, his cheeks red in the cold, and wander around the town, which is all sparkling in the snow. It's fantastic. Then Freddy walks me home and asks if we can go to the movies together. Maybe, I say, maybe, but how can I explain why I can't? I hint that my father is slightly mad and won't let me go to the movies with boys my age, but we could arrange to go skating with Liza and Roy.

Mama Humbert's bottom teeth are gone, too, except for a few, and the upshot is that his mouth is half numb, and his poor face looks like a watercolor blotted with a sponge. The bridges with the false teeth will be here in a week, and in the meantime he has to drink fruit juice through a straw and eat pablum for infants. I make it for him with all my maternal love. Now that he finally realizes how wretched he looks, he tries to see me as little as possible. He looks so pathetic I almost feel tender.

The book that Dr. Sharp gave me is really sad. I read it today and cried all night. There's a mother who knows she's going to die young, and she hides how much she loves her daughter, Jessy, because she thinks that afterward it will be easier for Jessy to love her father's new wife. But Jessy doesn't understand that her mother is being cold and distant for her own benefit, so when she sees other mothers being affectionate with their children she is consumed by a wild envy, she hates them. She's terribly unhappy, and when her mother dies in a hospital she says, Who cares, it's better that way. Then her father marries another woman, who you discover was chosen for her father by Jessy's mother because she was worried about finding the right person for Jessy. This second wife is a nice cheerful woman, and she sees that Jessy, instead of forgetting her mother, hates her more and more, and instead of growing up peacefully is tormented by rage at the fact that her mother didn't love her. So actually it's worse than if she and her mother had been affectionate, even if Jessy would have suffered more when she died. The good stepmother realizes that something is wrong, that Jessy is even more unhappy than if she had simply been orphaned, and that Jessy's mother made a mistake in deciding to hide her love for her daughter, suffering for nothing and torturing herself with this charade of not loving her. Now it all has to be put right, so the good stepmother tries to talk to Jessy, who refuses to listen because she hates everyone. Finally she gives in, and she finds out everything about her mother, who sacrificed herself so that Jessy would be happy, except she was wrong. So Jessy understands, and she hugs the good stepmother. They cry together like two fountains, then they go to the cemetery to put flowers on the grave of Jessy's mother, and they pray for her, and love each other, and up in heaven Jessy's mother can feel better seeing that her daughter has finally understood, and she's happy that Jessy has forgiven her, because being hated by the person she loved most in the world broke her heart. I don't even know where my murdered mother is buried. I've never seen her grave, and I don't have a shred of anything to help me understand what happened, or whether she was mean to me because she loved me to distraction and felt she was dying, or because she was just a bitch.

Liza is even more worried. It still hasn't come, and she still hasn't said anything to Roy. God, what a super big drag to be pregnant! Liza's mother tells her not to say anything for the moment. As for the baby, which should be born around September, she'll manage to make it pass for hers. Already they speak as if it's their baby. I don't know if I envy her or feel sorry for her, because it would be weird to have a baby but make it believe you're its sister, and then there's the complication with Roy, who still doesn't know anything, and could decide he won't go along and wants the baby to be his, which would be fine except that Liza isn't sure she wants to marry him. It turns out to be incredibly complicated. Yikes!

Second meeting of the drama club: since my part is mostly danced, in the afternoon I'm going to have a private hour with Miss Komar. Liza's going to have lessons with Miss Blumenau by herself, to learn the passage from poet to normal man.

. . .

"What are you so cheerful about?" Humbert asks hopefully, spitting because he's not used to his false teeth yet.

"I like the play. By the way, did you see the title? *The Enchanted Forest*."

"It was the name of a hotel, remember?" he says with a gaze full of senile sadness. I pretend not to remember anything about our first night, and Humbert feels really bad. I ask if he wants to read the play, but he won't even touch it. I try to tell him about it, and he pronounces judgment: "Worse than the worst of Hollywood, only more dust onstage." So much for the opinion of Mama Humbert. Miss Blumenau invited Filthy Sue to opening night. I have to be perfect, absolutely perfect. My guardian angel has to realize that I'm the best. I tell Liza that Filthy is from where I used to live, his uncle was our dentist, and I can call him Filthy Sue because he's a friend of mine. I'm so excited! If I do well in the nymph part, he's agreed to take me to a real theater. Liza has promised to help me keep Humbert out of the way. We have to have a bombproof plan of defense.

They're all annoyed with me, the clucking quartet of Bluedick, Ravensea, Slaw, and Root, because "I don't apply myself." But I don't have time I don't have time and I don't have time!!! I have a tremendous test to do in front of Filthy Sue. Blumenau's the only one who understands what a totally absorbing vocation is. And Komar a little, but the dance she's making up for me is stupid, so we're always arguing. I hate people who think a dance in a forest has to be poetic. I hate the whole idea of poetic.

It's Sunday, and I have to go with my dear toothless dad to the same old detestable Walrus Inn, where we see Miss Short, who applauds me from her table.

"What's that all about?" mutters Humbert, frowning. Eyebrows even thicker and more grizzled for the occasion, like a caricature.

"I wouldn't know. Go and ask her."

He gets up to say hello to Miss Short, and she tells him that I am really good, a great career is opening up, and as headmistress of the school she is extremely proud of me, et cetera, et cetera. Humbert stares at me full of hatred, and I, who know something about hate, never imagined you could hate someone so much.

"You're not happy that I'm doing pretty well at least in something, Dad?"

"And what is this play you're so good in?"

"I've told you a thousand times, it's a play that's already been on in New York."

"Don't use that tone, and above all not in this restaurant."

"You don't want to read it?"

"I don't waste my time on these Americanisms. I have to finish my book."

"Oh." Him and his stupid textbook. Three volumes of lousy poetic rehashings. I tried to read it once and fell asleep at the fifth word.

Damn. Financial ruin. No five hundred dollars. Not even two hundred or one hundred. The first prize from *Seventeen* went to a sixteen-year-old boy for "The Cocoon," the second to a girl younger than me who wrote a tearjerker thing about Siamese kittens. At least they could have given me third for my story about Nelson the Second. They must have preferred good feelings. Kittens are more popular than hamsters. I would have been better off writing the old story about the death of Nelson the First. All because I remembered that Mom didn't like me writing about that and I had this dumb idea of making her happy at least when she was dead. What an idiot. She even beat me in this. She must still be mad at me, she's up in heaven and cheating me, maneuvering from the beyond. She's taking revenge because she couldn't get Humbert to like her, only to marry her. And I let myself be taken in by that stupid *Mother's Heart*; obviously that goddam psychomanipulator gave it to me just for that purpose.

Amazing how the character of these jerks comes out at rehearsals: the bitch Holbrook, who plays the banker, which is perfect

(Miss Blumenau was pretty clever in how she assigned parts according to everyone's true character), doesn't want to let herself be seduced by me: she has a lot of trouble getting into the part, looking at me with dreamy eyes and then revealing to me how terrible her life is among all those businessmen. She doesn't sound much like she means it; instead of letting herself be overwhelmed by passion, she makes a face as if to say it's a great honor for me that she even notices my existence. She is a really pompous suitor. Miss Blumenau gives her a fake belly, just right for a banker. Kerlaw is also a disaster, as the mediocre writer, in the scene where she laments the life of an artist forced to publish, under pseudonyms, love stories between old romantic widows and retired pilots—she says this like it's absolutely the best kind of writing. Most absurd of all is Audrey: she's so fat, and she can't take off her metal-rimmed glasses even for a second, so she can't figure out how to run after me, and today, poor girl, she let out a big fart; hats off if she does that on opening night, because an undertaker with eyeglasses and pimples who farts while he dreams of winning a nymph would be super.

Filthy Sue is coming to Ithaca in May to watch rehearsals. God, it seems like tomorrow.

Humbert has to host a lunch for his colleagues, and asks me to help in the kitchen peeling potatoes. I say that a qualified worker like me, who can get nine dollars for a blow job with simultaneous anal penetration can't lower herself to a rate of twenty cents an hour.

"You could do it free and act unselfish for once." Look who's talking. Finally the shit guests arrive. Xavier, naturally, puts on an opera record, the mad scene from *Lucia di Lammermoor*, and, half drunk, he does some inspired gyrations with his fat ass, but his musical interlude is interrupted by the arrival of a Latin professor, a guy with snow-white hair tinted pink and a powdered face, like an old perfume seller. Humbert puts him next to me at the table and he talks to me sweetly about his grandchildren, though I don't know why I should be interested. There's also a fat lady professor whose nose is longer than her legs but less crooked; the whole time she pretends not to notice me, but I see her, and especially her nose, way too much, because she's on my right and emits streams of some fragrance which Humbert later explains is a disgusting scent that a French company sent to the vulgar United States before the war, and this scent, among other things, made his uncle's fortune. His American uncle. Take any hen and you will find in the middle the self-interested paw of some virile member of the house of Humbert.

Filthy arrived! At the rehearsal, he sat next to Miss Blumenau, who shook her hair and kept crossing her long American legs so that he'd notice her. The flirt. Then she got in the car with him to go to his hotel. Hateful. That's why she was so eager for him to be here.

But no. Miss Blumenau says that Filthy is enthusiastic about my performance. He comes in person, and says I am perfect but must be even more so. He gives me some suggestions, telling me above all to be careful not to try too hard, which you have to do at rehearsals, but then it should come naturally, as if I were simply myself, as if I had never in my life been anything but a nymph. After we talk, he gives me a ride in his car, and as I'm getting in Blumenau whispers, "Be careful, he has a weakness for adolescents."

"Don't worry, I've seen worse." Smile from Filthy Sue, and as soon as we're alone he mimics the scene of him going to see Humbert pretending to be the psychologist, and he imitates my toothless old dad sensationally. He asks how we're doing, the two of us, but then he stops me, he wants to guess himself, and hell, he gets it almost exactly, as if he'd been under the bed the whole time. A genius! We make a super-secret appointment for tomorrow afternoon at five in front of the Walrus Inn, which is when I'm supposed to be at my piano lesson, the stupid piano lesson that finally is good for something. I tell almost everything to Liza, who is stunned—she's never heard of such a farsighted courtship. "But how did he know you'd be in his play?"

I shrug.

"It's fantastic! It's like when you throw a bottle in the ocean . . . Can I tell my mother?" No! It's a secret.

27.

*H*UMBERT ALMOST FOUND out everything! That rotten old maid Vicompte—who would have thought of her—telephones tonight while Humbert is playing chess with Xavier, and complains that she hasn't seen me for a while. O.K., according to plan I explain to Humbert that I've been with Liza the whole time, practicing the scene in the forest. He sends Xavier off in a hurry, in the middle of the game—unheard of—and right away telephones the Websters for confirmation, and gets it, also according to plan. But instead of calming down, my dear dad gets paranoid, and even madder. He says we're in league, it's time to put a stop to it or else . . . and so on, down to repeating his ridiculous rancid threats of the reformatory and even the old warning about exiling me to the Appalachians with that shitbag Stinkhorn and so on. We have a really terrible fight, I mean so terrible that he almost breaks my wrist. Now I'm sure he murdered my mother—he's got at least one talent, for the perfect crime. A lucky ring of the telephone interrupts us. I go off on my bike and call Filthy Sue from a pay phone. I tell him everything—Humbert's discovered us, and we have to do something quick. He says, Listen, I have a fantastic idea, and while he's explaining it, he decides I can skip the play—who cares about Ithaca, you'll make your début in a real theater. Now tell your dear daddy that you love him madly and you want him to take you away immediately, but make him swear that you'll choose the route this time . . . And right at that point the adored daddy, who's taken a long time to find me because the car's at the repair shop and he had to walk, thank goodness, tracks me down. Though I still have only the vaguest idea of the plan, I go up to him like the most loving and remorseful of lovers: "My dear love! So that's why no one's answering. I was calling you, oh what a torture, let's go, we're not alone in this place, we're lost, let's get away as soon as we can. To hell with school and the play. I hate plays, I love you and only you, I want it to be just the two of us alone again, but I want you to promise one thing." Mama Humbert, face like an eager puppy, is at my feet: "Whatever you want."

"This time, no charade of your being my father. This time, we go as lovers—you're the man and I'm the woman, you're Tarzan and I'm Jane. Dear Dad, I'm grown up now and I have a lot of experience, so I get to choose the route. I'll take you on the most stupendous journey of your life and then we can get married in Mexico and never come back to the United States, and you can take me to see the South of France, and we can have fifty-two thousand babies, and there won't be any more Xavier to play chess, and no more plays or dances at the Academy, no nothing, only the two of us who adore each other." Humbert showers me with kisses, his heart goes *boom boom boom* with emotion, poor thing. He kisses my hands and feet and knees. What a pain. Come, my treasure, I say, it's going to storm soon, and if I get sick we can't leave. So we return in a warm romantic drizzle. I hold Mama Humbert tight and tell him to carry me into our love nest. He does it, his face radiant and flooded with joy, his false teeth dazzling white like ice cream. He closes the door behind him and abandons himself to the enthusiasm of love renewed, bathing me with tears and sperm all night long. The next day he comes home with an aquamarine, he gives it to me with I don't remember what nauseating lines of poetry. It's so painful! He even increases my allowance, to a dollar and fifty cents.

We're leaving soon. In the inevitable blue sedan, which Humbert, Lord knows why, calls his Melmoth, and now it's at the mechanic's again for a few last repairs. Humbert made up a story for Miss Short, about having to go to Hollywood to be a consultant on a film about existentialism, and he is inflexible in the face of requests to let me stay for the play: he refuses to leave me in strange hands. If something should happen while he is away, he would never forgive himself—he hasn't been able to trust anyone since his wife died under the lead weight of a car that came on her out of nowhere (blah blah) . . . A real melodrama of his great widower-paternal love, with Short and Blumenau and Komar desperate at losing the star of the play, while the evil quartet of Ravensea-Bluedick-Root-Slaw rejoices at replacing me with the awkward, lifeless, stammering younger Kerlaw, and I have to improvise in the role of affectionate daughter in tears at the idea of being separated even for a single instant from her dad: a child so sensitive, so needy for affection . . . If they were all like that, sighs Mrs. Hawk, Lord knows why.

A Bible salesman shows up, one of those unbearable types with a lumpy face like a boxer's and the frozen smile of a missionary. The good boy eager to do all he can for anyone, and with the money he earns selling Bibles he takes his girl to the movies Saturday night. He starts with Humbert, who's washing the car, and who gets rid of him by sending him over to me. I ask the guy what a Bible is, and, amazed, he starts explaining, but he doesn't do very well. It's the word of God, he says. And who is this Mr. God, I ask. He looks at me astonished but tries to explain that, too, and while he's stumbling I start my dance as the hunter of hunters, until finally he realizes I'm making fun of him. Furious, he marches over to Humbert, saying that his daughter dared . . . and Humbert sprays him with the hose. For once he shows some presence of mind, my dear dad. He forgot to worry about what people will say. Miracle of miracles! Effect of the word of God or of having one foot already out of Ithaca?

Sunday we leave! A real flash of lightning, Professor Guibert, settling everything, giving up the house to the Panzees, and groaning over the lost deposit and the reimbursement for the collection of blue porcelain lovingly broken by me. Saturday we pack. Wow! I saw Filthy Sue, and his plan is ingenious, really ingenious: at every stop I let him know where we're staying next, and he'll stay there, too, and then we agree on the next destination, or if we don't manage to speak I'm to leave a lipstick mark on the map. All this right under Humbert's luckily stuffed-up nose, and at the first chance we run away. Our final destination is Grace, where they're putting on a play called *Lightning Loves,* by him and someone called Andreas Nightingale.

Miss Blumenau sees us loading the suitcases and accuses my poor innocent dad of taking away the star of the show. And that dope, right at the beginning of our great journey of true and reciprocal love, gives me a lecture like a real pain-in-the-ass father about the fact that I am too impulsive and should control this destructive instinct that leads me to give up things before finishing them; that not being able to delay gratifying a whim even for a week is a dangerous tendency, if for no other reason than to properly finish a project I was so enthusiastic about for months—too enthusiastic, he continues, there must necessarily have been something not genuine in so much enthusiasm . . . Then he inflicts on me a summary of my "short life": I leave Goatscreek for camp, camp for a trip, and then my changes of mood, all my infinite caprices . . . He tells some real lies without even knowing it. He's a pathological liar. I can't believe he's preaching at me, but that big jerk speaks as if this person beside him really had decided herself what she wanted. He has simply forgotten that the hen sent me away from Goatscreek, he himself took me away from camp, and I have never ever had a say in any of it, and this is absolutely the first, and I mean the very first, time that I'm doing something because I want to. It's the first time I've arranged my own flight. The whole time Humbert's blathering I can see Filthy Sue's red convertible in the mirror, and every so often I wave hello without turning my head. Now that Mama Humbert thinks my theatrical career is over for good, he is suddenly curious about my play. I tell him it's the work of Geraldine Lou Guilty, an old lady who's been writing children's books for a million years.

We have to be in Grace in the middle of June; I tell Mama Humbert that we can't miss the ceremonial dances in Magic Cave, which are not like the ones he would call touristy but are authentic, he'll like it. This time the trip is fun; Mama Humbert at the wheel has the radiant face of a happy lover, with the metal hook of the bridge in his mouth always in plain sight. He even gives me a bottle of French perfume, until now totally forbidden. He doesn't realize that behind us is Filthy Sue's red convertible, ready to convert my dear Mr. Dad, who having eyes only for me doesn't see anything else. Filthy and I exchange notes with our impressions of the trip, and even manage a few kisses near the toilets in the gas stations, despite the fact that Rimbaud is really jealous and always works his way in between us, complaining loudly if we don't include him. But every so often Filthy has fun getting me upset: he vanishes for a while, then reappears, like he's blinking on and off. He's a great big blinker.

Mile after empty mile, the roads never end, the rain follows us like a peeing puppy. Which is good because the famous figure of Gerry Sue Filthy is all smeared by the rain—two dark lines for his mustache, a pink point for his lips, and the grayish patch of Rimbaud, sitting next to him all puffed up, pink tongue flapping in the wind. He's there and not there, now you see him, now you don't. It's a scream. Too bad that since Humbert thinks I'm in love with him he's even worse than before. He is all sickly sweet. He gives me the most pallid quivering caresses, he asks if I'm happy, really happy, if I like it, if I want to do it again. Then he is seized by this horrible mania for sniffing my toes, "to become intoxicated by them." The sort of thing I used to do with the hen when I was more or less a baby. The result is that it makes me sick. It's nauseating to see a grown man, with curls of white hair on his chest, thick eyebrows, and on his face that slightly doglike expression, with only one purpose in life, only one interest: to get inside me. That's where he feels alive—if he's stuck to me everything seems O.K.

· · ·

Filthy Sue and I initiate a new series of notes: Humbert's nick-
names. I list them while I'm sitting in the car, and the idea that he
suspects absolutely nothing gives me the perpetual giggles. Mama
Humbert mistakes it for the happiness of having him beside me.
Poor beast.

Where the hell has Filthy Sue disappeared to? We're supposed to
go to Whiskey together, to my old house, and he disappears. With all
the trouble I had convincing Humbert to go to a place that's so hot.
At this point who cares about Whiskey, better to stay in Cassava or
else we'll lose each other. I wanted to go back to Goatscreek, to the
book club, where Filthy Sue took me on his knees and held me in
his arms in front of the bright smiles and applause of all the ladies . . .
But on that Mama Humbert won't give in. Whereas he's happy to go
to Whiskey, and now he's almost sorry that I don't care about it anymore. I tell him I don't want to move on right away, I want to enjoy
the lawns and the woods and the swing, and besides I don't feel well,
so he goes out to get me some fruit. While he's out I hear the roar of
a car, and it's Filthy Sue, finally; his carburetor broke. We go into to
the garden, and sit on the swing; when we're back inside he scratches me under my dress, *prrrr prrrr prrrr*, while Rimbaud, not to be left
out, licks my ears, but no one must hear, we're secret lovers. I feel
weak, all bubbling with pleasure, but meanwhile we have to keep
watch out the window. Around noon Filthy Sue sees Humbert in
the chestnut-shaded street, with a bunch of bananas in his hand and
his hair sheared, so he takes off, with his tried-and-true theatrical
exit, beating his wings like a baby eagle and shouting Help, they're
raping me, while Rimbaud follows, barking with excitement. I lie on
the bed and hug my shoulders to hold on a little longer to the sensation of shivers up and down my back, until I hear a crunching
sound on the gravel outside the door. It's that shaved beast Humbert,
who had the astonishing idea of getting a haircut in town.
Unbelievable what he looks like—it's embarrassing to go out with
him. He glares at me perplexed, confused: What are you doing

dressed, he asks, then he examines me, makes his odious inspection like a police dog. You have gravel in your sandals, you've been out, you're not at all sick, then he strips me touches me smells me to find proof of betrayal. I hate him when he does this. Aside from everything else it's horribly undignified.

We continue the trip, amid huge thunderstorms that cause tremendous havoc. But it doesn't matter because we're having a swell time. Tonight Filthy Sue knocked on our door and terrorized Humbert, glimmering in front of him in white skeleton pajamas and the mask of Cutting Nose. Cuckoo! Too bad that after Cassava Humbert got suspicious; he suddenly realized there was a red car always behind us . . .

God, how far he is from the truth. He almost caught us at a gas station. Filthy Sue had come over to my window to discuss the route, and Humbert spotted us, though luckily he only saw Filthy Sue from behind as he was taking off. He falls on me panting and says, Who is that man? A guy who wanted to look at the map, I tell him. Mama Humbert sweats, he's afraid of the police, he decides the man in the red car is following us to arrest us both, and orders me not to speak to strangers because every word can be used against us . . . Poor, poor jerk. He doesn't see the danger when it's behind him, he doesn't even suspect that on this trip he is merely acting as a chauffeur, paid in special favors but with a time limit, a very short time limit. And then that peeled look he has now is painful. It's heartbreaking to see him.

Damn cop. Lets us go but stops Sue's car at a signal. Humbert accelerates to shake him, puts on a little smile of triumph for the occasion. Triumph like hell: we'll see each other in Grace, baby. It's still raining, and the lightning's terrifying. I'm in a bad mood—the storms make me nervous. Humbert's expression of relief at the idea of having lost Sue is unbearable. "Out of our hair!" he cries, pleased that he no longer sees him in the mirror.

• • •

Finally we're in Grace. Too bad, Dad, I was wrong, the ceremonial dances are over. Oh, I was so looking forward to them! Why don't we go to the theater, there's a play . . . Gosh, how dumb he is. He doesn't even realize that it's by Gerry Sue Filthy. Yesterday by accident we end up at the same restaurant, with Sue behind Mama Humbert. Every so often he turns and makes signals behind Humbert's head, which come out of the Chinese-restaurant shadows pretty clearly. I pretend to be laughing at whatever garbage Humbert's saying, and he notices nothing, nothing. He's blind, he rages like a blind man, he falls into the blackest, darkest impotence, he strokes and sniffs, in a terrific frenzy, but otherwise he's calm and cheerful and doesn't see a thing, really not a thing. It must be because he has only one thing on his mind: this never-ending desire to fuck me. He is hypnotized by the fury of the urgent red blood cells inside, and so he lacks the energy to see, the eyes of the great scholar Humbert are bloodless because of his monomania, but when he reaches out his arms and doesn't find me where he expects to find me he panics, his eyes are bloodshot, his body goes limp, and he quivers like a trapped bat. The thing is, he chose this horror of a life for himself.

Lightning Loves is a work of genius. Fantastic. Humbert doesn't get it at all, but when we leave, it turns out that he's not completely blind, the creep. Suddenly, he recognizes the name of Filthy Sue on the playbill, and that prompts a brilliant series of associations: "Look, your old flame!" (Thanks, gossiping hen.) I am indignant, incredulous, speechless: "How could you imagine that I could possibly ever like a dentist!" I don't think I completely convinced him. We go back to the motel, and there I get a real fright: Filthy Sue's picture in the paper! Little mustache and all. Luckily I see it first, while Humbert is in the bathroom, and hide it, or it would be all over.

I get a letter from Liza at the post office in Grace. Since Mama Humbert has the incredible delicacy to grab it from me to read it first himself, I make a run for it. It's so easy: in reality it's the simplest thing to do what you want. I could run away right now. I was an idiot to let Humbert and his idle threats frighten me. What was I afraid of? While he literally has his nose stuck in Liza's letter I slip away, right to Filthy Sue's hotel. He welcomes me with a wail of pleasure, takes me to the coolest ice-cream parlor in Grace, and we order an unbelievable sundae, with raspberry syrup and cocoa dust and then all kinds of nuts and candied fruit. I give the cookies to Rimbaud. We make a ton of plans for our future, and meanwhile he's scratching me with his clever little scratches, the ones under your dress that no one will notice. In November he'll take me to Hollywood for an audition. But why don't we run away now?

"Come on, let's have a little more fun like this, behind your father's back."

"But you know what he does with me?"

"Exactly what all the good dads in the world do with their daughters," he says, aping Mama Humbert perfectly. It's amazing: he can hear someone once, anyone, and no matter how much time has gone by he can reproduce the voice perfectly, better than a tape recorder. "Look out, get under the table!" Just in time, he sees Humbert, who has come in looking for me: we're safe by a hair's breadth.

"My father never did anything like that," I continue, now that the danger has passed.

"Maybe he was impotent?" with the voice of Truman.

"Don't you dare speak like that about my dad."

"Don't use that tone; if they find us they'll shut you up in the reformatory," in the voice of Mama Humbert. That's enough, incredible, too much!

"But if you love me, why not take me away?" He explains that I mustn't be an egoist. For you it would be fine to leave immediately, but I can't, I have to stay here at the festival. And then, consider the feelings of others: for me this business of following you and making fun of your father behind his back is terrific fun. It makes me write like a train. And you want me to write plays for you, right? Well, of course I do, but to keep putting it off, what a drag!

28.

GREAT COMPLIMENTS FROM Filthy Sue on the way I
resolved the situation: brilliant, totally brilliant. It happened like this: stupid Professor Humbert had taken one of those
endless roads full of sharp curves, and Filthy Sue had been behind us
in a gray car for at least three hours, under a dark-blue sky spotted
with big blinding-white clouds that little by little were turning into
a kind of foggy cotton wool, and on one curve he and Rimbaud just
missed ending up on top of us, gray against the gray fog. And
Humbert starts worrying again, thinking as usual of the police. He
thinks he's being pursued, but he's got the wrong target. He has no
imagination. The road is like this, a straight uphill stretch and then a
curve, and we go on until I point out to Humbert that we have a flat
tire, *tum tum tum*, on my side. He pulls up at the edge of a foggy
precipice, and in the rearview mirror glimpses Filthy Sue, who also
stops; he turns to get a better look, and sees him still there, not moving: cat and mouse. Humbert gets out of the car, slams the door, and
moves decisively toward Filthy. He has my dad's .32 in his pocket—
this is getting serious. So I sit at the wheel, and, concentrating hard,
as if I were about to go onstage, I say to myself: Dolores Maze, you
are now a woman with years and years of driving behind you, you
will do what you've seen Humbert do with this old car, exactly as if
you'd been doing it all your life, as if the drop below simply were not
there. With a determined, slightly bored expression, just right for a
sophisticated woman of the world, I disengage the hand brake, turn
on the motor, and let the car roll gently along the cliff, steering
toward the left so it doesn't go hurtling off. Meanwhile in the mirror
I see Filthy Sue backing up as grim Humbert advances, hand on pistol. Then he hears our old sedan sliding on the gravel. He slows

down, turns, stops, and seeing through the fog that I'm at the wheel he runs back, furious. "What are you doing?"

"Nothing, I was trying to convince this car not to kill itself. Not with me inside, at least." My old dad stops making objections. He realizes he's acting ridiculous. And while he's on his knees changing the tire I caress his balding head.

Filthy Sue plays a super trick. We are at Tripleview, one of those big resort hotels in the mountains. I've been playing tennis with Humbert for a while when Cindy and Will, two actors from the show in Grace, come over: Cindy is a blonde a couple of years older than I am, Will's a muscular type, shrimp-pink, he must be at least twice her age. They stand there watching us: I'm determined not to miss the ball, I get to fifty volleys in a row, which is impressive, before letting Mama Humbert win. Will comes over and proposes doubles. Perfect fake-casual expressions, that is, slightly awkward. Humbert accepts unwillingly, but just then a bellboy comes out, urgent phone call from Ithaca, he says. Terrorized, convinced he's been discovered, he hurries to the telephone, hobbling up the ninety-nine steps from the tennis court to the lobby, without considering how utterly unlikely it is that anyone knows we're here at Tripleview. Humbert disappears, Filthy Sue emerges, grabs the racquet, and the four of us start playing, a little preview of our future pastimes in New Mexico. Cindy and Will against me and Filthy Sue. While we're playing, Filthy Sue reels off a thousand and one insults about Humbert's stupidity: he can play all the chess he wants, the fact is he fell for this like the last of the innocents. Finally, after at least half an hour (who the hell could he be talking to?), we see Humbert rushing down the ninety-nine steps, all agitated, with a black, threatening face. Filthy Sue spreads his arms as if to take flight and clears off, with his baby-eagle cry.

"Who was that?" asks Humbert.

Cindy and Will look blank. "Never saw him. He offered to play with us while you were on the telephone. He was nice, he helped you win a lot of points. Now you two are ahead."

"Why did he run off?"

"He didn't. He suddenly remembered that he's expected in church because he's supposed to be getting married." Humbert turns pale, and even paler when later, really by accident, we run into Cindy and Will in the woods near the hotel having a sidesplitting laugh. So what, I'm going swimming. Humbert stays in the room to finish the index of his book, a boring job that's ideal for calming his nerves. When he comes down he finds me with Rimbaud and the shadow of Filthy Sue, who's lying behind a hedge sunbathing. He's about to stumble on him when he's stopped by an attack of vomiting. It's really gross, stuff the color of crushed cockroaches spurts out of his mouth, with an incredibly foul stink. It's like he's throwing up his rancid yellow-and-green soul. A lady looks at him in dismay and puts a handkerchief to her nose. To save face for my dear dad, I have to invent a story about a terrible tropical illness he contracted when he was a hero in the Pacific. The lady looks understanding and patriotic and then hurries off to complain to the management. Humbert is shaken, he spits yellow and brown, and then starts on a bottle of gin. I go back to the pool, and Filthy Sue calls me from behind a bush: "Don't you think it's your turn now?"

"My turn for what?"

"To give it to Humbert." He giggles.

"What do you mean?"

"You won't have many more chances to do what you want to him."

"But I don't want to do anything."

"Are you sure? Think how much fun it would be if he were asleep, anesthetized, he isn't aware of anything, and you . . . "

"And how would he not be aware of anything?"

"A sleeping pill," and he puts two big blue capsules in my hand.

"But I don't want to kill him."

"You won't kill him. With these he'll sleep like a top and tomorrow morning he'll be cured of his nausea and his paranoia, ready to deliver you without incident to the final stopping place, Urchinheight."

"And how do I get him to take them?"

"Open the capsules and dump the powder into his disgusting pineapple gin."

I go up to the room, and find Humbert sprawled on a chair, staring into space. He's not only drunk, he's worse: "Chéri, love, what's wrong, are you sick?" He doesn't answer, he's completely done in, out of it, gone. "Let's have something to drink. Stay here, I'll take care of it." I order our usual drinks down in the lobby, and while we're waiting I make him stretch out on the bed. You're sick, I tell him, lie here beside me. He lets me nuzzle him, he lets me, my big doll with the false teeth; I undress him, put on his striped pajamas, and the whole time I'm calling him Daddy. Poor Humbert, it was his favorite game, and he gave it up to make me happy. But now it's his last chance, and I have to let him enjoy his fantasy. After all, wasn't he always telling me that I should be more understanding of other people's feelings? And now, dear Daddy, I say very lovingly, get in bed, Daddy, are you O.K. like this? Here, the drinks have arrived, thank you, here's the tip. I close the door, open the capsules, and get in bed. He rests an arm on my shoulder, and holds me tight, my exhausted ogre, he has no more strength in him, he must have a foreboding of something—his flesh has already yielded. I make him drink his drink with a straw, my subnormal dad, and he sucks the pineapple gin, obedient, like a good child. His head lolls on my shoulder, he slides to one side. I push him over on his stomach, and climb on top of him and drink my rum and Coke. He's making bleats of sleep but also of pleasure, he mumbles words words words, French words that stink of perfume and toilets. When I finish my Coke I raise one of his arms and let it go, and it falls back practically dead. Here we are, he's in the deepest sleep, I can do what I want to him, but what is it that I want? Is there any use for that wreck of a man? I explore him to get some ideas, I pull his legs apart, I take off his pajamas. There he is stretched out in front of me, a hundred and sixty-five pounds of inert flesh, legs spread, face buried in the pillow, tufts of grayish hair on the moles on his back, the mark of his bathing suit and below it his whitish bottom spotted with tiny orange pimples. Well, he should know for once what it's like to be forced to feel when you have no desire. It's clear that he likes my finger, what harm can it do, I don't even have long nails so let's see how he reacts to having other things stuck in him— the straw from the Coke, a pencil, the fountain pen, once it's there I also empty the ink cartridge into him. Mama Humbert doesn't rebel, he goes along with everything, he enjoys it as he never enjoyed it waking, he is excited in his sleep, and it makes me sick, sick, only sick. I hear knocking at the door. It's Filthy Sue: "Are you having fun?" He looks at Humbert lying like a corpse, with tears of ink dripping out of his ass, he scratches him, laughs, then takes his false teeth out of his mouth and leaves them on the table along with a plastic carnation.

Finally, Urchinheight, but I had to take a big risk. We arrive at the bungalow, near the famous red rock, the suicide rock, which in fact is nothing special, and when we get to the room I feel sick. I've caught some sort of virus, but I'm so sick I have to be taken to the hospital, and all my stuff is at the disposal of Mama Humbert. I've had a fever for I don't know how long, and I seem to have been delirious. Humbert thinks I've got polio: what luck, to end up with one leg shorter than the other. He might like it, a woman with one child leg and one adult. But thank goodness it's not polio, because I don't want to be the President of the United States, I want to be an actress, and for that having polio would obviously be an insurmountable obstacle. So I'm in the hospital, where a cute young nurse named Julie keeps me company when she can. She's a great fan of Gerry Sue Filthy. I tell her he's my uncle but I have to travel with a French stepfather who has legal authority although he's a tremendous pain in the ass and a pig because he's always trying to touch me. Julie is outraged and takes our side. She makes friends with Filthy Sue, who gives her a signed copy of his latest book. Julie thanks him radiantly and promises to help us run away together. Humbert annoys us with his incessant visits, which are always outside of visiting hours, with that oily face of his, like a bitch in heat, that, though he doesn't know it, he got when the pen sprayed ink in him, and brought out his true nature—that of a toothless old whore. Julie finds the combination of convict-style haircut and pretentiousness unbearable, and for this she gets credit, even though, poor Humbert, I must say that starting in Ithaca he suddenly stopped being successful with women: a sign of his irreparable decadence, which ended with him losing his teeth. It's remarkable that in all this time no one, and I mean no one, has ever tried to take me away from him.

Today for the first time they let me keep the window open: I like lying with my eyes closed and feeling the mountain breeze caressing my cheeks and my arms. The mountain is gray and glitters with horizontal striations: some are white like ice, others pinkish orange or almost violet. After the sun sets, the mountain is like a big block of gray-blue air under a steel sky. I asked Humbert to bring me my suitcase and the hen's trunk the next time he comes, without making a fuss, and I asked Julie to get rid of the flowers and all those stupid heavy books Humbert brings.

He is sick, poor man. He couldn't even bring me my stuff. I got it all the same, from a friend of the motel owner, a guy covered with scars and tattoos who delivered it all as requested, the suitcase and the trunk, and even the pack of Kotex with my diary in it. Tomorrow, July 4th, Filthy Sue is coming to get me. When Humbert arrives at the hospital, Julie will tell him that I already left with Uncle Gustave. That will teach him a lesson.

On July 4th, as planned, Filthy Sue, alias Uncle Gustave, arrives in a big black car with the present I've dreamed of my whole life: a cocker spaniel! Rimbaud is hugely jealous of this puppy in my arms and he sits disdainfully on the back seat. The puppy doesn't mind him, he bites my wrists, licks me all over, and makes delightful whimpering sounds. Everything was fine except that Filthy Sue couldn't stop playing Uncle Gustave. It's like a broken record. He doesn't even give me a real kiss: "Good, little one, a kiss on the cheek for your dear uncle." It's obvious he likes the part, so I have to play along as that stupid niece Dolly who's just been in the hospital recovering from a terrible illness. To please him I invent a lot of dopey stuff. "Uncle Gustave, is it true that Rimbaud is the most intelligent terrier in the English-speaking world and the Queen invited him to Buckingham Palace?" I say, trying to make peace with Rimbaud. But he still won't look at me.

"Of course, Dolly, and not only that, the Queen granted him British citizenship and will make him a baronet of the United Kingdom."

"And she'll invite him to her next wedding?"

"Certainly, as soon as she's had enough of her present husband, she'll take a new one and invite Rimbaud to be a witness." Here Rimbaud raises an ear.

"Oh, Uncle Gustave, I'd so much like to go!"

"No problem, Dolly, you just have to marry Rimbaud and you can go, too."

"Oh, Uncle, but I wanted to marry you!" Rimbaud is offended again.

"Oh, oh, oh, Dolly, you mustn't say it, because the word . . . "

"The word is incest!" we exclaim together, and maybe at that very instant hopeful Humbert is heading to the hospital to pick up his daughter.

"And what shall I call my cocker?"

"Call him Bimbaki, which means child in Sanskrit."

"The child of me and Rimbaud?"

"The child of you and Rimbaud, and my grandchild, Dolly." Too bad, though, that Filthy Sue leaves right after he's brought me to the ranch. Walk around, rest, recover, return to yourself. Not even time to have a Coke together. He leaves me at the door of my room, which is completely purple, even the massive carved furniture. It is really ugly.

"Bye, beautiful prisoner of the purple bedroom!" he cries as I look out the window with Bimbaki in my arms watching him leave, him and Rimbaud. "Don't come down, I hate goodbyes, and we'll see each other in a hundred and seventeenth of a year." What? In three days point one one nine six five eight one one nine seven? That creep Gerry Sue Filthy, why did he leave me alone? I don't even know exactly where I am. It's a kind of Moorish castle, and the entrance is like a Greek temple, with a lot of columns, and palms and cactus. It's in the middle of brownish mountains, and everything is burned-looking except for some very tall tufts of dark grass. There's a light-colored winding road, completely deserted, and from the window my eyes follow his car as it goes off toward the northwest, becomes a tiny black dot and disappears behind the last hill. The sky is painted blue, with a single white-paste cloud, motionless and thin. I hear a violin; it hasn't stopped since I got here. And there's also a pool behind a wall of reeds, an empty pool, which some Mexicans are cleaning.

I must have fallen fast asleep. I wake up and it's dark. The door of my room is wide open and Bimbaki has disappeared. I go downstairs, where there's a living room with an enormous grand piano and a lot of light-green sofas and dark-green chairs. On the floor is a violin, on one wall are a lot of pictures of Filthy Sue: as a child, blonder than now; at school, performing in a gray donkey costume; receiving a prize; being applauded at the opening of a play. Filthy Sue to infinity. I'm dying of hunger, so I look for something to eat. The kitchen is blood red. Even the icebox. I find only pineapples and containers of yogurt. I hate yogurt. I peel a pineapple, and look for some cookies or crackers. I hear a strange whistling from under the big table, and when I approach, two black cats run away, leaping out the window to play in the garden under the full moon, among the palm trees. I close the window because I'm afraid of snakes. I stay there a while, in the red kitchen, then go back to my room. I have no idea who else is in this place. All the doors are closed and aside from the violin you can't hear anything.

This morning Cindy wakes me up, the blonde who was performing with Will in Grace. She sits on my bed with a glass in her hand and my Bimbaki in her arms.

"It's beef juice, but don't tell Gerry Sue Filthy when he comes back. He's a vegetarian and doesn't want meat eaten in his house."

"But when is he coming back?" I ask, taking my dog.

"Who knows. He always does this. He goes off and doesn't say when he'll be back."

"He didn't even call?"

"Yes, he did, he told me to look in on you. He wants my opinion."

"Why?"

"Because. To see what impression you make on me. So who are you, exactly?" What sort of question is that. Who am I, exactly.

"Who are *you*, exactly?"

"You know perfectly well. I'm Cindy Sailor, you saw me in Grace. When Gerry Sue Filthy is here I also play the role of vegetarian. Otherwise I drink beef juice and keep myself in shape working out with weights. So who are you?"

"You know perfectly well, too, we played tennis together at Tripleview. But if you're looking for a formal introduction, it's a pleasure, I'm Dolores Maze, I'm fourteen, and I'm a friend to male animals."

"Do you think you can make a career out of your friendship with Bimbaki?"

"To begin with, Bimbaki is my cocker, Mr. Filthy gave him to me, and you have no right to come and take him while I'm sleeping, and you don't understand, I mean . . . "

"I know, I know what you meant to say, but I've already heard it, it's old stuff. And your Tripleview companion, what happened to him?"

"I left him."

"I hope you're not left empty-handed."

"Not a chance." She shrugs her shoulders and goes away without even saying goodbye. What a rat. She comes to my room to drink that gross stinking nauseating beef juice, takes my puppy, then pretends she never saw me before and says my story is old hat. So I get dressed and go down to the garden with Bimbaki. There's Will, who's sunbathing beside the pool. He doesn't recognize me, either.

"And where did you come from?"

"I'm Dolly, you don't remember?"

"Oh, Dolly. You never said what your name was."

"But you don't remember at Tripleview?"

"Triple what?"

"Tripleview, Mr. Filthy was there, too."

"You mean Mr. Gerry Sue Filthy? Then you must be the one he was trailing. Well, poor guy, there's little to follow now," he says with a mocking smile. What a bunch of rude people. You'd almost say they'd gotten together to make my life impossible. I don't give a damn if they treat me badly. When Filthy Sue gets back he'll fix everything, and if they don't like my being here, well, they can leave, and besides I don't need their company. Bimbaki is a hundred times nicer than all of them put together. Will starts reading the paper and doesn't glance at me. I decide not to pay any attention to him, either, and I stretch out in front of him, to sunbathe, as if he didn't exist. I turn on the radio under his nose, I smear myself with lotion and ignore him, even though he's only about a foot from the tip of my nose. And when I've had enough sun I dive into the water and splash him all over, him and his newspaper. Will goes off in a huff, saying do I want him to throw my radio in the pool. But he doesn't dare. I hear the violin again from the garden. The sun is really too strong, so I go back in the house, waving offhandedly to Will, who's lying on a deck chair under a eucalyptus tree and pretends not to see me. In the living room is a girl with long black hair. She's the one playing the violin. After a while I recognize her. She was with Filthy Sue at the Enchanted Forest—it's his mute friend. If it weren't that she can't answer I'd ask her what the hell is going on here. Something about her reminds me of Mary Jo, the black hair and prominent cheekbones, but she's much thinner and her gaze goes way off into the distance.

This castle must have something like three hundred and sixty-five rooms, one for every day of the year. Every door is a different color. And above each one there's a brass nameplate that says: Purple Room, Green Room, Black Room, White Room, Dove-Gray Room, Canary-Yellow Room, and so on. This is on the second floor, where I'm sleeping. Upstairs on the third floor the signs say stuff like: Bile-Color Room, Pee-Color Room, Dog-Shit-Color Room, Girl-Vomit-Color Room, Tooth-Decay-Color Room, Dead-Person's-Eye-Color Room, Snot-Color Room, Bat-Dandruff-Color Room, and other really disgusting things. I see the mute coming upstairs. She goes into a room at the end of the hall. I go and read the sign on the door: Sperm-Color Room.

The mute isn't mute. I see her in the kitchen watching television, and she says hello. She has a deep, sensual voice. She gives me a hug.

"This chestnut hair is going to be a problem."

"Problem for what?"

"Don't you want to be a star? Well, I'm telling you, that hair is just no good." What does she know about it?

"But weren't you a mute?"

"Only when Filthy's here. He doesn't like me to speak. He doesn't want distractions when he's thinking. So I play mute. When he introduces me he says I'm deaf and dumb—that is, perfect. It's more convenient. People have no scruples in front of me and say whatever comes into their heads: since they think I can't tell anyone. I don't say anything, so I can pay close attention and I'm not distracted like most people, who when someone is speaking to them are already thinking about what to say next. I just listen, then I transcribe everything I hear into a notebook that's called the journal of indiscretions. Filthy uses it for inspiration. It's interesting what people say when they think they're alone. You want something to eat?"

She offers me a plate of raw vegetables with a piece of whole-wheat bread and a glass of milk, and afterward she gives me long smiles, without saying anything.

"Have you gone back to being mute?"

"In a sense," she answers.

"But do you have a name?"

"Joe."

29.

$\mathcal{J}$OE IS THE only nice person in this house. She takes me to see all the rooms in the castle. I ask her why the rooms upstairs have such ridiculous names.

"Filthy wanted them. When he was little his mother was choosing colors to repaint the house, so his father gave him a silver dollar to go and tell her to make it the color of shit. And he got a spanking for that. A really nasty spanking. He felt bad because it seemed to him a splendid idea, to paint the house the color of shit."

"But there are so many different colors of shit."

"True. Come and see the room the color of dog shit." O.K., but dog shit can be all sorts of different colors, too. I didn't say so, in order not to seem too pedantic. The room the color of dog shit is actually a color that the late widow Maze would have called noisette.

"Who stays here?"

"Filthy's father when he comes to visit, naturally."

"And where is he now, Filthy's father?"

"In a little town in New Hampshire, Goatscreek. In Hampshire hurricanes hardly ever happen. Try saying it."

"In ampshire urricanes ardly hever appen. That's old. Did you know that Goatscreek is where I lived before Ithaca?"

"So you must know Filthy's father."

"No, but I know his uncle—he was my mother's dentist."

"And who did you go to?"

"I never went to the dentist. I still have all my teeth. Not even a cavity."

"Then the cavity-color room will interest you. It's Will's."

"What's Will like?"

"An asshole. But he's really good in the plays in the role of the asshole all the women are wild about."

"And Cindy, where is she?"

"In the room the color of girl vomit."

"Perfect. That sums her up."

"Don't say that. Cindy's a good girl, but she practices playing tough. Imagine, just to be a success she drinks that disgusting red meat juice. The mere idea makes me sick."

We knock at the door of Cindy's room. She doesn't answer, so we go in. Girl vomit is a kind of pale pink veined with greenish yellow. A big book is open on the table.

"She's got it in her mind that if she studies the Kinsey report she'll learn to manipulate men."

"Let's see."

"Oh, there's really nothing to learn, that Kinsey is a tremendous bore. But every so often there's something funny." She makes me read some really incredible stuff. There are men who have violent convulsions when they come, so that their whole body, even their head, shakes, like a madman's or an epileptic's; their legs go stiff, with the nerves knotted as if they had cramps, their feet curl into a fist, the stomach muscles tighten, even the shoulders and neck stiffen: they're folded forward, and they can hardly breathe, or they pant, with bluish lips deformed in horrible grimaces, and their tongue hangs out, like an ant-eater's, or they make frightening barking sounds. Some even burst into tears, sobbing without stopping. Some spend five minutes ejaculating, and the whole five minutes they shake as if they were possessed, like spastics, like squid spraying ink, a real horror for the woman underneath, especially considering that after all this carrying on they can pass out on top of you or yelp like a werewolf, and in addition they have really stinky sweat. I had a luxurious time, if only because Mama Humbert's orgasms were silent, those of a well-brought-up professor, and aside from the habit of turning on the light to see how much my pupils were dilated and his poetic-patriotic perversions, he didn't have other eccentricities. This Kinsey's not very acute: he says incest is rare, and though he mentions boys who do it with their mothers or sisters, there's not a single case of father and daughter. To make up for it he's tracked down country boys who do it with animals, but what I would like to know is how he discovered an orgasm in a child of four. Maybe that famous case of incest between father and daughter he's forgotten to mention, maybe because it's his own?

"You really do have a dirty mind," Joe says reproachfully.

"I'm not the one who thinks dirty things, it's the dirty stuff that thinks me. He says here that men between thirty-six and forty do it on average twice a week. My dad did it every day with me, more than once."

"Your father?"

"The second choice, the one I was traveling with."

"That was your mother's husband. Your stepfather."

"How do you know?"

"Remember, I saw you at the Enchanted Forest."

"So?"

"Filthy told me he was your mom's husband, not your father. Don't you start taking these perverse attitudes—we've already got Cindy for that, and it's incredibly boring."

"O.K., but it was incest."

"Not at all. Because if he'd married you instead of your mother, he'd be your husband."

"But he married my mother, so he became my father, and so it's incest."

"O.K. Please yourself. If it makes you feel more like a victim."

"I've never acted like a victim. Show me some more interesting stuff." She finds the place where it tells about orgasms in farm boys:

in some places in the West sixty-five per cent of them do it with calves, sheep, mules, and even chickens, ducks, and geese (disgust!), and at night, when they dream, they don't dream of making love with some cute girl, but of embracing their favorite animals. Working-class people mostly hate deep kisses, manipulation of the breasts, and the sort of techniques that make Mama Humbert ecstatic; that's because they consider such things perversions. On the other hand, the farm boys, who, you see, don't think that way, love being licked by calves, sheep, mules, and so on, and some are so foolish they do it themselves, they lick the calves, sheep, mules, or whatever, or they masturbate dogs, and they claim they are so good that the dogs prefer to be masturbated by them than to go with bitches (and how does he know this? Has he interviewed dogs?).

"Well, a perfect book for the room the color of a girl's vomit, I'd say."

"It seems entertaining to me. Just to pass the time. Cindy has nothing to do."

"Why?"

"A couple of interviews went badly for her. Now she's waiting."

"Isn't she good?"

"She manages."

"I must admit that although I don't like her she was really good in Grace."

"That was a part that Filthy wrote just for her." Just for her! How many people has he written particular parts for?

"You haven't showed me Filthy Sue's room yet."

"Filthy doesn't have a room. He doesn't like to sleep in the same place every night. There are so many rooms here, he moves around according to his mood."

"Doesn't he even have a favorite room?"

"Yes, he has a favorite room. Why don't you ask him yourself when he gets back?" That's not very nice. Here they all seem to have a time limit on being nice.

"And where do you sleep?"

"I sleep in the Black Room. Come on. But leave Bimbaki outside. His color would clash." We go down one floor, two doors from mine. Bimbaki, poor thing, looks dejected, he doesn't like it that he can't go in because of his color. It really is all black. The furniture is angular and Chinese-looking, the walls have black wallpaper, the floor is made of polished black tiles, the curtains are black velvet, even the cat curled on the bed is shiny black, pleased that Bimbaki's crying outside the door—he must be the real reason Bimbaki had to stay outside. The only things that aren't black, aside from me, are Joe's milk-white skin and the green of her nail polish. On one wall there's the photograph of a statue of a woman from the waist up: one of her eyes is blank, no iris or pupil, and she has an enormous hat the shape of an upside-down trapeze, and a very long, thin neck, like the stem of a flower. Next to it, much smaller, is a photo of a boy.

"Who's that?"

"Nefertiti, the wife of a pharaoh."

"And the boy?"

"That's me, quite a few years ago."

"You look like a boy."

"I was a boy. Now sit down and tell me about yourself." I tell her about Humbert, and about Plasticmom, and how maybe he murdered her and maybe not, it's never been clear, about how I managed not to end up in the reformatory, about my dad, my little brother, all my friends, Liza Webster, Nora, everything, absolutely everything.

"And now are you happy not to be with Humbert anymore?"

"Incredibly."

"I hope you never regret it."

"You're kidding."

"No. We always end up regretting the people we run away from. At least for a while." She's crazy. Crazy. I don't regret a single thing. What is there to regret? My trip with Humbert? It was a huge bore. Our life together? All I did was dream of a life like other people's, and once when I saw a movie with that little creep Shirley Temple I cried all night because she had a father who did whatever she wanted without making her go to bed with him, while I had a pretend father who made me do what he wanted and never even paid me what he promised.

"What would there be to regret so much, Joe?"

"Oh, it's not things, certainly not things."

"When's Filthy coming back?"

"I don't know. When he's finished."

"And what am I supposed to do here by myself?"

"Do you feel like you're alone?" Yes, I feel like I'm alone, but I didn't say so. She could easily tell me that someday I'll even miss her. And I was sick and tired of sitting in that black room listening to her say things that didn't make sense to me. Like that she was a boy and I will regret leaving Mama Humbert. All just to be superior. Finally a gong sounds.

"Come on, let's eat." I pick up Bimbaki, the poor thing is lying on the floor with tears in his eyes, in despair at being abandoned,. Downstairs we find things set up on the patio. Cindy and Will are with two other people, who must have arrived while I was with Joe. They don't open their mouths the whole time. Mutes or fake mutes? Doesn't matter to me. One has flap ears, the other doesn't, otherwise they look like twins. I'm silent, too; I don't have anything to say. It doesn't matter to me if they want to keep their distance, not at all. And then Joe is right: if you're silent you have more time to observe. I eat my enchilada, I observe them and they observe me. Kind of hostile.

But yesterday I saw Joe coming out of the sperm-color room. Which isn't hers. I must find a way to see who's in there. I didn't succeed today. I knock and Joe answers. She's there again. Instead of letting me in she comes out: "What do you want?"

"Nothing."

"Then why did you knock?"

"Because. I wanted to know if you've heard from Filthy Sue."

"Are you bored?"

"Kind of."

"Do you have anything to read?"

"No."

"Try this." She takes me down to the living room and gives me an enormous book. The first volume of the Encyclopaedia Britannica. I go out under the eucalyptus tree to read it. I hope it doesn't mean that Filthy Sue won't be back until I've finished reading all the volumes of the encyclopedia. I wonder if there are any other books in this house.

To see the mysterious room the color of sperm I have to get up in the middle of the night. To tell the truth, it's a normal room, with cream-white furniture, like the kind you see in the movies. The bed is huge, king-size and a half; on the painted bureau there's an enormous white telephone; the bedspread is like plush and creamy white; the curtains are white silk, the chairs white satin, and the dressing table, with silver brushes and ivory combs on it, has a long chenille fringe that hangs down to the ground. In a big white ceramic frame there's a photo of Judy Garland in *The Wizard of Oz*. The walls are covered with white shelves, and they're full of books, which are the only drop of color in all that spermy atmosphere. Hidden among the shelves is a little door that opens into a dressing room. I open it, and try on some dresses; they're all too big—I'm swimming in them. They must belong to an enormous woman, wherever she may be now. In the chest of drawers there are silk-and-lace underwear, nightgowns, bathrobes, a pair of big white pajamas with slits in the crotch, silk stockings, underpants that cover nothing, garters, whatever, all the stuff that makes you wonder why this would be Filthy Sue's favorite room, unless he has a giantess bigger than he is for a lover. Suddenly the sperm-colored telephone starts ringing like a siren. Rushing out I stumble on a white satin slipper with pompoms, but huge, like size twelve or something. I close the door, the telephone stops ringing, no one comes, so I turn the handle to go in again and look at the books, but someone has locked it from the inside.

· · ·

Joe doesn't come around anymore. They've all disappeared. I eat by myself with the two Mexicans, who wait on me, and Bimbaki sits on my lap, a forkful for me, one for him. Joe can't be too far away, I hear her violin. All day I sit in the hammock leafing through the Encyclopaedia Britannica, and at the end of the day there's a furrow on my stomach.

Filthy Sue comes back but it's as if he hadn't. He continues to play Uncle Gustave. I can't take it anymore, this Uncle Gustave. He's so complicated, he and his inspirations!

"My dear little niece, is everything O.K.?"

"Come on, don't do that!"

"Uh, oh. What's the matter? Run over here quickly and give a little kiss to Uncle Gustave who loves you so much." Cindy and Will and Joe and the two unpleasant guys who were never even introduced are standing there, they're giggling. Filthy Sue is all glowing, pleased to be amusing these jerks.

"And now tell Uncle Gustave what you've been doing in the magic kingdom of Filthy Sue. Have you been resting? Studying?" I refuse to answer—it's too unbearable, this business of Uncle Gustave, which just goes on and on. Joe interrupts to make a report: she tells him what I've eaten, what I've said, what I've read, what I've told her, everything! Filthy Sue nods, with an expression of approval.

"And have you had nice dreams?"

"Do I have to talk in front of all these people?" I ask. Besides, what sort of question is that?

"Is there something about our friends you don't like? Aren't they fun to be with?" Hell. This is stupid. I go to my room and don't come out even when the gong sounds. Let him come and get me, surely this mania for Uncle Gustave will pass.

I'm dying of hunger. I could scream from hunger. Bimbaki is hungry, too, but at least he can go down to the kitchen without losing face. That snake Filthy Sue hasn't showed up yet. I don't know what he's doing. I won't leave my room until he apologizes. All those friends of his who are so amused by his banter. Impossible.

Tonight I sneak down very quietly to the kitchen and drink some milk from every bottle, so that it's not noticeable. I also take some cookies. But I'm still hungry. When finally I fall asleep I see roast beef and potatoes. Not the kind of dream I would admit to Gerry Sue Filthy.

In the morning I hear knocking. Finally, I think. Not a chance. It's Joe. Followed by one of the Mexicans with a breakfast tray. I don't have the strength to refuse. At least I didn't make the first move. Joe eats breakfast with me and asks if I intend to stay shut up forever in the purple room.

"I'll stay here until Gerry Sue Filthy comes and apologizes."

"Apologizes for what?"

"For making fun of me with this Uncle Gustave business."

"Come on, don't be a child. He's joking."

"I don't like jokes."

"Good heavens!"

"He promised to take me away to live with him and he told me . . . "

"Let's hear it."

"He told me that . . . "

"That he loved you?"

"Yes, that he loved me very much. That he found me adorable. That the two of us . . . "

"That the two of you would never be separated, that you had a great talent, that he would make you famous, that you are beautiful, intelligent, brilliant, you have a sense of timing, you are a natural comic, but you also have the depths for tragic roles, certainly you're photogenic, as if that's not enough you have a lovely voice and legs that are out of this world."

"How do you know?"

"A little man told me, who I met at the end, but I mean the end, of the rainbow, where the river stops."

"Anyway, he promised me all that and now . . . "

"What? Aren't you in his house? Aren't you living under the same roof? Why are you so impatient?"

"I don't like this Uncle Gustave stuff. I imagined something completely different."

"What? That he would take you in his arms and make you forget the whole world?"

"He did take me in his arms once."

"Incredible. It must have been the first time."

"The first time?"

"And made you forget the entire world? Seriously?"

"He gave me some super scratches on the back, he held me tight, he kissed me lightly on the neck and bit my toes."

"And that made you forget the entire world?"

"Yes." What's so funny? I was really stupid to tell her about me and Filthy. She must be jealous.

But still no Filthy Sue. He's working, Joe explains. He's working for you. And I have to let him play Uncle Gustave, because when he works he needs to imagine he's someone else, otherwise nothing comes out. They're all nuts.

It's terribly hot. And there's not a breath of wind. I spend the whole day sunbathing at the pool, but Bimbaki wants to stay in the shade and refuses to go swimming with me. Toward evening Filthy Sue comes down. With a fan of white ostrich feathers. "Come to Uncle Gustave and make peace."

"Come off it, please." Then I remember that when he works he has to pretend to be Uncle Gustave. I lay it on: "Dear Uncle, are you working hard?"

"I'm writing a part just for you. And you, my dear niece, are you studying?"

"What should I study, Uncle?"

"Aren't you reading the encyclopedia?"

"Yes, Joe gave it to me. I've almost finished it."

"Good girl, read it carefully. Because after you've read it all no one will be able to call you ignorant. You'll be able to say you have encyclopedic knowledge."

"Uncle Gustave, would you lend me your sperm-colored fan for a moment?"

"What color?" He starts laughing, a loud laugh definitely in the style of Uncle Gustave. And since he's laughing, the others also start laughing. On command. It's obvious, he's the boss . . .

30.

I'M ALREADY IN bed. I hear a murmur of voices from downstairs. I go down without being heard. They're talking about me. I squat behind the door. After a bit I can make out the words: some are saying that I'm no good as an actress, at best I could do some sort of television comedy; others say no, something can be done with her. Someone—Will, I think—claims that one could invent a new type, the four-foot-four-inch, ninety-pound girl who seduces men, takes the initiative. I should do well at that, seeing how I behaved with Humbert. Then it seems like Cindy's voice saying no, I don't think that'll work, aside from the fact that she's still growing and next year she might weigh twice as much and be the same ridiculous height. Just look how she dresses: the other night she was wearing that awful copper-colored blouse with the diamonds as big as walnuts. She was playing sexy but she wouldn't have excited a man condemned to death for serial rape. At this nasty remark Filthy Sue says, Come on, let's not exaggerate, while Joe says that ultimately my disturbed childhood could be useful. Don't pull that sort of stuff, says one of the mean twins who have never spoken to me, the one with flap ears. That won't work because she's only fourteen, and if you bring out her masturbated childhood now (laugh from Filthy Sue) you risk having her taken away to reform school immediately or to some family of well-intentioned Presbyterians who would adopt her. For that there's a friend of her mother's, a makeup woman in Hollywood who planted the idea in her head to be in the movies, certainly she could be named her guardian. Yes, that's true, says one of the mean twins, the one without flap ears. But a disturbed childhood isn't enough by itself, there has to be something uniquely hers—if not extraordinary beauty, then a flaw that can be emphasized—while to me that girl seems definitely insipid. There are a thousand like her, with freckles, straight nose, chestnut hair, the most ordinary type of all, the kind you might meet on any street in any city.

Come on, what do you mean, that little gap between her teeth is adorable, and then you should have seen how that Frenchman was attached to her—he wouldn't let her go for a second, Filthy Sue interrupts. What does that have to do with it, replies flap ears. It's because she was twelve years old, that's why, because she was forbidden, brand-new flesh, but now she's only a banal mass-produced fourteen-year-old, with mass-produced aspirations. Just listen to her talk. That's true, Joe says, but we don't have to leave her as she is. With her hair tinted blond, maybe platinum, and another name, say Marilyn, she could make a different effect, platinum and freckles can be sexy, and then we could have her marry Gerry Sue . . . No, no, really, Joe, I'm not marrying anyone. But it would be good for you to marry a young actress with a passion for scratching, Joe insists. But she's too young to marry, we can't keep her here until she's grown up. What are we going to do with her? I'm already bored by her, says Filthy Sue. By now I know her by heart. You could send her to school, says Cindy. After all, she's as ignorant as a goat—imagine, she was studying the encyclopedia. But we can't, says flap ears. We're not her relatives. We could send her to that friend of her mother's, says the one without flap ears. But we don't even know if she wants her, says Filthy Sue, I know these friends who take off just when you need them.

They are all saying such dreadfully nasty things about me—so many I can't even remember them all. I am totally stunned, until Joe, who, however you look at it, is the only one at all on my side, says they should at least let me try something, and then she tries to make me attractive: liquid gray eyes, like a frightened child's, and the fact that I always want to be seen naked but even when I'm naked I look innocent, and then the fact that I look sexy but defenseless, and she gets more and more excited as she explains how they could make something new of me, a kind of tiny kittenish woman who likes men who are older and stronger than she is, paternal types, something in the Shirley Temple line, a girl who's already a woman, a woman who's happy and trusting only when she has a man beside her, though maybe they'd have to make me a little near-sighted to give me a more defenseless look. Joe also says that my figure isn't bad; as for the fact that my hair lies flat on my head, which gives me a slightly monkey-ish look—you could always fix that, you could transform me into a kind of affectionate little beast with platinum hair. Yes, we know that, the little beast who is a friend to male animals, Cindy interrupts contemptuously, to which flap ears adds: An animal that doesn't understand anything, not even that her mother, with that worn-out Dietrich look, was a hundred times sexier than she is, right, Filthy? Filthy Sue tells him, Goodness, no, I only said that to make fun, her mother wasn't very sexy, but she had the appeal of an old, out-of-fashion shoe—a kind of plastic-and-nail-polish puppet, the kind of thing that both frightens and attracts. You know, all that decadence and stupidity have a kind of horrific fascination, and ultimately they are expressive, wouldn't you say?

Then the conversation becomes a murmur of indistinct voices, until someone says that's enough about that little hen, we can't go on anymore. I'd like to know why you brought her here, Will asks, and Filthy Sue, all satisfied, answers, Because you know how certain things interest me, and my astrologer advised me to follow the sign of coin-cidence: go right ahead and don't waste time thinking about it. So when I saw her in that hotel with that guy who seems like a perfect fag but doesn't know it, I remembered that I'd given her a kiss in Goatscreek. Later she writes me, and afterward I discover she's in my play in Ithaca. Then I say to myself, this is too much. Besides, I want to know what's happening with her fake dad. I have to say she is absolutely adorable. She trusts me utterly and tells me everything in the most intimate detail—it's amazing. And then she looks at me as if she expected to be saved: Take me away, she says, grabbing on to me like a newborn kitten. I think, This girl is fantastic, maybe I could set her in the South, in a sort of languid atmosphere. She's so naive she lets me listen at the door, to all the different ways they do it. The trip seemed like a pretty good idea, although maybe it would have been better not to go and get her out of the hospital, more sensible to let her stew in her own juice. Anyway, that's how it went. I was oddly fond of her; maybe the fact that it was July influenced me, because catastrophes or rash acts always occur in July—I thought, Who knows, maybe she'll make it, poor girl. The fact is I only saw the complications later. Now we either have to tell her the truth or send her somewhere. Yes, let's send her somewhere, says Will, she's got too many ideas about the leading-lady role, she won't leave us alone. Cindy says, She can stay as far as I'm concerned, it won't take much to make her listen to reason. Then Filthy Sue relaunches the idea of finishing that thing written just for me, with a foolish and whimsical girl who imagines she has the world at her feet, and an old man so lacking in imagination that he thinks the greatest thing in life is to fuck her, and then you could have this silly girl, who's convinced she's being used by this idiotic man who wants to make her a sexual slave, meet a poet who falls in love with her but when he gets to know her better and sees how empty she is he becomes friends with her lover. He, it turns out, is a man of depth who has been led astray by women, and the poet does his best to make him understand that the girl is better lost than found. Of course one can't write it, but one must feel intuitively that those two discover they are happier together without her, and . . . And they become lovers? asks flap ears. No, not lovers, how can they? Cindy objects. But in a strange way, which not everyone will grasp, you can make it understood that it will end like that just the same. Let's take a young woman, but let's say she's awful, because she's boring and plasticky and mean. Right, says Will. So then they all start discussing how Filthy Sue's new play will go. Cindy makes a stupid fuss and says that she wants to do the part of the horrible young woman, the twin without flap ears says, Do it, you'll see, you'll do it very well. Then I hear a noise as if something heavy had fallen on the floor with a soft thud, raised voices, and then loud laughter from Filthy Sue, footsteps coming toward where I'm hidden, so I run up to my room, prop a chair against the door so no one can come in, and finally fall asleep, but I get up right before dawn. A terrible burden woke me, I couldn't stand the stuff I was dreaming about. It began like this, with me knocking on the door of the sperm-color room. Filthy Sue was there and he told me to come in, come to Uncle Gustave, I want to show you something, and I said to him, Come on, stop it with the Uncle Gustave routine, I'm bored with it, and he said O.K., O.K., no more Uncle Gustave, but tell me who you are. I'm Dolly, I say, Lo, Dolly, Dolores Maze, Lolita, the daughter of Isabel and Gerald Maze, or rather I'm their former daughter, in the sense that they are my former parents. Anyway, call me what you like, it doesn't matter what you call me—you can even invent a new name if you want—just stop playing Uncle Gustave. O.K., calm down, I understand, you are all these people, magnificent, splendid, but who am I? You are Gerry Sue Filthy, Filthy Sue to your friends, I say. Ah yes, he goes, you want me to undress so you can check who I am? Get undressed, it must be time for you to get undressed, I say, after all it's good for the complexion. But how do I get undressed? he says. I've never tried it; explain how to do it. You're an idiot, Filthy. No, come on, seriously, you have to help me. Oh, if that's why. I open his pants and then I look to see if everything's O.K., but there's nothing at all there, it's empty.

Joe comes to talk to me. She tells me that Filthy has left again. "For me he can never come back."

"He said to ask if you want to audition."

"I want to go."

"Where?"

"To Los Angeles, to my mother's friend."

"But have you told her?"

"I don't have to. Her house is always open."

"Is it nice?"

"I've never seen it."

"So?"

"Don't worry." I pack my trunk. The copper-colored blouse, the one that would have made Plasticmom explode from envy, I leave for them. Since, as far as I can see, it's no good for special effects anymore, although I'm sure that it would have worked very well with the hen. Let Cindy have it for a keepsake. Maybe it will come in handy when she has to play the part of an awful, inept young woman who runs away from a fool who loves her so much he keeps her prisoner. At the bottom of the trunk I find *Wuthering Heights*. If I had remembered, I would have read that instead of the Encyclopaedia Britannica.

Joe's taking me to the train station. She gives me a cart to carry the trunk and a leash for Bimbaki. After we've been in the car for half an hour she tells me to look to my right.

"Where? I only see mountains and desert."

"You don't see that greenish color?"

"There in the background?"

"Yes, in the background. It's the Jornada del Muerto. I saw it that day."

"Which day?"

"Three or four years ago. One morning in July, more or less like this one. But much earlier, between five and six. I couldn't sleep and I was playing the violin, since I was alone in the house and I wasn't bothering anyone. It was raining, and suddenly I saw a glow in the sky and then a huge ball of fire that spread at tremendous speed, until it filled almost the whole western part of the sky. The earth shook, like when the buffalo herds go by in the Westerns, *tutum, tutum, tutum,* you felt like two suns were about to rise, one from the east and the other from the west. The sky was flooded with light from both sides, and I thought, My God, in a little while these two suns will clash above my head and there will be a disaster."

"And then?"

"Then nothing. Disaster averted. It was like a great cloud of light that suddenly stopped spreading and melted into the rest of the day. Now, at that point in the desert, which is more like a big field than a point, there near the Jornada del Muerto, the grains of sand have formed an enormous slab the color of jade, as smooth as glass."

Finally we get to the station. The train is really late. Joe stays to keep me company. Then as we're saying goodbye: "Write, if you want. Take this, it may be useful." It's an envelope stuffed with bills. Enough to last awhile, maybe until when the money from Grandma arrives. I'm sorry to see Joe leave. She was company, in her way.

On the train I sleep the whole time, without a single dream. At the station in Los Angeles Bimbaki barks like a lunatic, and I wake up and see a skeletonlike woman who is showing off all her gold teeth, but at least she helps me with my trunk and finds a porter. I get a taxi, but it takes a while to reach Nora's. She lives at the end of a long long canyon, and we pass houses of every type: Swiss chalets, a kind of Gothic castle, a villa built like a Greek temple, with gigantic palm trees, a kind of Arab palace and, right beyond it, a big green lawn almost all taken up by a swimming pool with orange tiles and a round cabana in front, and lots of other houses, all weird, and not one resembles another in the slightest. It's just the opposite of where I was before, and finally we stop in front of a small fantastic house, like something in a fairy tale.

"Who are you visiting, Rapunzel?" the taxi driver asks as he unloads the bags in front of the gate. I pull a cord and shake a cluster of bronze bells, and the taxi driver waits to make sure someone opens the door. After a while a big surly woman comes out, her head covered in waves of big green plastic curlers. Her knees are like colanders and they stick out from under her too short skirt. She covers her eyes with her hand, and won't let me come in until Nora gets there, who as soon as she sees me screams with joy, shoving her aside. The woman realizes it's O.K. for me to come in, and takes my things and disappears down a hallway where mannequins in old military uniforms stand. I hug Nora tight, and kiss her dimples. I'm taller than she is now, and she seems even younger.

"And that miser Professor Humbert Guibert? What happened to him?"

"He changed careers," I say, pointing to Bimbaki, who gives her a big smile.

"How dear! But what are you doing here by yourself? You're not going to tell me you ran away?"

"Maybe."

"Oh good heavens! And if he comes to look for you, what do I do?"

"Don't worry. He's definitely not the type to come and quarrel with an aunt who is a lawyer."

"What lawyer are you talking about?"

"Don't you remember, I called you aunt, because he didn't want to let me call? Well, I told him you're a lawyer and the terror of Los Angeles."

"But why?"

"Didn't you teach me that you should never tell the whole truth, that it's a good idea to leave yourself a way out, and a little lie every so often isn't the end of the world?"

"Oh, well . . . And so you ran away and you think he won't try to find you?"

"Of course not. You know, he really couldn't care less about me. The big trip to make me forget Mom, it turned out, was only an excuse to take me with him while he was writing a guidebook to the United States. He used me as his secretary, and now he's scared to death at the idea that I could get him arrested for violating child labor laws. Also, when I went back to school in Ithaca, you know, he made me waste a lot of time checking the English in his book. And the last straw was when he made me come here with him because he had a consulting job in Hollywood and I had to give up the play I had the leading part in."

"What a swine! But why didn't you tell me right away that he was exploiting you? We could have had him arrested and you could have come here."

"I didn't want to be a burden, and then, aside from his being such an exploitive pig, I liked the idea of going on a trip after Mom died. We saw a bunch of interesting places, I'll show you my travel log. I wrote down everything we did."

"But then did you come together to Los Angeles?"

"Yes. I took the opportunity to get in a taxi and surprise you." Well, Dolores Maze of the future, I hope you'll feel some satisfaction when you read this in seeing how magnificently I managed to improvise for Nora—without any plan at all—a seamless story, with the result that she immediately proposed that I stay and live with her. She promised not to look for Humbert, and now I am in a pretty little room in the city of my dreams and tomorrow I will be able to see everything I've always wanted to see. I didn't say anything about Gerry Sue Filthy: I don't think it would be a very good idea. I'll pretend nothing happened, since this notebook is on the last page, tomorrow is another day, and the bus goes by every five minutes.

Dolores Maze of the future who will read these pages, I think you will be grateful to me for having written here the chronicle of these years so you will be able to forget them with a lighter heart. And if you should happen to lose this diary, don't worry: sooner or later you lose or forget everything. There are a few more lines. I'd better offer some consolation to Plasticmom, who wanted to make me believe I could write to a dead man, and to Celeste, who said that though spirits can't send letters because pens are too heavy, they can read everything (as long as they weren't bad, because in that case they can't see anything you write to them). This is to make them happy: "Dear Dad, you never answered me even once. And so I won't write to you anymore. If you want to speak to me, find your own system. After all, you invented lots of things. At worst you can always slip into my dreams. That's always been the style of the dead."

It's pointless to send greetings to Plasticmom. Since she never believed in these things and that stupid *Mother's Heart* was just to confuse me. Now I'll finally be able to read *Wuthering Heights*.